HE WHO CONQUERS

"You won." He said it numbly, calmly.

"You're a strong man. You could out-wrestle anyone I've ever known. But you should not have listened to those who said you could win a knife fight...strength alone does not win a Death Match."

"You're a great fighter; I should have listened to my friends." There was a great sigh, and breathing stopped.

He bent down and chopped the rope. When he stood, his knife and axe were in their sheaths. "When you taste the flesh of this man in your kiva, his spirit will live in you to constantly remind you that you are coyotes, and he the true brave one among you."

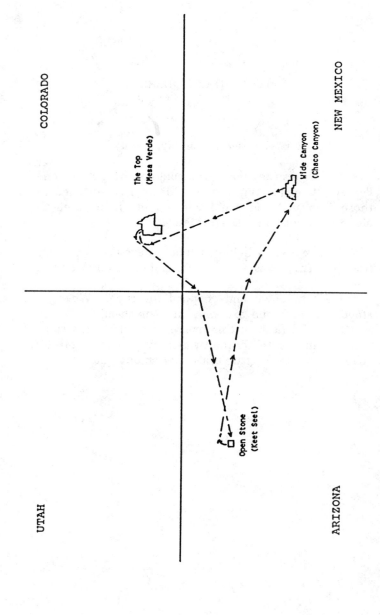

UTAH

COLORADO

The Top
(Mesa Verde)

Wide Canyon
(Chaco Canyon)

Open Stone
(Keet Seel)

ARIZONA

NEW MEXICO

HE WHO CONQUERS

THE ANASAZI SERIES: BOOK I

by

Wallace Burke

HE WHO CONQUERS
WEB PUBLISHING CO/1994

PRINTING HISTORY

This book was originally published as ANASAZI SERIES, BOOK I: PEOPLE OF THE TOP, in
1992, by Southwest Publishing Company, Sun Lakes, AZ.

Publisher's Cataloging in Publication
(Prepared by Quality Books Inc.)

Burke, Wallace E.
   He Who Conquers / by Wallace E. Burke.
   p. cm. -- (The Anasazi series ; bk. 1)
   Preassigned LCCN: 93-94266.
   ISBN 0-9639014-0-0

   1. Pueblo Indians--History--Fiction. 2. Indians of North
America--Southwest, New--Fiction.   I. Title. II. Series.

PS3552.U71H48 1994   811'.54
                                QBI93-22457

For information: WEB Publishing Company
                      P.O. Box 528
                      Westminster, CO   80030-0528

TO BARB

A wife is many roles in one, but mine went above the roles, dedicating herself to hours at the keyboard, the days too numerous to count. Without her faithfulness in the early typing, this book would forever have lived only inside my head.

PREFACE

* * *

ANASAZI! The ancient ones. The very name exudes a mystique, an enigma, a wonderment. The life and death struggle of these almost unknown peoples can only make the curious dream dreams. They traipsed the western regions of the Americas, following the seasons and the whims of man, leaving little by which to identify them or know of their passing--until...until by some strange anomaly which still has archaeologists and historians pondering, they began to settle in areas which to us seem too arid for good agriculture, there to eke out a living from the soil as the first farmers of America.

In the four corners region, the Mogollon, the Tonto Basin, and along the Grand Canyon, the Colorado River basin, the San Juan River drainage, these industrious people worked the soil for their corn, beans, squash, and other crops, then hunted and gathered berries and nuts from the regions around them. They flirted with drought, made friends with the dry winds, and slept with the canyons and rock out-croppings familiar to their area.

Their daub and wattle (in lesser degree), and their rock and mortar still survive in ruins, slowly losing to the elements of time. Still, because of the work of early men who discovered their disintegrating dwellings, and the on-going tradition of the archaeologist, when the last rock has fallen to the level of the soil that supports it, their memory will yet live. In pit houses, in primitive homes of stucco, and in masonry dwellings that amaze hundreds of thousands of visitors each year, they lived primitively and simply. We will forever see the genius of their passing.

Classic pottery, expert masonry, ingenious etching on sea shells and in rock, taming the wild turkey, hunting with atlatl and the emerging bow-and-arrow, these people lived, worked, played, fought, laughed, cried, hated, loved, enjoyed, feared, and died. Their story is still being studied, their civic and religious lives opening slowly to modern historians. Their history is nebulous and intriguing.

This book is fiction. It is meant to be just that. Yet, there is hope that through this medium, some of the reality of the Anasazi will come alive. Their community rabbit hunts, their changing construction techniques, their battle with disease and lack of medical expertise, their fight to survive, and their desire to learn...all these come in a social setting so different from our own we can but begin to understand it. While this is fiction, and many of the social customs which the author includes may or may not have been found among them, there has been a desire to show no discrepancy with modern archeology.

The mystery of the Anasazi will never be fully uncovered, though we find more artifacts and study carefully each new discovery. Perhaps that is all for the best, for it is the great mystery of a people that can best put our imaginations to work.

If this writing, or its planned sequels, help to make the Anasazi more real, then the project is a success already. You, as the reader, are fully as free as I to fill in the details of the time. After all, the writer who does not allow the reader to create enough mystery to whet the appetite of the imagination, the writing is, in fact, a failure.

I, too, have fun theories, such as those of the ancient palefaces who came to Anasazi lands, or the Ceremony of the Stick (see the Glossary). While I shy from trying to describe in detail any ceremonies or most superstitions, it is with hope that the writing captures a desire to imagine.

This book is based on activity around Far View ruins of Mesa Verde, Keet Seel near Kayenta, Chaco Canyon, and back to Far View. To assist the reader, terms found in italics (when used for the first time) may be found in the Glossary at the end of the book. The directions are found in hyphenated sun-set (west), sun-rise (east), no-sun (north) and mid-sun (south). If the term is not hyphenated, it refers to the time of day (see *sun*).

Enjoy!

ACKNOWLEDGEMENTS

My thanks go to the many who have, without seeing a single written page except to know my energies and aspirations were so directed, given words of irreplacable encouragement. How many times a venture of this magnitude goes wanting for the need of such things.

To my family, especially. My wife, Barb, for her typing, her work on the telephone, her encouragement. My daughter, Janine, who thought her father had some talent and ought to pursue it. My daughter, Jonelle, who helped with hours on the printer and in the setup. My last daughter, Jeanette, who stayed with her college hopes and gave me added reason to persevere.

To the extended family for their strengths.

To my acquaintances and friends, too numerous to mention, but who constantly asked about "the book"!

To the late Dr. Clifford Bennett, owner of Literary Services Agency of Colorado Springs at the time of his death, who was a great help in acquainting me with publication details, and who gave a great deal of stimulating advice as well as the idea to persevere.

To some helpful people at Mesa Verde National Park where I did most of my research, including Rovilla Ellis, Business Manager of the Museum Association, Valerie Wetherford who worked in the bookstore, and Linda Martin, Chapin Mesa District Park Ranger. Each of them spoke to me without even knowing my name or my project!

To these I am grateful, for without them this dream would never have stepped from the Hermes 8 to which I was addicted until I managed a word processor. Thank you, each one, for your help and stimulation.

1

Others were out there. He felt it, knew it. The great smoke could have come from no other source. They were there! Would they come here? Had his dreams of fear and anticipation come true?

As the lean, slightly gangly lad approached *The Rock*, his eyes, more hazel than the typical dark-brown, darted alertly. They absorbed the thinning shrubbery, the scattered cedars, the rock-strewn ground--and they noted the absence of smoke on the far horizon, where there had been a huge, flattopped, black cloud the previous *sun*. His eyes caught the Rosy Finch that darted through the nearby bitterbrush, the blackbird that worked from one branch to another in the juniper, and the collared lizard that darted from his path to stop beside a slab of stone, jowls pumping. A red-tail hawk floated on the upper breezes where the gods moved, its eyes on the ground far below in a continuous search for prey.

It would be an eventful sun; the presence and actions of the hawk told him that, and his somber expression gave way to a gleam of anticipation. A typical youth, he loved to see something--in fact, anything--happen to keep life from boredom. It mattered little whether the act be good or bad, just so there was action.

Little escaped the darting, pensive eyes of He Who Runs with the Wind, a man of fourteen *winters*, noted most for his keen eyes and swiftness of foot. And while his eyes missed little, his mind sought the watchpost, The Rock, which he pictured in his mind as clearly as though he were staring at it.

The Rock was not an anomaly on the sandstone-dominated landscape, being a shelf of stone that rose above the high lip of the highest part of the raised land *The People* called reverently "*The Top*." Below The Rock was a narrow shelf of gritty soil dotted with sparse grasses and wild flowers that showed the effects of the cool air, evidence of the changing season and the nearness of the first frost and snow. From the edge of that shelf the sandstone cliff dropped in a breath-taking sheerness to the flaring skirt whose hem lay on the *valley* floor far below. Sitting on The Rock gave a huge panorama to the sentry, reaching out to distant horizons dominated by snowy peaks that topped mountain ranges.

Runs with the Wind longed for the sentry duty almost as much as he longed for honor or water. It had become part of his lonely life. While most of the young men went to The Rock exclusively to escape the drudgery of work, he had a far greater incentive. Desiring idleness to the sweaty, back-breaking labor of the fields had not been invented by the newest generation, and he did not deny--to himself--an element of this in himself. That the task of watchman was equally divided among the young men who had been through the Ceremony of Manhood for their first three winters made little difference to him.

To Runs with the Wind, it was many other things. It was his chance to do one of the things for which he was respected...use his eyes. It was his opportunity to make the moccasins which bought him more times to be here. It was his place for sharpening his skills at axe-throwing, knife-throwing, and the bow-and-arrow, all of which were deadly serious skills to him.

Most of all, it gave him a chance to escape the barbs of his peers, most of whom considered him different in an inferior way, and to give his mind to the gods. Often he had spoken to the hawks, and sent messages to the gods through them, and on one occasion had caught a hawk and pulled a tail feather, which now dominated his headband. The tail feather assured him the ears of the gods.

He had been surprised to have met the sullen Gray Dog back along the trail, and his mind gave him a moment of recollection. Gray Dog had given him no greeting, which was not unusual, since he was one of the clic which made it almost a cult to hate him. But He Who Runs with the Wind had dismissed it quickly with his eyes on the hawk.

He amazed everyone, including his own uncle and his *mu*, by his dedication to devising methods to spend his time as a substitute for other youths at the post. He designed and made moccasins that were the envy of the young men. He honed throwing sticks to a sheen unsurpassed, and painted mysterious religious symbols that no one duplicated. He had learned and experimented with gut-and-resin until he could set the stone of a knife, arrow or *atlatl* beyond the ken of all.

But what brought him his greatest renown was his sight, and the good fortune that came to The People when he was sentry. Even the son of the chief, Boy with the Eye of an Eagle, failed to match his keen eyesight. In fact, over the past hunting season, Boy with the Eye had never given The Hunters a single lead that led to a kill, while Runs with the Wind had given them the lead to four herds of bison and elk, which had brought successful meat forays. The gods seemed to favor him, and his inner spirit was known by many to be conducive to success.

No smoke on the horizon. What had it been? Certainly far more than the smoke of a ceremony, or a burning lodge or kiva--a common enough event. When he had left the lookout post the previous sun, *Sun God* had long disappeared behind the smoke that had climbed high into the domain of the gods before the air movements had flattened it and sent it towards *rising-sun*.

Perhaps that was a tendril of smoke still hanging near the spot where the great darkness had been, but if so, it was quite indistinct. After a short stare at the area, he decided it was not worth the time. He stood on the shelf, buttocks against The Rock, and let his eyes play with the extended view for which he was responsible.

Satisfied there was nothing out there for him at present, he lifted himself onto The Rock and kicked off his sandals, being careful they landed flat below him and did not vault over the edge, which had happened to him but once, and that long ago. To retrieve it would have required almost a full sun, and to make a new one took much time. He never let it happen again.

His uncle had taught him long ago that staring fixedly for any time at all would reduce the effectiveness of sight, and he learned the lesson well. His eyes never stopped moving, constant and slow, and his greatest success had been from the periphery. A movement almost missed, but just "almost", for once seen, he was swift to identify the target.

How many times he had studied the far mountains he never considered, but he knew the gods would one sun take him there, or perhaps farther. He had no idea why or how, but to know it bore a fascination that never abated. What lay beyond them? Did other people live there, people like themselves? Or did the gods play there? Or did the dreaded Others dwell there?

Some said evil gods lived there, that no one who went there ever came back. But how did they know? He knew of no one who had tried. Certainly not in his lifetime. So was it fact or fiction? Fascinating.

In the hazy *no-sun*, the snowcaps were hardly visible, though the nearer ones to rising-sun were clearer. His people hunted there each season, and it was known the Others did, too. The highest was a sacred place.

Satisfied he could see nothing significant, he arranged his knife, axe and bow-and-arrows beside him, beside the prepared leather he had brought with him. Then he lay back in the warm sun, feeling the coolness of the breeze that reminded him of the freedom and sense of well-being he always felt out here.

Many winters ago, so the elders related to the youth in the kivas during the long, cold harshness of snowtime, warriors had come from no-sun, about two or three--some even said as many as four--hands in number.

No one knew for sure how many there were, for no one had seen them all at once. The attack on the People of the Top had come as Sun God rose, while men had been sleepily and without enthusiasm walking into the fields to work, their minds empty and their senses dull. Though Runs with the Wind had not yet been *dropped* into the land of The People, for it had happened two generations ago, the oral Traditions gave an accurate description to him.

The village at the time relied mainly on one large field for its crop, almost exclusively corn and squash, a field that stretched into *mid-sun* from the semi-ring of daub and wattle dwellings, and reached to no-sun behind the dwellings. The women watched in fascinated horror as the attack came with wild screams of the Others, and the partially armed men had been no match for the attackers.

After a short paralysis, the women had grabbed children and run into the cornfields to hide, and then had to scramble away with fire raging behind them and the Others laughing and shouting with glee, unaware the women were escaping.

Thirty-seven men had died in the single devastating attack, and only one Other had been wounded. They had been like the whirlwind, moving and deadly, bringing total chaos. A few women were caught, and many children were run down and killed. A few elders had been found in their dwellings, and slaughtered. When the Others had finally left, they took seven young ladies and several children with them.

The ripe cornfields had burned, along with the dwellings. In the ensuing snowtime, which had been uncommonly harsh, eighteen more people died from malnutrition and exposure. There had been no time to rebuild adequately, and their food crop was nearly destroyed.

It was that story which had filled his mind the previous sun while he watched the smoke far to setting-sun. It was that which filled his mind now, sobering him and causing him to sit up, his eyes seeking movement on the valley that lay below him.

Could it happen again? How many times had he asked himself that question? They had not returned, yet that fire had more than bothered him. That smoke had been ominous, though he could not have defended his unusual fear. His mind had played on it, turning it over and over long into the darkness after he had gone to his <u>mat</u>.

Who were they? Where did they come from? Why had they come here, so obviously distant from their usual haunts? Why had they passed by so many scattered villages and dwellings in the great valley to climb the steep hills to The Top? And how would his people fare against them if they knew of the approach?

His own people had once been nomadic, following the seasons and the animals, and Sun God. They had killed Others to steal food and for honor among themselves. They wandered and they hunted, and dreamed of heroic deeds. So to be attacked by Others was not surprising. But up here? On The Top? With so many other places in easier reach?

They would return. From the time he first heard of the attack, he knew that for a fact. It was not an if, but a when. The thought filled him with a mixture of fear and excitement, an odd blending of diverse emotions. The fear was the type to bring wetness to the palms of his hands and armpits. So where did the excitement come from? It seemed incongruous to have such strange thoughts. As though he wished for such a dreadful thing! Perhaps his uncle had been right. He did have a different inner voice from the rest of The People, and walked to the rhythm of a different drum.

So many questions, and no one with answers. Even the gods were silent. The sages of The People were without thoughts on the matter, though men speculated absently over the warming fires of the kivas. Their knowledge of Others came from the Trader, whose coming was both a celebration and an education. While he bartered and won, he passed along the things he learned from all the peoples with whom he traded. Even what he knew, however, failed to answer the most urgent question.

He had never learned where they seemed to come from. He did know where they struck, and loved the attention that came from the knowing. He had no idea why they went to certain places, sometimes in the midst of many villages without bothering the ones they must have passed to get there. He could not tell who they were. But they were deadly, and the horror stories that came from their raids brought many a darkness of sheer terror as the stories were told and re-hashed over fires while children and youth listened in morbid fascination.

The People of the Top, like those scattered across the great valley, or located in canyons near or beyond the mountains or far to mid-sun, were peaceful people. They had lost their need to go far to conquer, and indeed were too busy with their crops to consider it, anyway. They lived by the garden, gathering nuts and berries from the mountains, hunting game, and making occasional raids on the rabbit population. They had no intentions of assaulting other people, except to occasionally kidnap a young woman for the sacrifice to the Goddess. To live with the gods, to grow their crops, to be successful in gathering and hunting, to develop athletic skills for competition, these were the goals. Furthermore, their concern was not to kidnap other women to speed up populating, but to keep it within the bounds of the food they could produce.

They had no real defense against the Others. They had to be alert, to first see them, then to hide in the caves of the canyons. Let them burn and destroy; with the living, it could be made anew.

But Others had not returned. The great alarm once felt had degenerated into mere horror stories that gave youth nightmares, but otherwise were considered quite harmless. Runs with the Wind was the anomaly; his spirit knew. And he wondered why.

The People now made several fields for their crops as a defense against the great abomination ever happening again, but even that no longer reminded them of the once painful experience. Unpleasant memories fade, but for Runs with the Wind it was still very much alive. He had developed a vivid imagination, a long memory, and an active mind. Why he should think so much on it he had no idea, sometimes lying awake on his mat and wishing the thoughts would either go away or come true.

His alertness never abated while his mind ran its

circles, his eyes scanning constantly, for he well knew
the importance of seeing animals. How frequently he
had escaped the drudgery of the fields. Removing trees
for new gardens before each planting season was not his
idea of a good time. And each new area reminded him
of the coming of the Others, as real as the fear of
darkness or witches.

For how many seasons now had the People
feared being overlooked by Rain God? Others were
hardly a consideration! The common, everyday battles
with the witches of ill health and accident had become
their focus, their only vigilance.

But far more significant was his prestige among
his people because of his great eyesight. And how
precarious was his honor. Was not his *fa* the biggest
coward of all? Despised. Ridiculed. Lost from his own
people and an outcast among his chosen one. A man of
ill health and bad spirit. Runs with the Wind was the
son of such a man, and many watched to see if he might
not be of the same blood, a true son of his fa.

Runs with the Wind picked up his knife and
slipped from The Rock, wearing his moccasins in place of
his sandals, and eyed the much-abused trunk of a wind-
gnarled cedar which had felt the pain of many knives.
Suddenly his arm went back, then shot forward, the knife
released with a motion so quick and fluid it nearly defied
the eye. The knife embedded itself in the well-chewed
area he called his target, and he retrieved it with
satisfaction. As he returned to The Rock, he remembered
Boy with the Eye of an Eagle.

Their's had never been a comradery, though they
were but three suns apart in age, Runs with the Wind
that much the younger. Boy with the Eye was a caustic,
grating youth with deep-set eyes and huge nose, a
narrow forehead and jutting jaw. His normal
countenance was haughty, his mouth harsh and loud.
From earliest suns, he had taken to harassment and
torment of Runs with the Wind, and being the youngest
son of the chief put him where he felt utterly superior.

They had fought often while boys, until one time
Boy with the Eye had come at him with a knife. It was
his mistake, for Runs with the Wind loved his knife. He
had spent hours working with it, and in no time had cut

the adversary three times, one a deep incision along his cheek. It had ended the physical onslaught, but not the verbal one.

However, Boy with the Eye had lost the tip from his spear on three occasions, and his friends laughed at his inept ability to make a spear that would last. Secretly he came to Runs with the Wind to fix it for him, and the latter had done it--at the cost of four of his turns at The Rock. This was one of those, the next to last.

It had been exciting to watch the men and youth speculate on what had happened to give Runs with the Wind the turns normally due Boy with the Eye, who had thought the matter a simple give and take until the laughter began. No matter how many times he tried to convince people that he hated The Rock duty, no one believed him. And everyone knew his spear was better than new.

Runs with the Wind smiled to himself, picturing the sweat pouring off the visage of his nemesis. Perhaps it was not good to taunt the son of the chief, despite the personal enjoyment it furnished him, for in the end, it reflected on the chief. With eyes of laughter, he knew he would go on teasing.

And here he sat, enjoying his great pleasure, while the son of the chief harvested corn! The Rock became twice as friendly.

Planting was the hardest, and most tedious, chore of the men, for great care was given to each mound. Pulling weeds, watering when Rain God withheld his help, chasing out predators, thinning hillocks, each was part of the on-going labor. Then came harvest, the second most tedious task. And Runs with the Wind would not have to help once!

He smiled to himself again. How well he remembered the suns before his Ceremony of Manhood, when he had been part of the crew of boys who spent every darkness chasing predators out of the crops, the deer, racoons, rodents and other creatures of the dark. But to allow an animal to destroy part of a crop brought disdain and humiliation, something no youth wished to endure.

And those were times of terror, sometimes almost paralyzing. What thoughts a child could not invent in his own mind while wandering through his area of responsibility would be given to him in the telling of tales around the fires. Many the darkness he imagined every sort of trouble while he patrolled, certain that spirits of the dead were lurking behind that gnarled cedar, or in the shadow of the next serviceberry bush.

Well, he no longer had such duties, for he was no longer a boy, but a man; and Boy with the Eye labored for him in the chores of the men! The best of both worlds!

He stood and peered over the edge of The Top, down the steep drop at his feet, and could almost imagine he was soaring with the hawks. He felt good...so good he could almost see himself accompanying the Hunters on their next trip. How he wished he were one of them! But he was not. When the next snows were conquered by Sun God, he should be given the right to join them at their *Ceremony to the Goddess of Birth*, symbolized in the Moon at Spring Solstice. Then again, perhaps he would not receive the invitation. Antagonizing the son of the chief was not the wisest thing to do. Still, some of the elders received great enjoyment watching the developments, and some might favor his inclusion because of his success at seeing animals. The gods seemed to favor him in some things, but the decision would not be his in this dream, either.

He pitched a stone and watched it fall until he lost sight of it before it landed, and turned his eyes again to the vast span over which he was watchman. Nothing...a thin spire of smoke from a dwelling far out on the valley floor rose almost straight into the azure skies...but no movement anywhere.

He leaned back against The Rock, buttocks resting so he could cross his legs with one foot firmly planted. How he wished he could be a Hunter. Hunting was still of great importance to The People, and it carried with it the opportunity for glory and prestige. To harvest a crop, while satisfying, never brought an individual any accolades, but in hunting....

Every lad wished for--dreamed for--the chance to be a Hunter. And he, Runs with the Wind, now a man for having successfully endured the Ceremony of Manhood with all its serious challenges, would be eligible when the snows melted. He had no doubt he could pass the test involved.

But of course, there was another problem, his fa, perhaps more serious than his battle with the chief's son. It was deeper seated and of a more critical basis, and he was not a bit sure he could overcome that.

The frown of concentration was still on his face when he heard a sound coming from the edge of the scattered cedars behind and to his left. A quick glance caught the flit of movement that could only be Little Dove. Pleasant feelings surged through him. Little Dove, recently become a woman when Goddess of Fertility visited her. Petite, intelligent, quick, mischievous, daring, more than pretty, daughter of Medicine Woman and the traveling Kokopelli, daughter of the wealthiest clan on The Top, she was the desire of every son old enough to know what a woman could do to a man.

She ran from cover and darted onto the gravel where he stood, squatting immediately so as to be unseen by anyone who might be walking in the area. Her young, budding breasts heaved from her exertion, and her smile was typically coy and charming. He smiled in return.

She was a delicate girl, of small bone structure and dainty face, quite unlike the typically full, stocky build, and her high, more defined cheekbones in a narrow face were as unusual. Her coal-black hair was almost bluish, and her eyes favoring a tinge of blue with the predominant brown. Kokopelli, who visited The Top but once every five winters, was obviously her fa, and her mu never let anyone forget the honor of her high birth.

Best of all, she had eyes only for Runs with the Wind. He, too, was different, standing nearly a head taller than the average male, with slimmer, longer legs, eyes more hazel than brown, lighter complexion, and thinner face. He was an oddity, as was she.

But to no avail were their trysts. It had been decided that she, because of her high birth, was fit for no man but the son of a chief, and Boy with the Eyes was to be the one. Both knew their meetings were never to reach fruition, but both continued to enjoy their secret.

"He Who Runs with the Wind is glad to see me?"

Her eyes twinkled in anticipation of his answer.

He grinned. "Should I be?" He loved their word games. Reaching back with his two hands, he hoisted himself back and up onto his perch.

A band circled his head, adorned with tokens of achievement and spiritual connotations. Feathers from a bird kill, claws and teeth from small animal kills, his hawk feather, and a few trinkets. His necklace of small bones and teeth was its affiliate. His hand went to the band, a gesture he often used when insecure.

She was completely at ease with him, knowing well his small idiosyncracies. "But you are! Say it!"

He laughed, letting his eyes sweep the area below them.

"You've made no attempts to see me," she accused. "I have offended you."

He grinned, letting his glance sweep her before going back over the edge. "How?"

She was silent a moment, not sure how to play his game. His deliberateness was part of the mystery that intrigued her.

Seeing her uncertainty, he sobered. "You could never offend me if you worked at it, Little One. But you know, as well as I, that no matter where I go, I'm watched. Only here am I left alone. It's impossible to meet you."

Devilment danced in her eyes. She knew he was deadly serious, and she was satisfied. He was right, of course, but she liked the needle. She reached out and touched the ankle that dangled near her. "It's said that some of the 'boys' want to kill you. Is this true, my love?" When he looked down at her touch, the devilment was gone, and the eyes were somber.

"It is so."

"Then I must talk to mu about this."

He shook his head. "Who would believe it? I'm but a coward with delusions, like my fa. I see things that aren't there. So I let the talk lie, and consider it the waste of time of boys who will never be men."

"And you aren't afraid?"

"I'm fearful." His candidness, too, was part of what intrigued her. "I never walk the same trail twice. But who is there to believe me?" Again he glanced at

her, and then let his gaze wander into the distance.
Now, they were not focused on the great valley, however.
"Son of Happiness keeps me informed, but now they talk
less around him. Still, he hears."

"Then it's true you will leave...go away." The
statement served as a question.

She had caught him by surprise, and only by the
slightest twitch and sudden glance did she know the
truth of her observation. His eyes revealed nothing.

"Little One hears too much."

"Then it's true. I hear things, too."

He said nothing while his eyes moved, and then
he saw the two men below, climbing a steep skirt to the
one place along the no-sun side where one could get to
the top. As he watched, he knew one of them, and their
desperate climbing raised his curiosity, for they came
from where the great smoke had been the previous sun.

"It's not right," she finally said after a long hush,
not aware he watched the two men. "But I want to hear
you say it."

He nodded, and looked down at her, his eyes
showing his fondness for her. "I'll go."

It was like she had received a blow. Tears
welled in an instant, then pinched out at a blink and
coursed down her cheeks. "Have we degenerated to this
among The People?"

He smiled sadly. Her face dropped, and he
stared at her young, lithe body while she cried silently.
The visible development of her breasts intrigued him,
small but nicely shaped and stimulating. He wished he
could hold her against himself, and, at the same time,
longed for greater self-control. She could never be his,
and he had best remember that. But it could not stop
the desire.

He watched her intently, her hands lying relaxed
in her lap as though useless, her bare legs folded beneath
her. His eyes never left her, studying her shoulders, her
hair, her browned back. It was rare that one could study
a woman without her knowledge, and it was particularly
important that he take his opportunities to study this
one. Usually there were many youths around, and he
had to ignore her presence. To show much interest in
her would be bad for both of them.

She began to gain control, and he looked away again, unsure of what to say. She looked up through reddish eyes. "I will go with you."

He shook his head, smiling sadly. "That's not possible."

"Why?"

"Several reasons, and you know them...at least most of them." He looked down at her. "If I leave...or rather, when I leave, those who wish me dead may follow. Or they might manage to succeed and I'll never get the chance. That's the main one."

Her fixed gaze broke and she looked down at her knees.

"You are to be the mate of the future chief. It is decided. Honor is ever between us."

The tears, barely removed, came again. "It's not fair! I don't wish to ever see a boy with the eyes of a lame eagle!" Now they were tears of anger. "Why can't I choose a mate like all the other girls? Not another girl among The People has to take a mate which is not of her own choosing!"

She fisted away the tears, and her eyes came up to meet his. He gave her a warm but weak smile. "The gods don't will it, and the Great One hasn't told me why."

The Great One. No one else on The Top spoke of such a god, but to him, the Great One was almost like...well, a personal friend. He had tried to explain this to her more than once, but she could not grasp what he meant. A god was remote, not a shadow that followed one around. They cavorted, ignored men, played havoc when they wanted, and never got too close to any except Spirit Men. People paid them homage, sacrificed to them, sang to them, sent them messages, and then wished to be left alone. No one, be he a chief, medicine woman, or layman, fooled with the gods. And certainly, none spoke of or to a god as did Runs with the Wind. It was one feature of this man that truly baffled her. Yet it, too, led to the mysteriousness of him, and fascinated her as could no other man.

"How do you know such things? The gods have never told me anything that matters."

He studied her a moment. "But they have told

you other things about you and me."

"Yes."

"Then you know I must go, and alone. It'll be soon."

"And that doesn't matter?"

"I...yes, I guess I spoke too fast."

He smiled warmly. "Perhaps."

Her eyes averted, afraid of what he might see in them, she spoke softly, "Where will you go?"

He shrugged, though he knew, at least in a general sense. He thought it best she not know. "Away," he stated vaguely.

She turned and looked at the far string of mountains barely visible to no-sun. "That way?"

He smiled and shrugged. "Perhaps the hardest thing will be just to get away."

She dropped her lower lip to exaggerate a pout. "But you know where you go. Why won't you tell me?"

He grinned. "I can tell no one. That way no one will learn from another."

"My mu knows."

He shrugged. "Perhaps."

She shook her head. "She sees."

"As do you," he stated.

"Yes."

"Then, if the gods don't choose to show you, it's best you don't know."

"I accept that. But what I've seen leads me to fear for you. You'll travel far. You'll meet many people, and take a mate, but will be hated by a few who are ever dangerous. Beware of them. You will return one sun, but I haven't seen when, but a great event will take place just before you do. After you return, there'll be great honor for you. But it's the great event before you go...." She stopped abruptly, looked at him with soft eyes. "I speak too much."

She was on her feet, and he had been unaware when she stood. Her hand rested on his bare thigh, and the touch was like fire. "Mu knows how I feel, my love. She once had feelings for another man as I have for you...I'm sorry...I still say too much. I must go. Can you forgive me for talking too much?"

He smiled, but puzzlement showed in his face.

"What is there to forgive? You haven't offended me."

"You are a man, my love. Mu said you were, but I had to come and find out for myself. She said your honor would never allow you to consider taking me with you, and the reasons for my staying are many. But what you said is what I expected, and since you knew better than to accept my first request, I'd like to ask you one favor."

He shrugged, trying to understand why he felt a strong prick of uneasiness had just pervaded his mind. "If I can."

"Mu assured me you would, and she asked me to speak to you, though she isn't sure what your answer will be. I hope I do."

"It sounds mysterious," he smiled, trying to give it a levity he didn't feel.

"After this request, I'll not make another."

He stared at her, and his frozen smile was fake. There was something in her voice that gave him reason to think this might be something monumental, perhaps too big for him to handle.

"Before you go away, you must *Open* me."

2

The village faced mid-sun, a crescent of dwellings attached end-to-end, of *daub-and-wattle* construction, flat-roofed and chalk white, with reddish splashings of earth that made the base of the walls meld into the ground on which it stood. Doors were a vertical rectangle with a sill near knee height, keeping out snakes and other crawling and creeping creatures, as well as eliminating floor drafts. The well-packed courtyard was a hive of activity in the early sun, women grinding at the corn being harvested, using mano and metate expertly while children played games and wrestled for supremacy; old men worked on blankets or *snowtime* clothing with one eye on the tussles, chuckling at the obvious cheating and bullying which attended the games.

A Hunter stood on the top rung of the ladder which disappeared into his clan kiva below, watching his mate scold their neighbor's son for throwing dirt that had gotten into her ground corn, while he himself spoke back into the kiva to a youth who squatted half-asleep in the gloomy darkness.

"She returns, Boy with the Eye of an Eagle. There're three more with her. You're wrong again."

The lethargic youth replied without enthusiasm, "I know better. She went to see him again."

"So why don't you follow her? It's no trick to trail a woman! Or might your eyes not see like the eagle?" He chuckled at his analogy.

There was silence in the kiva, and he continued to chuckle, knowing he'd struck a raw nerve again. The son of the chief hated to be thought inferior at anything. The Hunter stepped up onto the courtyard, leaving his companion to simmer alone.

Little Dove paid no attention to the man as she climbed a ladder to the roof of her dwelling, where her mu and several other women were working at the piles of shucked corn remaining to be ground into flour.

Squatting beside the wrinkled, sun-hardened woman, Little Dove watched her moving the mano with the precision of years of work. "We talked, Mu."

The rhythm never varied. "So?"

"I'm not sure, but he nodded."

"So." She gave her daughter a glance of approval. "Then it will be done. Perhaps a bit of persuasion. A matter of honor is involved here, a lot of honor."

The other women were inauspiciously listening, trying to decipher the strange conversation which they caught only in segments. Most conversations among The People were known to all because of the close proximity of lifestyle, and privacy was nearly unknown and unpracticed. There were few secrets.

Singing Waters enjoyed talking in cryptic language for them, giving them morsels but little meat.

"I did all I could."

"I'll follow it up. Later."

"Yes, Mu."

Little Dove went back down the ladder and crossed the courtyard, rejoining her two friends. Before she could get to them, there was a loud call from behind the dwellings, and a few moments later two men came around the corner and entered the village, drawing all attention. Everyone was curious about strangers.

"Where's your chief?" one asked, directing his

question toward a group of men coming in from a field with baskets tied to their backs, laden with corn.

"Still in the field," one responded, "why?"

"We must speak to him."

"Then go down there," another said, pointing back to mid-sun.

"We were attacked by Warriors from no-sun. We come from Lion Village. It's gone. We were only a small village, and only five escaped. We lost the other three coming here."

"So why did you come here? Won't they follow you?"

"They need our trail to find you?" the second asked, his voice bordering on sarcasm as he responded to the obvious lack of hospitality. "Your smokes are visible far beyond where we lived. If they want you, they'll come."

The men deposited their baskets, then turned to face the two visitors. "They won't come here." The speaker, Keeper of the Corn, spoke with scorn. "No one has attacked us in over five generations."

"No one had ever attacked us." the first visitor responded. His voice was soft but firm, carrying a touch of unfriendliness, not unlike the attitude of the men. "Your smokes drew their attention after they finished with our village, because we were hiding and saw them point your way. We left after they went to their blankets...to warn you they'll come."

There was a pause, then a second villageman spoke. "More likely they'll follow you."

The unkind remark brought silence, which was broken by the arrival of two men. One, an older man with face painted to indicate he was the chief, glanced between the visitors and his companions.

"Welcome," he said heartily to the two men, putting his basket beside the others. "To what do we owe the pleasure of your presence?"

Keeper of the Corn spoke quickly. "They say their village was destroyed by Others, and that they're coming here. Ha!"

The chief gave him a withering glance, then turned to the visitors. "Your village was destroyed?"

The first spoke again. "I'm Blue Smoke. This's

Deer Slayer. We come from Lion Village. It is no more. Others killed all but five of us, and burned us out. The warriors pointed to your smokes before they went to their blankets. We came to warn you, and help you fight them when they come."

"Ha!"   This time it was Yellow Sapsucker. "Others never come here." The elder son of the chief was as haughty as his younger brother. "We're impossible to find...unless, of course, they follow your trail."

Again the chief gave a scathing look, this time to his own son. "To someone who is both blind and unable to smell, smoke is hard to see." He again turned to the visitors. "You saw them point here?"

"No doubt of it."

"Who is at The Rock?"   He spoke over his shoulder to the men behind him, his eyes glancing off to the unseen direction from which the men had come.

"Runner."

"You men are pretty sure they'll come here?"

"They'll come," Deer Slayer said softly, and Blue Smoke nodded.

Chief Roaring Lion stood a moment, then spoke as softly as Deer Slayer. "If they come, Runner will see them."

"If Little Dove doesn't distract him!" Yellow Sapsucker volunteered sarcastically, and Keeper of the Corn chuckled with him.

White Hawk snorted in disgust. "You two are like children! Your opinion of yourself is so lofty it shuts your mind to all intelligence! If Others come, I know of no one I'd rather see at The Rock. Perhaps better than the two of you together if you were there!"

There was a pregnant silence before the chief took the initiative again.   "You men will stay as our guests. We have a vacant dwelling, and women if you have need. With darkness, you'll be a guest in my kiva and tell us of all you know."

"We'll be honored, Chief Roaring Lion. You do your fame justice, for we have long heard of your generosity."

* * *   * * *   * * *

Little Dove was gone, but her last request still held Runs with the Wind--Runner was his name to the

villagers who often used the name as a term of derision
mostly--in the grip of shock. It was the last thing...the
very last thing...he had ever expected. After all, The
Opening was a female ceremony, not a physical union.
Never in his life had he even considered such a
phenomenon.

Still, that was what she asked. The Opening!
From time long past, tradition demanded that a young
woman be opened before mating so a man would not
have an unpleasant first experience after mating,
particularly because of an opening too small or blocked
by an inner skin.

How the women looked forward to *The Ceremony
of the Stick*! Any *mu-mu*, mu, sister, aunt, women of the
male mate's family, it was important for all to be there.
The mu-mu of the man who was to mate the young lady
would be the one to check her virginity, for no man
should unknowingly mate a woman who had been
promiscuous before her first mating.

He remembered having been told by his uncle
just what the ceremony entailed; to the men, it was a
titillating campfire or kiva story. The young woman was
taken into a private part of the mesa, with all the other
interested participants and spectators. Men were not
allowed, for if a man should see the Opening, it could
bring bad fortune to the young woman.

The future mate was placed on a blanket of
white deerskin on her knees, and given a drink that left
her with a feeling of well-being. The women chanted the
song of virgins and the song of fertility, then the girl was
stripped and ceremonially washed, the eldest sister or mu
burning the chastity belt. While it burned her mu sang
of a ripe young woman who longed for true womanhood
and children.

When only ashes remained, they were scooped
up, cooled, and poured over her head. Then came the
mu-mu of the young man, who none too gently checked
to see if the young woman had been opened prior to the
ceremony. When she was satisfied, an aunt produced
The Stick.

The Stick was about sixteen inches long, a
carefully carved and polished piece of wood, the top half
shaped like the male member, the bottom a wide base

that was placed on the ground. It was thoroughly coated with bear grease and dipped in water, then the aunt placed it butt down on the ground in front of the girl. She lifted herself as high as necessary, then lowered herself onto The Stick until it penetrated deeply enough to tear the skin of femaleness, or until her pubic hair touched the hands of the aunt.

With the hymen broken and the opening assuredly large enough for her mate, the girl was lifted from the stick by her family, laid back and washed again, this time because of the grease and blood, as well as spiritual purity. Then she was given a new chastity belt to wear until the mating, but this one had black fur on each side of the white rabbitskin.

Runs with the Wind remembered all this, and then recalled that if she were found to not be a virgin, she could be marked on her forehead with the image of a male member, forced from the village, condemned by Spirit Man, and left to fend for herself, unwelcome in any village. Never again could she enter a village of The Top, and surrounding villages would shun her. What if he opened her and this should happen? What could he do to help her?

She knew this, too, and yet she asked him! But while his head swam, there was yet another aspect even more significant. If she were telling the truth, and he thought she was, it was her own mu who had suggested it! Was she not allowing her daughter to be condemned to a death worse than torture? Or was there some method of which her mu was aware that would hide the fact of the Opening? She had no reason to lie to him? Or did she? No, she had not. She had never lied to him before, nor would she do so now. What she uttered was the truth.

It was all too much for him. He turned again to the vast distances below him, but even as his eyes read the country, his mind worked on the dilemma. The turmoil of thought that broiled threw a wild suggestion at him--one hardly worthy of consideration. He could leave now, just sneak away....

Some wanted him dead, some considered him no more than his fa and ignored him, and then...here was one...his love...his unattainable love...who wanted him....

What was that? He stopped, all thought suspended as a chill ran through him. Something moved far out. He watched a moment, nerves keyed. It could not be animals, for animals never travel in a straight line, at a steady pace, unless being chased, and even then they stopped to look back at their pursuer. Usually they wandered about, traveled in zig-zags and circles, stopping to browse or decipher possible danger, changing direction often.

This was a line of men, it had to be men, a spot on the great landscape, yet unquestionably men. Coming like the two men from the direction of the great smoke, there had to be a connection.

His heart racing, his head filled with the crashing of ideas, he studied the growing line until it took on the feature of individuals, coming swiftly in single file, following no trail but coming directly at The Top!

Who were they? Others? Was this the thing he had considered for so long, both fearful and thrilling to a young man with no experience but many dreams? Danger neared at a trot, and he began to count. Four hands and three. No hesitation...no turns...trotting... straight toward his homeland! Twenty-three men!

His excitement was nearly ready to burst when he realized his replacement was coming, and he turned to see Son of Happiness, his best and only friend, close to the rock. The young man, his junior by only a moon, was already busy trying to see what had rapt the attention of Runs with the Wind.

"What is it?" he asked as he rounded The Rock.

"Many men. Stay low and don't skyline yourself, and don't move. They're in line with Lion Village, and they come at a trot. I think they're Others."

"I see them. Did you see the two men?"

"From Lion Village?"

"Yes. They said Others destroyed their village and killed all but five. They told the chief the Others had pointed to the smoke of our fires before they slept after the attack."

"I must get to the village and tell the chief."

"You're faster, but let me go. You keep watch. It may be that later you will have to hurry back and tell the chief about them."

"Fine, but you best hurry. They'll be climbing the hill shortly."

The Others had turned for the first time, going straight to rising-sun. Son of Happiness streaked away, and Runs with the Wind squatted and watched. Twice the men disappeared behind low hills in the trees, each time reappearing with no change in speed or direction, until they were directly below. Still far below, he could not discern the paint on their faces or the colors in the feathers, but they were close enough to see their packs, spears, bows and arrows, and their naked legs moving almost in unison.

Just before they went out of sight behind the edge over which he could not see, they stopped. Bunching but staying in line, they gazed up his way, one pointing this way and that. Then he pointed around the side, to the easiest way to climb to the top.

He watched, frozen with fright and curiosity. Son of Happiness should be back at the village, or close to it. The thought brought him from his daze. What would the men of the village do? White Hawk would know, but what of the chief? Or Broken Nose, Hunter, or Maker of Defense?

The Others moved along the base of the steep hillside that rose to the sheer cliff behind which he sat, and went out of sight. For a moment he sat, wondering which of them knew of this place, or had visions from their gods. How did they know the easiest place to get on top?

Moving then, he approached the edge that looked down over the approach, and peeked over the edge. They had again stopped, only this time, the leader was pointing to the gap through which they would have to go. They knew definitely how to get on top, and they were coming up!

He could see their paint, their feathers, their unique clothing, their spears. They were awesome, fierce-looking men, even when they grinned or laughed. They were here, they were fighters, and they were beyond doubt the dreaded Others! His dreams had found reality!

He was excited and terrified. Why should he, a man of only a few moons, neither a Hunter nor a warrior, feel anything but sheer terror? He had no skills to face such men, and the Great One had told him nothing to assure him. Why wouldn't his Great One give him some indication of what he was to do? Now they were here, he was frightened, and he had no idea of what would be expected of him.

If only the Great One would speak! Instead, he felt only confusion. Should he follow the unwelcome threat, or return to the village to tell them the Others were now on The Top?

Then it hit him. He was the son of his fa, who was a coward. So he was probably a coward, too. If he returned to the village to merely tell them of the presence, which by now they already knew, would not everyone think he ran home to hide? The coward! "Ha! Here comes the coyote! Run, coyote, run! Hide beneath your mu's loincloth! Perhaps she will let you back inside!"

Still, the chief would expect him to return and tell them, wouldn't he? But what could he yet add to what Son of Happiness had already told them? And there were the two visitors, too. To add they were entering Deer Canyon would mean nothing.

The Rock was now a superfluous task. He had to follow, see what they did, where they went. The Great One didn't have to tell him; he knew.

Careful not to skyline himself or move while in their line of vision, he took his weapons and dogged them from high above. Each time he crawled to the edge to peer over, there were several whose eyes were scanning the hillsides while they walked. They were wary, but certain and obviously determined.

Dropping off the high vantage, he worked downward, staying out of sight but being sure to know where they were. Twice he sprinted to a new vantage point to be hidden when they reappeared. Hardly had he reached the second point, beneath an elderberry bush, when he saw they had done the unexpected. They were climbing almost straight at him, and were only twenty paces from where he hid. He could see their expressions, and hear only the slightest whispers of sound as they moved. None spoke; they knew they were deep into enemy territory.

Yet, what drew his stunned attention were the scalps! Some hung from the belt of every single man, with blood on the thigh and knee beside and below. New scalps, many, and he had to wrench his eyes away.

The leader was a sub-chief, denoted by the bobcat headdress, the lower jaw removed, the head resting on top of the man's head, the entire pelt hanging down over his shoulders and back. He was painted in black-and-white, his barrel chest covered with images. Bone carvings hung from his ears, more evidence of his station, and he had a majestic fierceness that commanded respect.

Never had the one simply called "Runner" felt such terror. He was as visible to them as they were to him should any of them happen to look in the right gap of the brush. His hands felt sweaty, and he clutched his spear with a grip that showed his readiness to bolt and run, although he had the feeling he would never get away from so many men. Where could he run to escape without leading them into a village or upon some undefended person?

But they passed, still in single file, angling slightly away from him until the last one went out of sight. The angle was what had saved him, of that he was sure. With a deep sigh of relief he vowed not to be so careless again. It was a vow that was to be short-lived.

Sitting a bit longer, he wondered if it were all a dream. After all, there had been no noise--only the apparition.

He knew better. In a few strides, he found their trail, and began to slowly follow, knowing this area as well as he knew his name. He began to cast about in his memory for a likely place they might stop and make camp. And he knew...he was sure of it.

A backtrail is always dangerous, because one or more might stop for any variety of reasons; he could walk into them without knowing it. Turning, he went over a knoll and down the next valley, then around another knob and up. Here he grew cautious, moving only when he was sure he could do so without fear of being seen. Fortunately none of The People wandered about; the closeness to sundown had turned them homeward.

He crawled on his stomach from under a serviceberry, moving to the next bush, sure he would see them very soon. He was right. There they were, in a small clearing just off the top of the hill, speaking softly so he could only hear a buzz and know it was the sound of men. On his belly, sweating from the nearness, with it's attendant excitement and fear, he watched.

Two of the Others walked into the brush and left to make a sortie of some kind, and three more were given the duty of guarding camp. One of these came toward Runs with the Wind and turned to the knob around which he had come. Would the man find his recent tracks? The tension within was building from the fear that would like to rob him of his senses, and he had to forcibly calm himself. His only other alternative was to leave.

Did these Others know his homeland so well? If so, how? It seemed they knew where to go, and how to guard from the best vantage points. Had they been here before? Though it was hard to believe, he had to wonder. Maybe someone had scouted the area for them. If so, when? No one had found spoor. Yet, maybe that explained the disappearance of the two young girls the previous growing season. Maybe witches hadn't gotten them at all. That was usually the accepted fact if one should disappear from time to time, even though most were taken about the time of the celebration of the Goddess. The two disappeared, however, in the time of the hottest sun.

Fear came again, this time from the witches who might be watching him. Did he do them wrong to think they might not have taken the girls? Would they attack him for his thoughts? Or did they know them? Maybe only the Great One knew.

His thoughts were recaptured with the realization the sun had set, and it was cooling quickly. The Others had eaten, and now were lounging around on their blankets, chuckling softly at comments they passed back and forth. They had no fire, and it was obvious they were going to wait for darkness before lighting any fire or making medicine to insure the gods help.

Slowly he backed from his hiding, looking for the

Other that was on guard. He was nowhere to be seen. Wondering what might have become of the man, he moved cautiously, listening and studying. He tried to picture every bush, but was uncertain, especially in the growing dusk, and determined to move only after knowing he had to do something....

The Other stood between two bushes, face averted as though he had heard something but was not sure what or from where. Runs with the Wind was instantly frightened anew. He stood downhill from the guard, and was difficult to see in the brush, but it would not be long before the man turned and saw him.

Could he escape? Yes, he knew the area so well, he could make a clean getaway--but..."Ha! The coyote! Find mu's breechcloth!" No, he was a man! Never would anyone consider him a coward again!

Deliberately he leaned his spear against a stiff branch, careful that it would stand still. Then he took the bow from his shoulder, placed the arrow, and applied tension to the string. It was his tree...his favorite target. The frayed area, long chewed from many knives, spears and arrows, was just below the left shoulder, in from the armpit. He let fly.

The man turned slightly in the deep dusk, like he was going to look at him. Then the knees sagged and the man went down as the life went out of him. He made no sound.

He had done it! He had killed his first enemy! A cry of triumph nearly escaped his lips before he caught himself. With a feeling he had never experienced, he knelt and put his knife to the scalp, doing what he knew They would be doing if They killed him. Never having done it, he was clumsy, and the cut jagged, but when he stood, he held a section of scalp with the long hair attached.

He tied it to his belt, feeling the blood on his leg as it dripped from the memento, then retrieved his own arrow, then took the man's arrows and knife before moving away. When he felt reasonably safe, he stopped and tried to think what to do next.

Where were the other guards, and what of the two men who had gone to spy out the villages? He had to be close to where the men would return, but did he want to be in their path? To kill one--and that somewhat between accidental and good fortune--was a far cry from taking on two at once!

And even as he thought of it, he heard a noise, however slight, and realized it was too late to run. His vow to be careful was as the wind. The second of the three sentinels stood only five strides away, looking right at him! His bow was unstrung, his arrows in their sheath, and all he had readily available was his knife!

3

Son of Happiness had burst into the village out of breath, frantically describing the presence of the Others, gathering around him the entire village. Questions had been asked to which he had no answers, and though no one would voice such a thing, fears aroused. The threat brought out questions whose answers were self-evident, and none seemed anxious to break out of the gathering until Broken Nose had taken over.

"It's doubtful they'll attack before the Sun God rises, so we have time to consider what must be done. They might not even come here. You've all been trained where to go and how to conduct yourselves, so remember well. Don't wander off and do something stupid.

"Be sure there's plenty of water on hand, since we don't know how long they'll stay around. No one should leave the village at any time, man, woman or child. Men will be posted nearby, and we will meet soon to discuss strategy."

The watchmen were assigned, the women and

children began getting water ollas filled, and the men went a short distance from the village and met. Workers were called in from the fields; there was no panic, but fear was evident everywhere.

Little Dove sought out Son of Happiness, and surprisingly found him alone and waiting the opportunity to follow the men to their place of meeting. "He Who Runs with the Wind, he will return soon?"

Son of Happiness, knowing her concern for his friend, shrugged his shoulders. "Who can predict He Who Runs with the Wind? He is like the hawk, alone and single-minded."

"But he's not afraid."

"Afraid? Probably, like the rest of us. But he'll do as the Great One tells him. He has a spirit you and I wouldn't understand."

She looked off toward The Rock. "I could wish for him to be here where it's safer."

"Is it safer here? Who knows where the Others will choose to go. Perhaps it's safer out there in the brush and trees. If I were in his moccasins, I think I'd stay out there and watch them. Much easier to stay where they aren't if you know where they are."

She turned and walked slowly back toward her dwelling, then helped her mu lift a large olla of water across the threshold into the dwelling.

"Mu, I fear for him."

Her mu gave her a slight smile and shrug. "He's a man, with the strength and knowledge of a man. He'll be as safe out there as we are here. I imagine he's tailing the Others at a safe distance to see where they go."

"But that's dangerous!"

"So is breathing. One can inhale evil spirits. So is walking, since it's easy to fall and break a leg. He'll be fine. Besides, you should be equally concerned for Boy with the Eye of an Eagle, you know." Her sun-darkened, wrinkled face gave the slightest of smiles, the spaces of missing teeth visible amid the discolored.

Little Dove made a face. "Never. I could almost wish him to be killed by Others. It'd make my life much more like the wild rose...able to move as I choose."

Argumentive voices could be heard from where

the men met, but the voices were too far away to understand. The women turned to watch for a moment.

"They'll decide nothing," Little Dove said contemptuously. "Two many minds, and most only half full." Disgust was plain on her youthful, pretty face.

Mu laughed, and the great difference in their faces would never indicate they were mu and daughter. She was stooped, her body skinny to the point of emaciation, her breasts gone with only folds of skin where they had once been. Her arms resembled sinews with a knob at the elbow, and her legs were bone covered with rough, wrinkled skin. Only her height gave credence to the relationship, for she, like her daughter, stood nearly a head taller than the average woman. Her eyes, however, were still alive and beautiful, and there was yet a lilt in her laugh that had given her the name Singing Waters. "You are too intelligent for your own good, my daughter. Just remember this. There are only one or two of those men who would not fight to the death to protect their women and dwellings. With what skill they can fight, no one will know unless The Others come, but for bravery, our men have as much as anyone."

"I suppose. But are there some who would not fight?"

"That, my Little Dove, is for you to find out. My suspicions are not going to taint your thinking."

"But the gods will be angry if all are not brave!"

"So? A man cannot be what he is not. If he's a coward, he's a coward. Coyotes live with the deer and wapiti, do they not?"

"And they run with the slightest fear."

"And the gods do not chastise them for their cowardice. In fact, the gods sometimes use them to give us messages."

"But they have a spirit different from a man. A man is to be brave. The gods punish men. Animals...." Her voice trailed off as she saw one of the men stand and point toward the Valley of the Deer. Other men shook their heads and one reached up to pull him back down.

"They argue about whether to attack the Others or not. Red Deer is old, and he's only the Designer, but he is brave. Perhaps foolhardy, too, who knows. But he'll not lack for courage when the time comes."

Little Dove shook her head. "If only our chief were younger, he might know how to fight. But he's much too old."

"Few men live to thirty-five winters. Even his once sage wisdom no longer is sage. Yet I fear for The People when he's no longer chief. Yellow Sapsucker is without a head, much less intelligence. His inner spirit's weak and fearful. The gods who lead him are stupid and wicked."

"I suppose that's your way of telling me I'm lucky to be mating Boy with the Eye of an Eagle, and not him."

"Life is often a choice between the lesser of two evils. And I'm told your soon mate will be renamed at the next ceremony. He'll be given the name Eagle Eye."

"Yippee," she responded with a complete lack of enthusiasm. "I suppose that means I should feel I mate a man instead of a boy."

"I had to mate your fa, you know. I had no choice, either. When the son of a chief is involved, neither will you. But you can kick him out later, if you so desire, though that causes problems, too. Few men want to mate a woman who was once mated to a chief, and especially if she gave her mate the hard toe."

"I wish I could run away with He Who Runs with the Wind."

"He will make a man. And a true man would never put a woman through what he'll surely face. No, he'd never permit it, and he has my respect for being so honorable."

"But I can still wish."

"Dream as you will. He'll open you. At least you can carry the memory of having known a man. I was even denied that. By the time I knew the joy of true coupling, the man had lost his manliness and become nothing more than the whisper of what I thought he was."

They lapsed into silence. The sun hung low behind the village, and the men still argued and cajoled. Cooking fires were started, and women were attending to the meals, two and three women around each fire. Singing Waters and Little Dove made no move to join any of them.

The growing dusk had a quieting effect over the women who worked at their meals, most with an ear and eye cocked to where the men were meeting. Occasionally a voice was raised high enough for them to hear a word or two, and they would stop and stare, trying to get the gist of the arguments over which the men fought. The sun set, and darkness came quickly, a typical feature of the country that lay on the sunrise side of mountains. Little Dove kept an anxious eye, glancing often at her mu. Singing Waters, now working at her meal, seldom looked at Little Dove, but kept a peripheral fix that allowed her to monitor her daughter.

"Why has he not returned?" The voice was soft but anxious.

"He will. I think he's a man with a mighty spirit. If I'm right, he'll be a hero before the men have time to settle their differences."

Little Dove stopped and stared. "What did you say? Have you seen something you aren't telling me?"

"Let us just say I have a premonition."

"Mu, you...."

"Hush! Just keep your eyes open."

Little Dove continued to stare a few moments, wondering at the mysterious words, then took a bowl of lentil soup. The bowl, however, was more a toy than a utensil, for she merely played with it, swirling the contents around and sipping only a few times.

He Who Runs with the Wind appeared from around the end of the village, almost as though he materialized from the darkness itself. Little Dove froze, drawing the curious glance of Singing Waters.

He stepped up to a fire where his mu stooped. She handed him a bowl with his evening meal. He sat in the semi-darkness away from the fire, glancing once at Little Dove. His look was one of interest, which she could not see because of the darkness, and then he fell to eating. Little Dove was dying of curiosity, but felt ill-at-ease in going to him, and refrained.

He finished eating, stood and stretched, and she heard the burp of appreciation before he wandered down the slope to where the men still met. She watched as he stopped behind the last of the men and stood watching.

"You finally come, coyote?" The raised voice,

audible to the women, was Boy with the Eye of an Eagle. "Been hiding?" He laughed, joined by a few others, including his older brother.

"He Who Runs with the Wind?" It was Broken Nose, who most often ignored him, seeming to hold him in neither derision nor favor. "You've been watching the Others?"

"I followed them," he replied nonchalantly.

"Come," Broken Nose beckoned with a hand gesture. "I can't see you back there, and I have a few questions."

He Who Runs with the Wind stepped between some of the seated men and approached the front, where a large fire lit the faces of the men. He was about halfway to the fire when he heard a man suck in his breath, and then another. Suddenly the four scalps at his side were like a screaming woman.

Unable to know what the men had seen, Broken Nose asked, "Have the Others come onto The Top?"

"They camp near the twin knobs above the Valley of the Deer." He entered the ring of firelight and stopped. "There are four hands minus one."

"But Son of Happiness said there were four hands and three."

"There were."

"But...." His eyes fell to the scalps for the first time. His mouth dropped open, and he stared as though fire rode the hip.

Suddenly He Who Runs with the Wind wanted to stuff the scalps down the throats of the chief's two sons, and without thinking he grabbed the four and held them away from the leg. Looking straight at Boy with the Eye of an Eagle, he said in a voice that carried to the women, "There were more, until I killed four. The coyote has struck! Perhaps boys and sapsuckers should learn what a man is before they stick out their chests like a prairie chicken in heat!" He pulled the knife of the first Other he had killed from his waist band and tossed it handle first at Boy with an Eye. "Here! A souvenir to remind you of who plays the coyote!"

Two men laughed as Boy with an Eye, surprised at the sudden missile, fumbled and dropped it. The laughter was enjoined by several more. Then White

Hawk spoke, his usually soft voice holding the men in total attention.

"Because of this, the Others will not attack. Their medicine is not good, and He Who Runs with the Wind has shown what it is to be the man. While we sat here since high sun arguing how to keep our women and children safe, another has won the battle for us. Yellow Sapsucker, do you still think we ought to hide in the caves until the Others are gone? Gray Dog, you still think we should set fire to our village to let them think we have run away? Twin Who Lived, do you think we can never attack them? You are the only one who might be right. We no longer need to. They'll be without spirit with the new sun."

He stopped and looked at He Who Runs with the Wind. "How many scalps do you have? Four?"

"Four."

"Then they won't stay. Let them go. To attack them would be to incur their anger, and they'd soon return. The chief and I think it best to let them suffer in silence, bury their dead and go." Several concurred, voices raised in assent.

He Who Runs with the Wind walked back between the men and headed toward the dwellings, ignoring the faces that turned to watch him. No one challenged him, and when he entered the courtyard, women and children watched him with eyes of praise. He entered his dwelling, stretched out on his mat, and soon slept. It was just before sunup when he awoke; his mu sat across the firepit watching him.

"My son has brought honor to his mu."

"I didn't think of honor."

"Which is what makes my son a man. I would hear the story, my son." She handed him a bowl of broth with a thick slice of cornbread and a cup of hot tea. "You will tell the story?"

He preferred to leave, but he briefly related how he had followed them to their encampment and killed four. Three guards and one who went out to relieve himself.

As he was about to leave the dwelling, unsure of what to do with himself, the Village Crier spoke into the dawn. "It is a sun to raise grateful hands to Sun God!

The Others, who would surely have been here to attack us by now, have found their medicine to be weak! Because of He Who Runs with the Wind, they will leave. We are yet safe! Rise and enjoy the travels of Sun God!"

He listened, and remembered anew, and felt the four scalps at his side. The decision was made. He would return to the Others and see what they did.

The chief sat at the doorway to his kiva, facing the lightening skies and having finished his morning prayer, enjoying the coolness and wrapped in a blanket. He noticed Runs with the Wind at the moment he stepped from his dwelling, and motioned for the young man to join him with a hand signal and patting the ground beside himself.

"You're up early for a hero," he greeted the younger.

Runs with the Wind was not sure how he meant it, and guardedly responded. "I don't think of myself as a hero, my chief."

"Ah, but you are, like it or not. You did what no one has ever done. You killed not one but four Others. That makes four more than any man alive on The Top, and four more than anyone for at least five generations."

"I guess I hadn't thought of it."

"You didn't endear yourself to many of the young men, my sons included."

"That's their problem." After a pause, he added, "I feel quite sure I've never been considered a friend to them, anyway." He said it quietly but firmly.

"Ah! Perhaps." He paused. "Perhaps what you say is true, but don't count on going unchallenged. You called them coyotes."

"Which is what they've called me for winters. It is good sometimes for a man to taste the bitterness of self-evaluation. I certainly had to endure and eat their words long enough."

The chief chuckled. "And it made a man of you. Now it's time for others to grow up a bit. But watch your step, my son. You made a pair of dangerous enemies."

"They chose to make me their enemy long ago. I only gave them a taste of bitter herbs, and maybe lifted their anger a bit. They needed no reason to hate me, since they started doing that a long time ago. I hope they hear a bit of the sarcasm and derision I've faced because of them for a long time."

"You could be right, but that doesn't solve anything. Perhaps nothing will. Everyone can see you walk with a different inner voice. Regardless, never underestimate them. They're bitter, and a little more than angry. You fueled their smoking fire."

"So be it. They earned the scorn; I'll be careful." He got to his feet. "I only wish they weren't your sons. You are my chief, but I would never accept either of them in your place. You have my respect. They have only my tolerance and disdain." He saw the slightest of smiles on the face of the old man, the twinkle of the eye, and knew he had nothing to fear from the old man. It was certain that he didn't consider He Who Runs with the Wind to be a rival of his sons, and even enjoyed seeing his sons challenged. He nodded briefly to the chief to indicate he understood the old one's attitude.

He picked up his weapons and left, and as soon as he was out of sight of the chief, he changed directions and began to run. He had a long way to go, and wanted to be there already. His curiosity of what was happening in the camp of the Others was overwhelming.

It was a voice that stopped him...the voice of a woman. He was not sure it was meant for him, but he thought he had heard his name. He turned and looked back, every sense alert that it might be a trap. But it was Singing Waters who stood between two cedars watching him.

"You aren't an easy man to catch," she said, smiling. "Come, I have some words for you."

She led him through an opening in the brush, then turned and sat on the edge of the canyon, looking down the steep hill toward rising-sun. He sat beside her at her signal. Only the length of a foot was between them.

"Little Dove has come to you with a request."

He felt embarrassed, but said, "She did."

"She has a very strong affection for you...perhaps it is love."

"No one seems to care," he replied bitterly.

"I do, but it has been decided."

He said nothing, so she continued. "You've proven yourself a man several times, and it is why I allowed her to approach you. You know of the Ceremony of the Stick."

He nodded, his eyes working on the valley before them in order to keep his eyes from hers, which he knew would befuddle him. He even felt embarrassment.

"She will, of course, go through it. But she'll be Opened before it, and it will only be held because of tradition, and because we prefer that no one knows except Little Dove, you and me. I can keep it silent, and you'll be leaving before the next moon darkens."

Surprised at her statement, he stoically said nothing. "You'll travel for half a moon before you find a people where you'll stop. But before you leave, you must do as Little Dove requested, and as you wish. She'll give you a trinket to wear, and you must not remove it until after you mate another. You will be a fa because of the Opening, but the son will be one you never understand. Some sun you'll return, and this people will be ready for a true leader. I shall see the time before I die.

"You must do what the gods tell you, being careful to listen harder than ever before. They can be difficult, but listen well." She stood and walked away.

After she was gone, he quickly turned down the hill at an angle, heading for the Others. While he ran, he thought of the two sons of the chief, aware that they were dangerous, and never more so than now that he had shaken their egos. He wondered at the temperament of the chief, but let that go quickly. More importantly, what had he goaded the chief's sons to do now?

It was possible they might try to do something immediately, while the Others were still on The Top, and let the blame fall on his being alone where the Others caught him.

He held no delusions. The People blindly followed their traditions, and the sons of the chief, while they walked to different voices from anyone else, could do little wrong. After the very serious incident when he brought the two to ridicule, he could expect no mercy from anyone. He had always been considered different by most, a bit strange and not particularly brave--though perhaps gifted. His fa was a nothing, a little, wizened man with no drive and no talent except to plant and to weed and to harvest...but despised for his cowardice in the place from which he came.

Son of Happiness was awed by his knowledge and perception, Little Dove loved him, his mu held him with a new respect, his fa was no doubt newly proud of his son, and White Hawk held him in enough esteem to listen, but he could not count any others on his side among the entire People of the Top. So it was imperative he be careful, and that he leave. The thought was frightening, even though there was an excitement in it.

Within the moon, Singing Waters had said. How did she know? And the part about his traveling for part of a moon before finding a people where he would take a mate. But he would return to his own people before she died. Surprising, interesting, and what else could he say? It tended to alleviate some of his fears, for if he were to return, he would not be killed out there. But that gave him no privilege to be stupid or unworthy, for the Great One would not tolerate such behavior. Visions could be wrong, especially if a man acted stupidly.

He topped a hill and turned along the ridge. It was no help that he was only fourteen winters, and Boy with the Eye of an Eagle, soon to be named Eagle Eye, was the older. But age was only one of the problems. Still, if he were to stay on The Top, he would one sun have need to challenge the enemy to the death, or face a life of watching every shadow and wondering where the knife or arrow might come from. It was something he would never do. Instead, he would go.

Even as the thought passed through his mind, he heard a word come through the air. "Coyote! Hide under your mu's loin cloth!" And they might be justified! Was that the reason he was leaving?

4

Smoke rose into the sky near where he had killed the four Others. At first, it was a single tendril, and then it grew and became two, then three and finally four heavy smokes that mingled into one. There was no doubt of the cause, and though his nerves tingled with excitement and his senses told him to be careful because of the alertness of the Others, he hurried to watch them sending the spirits of their four friends to their gods.

His uncle, while he sat at the feet of the man during his training time, had said, "Life is as uncertain at the time you feel great as it is when you feel terrible. When you feel the certainty of doom, you are no closer to death than when you are gaily dancing from joy. Never assume you will live forever. Only the gods have immortality. So, while one victory may lead to another, it can just as surely lead to death. Above all, carelessness does not make an honorable death."

On another occasion, he added, "Time for the greatest vigilance often comes at the very moment when you feel the best." The thoughts came to him while he ran, and he grinned. The Others had been feeling good, confident and even cocky. Destruction had come when they felt the best.

He felt good. In fact, he felt great. He stopped, listening, studying what he saw in his mind, considering the most likely positions of the sentinels, then proceeded more cautiously. He was close to where he had killed the fourth man, so he hunkered down to study everything before his next move, and again studied before another move.

He moved again, and stopped amid four bushes, where he lay on his stomach and peered through. The Others were on the far side of a clearing, many prostrated before the burning pyres. The stench of burning bodies filled the air, and the flames were high about four raised platforms. Heavy smoke billowed from the now leaping flames, evidence of the bodies that once were warriors...he had killed! He watched, fascinated. Some were dancing around the fire, chanting a language he did not know. A few were standing apart, their eyes busy studying lest they be attacked. He counted sixteen, which meant they had three guarding them elsewhere against a surprise attack.

Gradually the fires burned down, until only smoke rose from the piles of ashes. Silently, as by a signal, the Others picked up their weapons and headed up the valley, pointing for the place where they had entered. The three guards appeared from their spots of concealment to join the exodus. They were leaving.

He wanted to sing, to shout, to voice his joy at what the Great One had done for him. He was a man! He had driven the Others from The Top without a single one of The People losing a single drop of blood! He was a man! How he had longed for the sun when he could know for sure he was a man. And here it was! The coward did not exist.

He watched them disappear, and stood to follow. He took one step, and never felt the blow that put him on the ground. Unsure of what had happened, he lay motionless, a numbness in his left shoulder. Then pain began sweeping slowly out from it. Something warm ran down his shoulder and upper arm, and he felt rather than saw the blood. He did not realize that he was bleeding profusely, only that he had been hurt, the realization an incredulity. How had he been struck, or by whom? Had he missed count of the Others? As time passed, the pain began to intensify, but he knew he should not move, though it took effort not to move against the pain. He had no idea of the duration of time before he heard the movement of someone not too far away, and whoever it was approached slowly and cautiously.

My uncle was right, he thought. When I felt best, I was closest to death. Another sound...the man was close, in fact, he was standing only a stride away looking down at him. His eyes were like a physical touch on his back, and he clutched his knife in his right hand, unsure of how to move. If he rolled to his left, the pain might affect his ability to use the knife, but what other choice was there? Any move was going to require that he ignore pain, and in fact he determined not to be affected by it. It would take hard concentration, to which he committed himself. His deceased uncle would have been proud.

Through his nearly closed eyes he could judge the location of his enemy, and knew the man was debating if he lived or not. He wanted his death, not the scalp. It had to be one of his own people, for an Other would have never hesitated. And if he showed any sign of life, he would never feel the spear that rammed through him. He had to move fast when he moved at all, and did he have the strength to do it? He felt the tip of the spear on his back; it broke the skin again, and again. He had to use difficult discipline to lie still, though the three jabs of the spear were merely seeking muscular response, an assurance that the man was indeed dead and not decoying. The intense pain of his shoulder made it possible for him to sell his enemy that he was dead.

Trying hard to give no sign of life, he gathered his muscles and poised, then rolled left with suddenness, feeling pain shoot through his arm and shoulder, and flung his knife in a backhand that carried both power and accuracy. Even as it struck, he saw the contorted, startled face of Yellow Sapsucker!

The knife buried itself past its gut-and-resin just

under the sternum, and Yellow Sapsucker numbly stared at it, a blank look which rapidly turned to fear. As he fully realized what had happened, his tortured eyes went to Runs with the Wind, who sat watching, his right hand clasping the injured shoulder. "You...you...killed me!"

Runs with the Wind felt nothing...only tiredness. A desire to lie down and sleep. "You earned it." Did he say that, or just think it?

Yellow Sapsucker dropped to his knees, both hands wrapped around the handle of the knife, trying to pull it out but too weak to succeed. His face had gone pale, and his eyes closed; slowly he toppled forward onto his face.

Runs with the Wind sat staring stupidly at the body which lay lifelessly in front of him, then looked down to see his own blood. The arrow still protruded from the shoulder, having entered just below the shoulder blade, and almost half the shaft stuck through the skin in the front, the arrowhead covered with blood. Blood ran down his side, and he wondered if he, too, were about to die.

Somewhere in the back of his mind came the warning that if Yellow Sapsucker was here, Boy with the Eye might not be far behind. He had to move, and he was very tired, and very thirsty. He needed water. None was close.

He staggered to his feet and started back along his own trail, the arrow still in his shoulder. Ravens flew through his vision, dark birds of bad omen, trying to blind him, to keep him from moving much less reaching his destination. He stumbled, lost his spear but managed to grasp a branch with the right hand and remain on his feet.   He was swimming in a sea of ravens. Then he lost awareness, even the big black birds flying away. When he revived, the sun was at its zenith. He had slept for some time, and now his thirst was ravenous. He managed to sit up, his head thumping and a few ravens fluttering about, but his head cleared and he saw his spear lying near his feet. He had gone nowhere after losing it.

His face hurt, and a hand reached up to touch it, finding bits of rock lodged in the skin. He had fallen flat on his face...and there was dried blood. He could not move his left arm, and found the arrow was still intact. His own quiver and bow were still draped over his right shoulder, where he had last put them.

Memory began to return, and he saw Yellow Sapsucker lying only a short distance away. His knife must still be in the dead man's stomach. He tried to stand, but the sea of ravens returned, so he crawled the few feet to the body, with all his strength rolled it over, and retrieved his knife, which he cleaned on the loin cloth and skin of what had been Yellow Sapsucker. Then he slowly got to his feet, braced himself with his spear, and began to walk slowly and unsteadily toward home, gripping the spear so hard his knuckles turned white.

He was very weak, stopping several times to lean on his spear, his left arm useless. It was oozing again, but he ignored it and continued to walk. His legs felt flimsy like the grass over which he walked, but he kept plodding, trying not to go down hills so he would not have to climb again. It was farther, but he had no choices left. He kept at it, trying to stay away from trails where he might encounter Boy with the Eye, or one of his friends.

The sun was sinking quickly over the edge of The Top before he saw the backside of the village dwellings, yet a long way off, but seeing it gave him a boost of energy. He stumbled as he rounded the corner of the dwellings, and he heard several exclamations before he reached his door. His mu helped him inside, and summoned Medicine Woman. Grateful for his mat, he let the darkness come again.

"It's the arrow of Yellow Sapsucker! Why does he carry it?" The voice seemed far away, but he recognized Medicine Woman. There was someone touching his shoulder, a searing pain and he faded again.

When he regained his senses, White Hawk sat beside him, his shoulder was bandaged in a poultice and cotton-cloth binding, and his mu was holding a mug of hot tea for him. He gratefully sipped it.

"Well, now," White Hawk said with a feigned cheerful-ness, "I suppose now we can find the answer to the mystery of the arrow." He held up the broken arrow and added, "Yellow Sapsucker. I would suspect this might hold the answer to why the son of the chief has not returned in two darknesses."

Runs with the Wind nodded, though the effort took more strength than he thought he had.

"You want to talk about it?"

"He shot me." The voice was so soft and wispy he wondered if it were really his own.

"The arrow entered from behind."

"Yes. I had been...watching the fires...of the Others. They began to leave. I started...to follow...." His mouth was dry, so dry his tongue wanted to stick to the roof of his mouth. He sipped the tea again. "I had no idea what...knocked me down. I lay...to let...to let...." He began to see the ravens again. He tried to swallow, but it felt as though it were the tongue that was going down. "To let the man...who shot...come...and I rolled...." Was he still making sense? "I rolled...and threw...my knife."

"Yellow Sapsucker."

"I didn't know...it was he...until...until the knife was...knife...sticking...stomach."

"He's dead?"

Runs with the Wind closed his eyes. "Dead."

"Well, no one knows of the arrow except Medicine Woman, your mu, you and me. And no one else shall. Will his body be hard to find?"

"Near two knobs...where I...killed...four...." His voice was so soft White Hawk leaned to put his ear near the mouth.

"We'll leave him be a few suns, and then 'find' him when it's too late to see what killed him. The animals will have feasted by then. Just say you knew nothing of him, but you were wounded by an Other when you went back to see if they were leaving."

"Why? Truth is...easier."

"He was the son of the chief. He tried to kill you, but who would understand that, or believe it? Let it die like Yellow Sapsucker. He deserved what he got, and you live. Is that not enough?"

"Enough. As...you say."

"Good! Now you rest, and I'll get the story started about why you were wounded, without truth and not telling where the body is. No one will know of his death for at least three suns unless somebody sees the scavengers. They've been scouring the country looking for him...so far, without success."

When he was gone, Runs with the Wind swallowed some broth his mu spooned to him, drank two swallows of the tea made from yarrow, and slept. He dreamed of Little Dove, standing naked and beckoning him. He was still thinking of her when he awakened, his body responding in an embarrassing way. He wondered if all men had such dreams.

For ten suns he never went to the door, relieving himself into a jug beside his mat. He drank broth and tea, and ate only cornbread. Never had he felt so weak, and it frightened him. Again he remembered his uncle. "Time for the greatest vigilance often comes at the very moment when you feel the best." It had been so.

But now it was time to get off his mat and feel the sun on his face. He was surprised at his weakness as he left the dwelling, stopping just outside and slumping down against the building to avert the ravens that again raided his head. Once sitting on the ground, the ravens left, and he watched the activity around him without emotion, wishing he were on The Rock talking to Little Dove.

For the hundredth time he wondered about The Opening, which he was unable to do because of the wound. Was she still wanting him, or was she mated? He knew all the preliminaries had been made between Boy with the Eye and the family of Little Dove. All that remained was for him to decide it was time and move in with her. If he knew Little Dove, though, she had worked with her mu to stall the mating somehow.

Yet, he wondered how it would be effected between him and her...if it were yet to be. Somehow he knew it was.

On the other hand, he had another matter often racing through his mind--Yellow Sapsucker and the ambush. What was he to do about that?

This was the sun when either White Hawk or someone he had given an instruction to would find the decomposed body, unless the birds feasting on the cadaver had drawn attention to it. But he had heard nothing resembling an outcry, although it could have happened while he slept like he had been fed one of

Medicine Woman's potions.

Somehow he felt that, too, was yet to be. And after the body was brought back and buried, at least, what was left of it, he would himself take a leisurely hike back to the scene and survey where the Others had camped. Perhaps they had left a memento he could give to Spirit Man who could put a curse on its owner.

All sun he sat, speaking briefly to a few people, but most kept a distance. Why no one came near he tried to understand, but no answers came that seemed logical. Was he suspected of having done something to Yellow Sapsucker? While it was a most reasonable idea, no one seemed to be hostile. It was beyond him. Even the chief steered clear of him. Was it in deference to the warning at the sun when he was wounded? Did he feel compelled to act the part of the supportive fa? It was...well...hard to understand. But it was logical.

And if he took his walk on the next sun, what if he were seen and followed? Perhaps he should take a friend, though he preferred not to go if he were not alone. He had to speak to the Great One, to understand what had happened and why, and to discover what to do next. His inner voice had been silent too long.

It was near sundown when the cry went up as several men approached the village from no-sun. The decomposing body of Yellow Sapsucker had been discovered. The men came into the courtyard carrying what was left of it on a bison hide, some openly angry and some showing signs of sorrow. Where was White Hawk? His coolness would be necessary when some accusations were sure to fly.

Well, he had thought up his story, and if they accused him, he was ready.

It came just as the fires were being lighted for the evening meal. Boy with the Eye, feigning sorrow and accompanied by Gray Dog and Twin Who Lived, came to where Runs with the Wind sat alone.

"You killed my brother!" It was said loudly to gain the attention of everyone.

Runs with the Wind spoke quietly. "You lie...as usual." It was spoken laconically, disinterestedly. He watched them from his peripheral vision, but looked at Broken Nose, who watched from beside the nearest fire.

"You call me a liar?" The young man was nearly screaming, only a step from losing his self-control.

"If you aren't, then most of The People are deluded." His voice was quiet, with the same far-away effect.

"I call you! We will Death Match!"

"If you choose. I don't, since I choose not to kill the son of the chief. However, if you want, it shall be, and I choose that we fight not with knives or axes, but with spears." It was no secret that Runs with the Wind was far superior to Boy with the Eye in the handling of the spear...or its cousin, the atlatl. It was probable that he was very superior with the knife, too.

A look of fear crossed the face of the excited young man that faced him, but was quickly hidden. "Ha! So you choose the weapon of coyotes! It fits!"

"Coyotes? Who is the coyote? Have you any scalps to show The People you know how to fight? And the spear was said by your own fa to be the weapon only of the brave. It is the arrow that is the weapon of the coyote. Do you call your own fa a liar?"

Taken aback, Boy with the Eye lost composure, and spat venomously, "You lie! He never said that!"

"Then I suggest you ask him. It was to you he said it, when your spear was broken and you were unable to kill even a rabbit. Who was it that fixed your spear so you could at least use it?" It was a good time to rub salt into the wound!

Boy with the Eye stared at him a moment, unable to reply. In that moment of stunned silence, Runs with the Wind looked at him for the first time. "If not for your small intelligence, you would have known how your brother was killed, and I was wounded. But you can't tell truth from fiction, and your emotions control you again. If you want the truth, your brother and I were watching the Others, and they saw us. We were greatly outnumbered and ran. They caught your brother because he fell. They wounded me, but I managed to escape and hide. But you could never reason that out, and I can overlook your obvious lack of sense. Never could you have thought through the puzzle before you acted. It's against your nature to think. It's just another proof you aren't yet mature enough to be a leader. Perhaps you should pick better friends so you can grow up to be a man."

There was laughter from nearby, and the chief said, "Good advice, my son who is not my son. I must make amends for the words of my real son, whose mind still lacks maturity. Anger is the spoiler of intelligence. This darkness, while the smoke carries the spirit of my dead son to the gods, you shall be honored for your bravery. Council and The Hunters agree that you must receive recognition for having sent the Others back to their lands. It's enough that your aging mu and fa have a favorite of the gods to honor them, but you shall receive honor for what you have done."

The chief turned quickly away, and the speechless Runs with the Wind could only stare at his back. An honor? For him? The gods did indeed smile on him!

Angrily, Boy with the Eye spun and stomped away, followed by his two companions. He would have called Runs with the Wind a liar, knowing his brother would never have sat with him to watch the Others. It was a ludicrous thought. But to say so would have told the entire village that his brother was seeking to kill his village enemy. That would cause all kinds of repercussions.

The near disaster of a Death Match had been averted for the present, but Runs with the Wind felt an ominous aura surround the angry adversary as he disappeared into the fallen darkness. He might have escaped having to fight the man face-to-face, but it was quite certain a greater danger now existed. It was a task he hated, for running scared did not please him; however, he needed to be afraid, and ever so alert, for he had narrowly escaped the first ambush! It was obvious the sons of the chief walked to a different inner voice, since they were willing to kill without regard for fair play. He would have to be more than careful. It had nothing to do with being a coyote!

5

He had improved. Suns had come and gone, dawns were cooling significantly, bushes were dropping leaves while sumac turned flame red, and the breath of the gods was cold and sparkling on the landscape as Sun God arose from his bed. The strength in his legs brought restlessness, a desire to be out and doing. But while he felt the urges, his senses and alertness told him that Boy with the Eye was watching his every move...or one of his friends was. He felt like a caged animal.

He was up early. Sun God had not yet begun to make his appearance, frost sat heavy on the foliage, a myriad of stars twinkled overhead, and he looked out the door with longing. His breath formed steam that drifted up and disappeared. He had rested too long; it was time to go. Yet he hesitated. It was dark. The witches of darkness were not friends, and it was with trepidation he should consider going out. But he needed to be away from the village before the first stirrings by his people so no one would know he was gone.

Reluctantly, and at the same time purposefully,

he stepped over the threshold and stopped to pet a dog that had heard his stirrings and awaited his attention. Then he began to walk, quietly and carefully. Past the ever present guard and the last building, he was soon over the edge of the valley and following a path he knew so well.

There was no Moon Goddess, or he would have left the trail. But the lighter area of the trail was all he could see well. Carefully he picked his way along, his ears attuned to any night sounds which seemed out of character. Appeased, he watched for the turn of the trail where it started up again, and just as he took the first steps, he heard a sound from behind.

He froze and listened, trying to interpret the noise or hear it again. Puzzled, he stepped off the trail and squatted behind a bush, breathing slowly and softly. Time passed, but there was no repeat of the sound, until hesitantly he stood and inched back to the trail.

Fighting down panic, a desire to run or even hurry, he moved almost soundlessly, feeling each stone and twig with his feet, proud of his long interest in the moccasin footwear he had made. He went as fast as he could safely go without making noise, and soon topped the hill, where he gave no time for someone to see him skylined.

Down again, and up, and down again. The next ridge was his destination, but he wondered at the wisdom to go there if he were being followed. He planned to sing a song, one the Great One alone must hear, but so would anyone else in the area. He preferred to be alone.

On a whim, he stopped in the bottom of the valley, noting the slight lightening of the skies where Sun God approached, and left the trail far enough to get behind some mountain mahogany where he could sit. From there, he could see the trail in three places, in addition to where it came off the top of the last ridge. Liking the spot, he relaxed and became vigilant.

No one came and the skies grew lighter. His inborn fear of darkness began to subside, and he wished Little Dove were with him...a thought that crossed and left.

For a long while he sat, until it was fully light

and Sun God appeared. Relaxed as he was, and despite the chill, he slept.

Or was it sleep? He was watching a great scene, which he realized was the view from The Rock. And far out on the valley floor there walked a man, whose face pointed into mid-sun. It was far for clear-cut identity, but he knew who it was. It was impossible to miss the lankiness, the exceptional height, the ambling walk, the occasional stops to look back and remember the landmarks as they would look when he returned. The figure began to trot, and long after he was out of sight, the watcher still saw him, running, then sleeping under the snow and it could not touch him. The scene faded, and he pondered what he had seen. It was he himself, that was certain, but was it a dream? Or was it a vision? Would the gods play with him like that? He knew they would.

In fact, they had on many occasions, but never to the point he had been severely injured or killed. To be picked on by the gods proved he was a man! It was their way, for man was but a toy, a thing to use, to abuse or favor as they saw fit, and to do bodily injury if that seemed appropriate. They derived no enjoyment in bullying children. After all, they were gods, and had the right to do as they pleased. But for He Who Runs with the Wind, the Great One held them in check.

He was not strictly a monotheist, but held to the notion the Great One was above all. Perhaps even greater than Sun God. Such a thought was close to blasphemy, but he could not help it. It was a thought he had somehow learned as a beleaguered child, when his peers had teased him about his odd height, eyes, hair, and complexion. His mu had defended him often, until he had grown tired of her protection because of the added teasing it brought. But her defense consisted of telling him he was closer to the gods than they, that the gods had given him special favor.

He was not sure he agreed, but somehow the concept of the Great One had begun to formulate. Never had he shared his idea with anyone except Little Dove and Happiness. He had not been too surprised that she could not understand his thinking, because women did not know of such things. His biggest problem was that he did not know if the Great One and Sun God were one and the same. Happiness never argued with him, seeming to be more awed by his words, questions and logic than he felt himself.

He was about to creep from his covert spot and head up the hill when he saw movement along the trail. It had been at the top of the last hill, and his attention had been elsewhere. He sat still; it would be a moment before he appeared between some branches.

He fingered his knife, sharply alert, waiting. When the figure appeared, he was shocked. Son of Happiness! His friend...or so he always believed. Carrying weapons! For a moment he waited, having plenty of time before he would have to show himself. Happiness was still some distance away. He would step out onto the trail, keeping his hand casually on his knife, and greet his friend. It was best not to judge the motive for trailing him without hearing him out. He would confront him and see.

When Happiness turned across the valley floor, Runs with the Wind stepped out and stood. Two, then three steps, eyes glued on the trail and unaware of the one who now faced him, Happiness suddenly looked up. The first expression was of surprise, and then came the warm smile. All was well, his friend was true.

"Welcome," he said.

"He Who Runs...I mean, He Who Conquers! I've been trying to find you since before the skies grew light. You leave a poor trail."

"You found it. I suppose I should compliment you."

He laughed, then grew serious. "You are in great danger. I heard them talking in the darkness, far from the village so no one should hear. They plan to kill you before the sun sets."

"You were far from the village after darkness?"

"Incredible, huh! I followed them, because I knew they planned something drastic."

"You're a true friend, overcoming such deep fears to help me. I'm grateful."

"No need. We are blood brothers since we were tiny. You'd do more for me. I only did what I could."

"You've learned to track well."

"You're a good teacher. If I'd left it to my uncle, women could find you easier."

They laughed, but again Happiness grew serious. "Little Dove asked me to come. But I would have anyway." He leaned his spear against a bush beside the trail and took out a small leather pouch, which he handed to his friend. "She asked me to give this to you...said you'd understand. She tried to follow me from the village."

"Did she?"

He shrugged. "I think I lost her when I thought I knew where you were headed and left the trail for a while, and then came back to it. More importantly, Boy with the Eye intends to kill you far from the village. He thought you might return to the place where the Others were, and he still thinks you killed his brother. I think he's as addled as the old hag."

"No, I killed him."

Happiness sucked in his breath. "You...you killed him? Why? I mean...."

"He ambushed me near where the Others camped. But his arrow was too high in the shoulder. I feigned being killed, and when he got close, I put my knife in him. I live. If you doubt me, speak with White Hawk about how I was wounded."

Happiness stared at him, unable to comprehend. Then came the smile. "I'll be forever dark! I'd never have believed such a story had it come from anyone but you!"

"Tell no one...ever. Like White Hawk said, he deserved what he got, and I still live. Perhaps we'll be friendlier on the other side of *Sipapu*. If not, we'll fight again."

"I'll be silent. It's too much to know, but I'll never say a word." He grinned. "You are truly He Who Conquers!"

The memory of the great feast returned, and he stood like a tree remembering. For the first time, someone besides his mu called him by his new name. An honored name. Earned, the chief had said. He Who Conquers! A name to be revered, to be held in esteem...remembered!

It was truly his name. His friend had used it,

and for the first time it seemed as if it were his. But it would take some time to get accustomed to it, because He Who Runs with the Wind had been his for a long time.   He'd earned that one too.   But the new one...well...coyote be gone, the name said he was no coward, but a man.

He let the hint of a smile touch his face, and made a friendly gesture. "Boy-child would never believe that."

Happiness grinned.   "He'll not live it down, either.   He's the one who always bragged of his great bravery, and chided you about being the coyote. Yet his name still calls him a mere boy, and yours...well, it says it all!"

He Who Conquers.   He still would have to do some adapting!   He grinned at his friend's exuberance. "It's still a bit premature, I think, but I'm honored that my friend thinks it true."   Then he sobered.   "Do you know how they plan to kill me?"

"They think to surprise you along the trail.   I laughed when I heard that, because none of them could surprise anyone, much less you!"

"Your faith in me is too much.   But I'll be alert."

"And I'll return to the village the same way I left so they don't suspect I've seen you."   He took his spear and was down the trail and up the hill at a trot.

He Who Conquers watched him go, then stepped off the trail and again studied the hill.   His eyes had been alert during the entire conversation, not because he believed any treachery from Happiness, but because if Happiness had found him, so might someone more skilled in tracking.   Or they might have followed his enthusiastic friend here.

Again he sat, a patient man who had no reason to be otherwise.   Patience came with life on The Top, waiting for the seasons, for the crops to grow, for the weather to improve, for the food supply to fill adequately against the cold season, for the Hunters to select their new members, for the ceremonies that marked boys as men, and men as successes, for the gods to answer, for everything.   Nothing ever hurried.

Only a short time passed, however, before he saw movement again at the top of the hill.   But this time he

knew who it was at the first sign of movement. How did
everyone know he was here? It was scary! First friend
Happiness had found him, following nothing more than
the mere signs left by moccasins, and now Little Dove
was on his trail! Was she followed?

He glanced down at the small leather pouch. It
was deerskin, finely worked and painted with a picture
of a pregnant deer. In it was but one object, a very tiny
image of a pregnant woman. It had less length than his
big toe, of clear amber, with a small hole drilled through
the forehead where a string was attached for a necklace.
There was little doubt of its meaning.

She was running as she reached the bottom of
the hill, and across the canyon bottom. She was almost
to him before he stepped onto the trail. She pulled up
with a near-scream, put her hand to her left breast and
managed, "Great Earth Mu! You scared me nearly to
death!"

He smiled. "I surely hope not. Does your mu
know you came looking for me?"

"No! I can't tell her everything! She wouldn't
have let me go this far from the village."

"It's not the most intelligent thing you ever did."

"Neither were you to come here this sun. Don't
you realize how dangerous it is to be wandering about?"

He nodded, his smile still intact, and walked
from the trail to his hiding place. She followed, and
when he sat, she dropped onto her knees in front of him.

"You are He Who Conquers," she said softly,
though the breeze was beginning to stir the shrubbery
and make sound less dangerous. "I danced when they
named you."

He nodded. "Me, too, but it scares me to have
such a name. I think it will carry too much
responsibility."

She smiled. "You deserve it, and before you go
to Sipapu it'll be even more deserved. You've conquered
many things already. You killed the Others, and you
killed Yellow Sapsucker, and...."

"How did you know that?" He reacted by
reaching out and grabbing her arm at the biceps, his
eyes dark and questioning.

"Ouch! Please! I saw it in a dream!"

He released her arm, sorry for the strong grip that had hurt her though he said nothing. "A dream?"

She nodded. "On the sun when it happened. I was cleaning our dwelling when I saw it. It was like... like a...a painting on the wall...like a...well, you know what I mean. But I saw him shoot the arrow that went in the back of your shoulder, and I saw you fall. At first I thought you were dead, but then I saw you roll over and throw your knife. I saw it all."

He was enamored by her revelation. It was just as it happened!

"Mu knows, too. She made strong hints to me when Boy with the Eye accused you. You couldn't know how proud I was of how you handled him! You conquered him, too. You are a man...my man; this sun you must conquer me, too." In a moment, she put her hands up under the small skirt-like breechcloth and released the *chastity belt*. She held it out as though she were giving it to him.

He stared at her, his eyes flicking to the belt and back, meeting her eyes in full understanding of why she had come, and of the pouch he still held in his hand. Yet, with the moment arrived, he was suddenly uncertain, reluctant. He had no time to wonder why, but there was within his body spirit a block, a desire to escape, to look back on this moment as the very instant he knew his manhood was complete.

Expectantly, at the same time wondering why he had reacted as he had, Little Dove reached out a hand and touched his knee. It was a simple gesture, but the question in her eyes brought to it a significance he felt. He was immobilized, still staring at her with a shadow of doubt, unsure of how to back away from this thing. Yet he wanted her....

"What is it, my love?" she asked with a plea in her voice.

"I don't know? I wish I could say, but it's not easy for me to know." Her hand, still extended with the belt, began to sag towards her side.

"I've dreamed of this moment," she responded. "I never knew it would come under Sun God like this, or in this place, but I've wished for you since I was able to know mu and fa were not fighting on their mat, that it was their need and desire for each other. I knew you were the one, and only the fates have decreed it differently. You are my only love, and it's you who must fulfill my love before one whom I despise becomes my mate."

He continued to fix his gaze on her. There were more stirrings within him, but he could not understand them. Embarrassed by the enlarged male member pushing against and lifting his breechcloth, he wavered. He wanted her, more than ever...even feasting his eyes on her new female development had never aroused him like this. Why did he feel hesitant? He had known no woman, and she had known no man. It was for them to do, without the knowledge of anyone. Even her mu, who had given her blessing to it, had no knowledge it was this close.

"I have never wanted you more," was all he could say.

"But you will not take me?"

His hand went up to his headband, the other squeezing the leather bag. Dampness came to his forehead, and his eyes felt as though they were about to burst. His voice was so soft she could hardly hear him say, "I can't."

Tears were instant. Her hand on his knee, she began to knead without awareness. Then both hands went to her face, the belt lying unnoticed beside her.

"You don't love me like I thought?"

"I swear by the Great One that I love you more than life."

"Then...?"

"Am I a man to be manipulated? You ask me to do what no man should do to another, no matter how he hates. You desire me to make you a woman, but to do it would make me less the man. It's for a mate to open his woman if she doesn't have the Ceremony of the Stick. I can't take the place of even the one who is my enemy." He only half-believed what he said, yet he said it, and in doing so, gained only a more firm grip on ambivalence.

"Why? Is honor above love? Do you love me less? Is my body to be thrown to the one I can't tolerate, and you to leave here with my love and desire? Will I go through life like my mu, never having known a man?

A true man? You love me, and I love you. Is that not enough to allow us but one moment of true joy? You speak of honor, but you ignore what we've been to each other since we were infants. How often you would have been mine at The Rock had I but said the word, and now you say it can't be?"

Her voice had been low, pleading, filled with pain and compassion. His reply came as though from outside himself. "I've dreamed of you since I knew how little boys and little girls differ. Often I could've been one with you. I don't know why it suddenly seems so wrong."

She watched his crest-fallen face, his eyes now staring at the ground behind her. Something in her wanted to burst, but she kept her mind in control, trying to think how best to respond. He was lost in his sense of honor, something she had never considered as being eminent to their relationship. Now, of a sudden, it had become a domineering aspect of his character.

She stood uncertainly, looking down at her love. He was distant, unlike she had ever seen him. Was it the time of the sun, and required a more intimate time, such as when the many fires of the gods filled the sky? Was he too filled with fear of his life to think clearly? Was his body still too weak from the arrow? Or was there truly a different voice speaking to him?

He could see only her legs and the chastity belt that lay in a wad as she stood before him. He wanted to reach out and caress those enticing legs, to know the feel of the softness of the skin. But while his manhood continued to betray his wants, his body felt locked tight.

Her hand came down and touched his cheek, then his shoulder. There it rested, and he felt its lightness and warmth. She didn't move, and he sat as stone for some time; then his hand came up and rested on hers. A sob was wrenched from her throat, a soft, heart-rending sound, bringing his eyes up to see her face. Her hair hung down both sides, almost hiding her pretty features. The eyes were closed tightly, and her nose was running. She looked so helpless, so childlike, that he stood and wrapped his arms around her gently. She put a cheek against his chest, and the tears came. For a long time neither moved, then her arms came around his back and she held him as he held her. Her sobs stopped, her mind cleared, and she tilted her face up and, with tears hanging on her eye- lashes and her nose still running, smiled.

"I'm sorry, my love. I should have known you were too much the man, yet I've known you to be so gentle, loving...kind. I was selfish to want you to Open me, but I still do. I guess I dream too much...and talk too much. But I have truly wanted you for so long."

He flickered a smile, and their cheeks met. It was innocent, impulsive...soft. Then her arms tightened behind him, pulling his stiffened manhood against her breechcloth, and the embrace became more than just a meeting. It became a fire, demanding, sweeping over him in an encompassing heat, and all his arguments faded in an instant, his inhibitions gone. In a moment they were on the ground, groping awkwardly as two virgins, but seeking, finding, struggling, enjoining....

They slept. The sun was far to the setting when they awakened, and she smiled at him. "You've honored me."

His smile was warm. "You're a woman, and I a man. Long after I leave, you'll remember...as will I."

She stood and replaced her chastity belt, and he watched her with a look of compassion.

"You will live a lie from now on."

Her smile was quick. "And happy to do it. Sore, but happy."

He chuckled at her humor, which she had meant it to be. "You will still have the Ceremony of the Stick?"

She nodded. "It'll be necessary. Mu knows how we solve that problem. Did she tell you about her Ceremony? Or her Opening?"

"No."

"Mu loved your fa, but she was made to mate Hunter of the Deer, a man of spirits whom the chief and her mu feared. He was a hard and domineering man whom she never loved. She went to your fa and wanted him to Open her. He was afraid. So she went to him one darkness when he was alone and sleeping out under the stars...as he often did. And then she mated my fa. But for a time after she was mated, she still went to your fa. He had been mated, too. But she stopped because he became fearful they would be caught. He lost his manness." She held out her hand and he took it and stood next to her.

"But she said she had never coupled with the one... she said she never found...."

"What she said to you and what you understood were two different things. He opened her, and coupled with her several times, but to her it was all in her mind as to what he was. It was not until later that she discovered your fa was not truly a man, but a weak male who lived in fear and could not make good decisions. While he Opened her, she no longer considered him a man--and has not for many winters."

He stared at her, trying to catch the implications of what she said, as bewildering as it seemed.

"I must go." She started away, then stopped and came back. She grinned at him a moment, then stepped into his arms and embraced him, long and tenderly. "This will be our last moment of intimacy. Mu says you will be gone soon. Unlike her, I've been Opened by a man, and I'll remember you when I name our son." She was gone.

When she was out of sight, his mind had lost everything. His fa, the one who Opened her mu, was not a man. In fact, he was a coward. It was a shame that hung over the family like a toppling rock. All the while he tried to convince himself he was a man and not a coyote, he had the great shadow of the rock, leaning, poised to fall. For all his success, there was still that...that...thing. "Coward! Hide under your mu's cloth."

White Hawk, his uncle, his mu, all had told him he could be a man, a man of honor, held in high esteem. That being the coyote had nothing to do with being the son of his fa. That he was a coward only if he allowed himself to be one.

Was he? For all he had accomplished, for all he seemed to know and want, that was the ultimate question. Was he, when the final scenes of his life unfolded, a man? Or a coward?

The surest thing he knew was that Little Dove and her mu both thought him an honorable man, a true man. And for her mu, knowing his fa, that was saying a great deal. He had to hold to that, cherish it, nurture it, believe it with his whole being.

Anguish ripped at him, but he turned resolutely up the hill.

6

Sun God was setting behind the *Sleeping Giant* when a voice was heard near the ashes of the funeral pyres of the Others...a full voice, with just a touch of shyness in it.

O, Mighty Great One,
You have looked with favor
upon your servant.
You have made him
to conquer his enemy.
You have lifted his spirit
and given life to his aging Mu and Fa.

O, Mighty Great One,
You have raised up enemies
who seek his life,
Yet you lifted his spirit,
and sent a woman to make him a man.
Why do you toy with one
who seeks only to please you?

My heart is like the stones of The Top,
For I have little spirit left in me;
I desire to stay, but you send me away.
If I stay, trouble finds me.
    if I go, fear rides my shoulders.
How do I know right from wrong,
    when you make me see what I wish not to
    see?

O, Great One, mighty and sure,
    Give me answers to help me understand,
    not riddles, which puzzle me."

Silence settled, the cry of ambivalence and uncertainty stilled, and only the voice of a quail was heard to disturb the solitude of the one whose thoughts had been emptied. He Who Conquers lay prostrate on the ground, eyes open but seeing only what was going on in his troubled mind.

He was trotting across dry, sparsely vegetated earth, a deeply cut wash on his right, running toward mid-sun. The Sleeping Giant, rising on his right, had lost its shape, no longer looking at all like the story told in their training...or was it a fable?

A moment later, he was asleep, it was snowing, and he was dry and warm. Yet, he was in no structure. But his mind never questioned what he saw, for a moment later he was fully alert, though still prone. He realized he had seen the same vision a second time, and though it was assuring, he was saddened by the truth it described to him. He was alone, leaving The Top, traveling.

His beloved Little Dove was not with him. He knew it would be so, for her mu and she had both seen the vision that he was leaving alone. Or at least, her mu had. It did not make the going any easier...or more palatable. What he did not wish to see, the Great One was showing him...clearly!

He had little time left before he had to go. It was plain he was going to leave very soon, and there was no longer any doubt the threat to his life was the motivating factor. He was going to leave his proud parents...proud for the first time in their adult lives!

Their son was the hero of The Top, the very one whom the village had laughingly called Coyote because he could run swiftly and looked so different. Their pride was bursting, and he would not see them again...or more importantly, they would not see him again, this one they called their son, who finally made them wealthy among their own people. They walked with their heads high, their spirits soaring, their eyes bright and their bodies as erect as their physical problems allowed. They were parents of one who had saved many lives, and who had taken four Others in punishment sent by the gods. Did not his success prove the gods smiled on their son? They could sing, and they would sing many times, of their son's great accomplishment! For his fa, rightfully or wrongfully known as the ultimate coyote, it was a great salve.

Alas, he would never hear the song. He would never see but a small token of the joy they felt, the pride they showed to The People. He would know, but never see.

Still, had it not always been a dream to travel far beyond the Sleeping Giant? Had he not longed for such a trip since way before the times he was first called Coyote? Would he truly be running away when he was only bringing to fruition these long-dreamed dreams? And his emotions would run the gamut, from fear and sadness to joy and eagerness, many times.

He got to his knees, then his feet, cautiously studying where he was and whether he was alone or being watched. He looked back along the trail he had used, and knew it was not good to retrace his steps. However, could there not also be someone along the other trail he often used from this part of the mesa? It might be the better and wiser thing to take no trail, but go as his eyes dictated and his feet led.

Suddenly he felt like running, needing the wind in his face and air in his lungs. He began to run, his first stride as sudden as the feeling had come, never to know that with his second step the arrow that was meant for his left lung missed by only a scant step. He was exuberantly running down the hill, dodging around shrubbery and trees, up the next hill at a slight angle, following no trail. Past a pile of bones that marked a mountain sheep that had died of fever, the dried carcass of a long-tailed magpie, and a stumpy scrub oak that never knew what it was like to be a tree, he ran. His thoughts were on the terrain, on ducking the reaching branches of the juniper, the prickly spines of the cactus, or the dangerous spikes of the broadleaf yucca.

He never saw the disbelieving look on the face of Boy with the Eye of an Eagle, who stood and watched the runner disappear from view, or the disappointment in the eyes of Gray Dog, who stood behind a bush along the trail and saw the running He Who Conquers far away, untouchable.

He was breathless as he arrived at the village, but he felt good...like singing. But he thought of himself as a terrible singer, and spent his time making bird sounds or imitating the sounds of various animals. He was very good at both, but no one had told him, leaving him to continue practicing, not sure of his prowess.

A Perky Sue, a leafless stem with a yellow flower, grew at the corner of the first dwelling, and he noted it had lost its life to the coolness. The Blue Lupine had long been without a flower, and its green leaves hung wilted. It was only a couple steps away, as scraggly as ever, the traffic of people never allowing it much room for growth. Then he was in the courtyard and terribly self-conscious, aware he was being adored as a hero, and beside her dwelling stood Little Dove, watching him, the two of them holding a secret no one knew. Or did they? The thought made him uncomfortable.

His mu stood in front of her dwelling, and when he looked her way, she beckoned him to come. When he was near, she worked her way over the threshold, letting him know their conversation would be private. He felt a moment of panic, wondering if she had, by some roundabout means, discovered the great secret of him and Little Dove.

His mind was quickly put to rest. In a hushed tone, she spoke quickly.

"You must go somewhere and hide. I think you might go to the village of your sister near The Sleeping Giant."

"Why, Mu? What has upset you?"

"You know well, my brave son. Don't try to hide

your fears from me; I know there are many who seek
your life."

He stared at her a moment. "It's not so desperate
as all that. I can take care of myself."

"They kill from ambush! They are coyotes, and
not men! You are in grave danger!"

He understood her fears. Her voice, a hiss rather
than a whisper because of the terror that gripped her,
almost made him more frightened than he felt need to
be.

"Why did you not tell me that arrow in your
shoulder from Yellow Sapsucker was intentional?   I
thought you and he had been hunting and he must have
slipped. You think I can't keep a secret!"

"I thought you knew.   White Hawk said only
Medicine Woman, he, you and I knew.   But even if I
knew you had no idea, I would have said nothing.   I
preferred not to frighten you."

"I'm not frightened, my son! I'm terrified!"

"It's why I kept silence. I'm a big boy, mu, I can
take care of myself."

"Huh! With six or seven trying to kill you from
hiding, you think you can walk safely anywhere,
anytime? My son's more intelligent than that!"

"Who told you about all this?"   It was easier to
change the direction than defend himself, which he could
only do half-heartedly.

"I have my sources, but does it matter? After all,
it's true."

He shrugged, seeing she was not to be side-
tracked.   Instead, she stepped back and stooped to a
bundle lying in the corner, which she lifted and handed
to him.

"I've packed considerable food, two blankets and
a sleeping mat. You must go...as soon as it's dark."

He shook his head. "If I go as soon as it turns
dark, they'll follow and kill me.   I'll wait until the
darkness is half gone; they'll not be alert all through the
darkness. If I don't go early, they'll give up and sleep,
and I can be far away before they know I'm gone." He
set the bundle next to the door, overwhelmed by a
sudden sadness.

"My son does use his head sometimes," she said

dryly. "His weapons are in hand...what else does he need?"

He knew, but he said nothing, stepping out into the dusk and looking around casually, fingering the small leather pouch from Little Dove that hung from his neck, bumping the other pouch that also hung there, his fetish and amulet pouch. People moved about with the slowness of pointless activity, the sun gone and darkness settling. Children ran hither and yon, fighting, playing tag, or trying to escape from a situation they had pestered into being. Men sat about, talking of the recent successful harvest and gossiping of the Hunters, who were on their hunting trip just before the snows, and they watched anything of interest including He Who Conquers. Women were visiting or shrieking at the children, only a few working at something constructive.

He Who Conquers moved with the same casualness toward the kiva, and entered. Three men sat about the dead fire, saying nothing but smoking pipes that had the air blue with haze. He took up another small pouch he had tucked into a niche, and climbed the ladder into the fresh air.

He carried only his knife; his other weapons lay with the pack put together by his mu. Extra moccasins, waterbag and a pair of sandals were also with the pack. He was ready to travel, but would have to stop for water along the trail to not arouse suspicions by doing so now.

He walked to Happiness, who was separated from others his age and sticking his knife into the ground in practice for a game they called "*the splits*."

"You are led by the gods," Happiness greeted him, his voice low and his arm in motion to throw again.

"I am?"

"They just tried twice this sun to kill you. You were where the Others camped. You remember suddenly starting to run?"

"Sure, why?"

"If you had not taken the first step when you did, you'd be dead now. Boy with the Eye had an arrow meant for your heart, but when you suddenly started to run, it missed. Then you ran cross-country when there were three trails covered by six other men."

"You jest."

"And you live because you live and react to the urges of the gods. No, my friend, I don't jest. Jesting in a time for seriousness is for fools."

"I leave before the new sun."

The body of his friend went momentarily rigid, then he stepped forward and pulled the blade from the soil. Glancing at He Who Conquers, he said softly, "I'll miss you." He knew he could give his friend nothing more without arousing interest from gazing eyes.

"And I you."

"Where will you go?"

He Who Conquers shrugged. "Beyond the mountains toward sunset. It's hard to tell, since I know little except what the Trader said."

"It's a far place."

"I hope the snows don't come early." The memory of his vision edged into his thoughts.

"When will you return?"

He paused, thinking. "Perhaps I may never find my way back." He turned and looked back toward the emptying courtyard. "Maybe I'll find Sipapu before I can return."

Happiness stopped and looked at his friend. "No, you will never see Sipapu before that. It's possible, of course, that I'll be through Sipapu before you return, you know. Who knows what might happen? Chief Roaring Lion is old, and if Boy with the Eye becomes chief, the gods might destroy us all. One who tries to kill one of The People will likely bring ruin on everyone."

They fell into silence as Happiness threw twice more, the village becoming more and more quiet as the darkness settled and night sounds began to increase. It was a typical night on the mesa, clear and cool, the hush broken by the low sounds of voices in conversation, birds and bugs of the night, and the occasional cry of a child.

The People of The Top had long since lost the need to maintain constant silence after darkness. Their enemies were few and far away. Unlike generations ago when they were nomadic and in constant alertness to other moving groups, now they slept harder and with fewer fears. Even their guard duty, recently revived in spirit, had for a long time become lackadaisical.

He Who Conquers turned toward his dwelling,

ready to sleep, when Happiness said, "I'll think of you often, my good friend. Walk in the protection of the gods."

He smiled over his shoulder. "Burn some fagots for me from time to time. I'll appreciate it, and the hawks will let me know."

At the doorway, he stopped and looked at the several men who sat around the community fire which would burn in the courtyard until the first snows dowsed it. Boy with the Eye sat with his back to him, and Gray Dog sat at his right. He was obviously trying to ignore him, which made him want to laugh aloud. Twin Who Lived sat across the fire, overtly watching him, and Little White Cloud was speaking softly as though giving a step-by-step account of what He Who Conquers was doing.

He was halfway through the doorway before he realized there was a visitor in his mu's home. Singing Waters. A stab of fear went through him.

His mu dropped the elkskin over the doorway, then said softly, "The mu of Little Dove would speak to you."

He had already been hunched, the ceiling much too low for him, and now he sat cross-legged, saying nothing.

"The People now know you to be a man. Your feats are on the lips of The People, and they honor you. Will not your four scalps be remembered for generations to come?"

The celebration had been fun, but it would have been a success had it been nothing more than finding a herd of wapiti. Ceremonies began with an idea and a desire to celebrate, then fed themselves. It mattered little what the basis for the celebration might be, only that it was a chance for another good time...a dance...a time to forget the drudgery of life. Was not the Harvest Celebration held long before the harvest, and another held afterward? A feast was held to allay the God of Snows, and another to welcome rebirth in the new growing season. Some had a tradition and a purpose, but for others, they were but for a good time, and each good time was remembered, though the reasons might soon be forgotten.

So would his feat. When he left, it would not be

long before he would be a memory to only a few. Such
was life. Only a few great ones were remembered long
after Sipapu, feted in story and song until even the
names disappeared and only the distorted facts remained.
His scalp-taking would be remembered, and then the
name would disappear and the number of scalps would
increase.

He smiled to himself. Perhaps it would become
twenty scalps, done in a pitted battle in broad sunlight,
with a hand axe and knife. It would become another act
that would take on immortality because people needed
such stories in order to dream of greatness.

"You have truly become a man." The voice
brought him back to the present, and what she said told
him that she knew of The Opening.

It was good. She knew, and she was satisfied.
His fear fled. "You honor me to say it."

She knew he had read her intention, and smiled.
"Singing Waters will remember so renowned a warrior,
and surely his progeny will one sun sing of his great
feats." She glanced at his mu, her smile fixed and
knowing that the enigmatic statements were only being
read at face value. She and He Who Conquers were
tuned to a secret meaning only they knew. Like Little
Dove, she knew the single coupling had been successful
toward the procreation which was so important to a
people.

With the understanding of their previous
meeting, she relaxed and said, "You are leaving this
darkness." Her statement brought a look of surprise to
his mu, and He Who Conquers knew she had said
nothing to anyone. But Singing Waters had her own
source for information...not to mention the pack and his
weapons lying in the corner where his mu had moved
them.

"You are of mixed emotions, both heavy of heart
and excited to explore. Fear is there, for it is not easy to
travel alone so far from what is known; but you are a
wary man, one who knows to think ahead. Life will be
good to you, but always be careful. The gods will
sometimes play games with men." She paused, and he
was not sure what was to happen next. But she
continued.

"I had long wished you could mate with Little Dove. She, like you, is very different. Many generations ago, sometime after our people began to live here, men came from rising-sun. They had traveled a long time. One of their young men had been but a boy when they left home, and was a man before they arrived, from far across the shining waters that lie beneath rising-sun.

"Their skin was fair, their eyes were blue, their hair was light, and they had hair on their faces and chests. They stood tall--our tallest men coming but to their shoulders. They were strong men, fighting men, but they came in peace, though they had weapons and shields of a thin, hard stone. They brought many strange things with them, and traded for our blankets and trinkets. They mated our daughters, living among us for three winters.

"Then suddenly they were gone. But they left offspring with our women, children who were very different. Some were white of hair, some had blue eyes, some had pale skin; but mostly, they were taller and thinner.

"Over the generations, these characteristics began to dwindle, as the strength of their medicine lost its fight with the strength of our men. In you, as in Little Dove, it is still seen. Only a few know about why you are different, but you know that it's the medicine of the Ancient Ones.

"It was inevitable that you, so different, should be drawn to Little Dove, who is like you. Yet your mating is not to be, as you know.

"When I was your age, I loved a man. He was so gentle and kind, so understanding and wise beyond his years. I wanted him for a mate, and told my mu. She laughed, and told me love would come after I mated. Red Deer has been a good mate, but he was not like the one I desired. Only the one I desired I discovered to be less than a man who died in the shell. He was not the man I'd first thought, or he would have overcome the many setbacks and learned to live with them. But he could not, and became a man possessed by different spirits. Now he's a nothing among us, a man who is respected for his different inner voice, but shunned by all. A broken man is something to be pitied." He Who

Conquers wondered that his mu did not recognize her mate in the story, or perhaps she did. Was it possible she had long since learned to live with such a truth?

"Some sun, you'll come to know that all of life does not hinge on mating with one person or another, or of a fear of one thing or another, though I suspect that you already know that. You are a very healthy-thinking man, and it's this that makes me wish it could have been you who mated my daughter.

"However, since you go, you'll take this with you." She handed him a leather pouch, similar to the one Little Dove had sent to him through Happiness. He did not open it, but simply held it and dropped his hand into his lap.

"The mu of Little Dove is wise, and her story teaches me much. I will remember."

Singing Waters stood, stepping to the door, her left arm across her breasts to keep them still. Once very large, they were now but flat, hanging skin. "You'll mate one far away, and you'll love her greatly. Travel with the presence of the gods." She swept back the covering and stepped out, then said softly into the doorway before dropping the skin, "Choose one with smaller breasts. They're a great burden for a woman no longer blessed by the Goddess of Fertility."

His mu broke into laughter, her wrinkled face rent by a mouth too large highlighted by toothless gums, and he grinned, then he leaned back against the wall, his eyes flitting across the many items that hung from the walls and stood on the floor of the one-room dwelling. His mu was not a neat housekeeper, besides having too many things for the amount of space. But it was the determination of her wealth, since his fa rarely came into the dwelling now. He preferred the company of the older men, who accepted his strange behavior with the tolerance given those whose life was obviously spent following a god no one else knew. The tolerance was sometimes almost an awe, a suspicion that the gods were closer to such people. Being thirty-four winters, he was exceeded in age by only two men. The Man Who Chases Spirits was thirty-six, and Straight Arrow, the fa of Happiness, was thirty-five. Chief Roaring Lion was the same age as his fa.

People seldom lived long after attaining their thirtieth winter, and many did not reach it. Those who did, like the four eldest, generally had many physical problems. Witches attacked joints, bringing swelling and pain. Others entered the mouth, and caused swelling and discomfort, along with sores that drained with white or yellow fluid. Sometimes they took sight, or hair, and on occasion, the ability to know. Improperly healed broken bones and visits from witches in childhood that bent bones took on greater problems as people got older. Some got dizzy when they stood, or had hacking coughs. Some could no longer get around without the help of mates or friends.

Suddenly he came awake, and realized he had been sleeping for a long time. Carefully he looked out the door, and saw two men sleeping in their blankets beside the fire. He smiled to himself, for it was Gray Dog and Little White Cloud.

With care, he put on his pack outside the door, took up his weapons, glanced lovingly at his mu snoring on her mat, and slipped from the village. Moon God was of little assistance, only a sliver and far down in the sky. But he knew his way, and moved quickly away from the village.

Now that he was away, he felt good. It was up to the Great One to keep him that way.

7

As Sun God reached high enough into the sky to throw light on the big valley that stretched along sun-set side of The Top, He Who Conquers was pointed into mid-sun, trotting at his steady pace, long legs eating up the distance. Naked to the waist, he wore his moccasins, a breechcloth, his many pouches, and his headband. From his belt hung his knife and axe in separate sheaths, he carried his spear in his right hand and his throwing stick in his left.   A quiver of arrows was over his right shoulder, along with his bow, and on his back was a pack, a weight that had him sweating profusely, feeling the extra demand on his legs.

He slowed to a walk, then stopped and looked back at The Top he called home while he caught his breath and more importantly gave his legs a rest. He wondered if he would ever see it again, with a small numbness of heart when he thought of Little Dove and their secret tryst. Would Boy with the Eye ever find out? A humorous thought crossed his mind, and he chuckled. Perhaps it was repayment for the turn at The Rock he lost by leaving. It was the inanity of the thought that made it funny, and he was still grinning as he started walking again.

Singing Waters came into his thoughts, and his head was still spinning from the wealth of information she had given him. He was wondering if his mu had known of this all along and not told him, or if she was as ignorant of the facts as he had been.

His eyes followed the rim of the mesa, and suddenly came to a stop. Was that movement, or just imagination? He watched for a time, seeing nothing, and was about to turn away and begin walking when he saw it again. People. Right along the rim, but at a place where they could never get down. He counted three, no four...five! All men, and a long ways away. Was Boy with the Eye one of them?

He waited no longer, but turned and began to walk swiftly, a pace that would tire him less than running, but still too fast for a long haul. His empty water pouch hung from his neck, along with the possibles bag he had retrieved from the kiva, a small leather pouch that carried his important memories, along with spare arrow tips, and the two recently acquired pouches from Little Dove and her mu. It was the water pouch that held his attention, because he was getting very thirsty, and he had not found water yet.

Now that he was on his way, he was feeling nostalgic, his thoughts constantly returning to his lost love, his parents, Singing Waters, Happiness, and of course, the five men on the rim. But that was hardly nostalgic!

Everyone he knew was back there, on The Top, and he was here, on the last of the gently undulating bottom of the valley before it opened onto the aridness that was a desert, that extended far to mid-sun and up against the Mountain of the Sleeping Giant.

And before him was the unknown, that most fearful of foes. Was he really prepared for such a journey? He had passed all the tests for manhood, surviving fourteen suns in the rugged mesas that stretched off to sunrise from his familiar homeland. He had seen the vision of the hawk, proof of his totem. He had even killed a deer on which he subsisted, eating the crushed male gonads to ensure his fertility. He had even thrived, and returned to the village as fit as when he left. Then he had endured the Ceremony, in itself a test of pain, courage and strength.

Yet, did that prepare him to be out here alone, walking into he knew not what and still concerned for those who followed behind and wanted him dead?

He was a man, but did that qualify him for this? With less than fifteen winters behind him, he was just beginning to realize how much he did not know. But if he was lacking, when would he not? To turn back was out of the question; it would prove him a boy and a coward. Those who had accused him of being the coyote all his life would have won.

But what lay ahead? Was he really afraid of the unknown? Or was it just apprehension? He could break a leg and die of starvation, or be killed by a bear or wolf. He could fall into a hole and never be found. Or Others might find him, and alone he would not stand a chance.

But such thoughts could not hold him long, for he knew many of the fears he had expressed to himself could happen back home. He glanced back at the rim, but while he walked several paces, he saw no one. He increased his gait to a trot. There was no trail where he ran, but the vegetation was decreasing as he angled away from the mesa. He had no trouble finding footing, and he felt warm against the coolness of the early sun.

Grass grew more sparsely, barren earth became more prevalent, and he had to step around cactus more often. He wondered if he might have to stop and put on his sandals to keep from having cactus spines in his feet, since the tough yucca-soled sandals were almost impregnable.

He continued to move swiftly, and then, there was the water he needed. The *Water-from-the-Sunrise* filled his pouch, and then his stomach. He drank until he felt bloated. But never long sips without stopping to look around, little at a time, the eyes alert. When he felt so full he was nearly miserable, he stood and waded the stream, then began to walk again.

His legs were beginning to speak to him, informing him he was not really ready for so sudden and demanding a journey. The pack, something he had never had to manage except for the suns of his survival training while preparing for the Ceremony of Manhood, was swiftly growing very heavy.

It was midsun, he was moving smartly, but it meant concentrating on making himself go. He had motivation, not knowing for sure if those he had seen on the top of the cliffs were men hoping to catch him, but if so, he had to move on. They were likely carrying little or no packs, able to travel much faster than he, but it was unlikely they were prepared to go too far. If he could hold distance, having put time between himself and them by leaving in mid-darkness, he just might have a big enough lead they would give up and go home. He hoped so. He wanted no death confrontations with anyone, least of all from his village.

He became aware that it was clouding overhead, though the sun was out full. It would not be long, for the heavy bank overhead was swiftly moving toward sunrise. Even as he considered this, the sun disappeared. He felt the loss, the chill immediate in the breeze that was starting.

But he was out in the middle of flat country, where there was little to use for a shelter. The blankets and cured hide he carried would do little to keep him warm if it rained, because it would not be long before he would be soaked to the bone. He turned directly into the wind, at The Sleeping Giant, and began to trot. He was growing more than concerned.

He was alone. It had not struck him quite so strongly until now, when he looked desperately for shelter. Always he had been free to have people around or go off by himself. Now the choice was gone, and he was responsible for himself. It was a freedom he was not too certain he appreciated at the moment.

And what if the people he hoped to find were not friendly? That was a thought he had not considered, and he did not like it. If he met with hostiles, he would have to shuck his pack and run for his life...and what would his life be worth without that pack?

Should he return home? No, that was out of the question! If he ran into difficulties, it was up to his own wits to overcome. Whatever the consequences of his leaving home, it was his freedom and his choice. He would have to sleep with his decisions.

He was climbing, crossing a deep wash that he knew was a flashflood blowout, entering scattered sagebrush. Stopping a moment on the top of a knoll, he surveyed the country behind him and felt better. There was no one close...yet.

To sun-set, the land was quite flat, but heavier in sage brush. It was what he looked for, and he stepped quickly into the midst of the tall sage. Dropping his pack, he took out his axe and began to chop at some of the scattered bushes, building a pile very quickly. When he had a good pile from several bushes, he went to a place where there were four sizable bushes in a close square, leaving a manageable opening between.

Here he began to interweave the chopped branches between the live bushes, first making a thick wall and then building a roof. He went out and chopped some more, and thickened the roof, then added to the walls. When he was satisfied, he brought in the pack, dug out the hide and attached it to the ceiling. He could sit up, but no more. The thickness of the walls made a fair windbreak. He built a small fire, one he could cover with his two hands. He wrapped himself in a blanket and rummaged for the food his mu had packed for him.

It was dark, the wind was strong, and it smelled of moisture, probably snow. But he was full, he was tired from the long trek, he had relieved himself, and he was warmly wrapped in his blankets and the odor of sage brush. He slept.

He awakened in the darkness, listened to the wind whistling among the branches and leaves of his shelter, and slept again. And as he slept, the skies plied their wares in the suddenness common to this parched country. Rains and snows were infrequent, and often were "*gully-makers*". Had the snow been rain, it would have turned the entire area into a quagmire, with torrents of water running down washes and canyon bottoms. As snow, it piled up quickly, until the shelter looked like nothing more than another white mound of sage.

Waking again, He Who Conquers could no longer hear the wind, and wondered if it had died. Storms were often quick, hard hitters, and gone as quickly. The fickleness of Storm God was well documented by The People, who knew all too well the many torrential rains, windstorms and blizzards.

Sleeping again, he dreamed of Little Dove, and awakened fully aroused and wishing for her to be with him. But reason returned; he rolled over and slept again.

When he awakened with a need to relieve himself, he hated to crawl out of his blankets. When he did, he realized it was full-sun and his shelter was totally covered by a heavy layer of snow. Not wanting to fight through the snow and see what he was afraid he might see, he relieved himself into the wall.

It was time to find more food, and he did, keeping the blankets snugly against himself. He could see his breath...and in that moment he realized he was living his vision. He was under the snow, yet it did not touch him! It was exactly what he had seen. As had been his journey!

But what lay ahead? Who would he find on the other side of the mountains he had seen from The Rock? Others? Or the people spoken about by the Trader? If the latter, would they welcome him for two or three winters? Or would he have to flee from them too? But had not Singing Waters spoken something about his finding a mate among them? Did that speak of permanence, or would he leave without her?

He had always thought of Singing Waters as a special sort of person, probably because Little Dove was so much like her. She was friendly, knowledgeable and mysterious. The visions she saw had been true, so he had no doubts that a mate awaited him where he went.

So what was the significance of his bloodline, those Ancient Ones that Singing Waters had been so high on? Was it of any value to be of their medicine, or could it be a weakness? He had been considered a freak, as had Little Dove. Yet she was desired by every youth becoming a man, while he had been disdained.

It ultimately led to his being where he was, alone, under a pile of brush that supported a pile of snow, wondering about the future and the past, considering too many things.

Well, Little Dove was a memory. His mu and fa were part of his past, along with Son of Happiness and

White Hawk. And Boy with the Eye. He still held the right to another sun on The Rock from the spear repair. Ha! Of what good was an uncollectible debt. But Boy with the Eye no longer owed him anything, for his soon mate was with child from the one the son of the chief most detested. Such irony! Such satisfaction!

He rolled on his side and began to peck at a place slowly, to make a hole to the outside. It was reasonably warm inside, but he wondered what it was like outside. Besides, concentrating on finding his way out kept his mind from over-activity. He was tired of the many thoughts that kept going round and round inside his head.

He used his spear to work on the hole, and it took a time before he had cleared a spot large enough to see through. There was sunlight and blue heavens; it was quiet, and he wondered if the wind blew. His curiosity, however, was to weak to allow him to go outside. Besides, his muscles were very tired from the strain of the long hike with the heavy pack.

He opened the pack and sorted through it, but found nothing he could discard. His mu had packed well. So he would have to keep the weight, and eat the food to lighten the pack. That he would do carefully, because it might be a long time before he found a people who would accept him.

Suddenly it struck him. That last sun when Singing Waters told him the story of why he looked different, and of how she had gone through the same thing as Little Dove, there was something he had to consider more fully. Had not Little Dove told him that her mu wanted to mate his fa, but could not, and wound up with Red Deer because he was the Designer, and as such he was a highly respected man, one who consulted with all who planned to build? Singing Waters spoke of a man who was a nobody, a man to be pitied! Men did not get close to his fa, for the man was a coyote. Still, he was accepted as different men are. Would that be the only way he would himself be accepted or understood?

What was the truth? He had shown he was a man in some ways, but perhaps his fa had, too. What did it prove? There had been a rumor from long ago that his fa had moved to The Top from Wide Canyon, the

huge center of activity with its base far to mid-sun. It
was rumored he left to avoid a Death Match with the son
of the chief. Was it a rumor or fact? He had the gut-
feeling it was fact. It had been a long time before the
story followed him to The Top. When it came, he never
spoke of it, neither denying or affirming its truth. Why?
Had he loved Singing Waters, and then was made to
settle for his mu? It would explain some of the loss of
companionship that he knew they had suffered. It had
been long since fa had taken his mate to their mat.
Then had Singing Waters fabricated the story about...?
Ah! Mu was present! Singing Waters did not want to
make an enemy of his mu! Yet, she had expected him to
read between the lines, like when they were speaking of
Little Dove and The Opening. Huh! He had surely
missed that one!

Still, he had to remember that his fa was the
coward who would not face the son of the chief. Or was
it a simple matter of running away? Was there more
involved?

Somewhere from the back of his mind came the
incipient thought that he himself would one sun walk
where his fa had walked, to discover the truth of what
had happened so long ago.

He dozed, then awakened, drank a couple
swallows, and dozed again. Then it was dark again. He
slept fitfully, having been prone too long.

When it was light, he took the spear again and
worked at an exit from the shelter. Pushing out an
interwoven branch, he finally worked a hole big enough
to get through. Wearing his leggings and poncho, over
a torso-hugging underwear his mu had made, he slowly
wriggled through and stood up.

It was a white world, still and cool, with a slight
breeze that negated the heat of the sun. He was on the
foothills to The Sleeping Giant, and from here there was
no semblance to a man in the shape of the mountain
that lifted from him. Nowhere was there any movement,
but he could see a few small tendrils of smoke
demarking family dwellings separated and scattered far
to no-sun.

It was early sun, but he wondered at the wisdom
of taking to the trail again with it being so cold. He was

not used to making it by himself, and had no tutor to
instruct him. If he ran again, or even walked, what
could he use for a shelter against the cold come dark?
Did he dare start? What of those who followed him? He
thought he knew the answer to that. The Great One had
brought the storm to turn them back, and they had gone
home. He was safe from pursuit, but not safe. However,
his enemy was probably ahead of him now, and not
behind.

He walked to the knoll, and studied the terrain.
He knew he had to go back a ways and turn into mid-
sun, or he would come to the *Waters-That-Hurry-to-Sunset*
after they had entered the canyons they had carved. Men
had told how impossible it was to cross the river after it
once entered its walled canyons. He wanted to cross it
where the waters were broad. That meant mid-sun.

Satisfied he was making the right choice, he
exercised a bit, ran in the deep snows to work up a
sweat, and returned to his snow-covered shelter. He ate
ravenously, rested, napped, melted snow to drink and
refill his deer-gut waterbag, then ate again and slept.

It was a melting of his shelter that awakened
him three suns later, and he realized a *Chinook* was
coming from the mountains, a warming that meant he
could again travel. He needed to hunt, as he was quickly
doing away with the food his mu had sent. Perhaps near
the crossing, with water close, he would find game.

He ate a quick meal, drank until he was about to
burst, and got his pack ready. With first light, he was
out and moving, amazed at how the snow had settled
and crusted even during the cold suns. It made travel
tough until Sun God had softened the crust, although the
Chinook had done a good job. It was a warm wind that
had him feeling better than he had in a long time.

Tirelessly he trotted, passing the unknown
country and wondering what it would look like if it were
dry. He decided it was more deadly when it was dry,
because Others would be out and traveling. Right now,
he had the whole world to himself.

The gentle rolling of the land changed to
miniature bluffs of soil and snow. He avoided the
ravines, where the mighty puma hunted. The ground
became muddy, his moccasins and leggings soaked; but

he was working hard, moving and carrying the pack, and he stayed warm. He was glad he had dry ones to put on when he stopped. He peeled the poncho but continued to wear the rest of his cold-weather clothing. Though he would sweat more than he wanted, the once warm-feeling winds were cooling. He slowed to a walk, and let the clothing he wore dry while he moved so he would not get a chill once he stopped.

Breathtaking! The land suddenly dropped away on a slope that ended at the moving waters. It was a wide body of water...wider than he had pictured in his mind. How in the name of sense was he to get to the other side?

He stood on the top of the hill and watched for some time, but could come up with no ideas. He had to find something that floated, and he had to find a paddle. And he had to get some meat. And he had to be the man!

Was he not a man? Had he not passed the test? Did not his chest still have the two scars where he had been cut to insert the two faggots that held tenaciously while he danced? Was his hair not knotted in the back and his headband holding the feather of manhood? Did he not have a hawk feather to show he was a man? Had he not killed four Others? Had he not escaped the men who tried to kill him? Had he not Opened his love? Had not the chief said he was a man and given him a new name of strength and pride? Had he not breathed the spirit of his new name from the burning sceptre of Spirit Man? Had not his mu told him he was no longer her boy, but was become a man? Had not the Great One given him a vision and a trail? There was no doubt of it, he was a man. And what lay ahead of him, the moving waters with which he was so unfamiliar, would only prove another way to be the man, to show the gods he deserved the new spirit!

Perhaps it was the blood of the Ancient Ones. He certainly felt different from what he assumed his people felt about themselves. But was this feeling something for pride, or was it something to overcome?

Who could tell? Some sun his journey would be over, and he would forget the past, with its Little Dove, mu, and Boy with the Eye. He would forget that over which he had no control, and remember his dream. He would follow the Great One, and his new spirit, and he would do what he must. The moving waters would be just another step of many.

8

He could not believe his good fortune; the Great One was truly looking out for him. The dugout canoe had been concealed in tall grass and saplings, probably forgotten by the ones who put it there, because it had been there a long time. He was not too sure of its trustworthiness in the water, for mildew ran all along the bottom of the rough-hewn craft where it had partially settled into the muddy shoreline, and the log looked weak from dampness and age. But it would have to do, and it was certainly better than anything else he had seen while he wandered along the edge of the moving water. It was nearly dark when he had chanced to walk between the saplings, more concerned at the moment with chasing up a cotton-tail than finding a boat. He rolled the dugout and skeptically looked it over, and a moment later a rabbit bounded out from the base of a cluster of willows, almost at his feet, and he brought it down when it stopped to see what had caused the frightening noise.

Two goals in one fortunate move. Now he had

two squirrels and one rabbit for his evening meal, and he would need it all. He was starved, preferring not to dip into the pack again if he could avoid it, except for variety. But he was determined to have a meat diet to save his rations for emergencies. So far, so good.

His campsite was near the river in a stand of willows, where he had dug a small firepit and spread his blankets before his final foray along the moving water. He gathered dried twigs and built a smokeless fire, though in the growing darkness he felt calmly secure.

The weather had moderated quickly after the Chinook, bringing on a somewhat less than balmy dusk, though he was comfortable with his poncho and leggings. He roasted the three animals, grateful that the squirrels were small and heated fast. He had them eaten almost before the rabbit was hot. He took his time with it, spitting and slowly rotating it over a fire he fed for some time. It was good to feel the warmth, though he had to repeatedly turn to keep the heat even.

Feeling good, he ate half the rabbit, saving the rest for his early repast on the new sun, and let the fire burn out while he curled in his blankets and slept.

With first full light, he was examining the dugout critically, giving it a shallow water float test, and praying it would get him across. Then he beached it, ate, and reorganized his pack. He had just stepped from the trees when movement caught his eye, and on the top of the hill, right on the trail he had himself used the previous sun, stood five men. The first he recognized...Boy with the Eye of an Eagle!

He had made a couple critical errors. He had underestimated the resolve of his enemy. Because of this, he assumed the weather had driven them home. That was error number one. The second was predicated on that one. He had made no attempt to hide his trail. In the snow, and with the melt going on, it had seemed useless to try. They had found the clear trail and now they had found him.

For only a second he stared at them, that second of pure shock and disbelief. Then he sprinted for the dugout, fortunate to be holding all his belongings. He never looked back. His spear and bow were flung into the front of the dugout, and the pack, attached to his back as when he traveled, was no problem. He grabbed up the pole he had selected and delimbed, throwing it into the boat as well. Then he pushed it into the water and leaped in.

The momentum carried the clumsy craft well into the slow-moving stream, and he grabbed the pole and tried to aim for the far shore. The dugout sat low in the water, making it drag very heavily, which in turn caused him to misjudge the speed and strength of the water, but there was not much he could have done about that anyhow. The wild and frantic yells of the five men made him turn to look, and they were still racing through the high grass, brush and willows toward the water.

He was well out of arrow range, at least accurate range, before they reached the shoreline his pole still finding bottom but the soft mud making it difficult to progress. Slowly he crossed, but was carried much farther downstream than he had wished. His enemy ran along the river, trying but failing to get broadside of him.

He reached the far side, but the main current ran deep against the shoreline, and he struggled to beach the craft when there was only a cut bank to run against. The prow hit the muddy bank, sending the back out into the stream and around, and now he faced back upstream, though he was still against the bank.

Then a jut of the bank caught the stern, and he was jerked violently. The dugout pitched, and then rolled. In a moment, he was in the water, under the boat and then back up. His feet hit bottom, and he fought the current to get his balance, the pack giving him problems. His spear bobbed to the top, and he grabbed it, and in the grabbing was able to catch himself. Wading toward shore, spitting muddy water and coughing, he found his bow floating against the bank. He stopped and looked up at bare soil of the bank that rose quickly, seeing the struggle it would be to climb. Then he glanced across the wide river, and located the five who chased him. Two were holding small trees and wading into the water, preparing to use the wood for a floating aid while they swam. The other three were searching the dried, washed debris in an old backwash, hoping to find similar assistance.

Frantically, he climbed out of the water, slipping on the mud at water's edge until he finally got a foothold, then struggled up the steep cut. Holding on fast, he hurled the spear up over the edge, then did the same for the bow, which was useless with the gut string wet and stretched. Then he scrambled over the edge and stood panting while he watched the five men struggling with the water. Two were just getting a good start, and already they were being carried far downstream. He did not identify any except Boy with the Eye, who was still trying to get his limb to the water.

Gulping for air, he watched them until he caught his breath, then he picked up his weapons and began to trot up the side of the long hill. Had he crossed where he had hoped, he would not have had to climb the hill, but now it was the only way he could go.

He stayed to the sunny side of the hill, angling away from his adversaries, continuing to trot though his legs were beginning to feel like wet logs. The pack was wet and heavy, and he wondered if he were in for a tough, even sleepless darkness. If he managed to escape!

The snow was gone on the mid-sun side of the hill, and he angled back downhill as he turned toward setting-sun. Behind him, the sun was lifting into the cloudless sky, and it was warming. He wished he could stop and put out his blankets to dry, but he did not dare. He labored on, finding it much easier to angle down than up, and wondering how much distance he had gained on the five.

Now he could see far ahead, though barren mountains raised toward mid-sun, and the line of hills that fronted the moving water rose on his right, falling away toward no-sun. He wondered if the five had managed to get out of the river, where their packs were, how they planned to catch him if he managed to escape another sun. It was unlikely they had any food when they swam the river, and only bows and arrows to hunt. Their spears had been left somewhere behind them. It was comforting to know they were limited in how long they could chase him, but his immediate problem was acute. He had to escape...now.

He reached the bottom of the hill, and the wide,

flat country stretched out before him as far as he could see. He wondered how far it was to friendly people, and how he would be able to tell friendly from unfriendly if he met anyone. Of only one thing was he certain, he had someone on his backtrail that was dangerous...and unyielding. And they, too, once they reached this spot, could see as far as he saw now. He would be out there, in plain view, and there was nothing he could do about it.

He dropped into a ravine, then followed it for a time, since it went in the same direction. He would remain unseen, though the melting snow had made the bottom a small stream and the ground muddy. He walked, then ran, then walked, and when the wash bent back toward mid-sun, he found a small adjoining gully and climbed out. Taking a moment to rest, he studied the country behind him, but saw nothing of the five. Then he began to walk again, angling between mid-sun and setting-sun.

Were they still behind him, and had they managed to cross the moving water? How much longer would Boy with the Eye continue? He had no answers, and stopped thinking about it. More necessary was what lay ahead...or was it? One thing was sure, in the mud he was leaving a trail a blind man could follow with ease! As he walked, he turned and looked back several times, and after a time he felt the urge to trot. The sun climbed into full heat and he spotted a small herd of antelope, but they had seen him first and were moving away, wary and giving him no chance to approach. A rabbit bounded away before he could get his spear out of hand and the throwing-stick into action. The gut of his bow was nearly taut again, and he would be able to use it before darkness.

The sun warmed him, he felt good about having lost the five men, though he walked in wide-open country that was beginning to undulate and show rents and ravines, and he watched a hawk lazily soaring in the heavens, knowing it was anything but lazy. Its head was working, and he knew it saw every movement on the ground ahead and around him. He wondered what the presence of the hawk portended to the rest of this sun.

He carried his throwing-stick in his right hand

now, ready to drop his spear if a small animal moved near him, but it was long into the warm sun before he had a chance, and he missed. The pack was a hindrance to fluid motion. He was feeling the pangs of hunger, but glad to be alive and traveling. He had lost the five, at least for the present, but he still felt them. They were still there, but he was going to ignore them. For now.

He came to another hill, and skirted it rather than climbing it. As he rounded the mid-sun side, he found a deep cut into the hill, a washout that was only a stone's throw deep, with a sheer upper end. The bottom of the cut was sand, and had a trickle of runoff water in it. The sides were sheer and had begun to support small plants. The slight bend to the opening made the back walls of it invisible to anyone who did not take the time to try it. He entered, dropped and opened his pack, and stretched his blankets on the drying mud, in full sun.

Then he went out the mouth of the wash and climbed to the top of the hill, where he studied the surrounding country again. The hawk he had seen was still there, now far behind him, and he could see nothing more. For some time he sat and watched, letting the sun warm him and feeling the tired muscles relax.

Finally he went back down, checked the blankets, one of which had not gotten very wet, and found them drying well. Then he took his bow and arrow and went out again, checking for rabbit tracks. He found coyote tracks, and then the large pad prints of a lone wolf. It was the first such track he had seen in over a winter.

He studied the sun-old track for a time, then circled out before heading back for his camp. He jumped a jackrabbit, and shot it. As he headed back, he saw a second, and killed it. The first was good size, but the second was huge. Thrilled by his good fortune, he hurried back and began to search for campfire fuel, not an easy task in the treeless, shrubless terrain. He settled for some dead cactus and ancient buffalo dung.

He waited for dark before making his fire, spitted the first rabbit and watched it carefully. It was cool, and he donned his leggings and poncho again, and was glad they were dry. Hungry, he reached for the spit to take a piece of meat that was not done, and heard a slight sound. Turning only his head, he looked into the icy gray eyes of the largest wolf he had ever seen, teeth bared and tail straight back. It looked from him to the meat, then back, its tongue lolling and slobbering. Fear leaped within him, but he swallowed it and spoke.

"Welcome, old wolf-man. Smell my meat? I suppose you would refuse to settle for less than the whole thing, right? Well, I tell you, friend, what else is a meal for? Share my meat. Sit right there, and let me tear off some of this. Here. This okay?" He jerked off a leg and tossed it over the head of the wolf, who winced and turned to sniff out the meat with a peculiar odor...fire smell and man smell. He lifted his head and looked back at the man, then leaped aside...but too late.

He Who Conquers had grabbed his spear and thrust it hard into the side of the old wolf. It penetrated the body cavity in front of the left hind leg, rammed up through the intestines, and the point broke the skin on the right side above the front leg. A slight "yip" escaped the wolf as it collapsed.

He Who Conquers was instantly on his feet, and his voice rang into the darkness and sounded full in the water-hewn gully.

> O Great One, riding the moontime
> > as well as the sun,
> > You have selected this learning man
> > > as an object of value.
>
> In times of need, you have seen fit
> > to reward his effort,
> And to smile on a servant
> > who is humbled by your attention.
>
> Four warriors you have placed
> > on my arrows,
> Evidence of your overseeing eye.
> A shelter you showed to me,
> > and protected me from a storm.
>
> Rabbits you fed to my keen eye
> > and accurate weapon,

And now you have helped me
    to overcome the mighty wolf.

My sadness departs,
    my eyes fasten upon what lies ahead,
For now I know you lead me
    and indeed go before me.

The meat the wolf would desire
    I leave for another.
Perhaps there is one in need
    more than I.

My heart soars that you walk
    the path where I must go,
My spirit is overwhelmed
    by your protection.

O, Great One, let me continue
    to know your trail.

He sat down, looked at the meat he still held, pinched off a small piece to drop into the fire and then a second which he tossed toward rising-sun, and began to eat.

His sleep was marred by a dream, but when awake, there was no memory of it. Only that it was horrible, with images and events that held no joy. Lying awake listening to the sounds of darkness and trying to remember what had upset him, he fell again into a restless sleep.

He was back on The Top, walking hand-in-hand with his mate, but her face was lost in the long hair that hung on both sides. They stopped to make love, and he recognized the place where he had been felled by the arrow, but when it was over, he saw ever so briefly the face of Singing Waters, and was horrified. She got up and began to run, and he chased after her, both of them laughing merrily, when she stopped and looked at him. It was his mu! She shrieked and looked down, and there lay his fa, dead and somewhat decayed, and he glanced up at his mu, only she was no longer there, but was also dead and decaying at his feet. Then Little Dove was

there, and came into his arms, watching him soberly, and
Boy with the Eye was smiling and waving from a
distance. He discovered it was another he held, and not
Little Dove at all. There was an aroma... what was it...a
sweet scent...but before he could pinpoint it, he was
running, down canyons and along sheer cliffs, through
fields with wild animals and then deep snow with no one
around. Always he heard the wailing of his mu, but how
could that be? She was dead! Then he was quietly lying
in the arms of his mate, and Little Dove was nodding
and smiling while he reached out for her, only to have
her disappear and many people...his village people!...were
calling out for him to come help them. They were
helpless and needed He Who Conquers!

He awakened in a sweat, deeply disturbed,
blankets in a heap beside him. He remembered; it was
not pleasant. It was all so horribly confusing--the swift
changing of personages and scenes--but more than that,
it was ugly. He was not sure if he wanted to know what
it meant, though in the end he must, nor did he wish to
think on it. But no matter how he tried, the dream--or
was it a vision?--continued to dominate his mind.

Who was the mate he coupled with at the site of
his injury, and how did Singing Waters fit into the
scene? Why were his fa and mu decaying? Why was
Boy with the Eye smiling and waving while he held Little
Dove, and why was she so sober? Or was it Little Dove
he held? And the aroma he smelled, different from the
sweetness of a woman, what was it? And why the racing
over great distances? Was the sight of wild animals
significant? And why the screaming of his dead mu?
Who was his mate, and why was Little Dove smiling
while he reached for her? And why did she disappear?
Was she his mate, after all? And what was the problem
with his people, and why were they calling to him, The
Coyote, the one who left them to escape death at the
hands of their soon-to-be leader?

Did all this portend the future, and should he
return to them now? His resolve wavered again, but
once more he consciously set aside his misgivings. He
could not go back, and the certainty was even more
strange than his desire to keep on going toward an
unknown destination.

What lay ahead? And why did he feel this compulsion to be in such a search for something of which he was not sure? With its many inherent dangers, the journey seemed absurd, although those who followed him gave him reason enough to keep going. Yet, the real desire was to be moving, traveling, seeking, and the danger behind him was only the time factor that made him leave now, instead of down the road in time.

He sat up and pulled his blankets around him, chill reaching him after the arduous vision began to lose its grip, and eyed the embers still reddish in the ashes of his fire, clear because of the deep darkness that still held the land. He lay a few pieces of dung on the fire, then stirred it with the point of his spear. It flamed, and he sat watching the fire, knowing what it meant to be looking into a fire if he had to suddenly focus on something out in the darkness. He stared at the bloody carcass of the wolf, and remembered his deliverance from it, then at the hide that lay on the other side of the fire. The Great One was with him, and had already shown him he was going to be protected against every adversary, and he wondered what might be next. It was almost an excitement to think of what the next marvelous act might be. The assurance of the Great One was also a strong incentive for him to keep going. He was on a mission, whatever it might be. Only the Great One knew!

After the fire burned down, he watched the blues and oranges that winked and floated among the bigger embers, wondering if he dared try to sleep again. After the last two sudden awakenings, he hated to think there might be another. Yet, in but a short time, he slept.

9

He awakened with a start, and found it well after sunup, though the walls of his ravine were keeping him in shade. It was the reason for his instant alertness...a voice...or rather, a shout...was it real or imagined? With his sudden attention came the realization that a hawk was again floating overhead!

On his knees, he quickly stuffed his pack together and roped it, prepping it for travel. He may have to leave in a hurry, and was sure of one thing, he did not want to go without his personal belongings. It was while he finished the tying that he heard it again.

It was significantly close.

"More tracks over here!"

Twin Who Lived? It sounded like him, and it came from near the mouth of his gully. A responsive shout came from somewhere over the edge of the gully.

"None here but the trail. What you got there?"

"Too sandy. Some animal, but some human. Come on over here." There was silence. He frantically looked for a way up the sides of the gully, but the only way out was the one he had used on the previous sun, clearly visible from where the voice came. Because he overslept, he was trapped, and there was nowhere to go! It was a lesson to remember: Never sleep in a dead-end canyon.

The voices were more conversational as the men drew closer together.

"Too many tracks here. Fresh wolf over there, and it went into that gully. These human ones are hard to read. One set leads into and out of that same gully, but with the fresh wolf going in, he wouldn't be in there."

He Who Conquers held his breath. Gray Dog's voice came from farther out.

"Here are his tracks...out here. Kind of meandering. And blood...rabbit, I think...yes, here is where he killed it. Blood trail leads your way."

"No blood over here. Those tracks going that way must be his. Should we follow them?"

He Who Conquers moved closer to the mouth of the ravine and snugged in against the bank where he could see some of the flat country directly in front of his hiding place. Far out was Gray Dog, but the other two were too far to his right to be seen. It was where he had returned to the gully. No blood? He wondered why it ended, and then remembered shifting the rabbit to his other side and lifting both a front and back leg. The blood had to find a new trail down through the hide, and that insignificant move had saved his life! The Great One had done it again! Perhaps Son of Happiness had burned a faggot for him!

Across the entry, hardly but a stone throw from him, strode a fourth member of the group. He was shocked, far beyond his ability to comprehend! Broken Nose! One he had admired from his earliest memories...a man of honor, integrity...a leader of The People...one he thought to be his friend, or at least not an enemy!

Why Broken Nose? What had he done to deserve such hate? It was a blow that numbed him. When he returned to reason, a gradual process that began when his unseeing eyes took note of the hawk so high it was almost out of sight, the four men--or was it five?--were gone.

He Who Conquers stole to the mouth of the wash and carefully eased far enough to see out. They were far out, separated, and casting back and forth for sign.

He stood a moment deciding. If they found nothing, they would retrace their steps to the last sign they had seen. That would be here, and this time they would no doubt enter the ravine to check on the tracks that had come this way.

He trotted back and shouldered his pack, took his spear and bow and quickly left the mouth, wiping out his tracks as he went, until he was well away from the opening. Then he back-stepped himself and turned toward mid-sun, the land having dropped enough so he was not able to see the ones searching for him, and more significantly, they could not see him.

He trotted, beginning at a good pace, pushing himself hard for the distance he felt he needed. The land was so flat despite the hills and ravines that one could be seen for a long distance whenever topping a hill, and only space could give him any sense of security. He could feel the hair prickle along the back of his neck as he ran, wondering if they would spot him.

Sun God was halfway to his zenith, which, at this season, was a very flat trajectory. He wished it were nearer dark, an advantage to him in such country, unless they out-thought him and kept going the same direction. That was possible, mostly because he had set such a course. If he changed, perhaps it would throw them off. But that would make the trip that much longer, and perhaps he would still run into them.

Mid-sun...moving...toward the barren mesa visible but falling away in the place where Sun God would rest in his near-snowtime orbit. In the new sun, he would seek the Great One and send him a message in the smoke of his fire.

Then it hit him. There had been only four! Why? There had been five at the moving water. Could the God of the Moving Water have taken one of them? If so, why had they not taken time for better medicine? What had he done to give them such incentive?

His legs were growing very tired, and he slowed to a walk, checking the landscape as he did, first in the direction he went to avoid someone he might not want to meet, and then back to where the four were still seeking his trail. He did not see anyone.

He walked for a time, then ran, then walked, each time looking back and ahead.   It was barren country. Turning more toward setting-sun, he angled up the back side of a knob that might give him perspective on the country from which he had come.

He stopped before he skylined, and stood where he could just see over the top of the hill.   There they were, the four of them, far back and near the horizon, standing in a cluster so small they appeared but a dot. They had not found his trail, but still traveled in the direction he wished to go.

Then he saw movement, far to sunset.   Men. Many men, strung out in a line and traveling at an angle between no-sun and rising-sun.   In just a moment, they would be where they could see the four skylined men. What would be their reaction?   And that of the four?

He stood a while, then checked behind himself and around the wide scope he could see and be seen. Nothing drew his attention.   He turned back to the moving line of men, and it was at that moment the four saw them.   They stopped, stood a moment, then lay flat on the ground.

Had the line of men spotted them before they got down?   They made no alterations in their step, or their direction.   Where were they headed, and who were they? There were eight hands less two, a long line that made him think of getting to better cover.   But they were far away, and their angle would take them even farther. Unless they saw the four.   If they backtracked them, they might find his solitary track headed into mid-sun.   Would they come?   No, one man was not a big enough quarry for so many.

Tensely, he watched.   Suddenly the line stopped and stood for a time, the front four or five bunched like they were having a conference.   Then they turned, and the four suddenly rose and fled.

It was only a short time before the line took up the chase, but the four had a good lead.   Only Broken Nose had a problem, being much older and not as agile.

The distance between them stayed the same as far as he could see them, then the four were over a hill and out of sight, and after a time the line of men was, too. He wasted little time wondering at the outcome, heading directly into setting-sun of the hot season.

His legs were tired, but he walked at a good pace, forcing himself to keep going, his eyes constantly moving, watching the area in front and to both sides, with an occasional glance at the backtrail. That was to remember the country if he should come this way when he returned.

The sun rounded to his face, and he looked for a camping place, but found nothing. Sun God sat on the horizon, then dipped, and he stopped, having nothing around him but open spaces, and a small puddle of water in the flat land that came from snowmelt. He did not care. It was water. The ground here was almost all rock, but most of the small pocks and tanks in the rock were empty. He stretched out his blankets, pulled the strips of cold wolf meat from his pack and paid obeisance to the gods before beginning to chew, drinking often from the puddle of water. It was food, but he chewed mechanically.

He wondered about the four and their run for freedom, and the identity of the line of men. And then of Little Dove and Son of Happiness. And of mu, and Singing Waters. And his vision--or dream. It was both, in all likelihood.

He fell asleep thinking of what the various scenes meant, and his sleep was uncluttered by dreams. He awakened in the coldness of the first inkling of dawn, stiff from the rocky bed, ate the last of the rabbit, packed his things and began to walk.

He had not traveled long when he came to a sheer drop and a wide chasm, the sides and the top, including what was at his feet, being slabs of stone--huge slabs, rounded and broken, like the ground over which he had been traveling. The ravine had a sandy bottom, and in it running water. The stream angled into setting-sun of snowtime, and he looked for and found a way to the bottom. He drank heavily, then followed the stream, seeing many animal tracks but no human ones.

The bed wandered a bit, but held its same general direction, and he saw no good reason to climb out, though once he found an easy place to climb and

went up for a look around. When Sun God cast long
shadows from the rim, he began to think of camping,
and found a small spot to one side, on a ledge. There he
built a fire using wood found along the bottom, and
cooked a rabbit he killed.

Another sun he followed the stream, then
climbed from it and angled directly to mid-sun, toward
the end of a flat mesa that was ringed by scattered trees.
It was late when he got to the trees, and he camped,
again eating a rabbit he had killed, along with spitting
two more.

He awakened to see sixteen deer foraging not far
away in the trees and a hawk circling overhead--it was to
be another eventful sun! He was about to stalk them
when he saw four men entering the trees. His pack
together, he made no attempt to move, because the men,
who had as yet seen neither him nor the deer, were
obviously hunting. Then, he realized that from their
perspective, they would not see the deer at all, and an
idea began to formulate.

It was interesting country, but he had no interest
in the line of redrock spires that were in the background
outside the trees, nor in the sage country that he had
traversed the previous sun. He had studied the two
mesas that seemed to converge farther to mid-sun, and
had taken to the trees where the closest one turned
toward it. The men had come across the large opening
from the direction of the other mesa, to the mid-sun side
of the line of spires and pinnacles that had him
wondering if the gods dwelt near here.

Junipers thickened as they approached the mesa,
and it was in the thickening of the trees where the deer
fed, oblivious to either the single man who watched, or
the four hunters who were passing them by, staying near
the scattered edge.

He Who Conquers stood and scrutinized them.
They were built much like the People of The Top. Short,
well-built, dark of hair and complexion, dressed in animal
hides against the coolness, wearing leggings and sandals,
carrying atlatl and bow. They saw him and stopped,
muttering among themselves. He kept a careful watch
but made no moves until they had talked and turned
toward him.

"Hola!" he called out, giving them the palm-up sign of friendship, watching their reaction to see if it might be better to run or stay. He felt he could outrun them if necessary, but they had shown no signs of hostility. He again raised a hand, palm up, and they responded the same.

They stopped a *stone-throw* away, and one said something he could not understand. They awaited his reply, so he shrugged and said, "I don't understand."

They spoke among themselves again, and then one motioned for him to come to them.

He pointed to himself and said, "He Who Conquers," but made no move to approach them. He motioned toward the sun and made ten circles across the sky, then pointed to the direction of his people.

The spokesman walked toward him, said some words he did not hear well, though he thought he understood one of them to mean trader. He shook his head, and made the signs for a trader, then shook his head again. One of the men pointed to him and then back to the direction from which he had come, then formed his hands to show the flat top and sweeping steep sides of the mesa.

He smiled and nodded. The man asked in broken words of the People of the Top, "You travel alone...so far?"

He Who Conquers nodded again. The man smiled in response.

"You He Who Conquers?"

"Yes. And you?"

They came to him with smiles, and clasped forearms. The curiosity and welcome of their eyes were evident in the firmness of the clasp. They spent time talking, the one man somewhat familiar with his tongue, and he quick to find many words of similar sound and meaning.

He related his travels with the use of signs, and said it was because his intended mate was given to the son of the chief. The men laughed, understanding what he meant by that. A son of a chief often had benefits that brought jealousies and conflicts.

They discussed their hunting foray and He Who Conquers understood they had been hunting eleven suns,

with nothing to show for it. They had been told there
were many deer, but they had seen none. He learned
their names were Hawkeye, an older man of about
twenty-five winters, who was the craggy-browed leader of
the hunt. Moccasin Maker, about twenty-two winters
and muscular like a *lifter of the rock.* He Who Tracks, a
quiet and reserved man of nineteen winters who had
found many tracks but not the animals that were making
them. The last was Dog Man, whose specialty was the
atlatl, a man of twenty or twenty-one winters with a
hunched back and misshapen left leg.

As they talked, the eye of He Who Conquers was
drawn to the strange breechcloth of these men, because
it was not the short flap worn front and back by the men
of The Top--and even the Others. The flap was the same
on the back, but on the front it was another story. A
shallow cup hung from the belt, covering the sac, and
from the disc-shaped skin projected a tube for the male
member. The entire cover was larger than would be the
male member when aroused, and each of the men had
painted the large projection with white and black colors,
images of pregnant women and well-endowed bison bulls,
the male member greatly exaggerated.

It was obvious to him these men were of a
people that greatly honored the Fertility God. There was
no way the male member could be so large, but they had
certainly made its extreme importance obvious with their
artwork. Never having seen such a unique way for the
reverence of fertility, though the people of The Top had
their fertility symbols and rites, he was a bit unsure how
they would accept him with his lesser emphasis.
Humorously he wondered if the women of these people
were impressed by the cover, wondering which of these
men wore the covering in greatest oversize compared to
what was inside. He had to suppress a smile as he
thought of it.

What did the women do for special emphasis?
Or to invite their men to such practices? Or were these
men competing with one another for honors from the
Goddess? Or was this a successful means of insuring
fertility?

And another thing impressed him. The backs of
their heads were flat, and the head wider. The Trader

had told The People of The Top about such people. They made boards for the infants back-carriers, cradleboards the women wore to carry the children while they worked. They had the boards rather than the softer animal hide for a reason. Some people from far to mid-sun had come among them in generations past, a people of great intelligence. The women were very jealous of such knowledge, and felt that with the wider heads their own children would become wise like the "Broadheads" from the warmer lands to mid-sun.

He wondered if it were true, but until this moment had not given the story credence. Now he knew it was a fact. If indeed the people were wiser than others, or if the cradleboard had just become so common they thought nothing more of it, he was unsure. But these were the Broadheads, known to be friendly and very social. Those from whom they copied the use of the cradleboard were far from being so friendly, raiding the area from time to time to capture slaves to use in their tribal grounds. They knew of this from the few who had escaped.

"Our harvest is over, and it was good," Hawkeye told him, but our people are low on meat. We haven't seen a bison herd in almost two winters. We've found wapiti and a few deer, but so little meat for so many."

"How many people are in your village?"

"About twenty hands, some are infants."

Less than a hundred people, but over an entire snow time, that could take a great deal of meat.

"Do you have other groups out hunting?"

"Most of the men are out. In groups of four and five. If this hunt isn't successful, the men think to go to the swamplands far away and hunt the shaggy beasts, or even try to find the animal with the long nose."

"Then I'll make you the most successful of them all." He Who Conquers spoke firmly, and they reacted by merely staring at him.

He Who Conquers stooped and smoothed the ground, then drew a quick map, showing the mesa that rose up beside them, the pinnacles and their direction, and the trees where they stood. Then he showed how they could deploy, and if they were truly hunters, get some venison.

Where he sent them, he could run the deer
directly through their posting, and the way he put it, the
men took it as a dare. He had but one uncertainty, and
that was whether the deer had stayed to graze in the
same place where he had last seen them.

The men left in single file to take their places,
and He Who Conquers waited to give them plenty of
opportunity to be settled and alert, then he circled
slowly, soon seeing the deer, some feeding and some
lying down. He stopped behind a tree, studying the
location and the lay of the trees, deciding how he might
approach closely enough to one before he ran them off.
It would be a tough stalk, but he felt confident.

The trees were scattered far enough to insure
safety in the minds of the deer, and they had not been
disturbed, their watchfulness not as sharp as usual. He
Who Conquers moved very slowly when in the open,
trying to line up behind trees from the two who were the
most alert. When one would turn to stare at him, he
froze, and if it looked away, he took a step or two.

Gradually he closed the gap, noting a huge
boulder just to the far side of the deer, which meant that
when they bolted, his direction of approach and the
location of the boulder would turn them in the direction
he intended. The boulder was more significant than the
steep hillside which he had pictured in his mind.

He stopped behind a large tree, and was
surprised to see a large doe lying nearer than any he had
seen, looking away. There were no bucks with the herd,
which meant the rut was upon them, the buck nearby
watching his herd.

He fitted an arrow and watched the doe, careful
not to make a move while another watched. Slowly he
raised the bow, sure of his short shot of five or six paces,
and let fly before he could over-react to the tension he
felt.

The arrow was true, entering the neck just
behind the head, and other than a slight jerk of the
body, she simply laid her head down. It was so quick he
hardly had time to realize he had done better than he
had even considered.

The arrow made little noise, and the string only
a slight twang. It was so quiet, the head doe of the herd

merely glanced at the one he had killed and looked
away. The wind was right until he went perhaps four
paces past the dead doe, and he realized the Great One
had indeed led him here. He could yet get another!

He studied those he could see. The nearest was
almost fifteen paces away, a long shot for an arrow and
beyond accuracy for his spear. He would have to get
closer, but now he felt tension, wondering where the
buck might be. He kept scanning the trees as he moved
each step, trying not to alert any of the animals. Earlier
he had seen sixteen, but now could locate only twelve,
counting the dead one. Fearful lest he lose his contest
with them, he eased around another tree and stepped
one, two, three paces, each carefully chosen.

Another step, a long wait while two does stared
at him, then another. He was nervous, the wind very
weak but crossing his path, and soon to take his scent
into the herd. Another step, a tree well-positioned, a
step and another. Only seven paces, but the closest one
was a small yearling, not the one he preferred. It stood
quartered away from him, head down and feeding.

A step, and the head of the watching doe came
up and fixed on him. He stood as stone, not blinking,
watching, his bow in his left hand with an arrow strung
but loose, his right hand steadying him on a sapling.
She watched him a long time, unsure what was wrong
but mildly fretful.

Then a different one moved, one he had not
seen, around to his left. He had half-circled it, but it lay
behind three trees, out of his line of vision. But now his
scent was among them. Ears erect, tails up in alarm,
the entire herd was now alert, watching him.

He was not sure what to do. If he went for the
shot, they would be in full flight in one bound, and it
made for a tough shot. If he stood, they would most
likely move away from the smell, but not flee. If they
panicked, they would run back to his left, following the
one who had picked his scent and was fidgeting. The
main doe stood broadside, her gaze fixed on him. His
first move would send her into flight, and most of the
herd would follow.

Perplexed, he remained fixed, watching, trying to
keep a perspective on the trees in case another was

there. The herd moved a few steps, nervous and ready to bolt. Then the unexpected happened again.

The buck moved. He was back to the right of He Who Conquers, near the base of the huge boulder, where he had been lying. He had no idea what had the herd jittery, coming from upwind, head high and tail twitching. He would follow the herd when it ran, but his path brought him within five paces of He Who Conquers.

The arrow was released so quickly, the doe had taken only one bound when it flew. She moved along the base of the steep side of the mesa rather than following the one who leaped into action and went directly away from He Who Conquers. The main herd followed, only one going with the doe he had not seen.

The buck never saw him, and the arrow entered just behind the left shoulder, puncturing the lung and heart. It staggered, then bounded five times before the left front leg collapsed and he nose-dived, struggled to his feet and jumped twice more while reeling sideways, then went down.

He Who Conquers threw back his head and shouted his joy, knowing his cry would be heard by the posted hunters. The main herd was going directly toward them.

He turned and ran to the doe, rolled her on her side, cut into her chest cavity and pulled the heart from the body, then cutting out the liver and the female organs. Taking a cupped hand, he scooped out a palmful of blood and sucked it into his mouth, and took a bite of the warm liver. Laying the heart, female organs and the remainder of the liver on a log, he went over to the buck, where again he took the heart and liver, then the male organs, and again drank a handful of blood. His heart soaring, he gathered some inner bark, shredded it, and started a fire. Once the fire blazed, he laid the remainder of the two livers in it, bent his head back and sang another song.

O Great One, You have spoken to me again!
   How do I understand the marvels you
     perform?
   First the mighty wolf, and now two deer,

Including the mighty buck!

My fire burns, and the smoke is strong!
The aroma of the liver lifts to You,
The scent of it comes to Your nostrils.
See Your servant in his ecstasy!

See the mammaries of the doe,
Take her strength and fertility,
Place her strength in another
That has been without young.

Here, I offer the maleness of the buck,
See the great size and strength,
And give me its great power
While I feast on its richness!

O Great One, come feast with me,
And share in the success you brought!

Taking the gonads, he placed them on a bare
fallen bole and crushed them with a flat rock after
cutting several slashes. Then he scraped the mushy mass
into his right hand, threw back his head and ate.

He returned to the fire, fed it again, then
watched the liver of the buck turning black. He had
nearly forgotten the men whom he had posted, so intense
his reverie, but while the meat sizzled, he was suddenly
aware that Hawkeye and Dog Man stood at the side of
the big buck, staring at him with both amazement and
admiration.

He motioned for them to join him, but they
shook their heads and stayed in place.

"Did you have success?"

Hawkeye was speechless, forming words but
saying nothing. Dog Man first made a sound, tied to a
nod that said they had animals down where they had
been posted.

"How many?"

The fingers held up indicated three.

He Who Conquers smiled and nodded, then said
again, "Come. The liver is being sent to give new life."

Hawkeye finally found his voice. "The animals,

you have not opened the stomach for the great delicacy. The God of the Deer will be angry."

He Who Conquers looked puzzled, not at all sure what he meant. He had done what his uncle had taught him before his trip to Sipapu--taken his sip of the blood, a bite of the liver, laid out the female parts for the earth to take in its cycle of nourishing the female deer of the future, and thrown the heart out toward rising-sun where Earth Mu could use it to regenerate life. What else was there? Were not the gods pleased with his offerings?

"It must be done," Hawkeye said with a degree of urgency. "The gods will not be pleased," he reiterated.

"Then, I give it to you to do," He Who Conquers agreed, his hand going out to invite them to the animals.

Instantly, each man went to an animal, and while his meat spit and scorched, he watched them with uncertainty. Shortly, Hawkeye stood up, holding the intact stomach with tubes attached to each end. He squeezed some of the contents of the stomach into his hand, and fed himself, then brought the sac to He Who Conquers with the obvious intention that the successful hunter was to do as he.

He took some, hoping to keep it small in case he did not like it, but found the grassy contents of the stomach not unpleasant. When Dog Man came with his hands full, he took some of it, too. It was then the two men smiled, and relaxed.

"The gods walk with He Who Conquers."

"The Great One has given He Who Conquers success."

Puzzled, Hawkeye asked, "Who is the Great One?"

"He is the Leader of the gods, God of the Sun, the Maker of all life and Giver of success. He guided me here. I honor him with the smoke of two livers."

"He Who Conquers speaks strangely. Yet I will follow him in any hunt. His god is wise."

10

Being the object of a man's adoration brought strange sensations to He Who Conquers. Primarily, he was elated. He had been humbled among his own people, since the typical young man was traditionally presumed to be short on wisdom--and therefore to remain silent--and he had only been venerated for killing the Others. It was his only claim to fame among his people. Now, thanks to the Great One, he was being entrusted with a boyhood dream, becoming a man. He liked it. It was uplifting. He was becoming what he dreamed of being--a man. He was a bit puzzled that he had often been ignored despite the other things he had accomplished, things that required motivation and skill. Yet, no matter what he accomplished, in the eyes of his village superiors, he was still a boy working to become a man. Until the Others came.

But killing four Others had required only two things, stupidity...the stupidity of not realizing his great danger--naivete, at the very least--and weapon skills that had previously brought some recognition but no respect.

He had been given success by the Great One despite his blunders. Yet, four scalps formed the achievement that brought the recognition every man wanted. And now his selfish but successful ploy had won the admiration of new friends. They, without reservation, accepted him as a man, a mature man!

It never entered his mind that stupidity was not in the thinking of his people. All they saw was the result, the four scalps, the proof that he was skilled, brave and successful. While the coup he counted was dead before he touched it, it was nonetheless the greatest feat of protection accomplished among his people since their settling to become crop raisers.

He had been taught from his earliest childhood that The People were superior, that the gods had elevated them above every other peoples. He accepted it outwardly, but he wondered about it. If that were true, why had Others managed such success against them in the past. And why did Singing Waters believe that the Ancient Ones' bloodline somehow made him superior? It was illogical that if The People were the favorite of the gods, and the greatest of them all, that the blood of a lesser people made them superior! Or could it be The People were inferior until the god-like people had come among them? But the teaching was that they were of a different bloodline than all the other peoples around, and isolated on The Top to preserve it and keep it pure.

Strange beliefs. Beliefs that made him wonder if the inner voice of some was out of tune with the gods. Did this mean that if he believed something, it was right, regardless of facts which might prove otherwise? How could one say that any people was superior to another simply by bloodline and location? Could not these people, these of Open Stone, be as good as his own people? Did their veneration of fertility and the broader heads make them greater or lesser than his own?

He shook his head, wondering about the real value in becoming an adult male. Having become one, he had no choice except to refuse to be like all adults thought they ought to be. Receiving accolades for his bravery and achievement was fun and nice, but it scared him, too; to carry a name such as he had been given made him not only a man, but a target, one who would be both recognized and scrutinized, buried in derision should he somehow fail! That carried with it something else.

Responsibility. It was not that he had merely accomplished, for it was a statement that he must continue to accomplish. It meant he would be constantly evaluated, and if he failed to perform to what was anticipated of him, though he be twice the man that others were, he would be criticized and even shunned. Once he had climbed the pinnacle of success, he had to keep himself there.

That was awesome. How could he maintain such a lofty height at all times under all circumstances? Especially when he would be pushed into the role of making decisions by the very fact of his success. So far as he could see, many of the decisions he had already made left lots of room for questions, and even accusations!

He Who Conquers pondered these things as he staggered along with the other men on the way back to their village. Each man carried a huge load, a deer apiece, each man carrying his weapons and his pack. He Who Conquers, his muscles not yet fully developed though he was sinewy, soon realized how long the trail would be back to the village where he would become a famous man in but a moment--if he could manage to carry his load and keep up with the four men he trailed. He hoped the journey was short.

He strained under the load, but could soon tell the others did, too. Their loads so great, they only made about five miles the first sun. His time on the trail with his pack, and running as he had done, had helped equip him for this trial. They slept the sleep of the exhausted, and on the new sun were stiff and sore, then tired sooner as they continued across the level land toward the rising mesa He Who Conquers had watched as he traveled, which now appeared as an adversary!

Directly toward sun-set, their trail was straight and long. They stopped often, sometimes just standing with their loads still on their shoulders, then walking again. Most often, they dropped their loads and had to struggle to reload. They slept at the base of a canyon that split the side of the mesa, a broad, sandy bottom that promised a tough climb before reaching the top.

The mesa was accessible from any point, unlike The Top, where the sides were steep and the top edge was most often a sheer cliff. On the third sun, he found that his legs were getting stronger, though the trail was tougher as they left the floor of the desert-plain and began to go up a canyon.

Progress was slow, the men struggling even more than before, their way often blocked by boulders or fallen trees that sent them on short detours or climbing over deadfalls. He was curious to see a hawk circling above the mesa near their canyon, not once but twice! What was it that was to happen? It had to be stupendous for there to be two hawks to alert him! Throughout the sun, his mind retraced the excitement of wondering what the Great One was planning this time.

Each time a hawk had appeared to him, something had happened to or for him, and he recounted the ways in the long trek up the canyon. His eyes often flicked up at the birds until they were gone, his curiosity bursting.

That sunset they camped in a narrow defile on a small patch of sand, an offshoot of the main canyon which was growing more shallow but littered with too much debris from flash-flooding to find a place large enough to camp. Early in the sun they had heard a pack of wolves howling not far away, and it seemed to come from their backtrail, though the direction was deceiving.

They stretched out the deer for airing, ate and spread their blankets to sleep when Hawkeye turned to the edge of their camp to relieve himself. With a shout of warning, he almost fell back into the fire he had just stepped past.

He Who Conquers was sitting on his blanket looking at the small figurine given him by Little Dove, hanging around his neck by the leather string he had made. The sudden cry and leap of Hawkeye ran a chill through him and he jumped.

A wolf stood not four paces away, and behind it stood several more, hard to count in the darkness. They were small and lean, and it was plain they were hungry. Tongues were hanging and dripping, reminding him of the old lobo he had killed a few suns earlier. The curing venison had drawn their attention from far back along the trail, and there was no doubt of their intentions.

He Who Tracks was the first to react, grabbing the spear at his side and throwing it at the lead wolf, but he missed, nicking the one standing behind it to its right. He Who Conquers had no desire to throw the weapon he would use if they charged into the camp, but instead was almost instantly on his knees with his bow and a strung arrow.

It was like being back on The Rock, with the well-frayed tree about the same distance as the first wolf. He took no time to consider his aim, unconsciously certain that the wolf was as easy to hit as the small place he had slivered so often, and he let fly at the dead tree- -only this time it was the bared fangs of the leader.

His shot was true, entering the mouth after clipping the fang on the upper left side of the mouth. The leader spun around, rolled over, got up shaking its head, then dropped facing the pack and lay still, twitching a few times before its blood-smell aroused the rest of the pack. In moments they were on their leader, snarling and growling and ripping at the carcass.

"Kill them!" Hawkeye said into the din, and loosed an arrow at one of the savage animals. As he spoke, Dog Man killed another, and then He Who Conquers killed yet a third. There was a sudden pause in the noise, and the remaining animals realized death was striking them quickly. They fled into the dark, one carrying an arrow in its hind quarter.

The men stared at the dead animals almost numbly. "They will return," He Who Tracks said calmly. "They starve."

"Why should they starve? There is plenty for them. We have seen deer tracks all over." Dog Tracks said what He Who Conquers had immediately thought.

"Who knows? But they were gaunt."

"It was like one I killed a few suns ago. He too was thin, yet he did not act starved. If they starved, they would not have run. Their senses wouldn't let them." He Who Conquers still stared at the dead leader.

"If they were not starving, would they have come so close?"

"Maybe they have never been confronted by men

before? It seemed to me they just thought we were other animals who had meat they wanted. The god of the wolves lives in the wilderness; maybe they have never seen humans before, at least when the humans had something they wanted."

"He Who Conquers speaks with wisdom. I'll listen," Hawkeye responded to end the discussion. "Right now, we must get those skins and teeth. Does anyone want the toe nails?"

"I will take them," Dog Man said.   "My ceremonial necklace is still growing."

Suddenly He Who Conquers moved. From standing with bow and arrow, he suddenly dropped to his hands and knees and pitched several handsful of sand on their fire, killing it though smoke rose thickly. At the same time, he said, "Sh-h-h, quiet!"

The men froze in position, standing alert for several moments before one whispered, "What is it?"

"We must get away from this smoke! There are men coming across the top of the mesa above us!"

"Perhaps it's some of our people," Hawkeye said in a low voice, not knowing how to whisper.

"There are many. You said your hunters went out in fours and fives. There's a large group up there."

"How do you know? I hear nothing."

"It is so! Come, get these animals away from here!" He was in motion immediately, putting his pack together, tying it to his front and struggling the buck over his shoulders. Its stiffness was an assistance. As he left the area, crossing the main ravine and going up the other side, his urgency sent chills of action to the others, and they blindly followed.

"How does he know?" Dog Man complained, though he reacted like the rest.

"Maybe he leads us on a wild goose hunt." Moccasin Maker had no love of moving again. He was ready to rest.

"Then why follow?" Hawkeye snapped. "He is led by the gods, and I'll do as he says! He proved himself to us already; do what you want, I'll follow."

They exerted hard climbing out of the ravine, then nearly ran as they staggered among the scattered trees. A large rock appeared to rise like a black hole, and they circled it quickly; He Who Conquers dropped his deer.

"One must stay here with the deer to keep animals away. The rest, come with me. You shall soon see why we had to move."

He turned and trotted back in the direction from which they came, and Hawkeye spoke quickly. "Follow him. I'll stay with the animals. My knees betray me."

The three quickly caught up and followed He Who Conquers back to their previous camp, where he had them get the wolves dead carcasses across the ravine and on top, then they lay down behind a pair of gnarled trees and waited.

The wait was short. A rustling of a bush, then the sound of someone sliding in sand, then a grunt. A quiet voice spoke into the calm of early darkness, and men swarmed into view as black ants across the ravine. There were too many to count in the dark, but they teemed around the smoldering campfire, spreading out to look over the area, then returning.

They talked together in a large mass with many voices before one took over. He gave instructions, and while most of them settled in, one went down the ravine a short distance, one up, and one went to either side. One of those came toward the four men who lay silently, stopping but five strides away, sitting on the bank with legs dangling into the sand.

Soon the fire was re-lit, and in the low glow, He Who Conquers counted sixteen. That meant there were twenty men in all, and he felt the tension of those beside him who did not dare to move with the Other so close.

The guard turned and looked around him, then back at the men near the fire, who were below and nearly a stone's throw away. When he looked back, He Who Conquers began his stalk.

Leaving the three to watch breathlessly, he stood, grateful again for his moccasins, and moved ahead like a wraith, the ground underfoot gritty like his Top with only scattered vegetation. He took three, then four steps.

The guard, either hearing or feeling something, turned...too late. He had time for neither movement nor a shout of warning before his neck was nearly severed with a hand axe.

He Who Conquers, now somewhat of an expert, took the scalp and toppled the body into the sand, then stole back to his watchers.

"Come. We'll have to move again. They will follow with the new sun." He picked up one of the wolf carcasses and headed back toward the place where Hawkeye waited.

Hawkeye was standing when they returned, and asked, "Was he right?"

An awed Dog Man responded. "He was right! There are many, as many as in our Council. They'll have one less when they meet at the new sun. He Who Conquers took a scalp."

Hawkeye chuckled. "You'll follow him when he says something again, am I right?"

"He has the senses of the gods! We would all be in search of Sipapu right now if not for him!"

He Who Tracks nodded. "He's like the wind! No one hears him until it's too late to escape! No wonder he killed two deer while we killed three! The gods are in him! Or he is one!"

"We must go. They'll come with the new sun. Is there a place near here to hide?" The voice of He Who Conquers was neither insistent nor alarmed.

"What of the wolf hides?"

"It depends. What of a place to hide?"

"I know of nothing," Hawkeye said. "This place is only a lot of scattered trees and a few rocks."

"How far are we from the village?"

"We have to get around them to get there...not a good thing to contemplate. If we left now, we'd arrive about the next darkness if we were lucky. Who knows?"

"Then we must hide somewhere."

The four men stared at each other, but none spoke. Finally, Dog Man shook his head. "This is not a good place to hide. There's nothing here. What can we do?"

He Who Conquers squatted, cleaning blood from his axe as he spoke. "Then I will seek the advice of the Great One. Perhaps I angered him when I killed the Other. I must make medicine."

He disappeared into the darkness, away from where the camp of the Others stood, but once out of sight he circled quickly and headed back to where he knew three guards to be located. It was not medicine he wanted, but scalps.

Hawkeye sat with his back against the huge rock while his three friends took the hides from the wolves, then broke out the teeth and cut off the paws so Dog Man could take them with him and remove the claws later.

"What must he ask of his god?" Moccasin Maker asked as he cut through the throat of one of the wolves to keep the head intact and attached to the skin. "Does he think they will make us disappear?"

Hawkeye, who was in good spirits for having escaped a hideous death at the hands of Others, chuckled again. "I will not question him or his gods. He saved us, he found us meat, and he killed two of those three dead wolves you carve. He's more than a man, I think. Perhaps you are right, He Who Tracks. Maybe he's like the wind...or maybe he is The Wind. How can I know, but he's more than we are, and where did he come from? I mean, here we are walking in a favorite hunting spot seeing nothing, and suddenly someone stands watching us. He says he came from The Top, but maybe that's where the gods live. I think it's not a place where you or I could go, because humans can't get there. How do we know he didn't make up the place where he came from just to keep us from knowing?"

He leaned back and listened to the few sounds of the working men, but no one spoke again. The quiet stretched out as the men finished their chores and rolled the hides, tucking them into the cavity of the deer and tying the cavities shut with strings from a yucca plant near at hand. The moonlight was brilliant, giving them plenty of light by which to work.

After they were done, they squatted together near Hawkeye, their minds at work but saying nothing. The darkness did not please them--not knowing where their protector was--and time moved slowly.

Impatient, Dog Man spoke, his voice giving evidence of his fear. "Why is he so long? If we don't move soon, the Others will be close behind us come dawn. The gods must be speaking to him in long words."

Hawkeye had a soft laughter in his voice as he responded. "You're still too young, Dog Man. You don't hurry the gods; he'll know when he returns what we must do. Why don't you just lie on your blanket and rest so you'll be ready if we have to travel fast?"

He Who Tracks chuckled softly. "I think we'll camp here. If his Great One, or whatever he calls his god, does as he has already, we'll sleep here long into the new sun. I think he's recently from Sipapu, to teach us many things. The Others won't bother us again; maybe they'll just leave come the new sun. When they see The Wind has destroyed some of them, they'll go back to their own."

"Some of them? You think more will die than the one we saw?" It was obvious the idea was new to Moccasin Maker, who was awed by the thought.

"They'll sorrow for more than one." The voice was one of confidence. "Sun God will smile on us."

Again they lapsed into a long silence, lying on their blankets and wondering what was happening to He Who Conquers and his medicine to the gods. Hawkeye continued to sit with his back against the rock, using a dried shaft of a dead flower to pick at his teeth.

"He comes," Hawkeye said. "Like the wind, he comes."

In a short time, He Who Conquers came back, but he returned from the direction of the Others, not from the direction to which he had gone when he left. He said nothing, but dropped something on the ground near Hawkeye as he went past, opened his pack for his blankets, wrapped them around himself, and fell asleep instantly.

The four men looked at him and one another, wondering about his cryptic behavior. Then Hawkeye reached over and picked up the thing he had dropped, and in his dry, humorous chuckle said, "Sleep, my friends. There are four scalps here. The Others will have to make new medicine come the new sun; they'll leave us alone."

He Who Tracks stepped away and relieved himself, speaking back over his shoulder, "Is he truly The Wind? No, not just The Wind, but Death Wind." He shuddered at the spooky tales he remembered hearing as a boy, when the men sat around a fire late into the darkness and told stories to keep away the terror of silence. 'When he's here, I feel odd, like he's more than a man. Is he part god? Did he come from where the gods dwell, and not from some other village at all?" He stared at the sleeping form of the strange one no one knew or understood, then stepped back to his blankets and lay down.

The silence stretched until they finally all slept, no one even staying awake to keep watch. It was severe aches in the shoulder that awakened Hawkeye as the first light came from rising-sun, and he rose with pain, but cheerfully. The God of Snows was coming; he could feel the change in his joints as he stretched and walked to the rock and relieved himself.

Memories of the long vigil returned, and he stepped back to confirm the events by seeing He Who Conquers, who still slept soundly. It confirmed what had haunted him in his sleep. He remembered the scalps, the nonchalant and even disinterested way in which He Who Conquers had dropped them on the ground at his return, and he wondered at this young man.

Who was he, and where did he truly come from? Was he, as He Who Tracks thought, more than just a man? Had he come from the gods to help this people, these struggling people who lived at and in the mouth of a cliff they called Open Stone? And what really happened in the canyon during the darkness while he was gone?

Curious, he limped back toward the campsite abandoned so hurriedly at the insistence of their new savior, until his legs limbered and he was able to stride without pain. At the edge of the ravine where He Who Conquers had killed the guard in front of the startled eyes of his friends, he laid on his stomach, seeing the Others in a huddled group with their fire out. They were excited and frightened, many pointing and speaking at once. They had no doubt just discovered the dead guards and awakened the whole camp with the news.

He searched among them for their leader, the one who had directed activities, appointing the ones who had left the smoking fire and posted as guards, and could not find him. He remembered the man from the way he spoke so authoritatively the previous sun, hushing all general discussion. But he was not in evidence in the early dawn, and no one seemed to be in charge. Hawkeye lay still, wondering if the man were out relieving himself, but after a time the chief still had not returned.

The voices grew more insistent, until one of the men called for quiet and spoke imploringly. The voices were far away, and the tongue was strange, but he realized the import of the talk in but a moment, when five bodies were laid out and the men went up the bank in search of wood. Astounded, Hawkeye realized that one of the dead men was the chief!

Numbed, he watched them bring wood, build pyres, lift the bodies onto the stacks, put each man's weapons and belongings with the body, and light the fires. Fire bit into the dead fuel, then glowed, and grew huge. Blackish smoke began to rise, then turned gray as it rose into the early sky, the bodies burning hot.

The Others prayed, danced the Dance of the Dead, and all the while Hawkeye let his eyes watch but his mind wander over the scene that must have occurred here while Moon Goddess watched. He Who Conquers had killed all four guards, one while he and his men watched, and then must have sneaked into the middle of the camp to kill the chief! No, he merely floated into the camp, for he was Death Wind among the Others!

He involuntarily shuddered. What if they had tried to kill him when they first saw him at the foot of the mesa where they were given the deer? They had thought to do so. It had been the first words of Dog Man! Would they all be dead now? Fear stabbed him, a sharp contrast to the lightness he had felt since moving to safety in the darkness. He knew the gods smiled at his people, for had Death Wind come to be an enemy, they would all be dead!

He let himself back until he could stand without being seen from the bottom of the gully, and turned back toward the camp beside the stone. His mind was a turmoil of ideas and events, all mixed into a hodge-podge he did not control.

When he returned, He Who Conquers sat beside a small fire with a piece of venison spitted, and the other three still slept.

"They go," he said to He Who Conquers.

"I have seen their smokes."

"They honor their dead. You killed their chief."

"It was necessary to convince them to leave."

Hawkeye stared at him, wondering at his unpretentiousness, his display of disinterest. "It's safe for us to finish our journey because of you." He watched the meat sizzle a moment. "Why did you come?"

He Who Conquers looked up at him and smiled. "I look for a mate, and a people who will become my people."

"Come and find both among us." He wondered at the awe he felt, the tinge of fear that inspired it. "I wish to be your friend."

He Who Conquers laid the meat on a flat rock beside the fire and stood to face Hawkeye. "You are my friend. I wish for more among your people."

He Who Tracks sat up and looked at the two men who stood facing one another. "We can return home?"

Hawkeye turned and nodded. "The Others leave."

Dog Man rolled and got to his feet. "You sure?"

"I watched them honor their dead, and they go. Their medicine is bad; their chief is among the dead."

There was silence until Moccasin Maker spoke to break it. "It'll be good to get back. I'm weary of this hunt. If not for the help of the gods, we would all be in the smoke of this sun." What he said was not the real feeling any of them had, but was rather a means of getting past the unanswered questions they all had, and the awkwardness of having one with them they did not understand. Not knowing what else to say, the subject was made indifferent and impersonal.

"We'll eat and go. It'll be yet a long sun." Hawkeye caught the intent and closed discussion. None of them wished to begin the hard work ahead, but it was there, and it took their thoughts from things they could not understand, and thus feared.

11

The trip to the village took longer than they had thought, due in part to their fatigue. Only Moccasin Maker, muscular and powerful, still walked with a somewhat lively step. The sun ended as they dropped down a steep bank into a shallow gully that would eventually open into the great canyon. It had turned raw cold, a heavy over- cast promising snow to the arid country, and as they huddled around a guttering fire with their blankets wrapped tightly about them, they felt the weariness that was honed by their disappointment at not making it home.

"They will wonder by now if we will return," Dog Man ventured. "We've been gone a long time."

"Almost a moon," Moccasin Maker responded. "Our animals are cured and ready to be dried."

"They'll freeze hard this darkness. It'll be like carrying cordwood on the new sun."

"Be sure your animal lies in a position that makes it easy to carry," Hawkeye warned. With his usual optimism, he added, "With good fortune, we'll be home by mid-sun."

It was a close estimate. They broke out of the side-canyon below the village, unable at first to see the main cave, which was above the valley floor. The people of Open Stone swarmed about their dwellings preparing for the snow that was coming soon. Dormant fields, split by a meandering, shallow stream, lay along the canyon floor, shorn of their crops. Several children played near the water. Then someone spotted the hunters.

There was a cry of welcome, then men and boys came running toward them. Eyes wide and taking it all in, He Who Conquers saw the curious glances sent his way as many helped relieve the loads of the men, noting the glances at his simple loin cloth which showed no signs of honoring the Male God of Fertility. Perhaps the only other person they had ever seen with such dress was the Trader. He felt a stranger among them, and though they lifted his load and carried it for him, he knew already that he would always be the alien.

It is near the time of snows, he thought, **and they wonder if I'm but another mouth to be fed for the many moons.** He ignored the stares and noted the daub and wattle buildings that stood below and inside the great cave, but something curious inside the cave itself. A few buildings that he thought looked like more than storage were built from rock, something he'd never seen before.

As they neared the village, he saw the old men staring at the meat, the hunters, and the new man, and above them, several women greeted the hunters with calls that told him a few of them were mates of the returning men. Then he saw her.

She was near the corner of the field-level dwellings, wearing leather leggings and a heavy blanket across her shoulders. Her hair was coal black, like most of them, and there was nothing particularly distinguishing about her. Only, she was pretty...in fact, she was most beautiful. And she was staring at him, fascinated.

Was she mated? he wondered. Could this be the one meant for him? He smiled, and she smiled in return, then turned coy and entered her dwelling. An old man, standing with three other elders, witnessed their exchange, his old but shrewd eyes evaluating the young man who stood looking over the village as appraising as his own.

"He's brazen," one of his companions offered, "afraid of nothing."

The oldster chuckled. "Reminds me of the way I acted at his age. You remember how I was. Owned the world. Funny how we still wind up old and decrepit."

"Kind of a different looking youngster, if you ask me. Even looks a bit like an Abnormal. Wonder where they found him?"

"Don't underestimate that young man. He'll make his way very well. He has no funny long-necked dogs, so he isn't a trader, but his build is one of leadership. Mark my words, Cornkeeper. The gods are smiling on us."

"Huh! Another mouth to feed, if you ask me. You watch that granddaughter of yours, too! He saw her first thing, and she needs a good mate from her own people."

"And which one is that?" he asked with a touch of sarcasm. "I've looked over our boys and young men for a long time, and it's impossible to find one worth spit. You just may discover he's much more than any of our youth when it comes time to be a man."

"Huh!" Cornkeeper snorted again. "His breechcloth tells you he may not even be a man! You watch out!"

The old man turned to study the young man again, and He Who Conquers felt the survey. He saw the three old men looking his direction and conversing, and it was easy to know who their subject was. Old men were as gossipy as old women. For his part, he continued to scan the area and evaluate what he saw.

The climate here, though perhaps a bit dryer, was similar to what he had always known, for the pinion pine and junipers were king of the plants, splattered generously in places with quacking aspen. Corn was their main crop, but here there was no protection from raids for the crops which were planted down the main canyon, wide open and one huge field. Did they not have to worry of such things?

The canyon floor was largely unbroken, with only a few huge boulders dotting the edges near the steep rock walls, where a few spires rose from the valley floor as well. He wondered if there were many ways to exit the canyon, unable to see up-canyon very far. Then he saw toe-and-hand holes chipped into the wall to the left of the cave, leading up to a ledge, then farther over, on to the top. That partially answered his query.

The buildings were like the village of his people, but the number of dwellings exceeded the number back home. There were more scattered dwellings back home, which meant these people were more centralized, though he had seen a dwelling down-valley earlier. Perhaps they were more capable in defense because of it, but it also made them especially vulnerable to crop failure, maybe to the destruction of those crops by Others. The field he could see running down the canyon was as big as any single field on The Top. Of course, there were more fields elsewhere, most likely. The running water was, however, a key.

While short stalks showed the corn fields clearly, he noticed a huge area so denuded it was impossible to know what had been raised there. If it were beans, then these people raised a much larger crop of beans than back home. Perhaps they had a better way of using the beans. Then again, maybe it was squash, though squash was most often planted among the corn hills. Back home, so were the beans, because they were light on those plants.

On The Top, their pottery could not stand the intense heat long enough to cook beans, and beans had to be ground into flour for eating. Being so hard, they were next to useless. It was something he would have to study.

Caves were frequent in the canyons back home, but no one was interested in living in them, mainly because they were less accessible, but also because they were cold.

When he had run the course of initial observations, he again looked at the people, to again become aware of the curious stares of many. Hawkeye had greeted his family, and now approached.

As he neared, Rain Water called out, "Hola,

Hawkeye, a good hunt!"

"A good hunt, indeed! With thanks to the gods for sending us my new friend, He Who Conquers. Does Council meet this darkness?"

"When the gods light the fires in the sky."

"Our friend will have much to tell us. He'll be my guest."

Rain Water hobbled to them, his dark eyes peering out from under bushy eyebrows that topped and hid deep-set eyes. "Good! We need some new stories. Boredom has overcome us." The sharp, penetrating eyes belied the withered body below. The loose, warm clothing and over-blanket could not hide the emaciated, skeletal man whose every move appeared to be in pain.

"This one will twinkle as the god-fires of which you speak, Rain Water, for I've seen the gods visitation. We need to find a place for my friend to stay. You still have that room?"

"My granddaughter has need of someone in one barren room. He can use it as long as he desires, I'm sure. It's lonely in the silence of memories for one as old as I, and perhaps we can offer him *The Hospitality*."

"Then if He Who Conquers agrees, he has a place to stay." He turned to the one of whom he spoke, "See what he offers. It's not large, but none of our dwellings are. Rain Water has offered."

"I accept the offer," He Who Conquers replied, partially signing, giving the elder a scrutiny that showed approval and gratefulness. "He's being most generous; I see a man who can teach much to youth."

The old man smiled broadly, understanding enough of the strange tongue and signing to know he was being extolled, and from the selectivity of the words knew the youth was quickly catching their own dialect.

The animals had already been skinned, and the women were cutting the meat to get it drying over the smoking fires, and one of the women approached He Who Conquers shyly, another coming to Hawkeye. Each carried a tongue, and He Who Conquers watched Hawkeye accept his, realizing the hunter of the kill was given the honor of this choice meat. The rest of the meat became community property and was dried.

After accepting his, he turned to Rain Water. "I

stay in your dwelling, the meat is yours. We'll feast when the sun sets."

The old man took it, excitement in his eyes, blood running through his fingers. "It's long since this old man tasted fresh tongue. I've been rewarded already for doing nothing. It looks like I'll be the one who benefits from having one stay with us."

Rain Water looked back at his dwelling, and a funny feeling coursed through He Who Conquers. It seemed he looked at the one where the young lady disappeared.

"I'll take this to my granddaughter. She'll show you how good tongue should taste." He turned away, his stiff joints greatly inhibiting his actions. He Who Conquers almost held his breath as he realized how close to the dwelling of the young woman he was going, and then was stunned when he entered the same one!

Hawkeye saw the look on his face, the eyes following the old man, and smiled. "To the youth go the spoils."

A touch of embarrassment touched He Who Conquers. "I enjoy beauty wherever I see it. The beauty of sunsets is rare, and most scenery is found by traveling, for the rest becomes mundane. The beauty of youth, too, is fleeting. One must always enjoy it while it's with us."

"Ah, a philosopher! But one who certainly knows the most of true beauty! Perhaps you'll do more than see beauty!"

"You do me honor by allowing me to meet Rain Water. His mate is dead?" His abrupt change of subject was not lost on Hawkeye, but accepted without rebuttal.

"Last cold season. He was especially fond of the old woman, and it was hard on him to watch her suffer so long. Three winters she hung on while her body ached by the same witch that attacks most of us while we're still relatively active. The Witch of Pain can be most debilitating. Anyway, she couldn't walk for the past two winters, and he carried her little, withering body all over so she'd miss nothing."

"He's none too large himself."

"It was a struggle for him. But he did it. He's one of a kind, my friend. When he goes to Sipapu, it'll be a sad, sad sun."

He Who Conquers listened intently, then asked, "That was his granddaughter who stood near the corner?"

"It was. She has no female relatives to speak for her, and the old man is very jealous to see she mates well. He's not been satisfied with any of the youth of the area, and most shun her because of him, and he's too old to go to other villages to find a mate for her. She's fourteen winters, when most are mated and have children by twelve or thirteen. Some think she has a witch and won't let their sons speak for her. There's been talk that if a captive isn't found before the Goddess of Fertility rites after this snowtime, she might be the sacrifice."

He Who Conquers stared at the vacant doorway. "She's too pretty. Back on The Top, if we can't find one from among another clan and steal her, we take one of a set of twins or one that's from a family with many." He looked at Hawkeye, and then back at the doorway. "And what's your opinion?"

He grinned. "Were I your age, the old man would have to fight me away. I've even thought of a second mate!"

"The witch claim, it's because of jealousy?" His voice was just a bit more husky.

"More of retribution. A mu getting even with the old man for turning down her son."

Chuckling, He Who Conquers asked, "And what about rumors when I go there to stay with the old one?"

"Guess!"

"Then I'll go and get them started. Perhaps the old man and I'll have a talk."

Hawkeye laughed aloud. "You are a rebel! I hear stories the old man was like that when he was young. In fact, once he was banned from the village for a moon for some alleged indiscretion."

"Sounds like an interesting old man. I might enjoy my stay more than I first thought." He chuckled and turned to see the old man stick his head from the doorway and motion for him to come.

"He wants you to meet the young woman. I wish I were wearing your breechcloth right now. You go; I'll see you at Council when darkness comes."

* * *   * * *   * * *

Little Dove stood in the courtyard combing her

mu's thinning hair, checking for lice and picking out those she found. "Is He Who Conquers among another people now, Mu? I worry about him, moreso since the men haven't returned."

"The longer they're gone, my daughter, the better the chances he's safe. Those who return quickly have gotten their prey. Besides, the vision didn't indicate he'd be injured before he got there."

"Will they follow him all the way? I mean, why do they have such hatred for him?"

"You don't know? I'm surprised! You, my child. You started it all when you found him so fascinating. Boy with...I mean, Eagle Eye...has had jealousy festering for many winters."

"That's no secret. But what of Gray Dog, Twin Who Lived, and most of all, Broken Nose? Or Sitting Bear, who's not even from our village? Are men just that way?"

Her mu laughed softly but deep. "Some are like that. I sort of categorize Gray Dog and Twin Who Lived that way. Neither has a brain that could challenge a worm, but both are dangerous as rattlesnakes. Sitting Bear's a cousin of Yellow Sapsucker, and took the *Oath of Retribution*. He's the most dangerous of them all, being sworn to kill He Who Conquers or die trying. Only Broken Nose has me puzzled. I know of nothing that would make him want the death of He Who Conquers, but then, I don't live inside his head. I suppose there's something he hears inside, but we never hear the voices of another."

Little Dove stopped and stared across the hillside, then her hands froze, the comb pausing. Twice she tried to speak, and finally managed a whispery, "Mu, look!"

Her left hand moved a bit to indicate the direction, and Singing Waters turned her head. In but a moment, the entire village watched four men returning from a long absence. Gray Dog and Twin Who Lived supported the sagging body of Broken Nose, who only managed a few one-legged steps to assist them. Eagle Eye, his name changed at a secret meeting of Council the darkness before He Who Conquers left, walked in front of the three, looking haggard and sheepish.

It had been the next sun, with Eagle Eye already

trailing He Who Conquers, that the entire village learned of the name change. They also were told that the five men were hunting, until rumor brought Sitting Bear into the picture, and finally the story came out that it was a vendetta against He Who Conquers.

The men entered the village to silence, and no one welcomed them or even spoke. The men went directly to the kiva, after which Man Who Chases Spirits was called.

The women stood around, speculating, and no one knew of Sitting Bear. Had he returned directly to his village, was he still on the trail, or had something happened to him? The first was unlikely, with the oath he had taken. The second was a possibility, but the most logical was the last, since the others had returned, and in obviously bad shape.

"He's alive and well," Singing Waters said softly as Little Dove unenthusiastically continued her chore. "Perhaps they met in battle somewhere, and Sitting Bear is no more. Maybe they never found him, but ran into his protective gods. Who knows? We'll find out with time."

On the third sun, Eagle Eye came with his blankets to mate with Little Dove. Since she was pregnant, she wanted him to mate her to keep everyone from knowing it was the child of He Who Conquers, though the thought of *coupling* with him made her skin crawl.

"You made it through the Ceremony of the Stick," her mu had warned her several times. "Do nothing to ruin your plans, now. Play the woman. You can kick him out later if you must, but do nothing to reveal our secret."

She accepted the advice as necessary, to await the time when she could put his belongings outside the door and make him go away and leave her alone. First, she must have her child...the son of He Who Conquers.

"You're now my mate," he said as he dropped his mat beside her. "You'll know often what it is to be coupled with a man, and will have strong sons and daughters."

She said nothing, allowing him to touch her shoulder as he spoke. She did what she had worked so hard to do, think of He Who Conquers and pretend it was him. But she found that, with the dreaded time come, it did not work. It was not he, but another, and try as she might, she could do nothing to make herself respond.

He was not rough, but neither was he gentle. His entry was with little foreplay or thought, and she simply lay and let him satiate his appetite. It was somewhat dry and mostly unpleasant, unlike the firewater that had risen when she possessed He Who Conquers. When he was through, he rolled off.

"Is that it?" she asked, trying to sound innocent and unknowing. "Is that all there is to it?"

He was speechless for a moment, then grinned. "You want more?"

She shrugged, sitting up and replacing her breechcloth. "It seems of little significance. I thought there'd be more to it. I mean, everyone talks so much about it."

"It was good. Didn't you like it?" There was a boyish quality to his voice, an insecurity that made her pleased with herself. "What did you expect?"

Again she shrugged. "It did nothing for me."

He smiled, trying to regain his shaken vanity. "It'll come with time, I promise."

She handed him a cup of tea brewed from a plant found near the *Rock of Prayers*, which held magical powers to heal but also tasted so good it was often used as a social drink. He sniffed it and grinned, then sipped.

"You'll make a good mate," he said.

"What happened when you and the four others went hunting? Did you get nothing? I mean, you brought back nothing." He was taken back by her sudden question, and before he could answer, she added, "Sitting Bear went with you, didn't he? Wasn't he sworn to kill He Who Conquers? Why did he go with you, and not return?"

"It's not for women to care!" he snapped, regaining his composure and speaking forcefully, almost angrily.

She smiled. "Then this dwelling won't be welcome to you! It's my house, you know! If I'm unfit to know what happens to our people, especially when my mate's involved, then perhaps I'm not fit to be a mate, either! I'll know what's going on among us, or I'll withdraw from everyone and become a Medicine Woman! You can find another mate!"

He was aghast at the tirade, and for a moment felt like striking her, but changed his mind quickly when he saw the fire in her eyes. Then he realized how tenuous was his mating unless he made amends.

"I'll tell you what I know." He tried quickly to think of some way to relate some things without telling her the truth. "We hunted bison near the Waters-That-Hurry-to-Sunset. We were heading in the same direction that Sitting Bear was going, so he went with us. When we got to the waters, he went across and kept going. We found nothing and returned. Broken Nose fell and broke a leg, and we had a hard time getting him back."

She smiled. "Now, see, that was easy. Only I wish it were the real truth. Gray Dog already has told many that you looked for He Who Conquers, but never found him except when he was crossing the moving waters, and you never saw him after you finally crossed. He said Sitting Bear lost hold of his log and was swallowed by the God of the Waters. Then you were chased by Others, and Broken Nose broke his leg after you got back across the waters, and the Others gave up there. The truth is always easier to tell than fiction. You don't have to remember which lie you told, and never have to cover it with more lies later. You're not starting our mating in a very promising way." Every word was spoken quietly and indifferently, his mouth falling open as he realized she knew all along what he thought was a secret.

"You believe everything Gray Dog speaks?"

She smiled lightly. "He had no reason to lie, and the story is very logical...unlike yours. You think me stupid, but I can assure you otherwise. The next time I catch you in a lie, you'll find your clothing outside the door. I have little feeling for you, Eagle Eye. You're a stranger to me, and if it were not for our traditions, you'd never have entered this dwelling. However, I have pledged myself to try to make it work, if you act like a man instead of a five-winter child that has to lie to cover truth. You're not a god, nor are you some great man...not yet. Maybe you will be, sometime, and maybe not. The gods control destiny. But don't try to be a god with me. I've not seen you among the hawks, nor controling the ways of Sun God.

"I'll keep trying, but I expect you to be a man, not a boy. I expect to be treated with respect. Don't destroy my hope, or I'll put you outside...even if you become chief of this people."

"We had no choice but to go after him!" he blurted, his anger hot but his thoughts cold as ice. "He told the younger boys he intended to be the next chief, and that's contrary to our tradition. To do that, he had to kill Yellow Sapsucker and me, and I think he was the one who killed my brother. I had a duty to kill him to hold our traditions in honor. Don't speak to me of greatness until you know what it really is."

He stared at her while he spoke, and for a short time after, wondering where he had found such a story among his thoughts, then left the dwelling without a word. When he was gone, she drank his tea slowly, leaning back against the wall and staring at the deerskin that hung on the wall next to the door. She had laid out the facts, and she smiled to herself to have been so forceful. She knew his last story was a lie, because no one knew He Who Conquers like she did, and he never mentioned such aspirations. It didn't make any difference. She could never love the man, and she would even have a difficult time tolerating him.

Singing Waters came inside and broke her reverie. "You were a bit hard on him, weren't you? He's trying very hard to be a man, and you surely sliced him to pieces...little tiny pieces."

Little Dove continued to stare at the skin, never giving thought to the fact her mu had stayed so close to the doorway in order to hear their conversation. "He'll treat me differently from now on, Mu. I'm not going to let him lie to me, or mistreat me...ever!"

Her mu smiled wistfully. "Were I your age, I could have wished to speak my mind so clearly. Just beware his anger; he's vindictive. Be careful."

"Oh, I shall, Mu. I shall. But I'll never love him, not now, not even beyond Sipapu!"

12

It was like back home. The smell of bodies, of hides, of cooked and uncooked food, of smoke--the myriad of odors that made life. He had not smelled them in many suns, and was warmed by one of the aspects of life he suddenly found he had missed.

Rain Water lived with his granddaughter, the dwelling having become hers through her mu. No longer able to hunt or travel far enough to fish, he had not tasted fresh meat in many winters. His teeth were gone, but one never replaced the longing for a taste of fresh meat.

They were sitting in the main room of the three-room dwelling, one of the few that had so many. At one time, two generations ago, this had been the most powerful clan in the village. Then the Witch of Sickness came, and in just one generation, only the fa-fa, his mate, their three daughters and a son still carried on the family clan. The son was killed in a fall while climbing those footholds he had seen on the canyon wall, and one of the daughters inexplicably disappeared, though it was

likely another people had kidnapped her for their fertility
rites at the spring equinox, when everyone honored the
Goddess of Fertility. Among those of Open Stone, it was
agreed that the gods took her. The remaining daughters
mated.

The first daughter gave birth, and in the giving,
her life was taken by the gods. In his grief, the fa
denied his daughter's existence, and shortly after was
punished by the gods. In a simple wrestling match, his
neck was broken and he forfeited his life. Two suns
later, a witch attacked the infant girl and stole the spirit
of life, her breath.

The second daughter was constantly critical of
her mate. She dropped a daughter within the first
winter of their mating--Scent of Violets--but continued to
berate him, finally to drive him from the dwelling for
long periods of time. She became with child from one of
the few times he coupled with her, but she never told
him. One sun, he went hunting, and never returned.
Unable to control her grief when she realized what she
had done, she gave premature birth to the infant, and
entered Sipapu. The infant followed her two suns later.

A half-moon later, the old man's mate began to
cough. The witch that brought pain to the joints entered
her, and within six moons she was unable to walk and
occasionally coughed bloody phlegm. She hung on to life
tenaciously, long after she could no longer walk. He
carried her. For two winters she managed to live, until
one darkness she gagged to death on her own mucous.

The lonely old man, still speaking to his departed
mate at odd times and under any circumstance,
remained, determined that his granddaughter would be
treated properly by the villagers. Their power had
dissipated with the decline of family and the loss of
working capability, until now they were considered by
many to be mere faces to feed. He wanted more than
anything else to offer himself for the *Rite of Perfection*,
but until his granddaughter was mated, he felt she was
his first duty. This made Scent of Violets feel guilt, often
considering the possibility of mating one of the village
youths or even offering herself to the Goddess for the
fertility rites.

Their situation was not explained to He Who

Conquers, though they told him of the reason for them
to be living as they were. He pieced it together through
comments from Hawkeye and reading between the lines.
The old man was candid, though never complaining.
The girl was mostly silent, watching their new roomer
openly.

"I'm grateful for your offer to stay here. I wish
to learn from one of so many winters." They had
finished eating, and he was leaning back against the
wall.

"Or get bored," the old man chuckled, seemingly
never far from humor.

"I'll never be bored with one of so much
experience. Besides, boredom is a sign of laziness."

The old man hunched forward, sitting cross-
legged on the floor. "Our guest has a mind, Scent of
Violets, one that actually works. It's been a long time
since anyone told this aged one that he was anything but
a burden." He laughed. "Imagine, I, who killed more
buffalo and elk than anyone in the village, and hunted
alone many times so there was meat...a burden, now."
His laugh revealed his toothless gums. "Fame is fleecy
clouds, and renown like early fog. If I had it to do over,
I'd...." He stopped and chuckled. "I'd probably do the
same thing again."

The girl watched He Who Conquers as her fa-fa
spoke, then asked, "Is He Who Conquers staying long
with our people?"

He shrugged and signed, "I don't know, yet.
Who can tell what the gods will ordain."

"You may stay with us forever," she said softly.
"No one will dare to run you out or harm you while you
stay with us. Fa-Fa makes you think he's considered
useless and without authority, but when he speaks his
voice is powerful in Council."

He Who Conquers smiled. "One who can laugh
at himself never lacks for admirers. I think your fa-fa's
an important man here. He's only hard on himself
because he feels his loss of physical strength, but I've
seen old men with no ability to walk still make a whole
Council bend. My fa was like that."

She smiled at his commendation, and the old
man scowled, though his eyes revealed the pleasure he

took in the compliment. "Maybe the young man's not as intelligent as I thought," he said gruffly.

Scent of Violets laughed, and He Who Conquers watched her with a smile of his own. He liked her full laugh, and the smile in her eyes that accompanied it.

"Fa-Fa would never admit he deserves the flattery he receives. He's too much a loner now to appreciate how everyone regards him."

The old man snorted. "It's time for Council. Enough of this bull-roar."

He Who Conquers grinned, and Scent of Violets gave him a big smile, which he remembered as he walked behind Rain Water, in deference to his age, to the place of Council.

It was in a short, steep-sided canyon across the valley floor from the village. From the main cave, it was possible for spectators to see some of the ceremony. They could not, however, hear.

Among the rocks, a giant fire burned, and most of the men were present before the two arrived, huddled in their blankets to ward off the icy stirring of breezes. The wind blew hard outside the protected Council chambers.

As when he had first arrived, He Who Conquers felt the eyes of the men on him, but kept his eyes on the move and never gave them the satisfaction of knowing he was uncomfortable under their stares.

When they were seated near the fire, the old man said softly, "I'm quite anxious to hear of your exploits, young man. It's many moons since we had anything interesting to hear, much less talk over, save the recent scrape with some warriors passing through from a strange tribe that lives far to no-sun. Even that proved to be more of argument and accusation than interesting."

He Who Conquers began to return stares, until some of the men broke contact and found another sudden interest. He responded to Rain Water in the same hushed voice, signing in a way not everyone could see.

"Don't expect too much, Old One. I'm but a youth who has traveled little. I would sooner learn than speak, for I've accomplished nothing."

"Every time you open your mouth, I hear

evidence of wisdom. When someone beats his chest and boasts of much, I cringe. When one is humbled by life, I listen. It has been many winters since I last listened to a youth who had enough wisdom to make the listening worthwhile. I think I've lived just long enough.

"When I was young like you, I enjoyed the hunt like Hawkeye and He Who Tracks. They're good hunters, and I was like that. I detested the drudgery of the gardens, though I aptly took my turns. One sun we were surprised by some strange warriors, and I took this wound in the fight." He pointed to the now whitish scar along his left hip, just under the rope that held his loincloth. "You noticed how I limp. It's not all from the witch who attacks the joints, I can tell you. But these old joints squeak now, and I alone know how painful it is for me to move. But I get young again when I hear the exploits of those who are successful, and your story will become to me a new inspiration. It would give me new spirit to be able to honor Sun God in the Rite of Perfection."

The old man stared into the fire a moment, and before he could speak again, He Who Conquers said in a voice so soft it was almost unheard.

"You honor me, Old One. I can never live up to what you expect. I only hope you'll not be too disappointed."

The men hushed around them, and a man entered the ring of light wearing an entire elk hide, with the antlers fastened to his head, moving around the fire with the gracefulness of running water, the antlers barely moving. As the man danced, his voice was almost like an echoed monotone of syllables, his feet light as the wings of the sparrow. The hide whorled and shook.

He went several times around the fire, and when he stopped and went into the shadows, a man wearing a headband of feathers stepped forward. He singled out two men who joined him, and they began to emulate the man of the elkhide. Then the first man returned, and soon there were many who joined them. He Who Conquers watched, as usual fascinated at the dance of the hunt. They were acting the hunt for an elk, first simulating the hunt, then the stalk, and finally the kill.

Hawkeye appeared as the spear stuck in the

ground next to the man who acted the slain elk, standing at the outer edge of the fire ring, his eyes watchful and his attention on the men who surrounded the "kill". Then he stepped forward, and the dancers withdrew. He stood for a time, letting the expectations build, then began to dance slowly toward and then around the fire, his agility a surprise to He Who Conquers, who had often seen him almost hobble from the attack on his joints. After he had circled the fire four times, each time changing his pace and method, he began to sing.

> Out we went, we men of weapons,
>> To hunt the deer and elk.
> Harvest was over, and we did well,
>> The gods smiled on our work, and so did we.
>
> Many went out, to the four winds we pointed,
>> We prayed and we hunted six suns.
> Other men in other places, hunting just as we,
>> Found nothing at all, though they prayed.
>
> The gods were silent, we thought they had heard,
>> But we found nothing to take for meat.
> We were tired and down-hearted, and we thought
>> To give up, like some others, and go home.
>
> Then, among the trees beside Mesa of Death,
>> We saw a man who spoke to us.
> "Go over there," he said, "and deer will come,
>> Only shoot well, or they will laugh at you and run."
>
> We did as we were told, for he came to us from the Sun,
>> And the deer came to us, and three fell at our arrows,
> So we were successful to have found meat.
>> And two of us returned to the stranger.
>
> We found him among the deer beds, and he, by himself had killed two!
>> Alone, this man from the gods,
> Had killed as many as had we four!

And then he gave to us what he had killed!

Then, to our sheer astonishment, this one of the
gods,
    Helped us to carry them back!
And while it was good to have him help at that
chore,
    What came next is shocking to tell.

We stopped for a darkness atop the hill,
    In a gully where wolves soon came.
While one of us managed to kill one of the
many,
Our god-man killed two--twice what we had
done!

Before we had time to skin the pelts,
    Our leader hurried us away.
We barely had time to kill the fire,
    And carry our animals to another place.

When we went back to see why he led us away,
    Our campsite was filled with Others!
If we had not fled as quickly as he spoke,
    None would have returned to you.

We watched as our leader sneaked up on a
guard,
    And we watched as he slit his throat,
But we returned to our animals fearful to know
    That come Sun God, they would come for us.

But in the darkness, while we four fretted,
    Our protector slipped away to see his god.
He returned before Sun God opened the skies,
    And in his hand he carried four more scalps!

So we escaped, we four, and we brought back
meat,
    The most successful of hunters among The
    People;
And now I introduce to you, my friends,
    The one whom most of you have seen.

He Who Conquers is his name, and it is
certainly true,
   For we four came back because of him;
Is he man, or is he god, is he human or spirit?
   We cannot tell, but he is Death Wind.

He passes by so silently, even we who knew he
was there,
   Heard nothing of his passing...nothing at all.
He is the Wind God, who walks among the trees!
   And death he dealt to five Others!

As he came around the fire, he stopped in front
of He Who Conquers and looked down at him. Then he
dropped his arms and pointed both index fingers at him,
and said, "This is he.   This is the one who worked
miracles for us, who protected us, who gave us five
animals to eat and three wolf pelts to use. Know him,
learn from him. He is mighty, and he is my friend. One
who fails to show him the courtesy of our people shall
answer to me!"

He turned and walked from the ring, leaving
silence behind him. Rain Water sat with mouth agape,
and when He Who Conquers looked around, many closed
their mouths to keep from showing awe to this one they
hardly knew.

When Rain Water regained his composure, he
said, "Speak, my young friend. The men await you."

Before he could do so, however, the pipe was lit,
and the man who lit it looked like a clan chief.   He
brought it to He Who Conquers first, and then, after he
had taken his four puffs and blown in the four directions,
it was passed on. Around the circle it went, having to be
repacked several times until Rain Water finished the last
four. Each, like He Who Conquers, blew the smoke in
each of the four directions.

Then He Who Conquers stood to speak.   Sweat
was running from him, though it was cold. The winds
were kicking up, the fire was guttering, the men were
huddled in their blankets or large skins, and it smelled
of snow.

"I am but a man.   I come from the People of the

Top, who live on the mesa far above rising-sun. I'm not a god, nor a wind. In my lifetime, I have accomplished little." Suddenly he realized how negative he was sounding, and he cast about for something positive to say, and it came to him in a flash of inspiration.

"I have come among you to let you know that serving the needs of the gods, and especially the Great One, will mean special things to you in your future. Let me tell you how He has often come to help me."

He let his mind cast back into what had happened to him, and wondered how much he dared say about the members of his own people who wanted him dead. Nothing, he decided. They might never really understand what he meant to say. He decided that each of his scrapes with his peers would become scrapes with Others. That they could both appreciate and understand.

"A couple moons ago, Others came to our mesa. They were four hands and three, and when they came I was on The Rock, where we can see great distances. I saw them, and followed them when they came up among us. The Great One directed my feet, and during that darkness I took four scalps."

There was a murmur among them, and He Who Conquers wondered if it sounded too boastful. Realizing they might not believe him, he reached into the pouch he carried under his left arm and pulled out the four scalps, now dried and shriveled, though the hair was still in perfect condition. He held them out, and separated them one at a time, dramatically, in response to the growing murmurs that indicated they were amazed.

"However, when I was about to return home, one of them saw me and put an arrow through my shoulder right there," and he turned to let them see the scar that was still red and healing behind his left shoulder. "The man who shot the arrow came to investigate, but the Great One had kept me conscious all the time. I had only my knife, so I lay still until he came near, then I spun and threw the knife and implanted it in his stomach." As he said it, he spun with his knife suddenly in his hand and flung it at the aspen tree that grew five steps away. It buried itself into the soft trunk and stayed there, in the center of the tree and only the width of a finger from a large knot.

There was a babble of surprise among them, then more talk as he retrieved his knife. It was doubtful any of these men had ever witnessed such skill with a knife.

"I was too weak to take his scalp, but I managed to crawl away and hide, then to return later to my village where Medicine Woman mended me. But it was then the Great One played with me, and gave the young lady I wanted to another. I would not stay to live such sadness."

He saw smiles that told him they were listening carefully, and even sympathized with him.

"It was the son of the chief." The pause he made before that statement made it dramatic, and it was intentional. It brought smiles and nods of understanding. He had scored points with them, and in the scoring felt vindicated. A man was often more appreciated as an alien.

"I had been gone half a moon when I found men were trailing me, from where I don't know. When I crossed the Waters-That-Hurry-to-Sunset, they chased me, but I ran and hid in a washout. They came close, but never found me, and then they in turn ran into a larger group of Others and had to run. What happened to them I'll never know.

"A few suns later, I met your four hunters, and Hawkeye has told you some things about what has happened. But as I said, I'm not a god, and I did not come from the skies. I'm not the wind. I'm a man, who was dropped into this world like all of you. I am only in one place at one time, and I don't move silently. I have studied the way of quietness, but I do not float over the land. I must walk...just like you. And I eat and pass water like each of you, too!"

With that, he sat beside Rain Water. The men laughed at his final statement, realizing he had meant to be humorous, and then smoked the pipe again.

Shortly, two men spoke on needing more meat. He listened to the various men, and when he was walking back to the dwelling afterward, Rain Water beckoned him to walk beside him.

"You have nine scalps, my son?"

"Yes."

"Then you are truly a warrior worthy of renown.

No one in our village has more than one, and those who
do have scars to show they were in a fight. Yet you only
have the one arrow wound. I think your Great One
might be as you say. I would talk to you again about
Him, though I fear my suns are limited. Why did you
come among this people, of all those who are around?"

"Your men found me, Old One. I was wandering
and looking, and trusting the Great One to find me a
place to stay, perhaps to live. This is where I came
because this is where I was led."

"We are most fortunate. Will you lead our
hunters before the snows come heavy? The village needs
meat, and your Great One might help us where our gods
have not. Everyone here knows how fickle they are."

"As do I. It's no secret they toy with men, but I
haven't had the Great One do that...except regarding the
girl I wanted to mate."

"Then he saved you for one reason, my son. You
must mate my granddaughter."

He Who Conquers lost a step, then regained his
composure. "I'm not sure of the wishes of the Great One,
Old One. I can't mate unless he gives me the signs."

"As it should be...and will be. You'll know before
long. However, there's a more important thing that must
be done, and that's to offer you The Hospitality."

Wondering at how best to deal with this, He
Who Conquers followed the Old One into his dwelling
and stretched out on his mat, realizing Scent of Violets
had arranged it and his blankets while he was gone. She
slept in the next room, which doubled as a storage room,
while Rain Water slept across the fire from him.

He lay awake a long time. Scent of Violets was
near, in fact, separated by a mere wall that had a door
in it, and the old man had said he should mate her. And
well he might, but not until he knew her better and
knew the Great One meant it to be. The feeling that
came over him when he first saw her was stronger than
ever, but he was confused about how best to deal with
The Hospitality. It was titillating to the mind, and that
did strange and enjoyable things to his body; but he
wanted Scent of Violets to know he was a man of honor,
and that he wanted to choose her as a mate or reject her
as a mate before an Opening. She was a virgin, and one

Opened a virgin with care. If she had been or was still mated, the offer of The Hospitality would be accepted without question. The thought stirred the loins.

He thought on that a time, then turned his attention to the request of the old man that he lead a hunt, and the idea put fear into him. What if he tried, and they found nothing? It would probably undermine his desire to stay among them. Still, if he were successful in such a venture, it would mean great prestige. Did he seek that?

Or was he, as he had told Rain Water earlier, truly wanting only to learn? If so, then could he be honest and tell them he planned to stay among them for only a winter or two? And what would that do to his finding a mate?

His head full, but again beginning to cycle through the same thoughts, he fell asleep.

And again he was running through fields with wild animals around, and along cliffs that were strange to him. Then he was back on the mesa, and his mate was with him near the place where he killed the Others and Yellow Sapsucker, and they stopped to couple, but he could not see her face. Who was she? Little Dove? Scent of Violets? That aroma came again, and he was more than a bit mystified as he tried to identify it, but could not. And then the scene of his parents came to him again, and he wakened in a cold sweat, breathing hard.

Again he lay and tried to piece the images together, but failed. And he wondered about the fragrance, and why it came up again. What was it, and what did it mean?

Almost numb with drowsiness, he fell asleep without seeking answers, and this time, when he awakened, it was to an open door and sunlight, and Scent of Violets holding for him a cup of tea. He took it, and she smiled shyly as he sipped. It was good tea, and he wondered if she were seeking to impress him with her ability to cook. Perhaps her fa-fa had told her what he had told him. If so, matters were becoming more complicated.

13

It was snowing. Large, wet flakes were sifting down without the benefit of wind when he left the dwelling to relieve himself. After watching the steam rise from where the urine melted the snow, he looked down the canyon and wondered how far it went. Above the canyon, he could hear the wind blowing, though in the bottom it was relatively still. Few were out, mostly those arranging firewood for their dwellings, and he pulled his fraying ramskin coat tighter around his shoulders and walked the way he had been looking.

The small canyon dead-ended on his right, and as he glanced at it, a whim made him turn and head back up the canyon, past the village, until he came to another high wall. It was a dead end. In the gentle flaking, he could see what appeared to be a means of ascension to the upper level, and he went up it quickly, wondering at his compulsion as the snow made the climb dangerous--not to mention he had no idea what was at the top. Several times he stopped to catch his breath, studying the hard climb before him, until he arrived at the top, and found a denuded mesa top, wide open spaces where he could see more fields that had been harvested. Short cornstalks, less than the height of his foot, stuck through the snow that was about to bury them.

Were it not for the snow, he would be able to see a great distance, to a round mountain he knew was there but could not see. He thought that was like himself. He could ponder the many events of the previous sun, and then realize how little he could really see, merely because he had only enigmatic visions of what lay ahead, puzzling and even baffling. Most people had none at all, which made him think that to know some things before they happened was more a bane than an benefit. **As usual,** he thought to himself, **I wait to see if the Great One is still with me.**

A movement caught his eye on the fringe of his visibility, and he studied it for a time. Something was out there--he had faith that his senses were not playing tricks on him--but he was not sure what. He had only his knife with him, and wondered if he dared go out to see what it might be. He decided against it, but continued to scan back and forth through the snow.

He was feeling the bite of cold. Snow was falling harder, though the size of the flakes diminished. Worst of all, a breeze was picking up, quartering in from over his left shoulder, showing signs of gusting. He stood uncertainly before turning back. When he had taken but a few steps, he changed his mind again, and faced about and began to trot.

Then he drew up hard. An entire herd of buffalo stood facing the driving snow, heads down, like statues! What had he just heard that previous sun? Something about there not being any bison in the area, and had not been for a few winters? And they wished him to lead a hunt?

He felt the excitement begin to grow inside as he turned and raced back to the way into the canyon. As if the Great One had laid out his itinerary, Hawkeye was just returning to a kiva from a walk somewhere, and he shouted to him. The man drew up, waiting for him to arrive.

"Bison! A herd of bison stands in the snow just

a short distance up there!" He waved his arm to indicate the direction.

"You were up there? Just now? You've seen them?"

"They're up there! They stand like great stones!"

Hawkeye was instantly in action, stopping at a hole that led down into the kiva. Leaning down he said loudly, "Bison! Come...hurry!"

Six men came up the ladder, and Hawkeye spoke again. "Notify all the men to get out here immediately! We have meat just a short ways away!"

Men scattered, shouting as they ran, until many came boiling out of kivas and dwellings, running to where He Who Conquers and Hawkeye stood.

Thirty-one men of hunting age soon milled around, along with many younger boys who wanted to watch the excitement. When the last of the men arrived, Hawkeye spoke.

"He Who Conquers has spotted a herd of buffalo. All you men know what that means to us. They are...well, let He Who Conquers tell you. He saw them."

"They are just a short way to no-sun on the top up there. They stand facing the snow and wind, like stones. There are many. Is there one among you who has hunted a herd of buffalo before, who knows the land better than I?"

A man of about twenty-five winters stepped forward, and He Who Conquers recognized him as one who danced at Council. They looked at one another for a moment, then He Who Conquers said, "You wish to lead the hunt? It's for you to decide."

"How far are they?"

"Ten, maybe twelve stone throws from the rim at the top of the canyon."

"So close?"

"That close."

The man stood a moment, then said, "I will plan the hunt."

He Who Conquers nodded.

"Did you see how big the herd is?"

"No. There's too much snow falling, but there's a large herd."

"Then we'll circle around and come at them from

downwind. We'll try to get past them, so if they run, they may fall down over the edge into our canyon. Then we can get all we can handle and then some. To do that, we need to get all the way around the herd, and keep our line well. If we come at them from downwind around to no-sun, they might run this way, though they're hard to predict."

He looked around. "Every man must get his weapons and return here. Move quickly."

It was only a short time before they were all back, carrying bow and arrows, and atlatl or spear. In but a few more moments, Running Bison led the line of men to the end of the canyon and up the same place He Who Conquers had used. Once on the top, they saw the bison almost at once. None moved in the lighter but driving snow.

The herd was huge, so large they could see no end to it. Circling to rising-sun, they traveled toward no-sun for some time, still seeing no end to it. Finally Running Bison stopped and gathered the men to himself.

"It's too big. We can't drive them over the cliff when there are so many." He thought a moment. "We'll sneak up from the back, and kill what we can. With this snow, perhaps they won't run, and we can kill many more before the sun is long."

"Spread out that way, each man about three strides apart, and get down. Cover yourselves with your white blankets, and we'll stalk them slowly. Stay close, and don't get ahead of the others. We'll begin the kill soundlessly. No yelling or shouting. If they stand, perhaps we can each kill one or more each. If they begin to move, try to drive them toward the cliff with lots of noise. Don't lose your self-control. Be smart!"

Soon, the long line of men was crawling toward the edge of the great herd. The wind carried the strong odor of the herd over them, raising their excitement even higher. The animals paid them no mind as they came within ten, then eight, then five strides. Then they stopped, strung arrows, and let fly. Then again, and again, and yet again.

He Who Conquers, about halfway up the line, emptied his quiver, and then waited for others to do the same. When animals began to fall where they stood,

without running or making noises, his pulse was
pounding. Soon the entire line of men had emptied their
quivers, and almost as at a signal, they threw off their
blankets and ran at the herd with spears raised, then
thrust into whatever animal was closest. For the first
time, the animals realized danger. A few snorted and
began to push at those ahead of them. Some were
foundering, many were down, some lying still, and even
more simply stood with their sides pricked with arrows.

Finally the herd began to move, showing no
panic or hurry. But try as they might, screaming and
waving their arms and blankets, the herd simply moved
to sun-set. The men glanced around them, and began
the count. He Who Conquers took no time to count. He
knew he had at least four animals down with his arrows,
and one was sagging with his spear. Standing next to
his wounded animal, he grabbed the spear and tried to
jerk it free, but the animal suddenly turned and lunged.

He leaped back, and fell over another animal that
lay dead. He rolled, then scrambled to his feet, but the
bison had stopped and stood looking at him from small
eyes that hardly blinked in the snow, then the front
knees bent and it went forward onto them. For a time
it stayed like that, and He Who Conquers circled around
it and again grabbed the spear, only this time he pushed
hard.

The large beast rolled slowly away, and fell on its
side. He again circled to get behind it, then tried a
second time to remove the spear. The animal bellowed
and tried to struggle, and he jumped back, then grabbed
the spear again. This time it came free. But when he
turned, the herd was lost in the snow, and only dead and
dying animals lay around him and the other hunters.
There was no chance for him to use the spear again.

He had killed five! Maybe more! He would eat
fresh meat again, and Rain Water would be grateful
again! And Scent of Violet would have eyes that
sparkled, again!

Some of the men had already headed back for
the village to tell the women and have them help skin
animals and get them to the drying racks. Several men
were dragging carcasses toward the cliff, where they
could push them over and allow women below to do the

butchering.

Hawkeye came wandering among the dead animals, speaking to the men who were busy removing horns and heads, cutting into the cavity for the stomach contents, or just looking around in amazement.

"There you are!" Hawkeye stopped near He Who Conquers. "I wondered what happened to you." His eyes fell on the arrows sticking from the three nearest animals, and he exclaimed, "The gods...you are one of them!"

He Who Conquers smiled while he worked, but said nothing. His friend moved among the dead bison, counting them and seeing the placement of the killing arrows. "Five! You killed five! No, there another!"

A few men nearby stopped their work and looked at Hawkeye, who stood among the dead bison and stared around him. One by one, some came to see for themselves, then stared at He Who Conquers.

"You think he is a god?" one of them asked in an awed voice. Hawkeye never looked at the man, staring down at one killed by a single arrow. "If he isn't, that's not a dead bison. Do you see it running away? Answer your own question."

He Who Conquers sat on his knees working with his chert skinning stone at the head of the animal he had speared, his own head whirling at the words being tossed around, knowing denial was useless to men awed by another's good fortune. The Great One had done it yet again! Afraid any denials would merely foment further discussion he preferred to see end, he ignored them and continued to his task with head down.

Women began to appear, snow still falling heavily, and in the first group that came he saw her again. She came out of the snow that screened the animals from the village, looking around at all the men and animals, but it was obvious she hunted but one person. She was very close when she first saw him, and there were seven men nearby talking. She merely glanced at them, stopping across the carcass from him, almost shyly, watching until he glanced up. She knew she had been seen earlier, but she also knew he would say nothing to her in front of all the men.

"You have an animal for me to butcher?"

He looked up soberly. "The one there, or the one over there." He nodded toward each to indicate the ones.

Hawkeye spoke immediately. "Or that one over there, or the one over there. He killed six."

Scent of Violets looked at Hawkeye, at the bison, at Hawkeye, at He Who Conquers. "How can one man kill six?"

"If he is a god," Hawkeye returned, watching Scent of Violets for her reaction.

She stared at Hawkeye to see if he were serious. When she decided he was, she gave He Who Conquers a wondering look that bordered on amazement. Then she pulled a sharp skinning stone from a pouch tied to her waistband and went to work.

It was a long, hard sun. Meat was cut from hides that were being covered with the driving snow, carried back to the village, and more meat cut. Hides were freed from the meat and given an initial scraping, then allowed to cool on the snow. Once carried down the now treacherous path to the bottom, children carried meat back to the drying racks, and at the bottom of the cliffs, women skinned, cut, carried and sang while men skinned and talked. Everyone was spackled or smeared with bison blood. While the work was long and tedious, and the hands grew cold and were often thrust into the guts of the animals to rewarm them, attitudes were high and laughter frequent. Singing could be heard throughout the two areas where they worked, and occasionally a man would stand and dance while he chanted some bawdy tale of victory.

Hawkeye was the first to spot the snow-flecked dark objects sitting on the edge of their visibility. Wolves. Smelling blood, they had come, probably having followed the herd for some time. It became necessary for men to stand guard over those who worked, keeping the several wolves from getting too close. The beasts were brazen, but stayed well outside spearpoint perimeters.

Dark had long fallen before the work was done, and snow sizzled around the racks that sagged under their loads. New ones had to be constructed because of the enormous amount of meat, and women had been slicing meat into strips most of the sun, while others came from the field with more, guarded from the wolves that followed them, tongues dripping.

It was a community project, though Scent of Violets made sure her household was given the tongues from each of the five bison He Who Conquers had killed. Fires burned under the racks, and smoke billowed from them. Shifts were set for women to keep the fires burning continuously for however long it would take until the meat was cured for storage. Always there were at least three women, one with a spear in case the wolves got too close. The cooled hides were stacked, frozen, inside a vacant dwelling to await opportunity for working into cloaks, leggings and blankets. Bones were stacked for utensils, for making trinkets and religious artifacts, and stomach and intestines were saved for bags, string and thread.

Rain Water was everywhere on the lower level, acting like he was half his age, carrying meat, hides, bones, everything he could do. His pride was so high there were those who chided him that he had no reason for boasting. His response was short and jokingly curt.

"My new son did more than all of you. Without him, there would have been no meat at all!"

"Ha! He's not your son, Rain Water!"

"Ask him! He will tell you!"

Arguments ended there. No one was audacious enough to ask. Rain Water would continue what he was doing with a chuckle, bringing sidelong glances to those who accused him. Several times he was heard talking to his dead mate, laughing as he spoke.

When it was dark He Who Conquers finally returned to the dwelling. He was nearly exhausted, his eyes revealing just how tired he felt. He had used snow to clean the blood from his hands and arms, leaving his skin raw. Snow was almost halfway to the knee, and drifting in against the front of the village as it swirled down from above the huge rock.

Rain Water was chewing on a piece of fresh buffalo tongue, watching the young man with interest. "You'll mate my granddaughter."

He Who Conquers felt too tired to think about it, though again the thought was titillating. He would dream about it later, but just now he had no desire to do mental gymnastics with Rain Water. He said nothing, leaning back with his eyes closed.

"Let it drop, Fa-Fa," Scent of Violets said as she entered the room with meat for He Who Conquers. "It's for him to decide...and for me." She added the latter lamely, as though her own mind was already set and she did not want him to know.

"He needs to know," the old man said frankly, then he lapsed into silence, watching his new roomer eat slowly.

He Who Conquers savored his meat, remembering the kill, the blood-ritual and sampling, throwing the hearts in all directions to scatter them on the newly fertilized earth, tossing the female reproductive parts to Earth Mu to replenish her strength, the taste of liver when he took his single bite of each one, and the smell of the smoke as he burned the livers to the Great One. Eyes closed and leaning back, he took one bite after another and chewed each slowly. The other two in the room watched him with silent interest, and when he drank the tea she handed to him he saw their stares for the first time.

"It has been a hard sun." He spoke to break the awkward silence.

"You have earned your stay among the people of Open Stone. No one can ever think of you as just another mouth to be fed over the long snowtime."

A slight smile touched his face, remaining as he finished eating. When he completed his meal, he burped his appreciation and went out to relieve himself, then stood back against the bottom massive rock that fronted below the cave, where there was some protection from the wind and snow fell almost straight down. It still fell heavily, and the women who tended the fires at the drying racks were merely blanket-covered dark lumps against the light of the fires, the wolves bumps in the snow where they watched. The village dogs cowed between the wolves and the buildings, snow slowly burying them. He stood a long time, feeling the cold creep into his body, the wind nip at his face, only partly conscious of his discomfort. The fires flickered and guttered; the women occasionally added wood; the snow swirled down off the face of the cliff and piled against and atop the line of buildings below the cave.

A few people came out to relieved themselves, but otherwise there was no one moving about. He hardly noticed, his mind working on what Rain Water had said. "You will mate my granddaughter." Was it true? She was a lovely young woman, and she seemed to like him. She was truly amazed at him, which both thrilled and bothered him. She was half-believing the stories about him that were flying around. He had even heard most of them himself. And the ones who brought him to Open Stone were sounding off the most and loudest. He was almost grateful for the voices raised in protest, but wondered if this latest development might hush even those.

He had no idea how he would stop the rumors now. He had been too successful too quickly, before they had the opportunity to see him as nothing more than a man. Their conclusions could make it impossible for him to stay, though he was already aware of the unlikelihood of any length to his stay. There was no way he could continue to live up to the high archetype already set. Having come to them after a successful hunt and getting five scalps along the way was enough to make him something different, but now it was the great bison kill. If he did not know himself so well, he could almost wonder himself!

And maybe, just maybe, the truth might be that he was different! He sighed audibly, and the sound made him realize where he was and how cold he was. Yet he was reluctant to return to the room where he would sleep. He wished he could see past the adulations that were coming, to know if he would be staying. If it became impossible, he had best not mate here either. Like when he left The Top, it would be to his advantage to have no mate when he traveled. To make it on his own from one place to another was enough of a fear; to have to protect another who would be useless in a fight would be beyond his worst thoughts.

He wanted that girl, and that was the problem. So why could Rain Water not leave the subject alone and let things work in a natural way? The girl wanted him to stay in the background, too, but it was obvious he never would. Why? Perhaps the rather abrupt mention of The Rite of Perfection had something to do with it.

Was the old man serious...yes, he probably was!

Finally, thoroughly chilled, he shuffled through the snow back to the dwelling. About to push the heavy bison hide aside and enter, he was stopped by a sharp retort. He stood a moment, wishing he had heard what was said, but a few moments later her voice was clear.

"No, Fa-Fa, just forget it!"

"I've only a few suns left, little pretty one, too few to think I might make it to the Rite of Snowtime. I promised your mu that I would see you mated, and I have failed. This is your last chance at someone special, not just one of the tasteless puppies from here."

"Perhaps you just know the ones from here too well."

"And already I know He Who Conquers. He's a man, one who will take care of you, give you prestige. One sun, his name will be sung by his people as a champion. Most of all, he makes no attempts to show off. He had a chance to boast at Council, but did he? He spoke cautiously and was humble, instead. He has character. You may think so, but I know you will never find better."

There was a pause, then she said, "I like him, Fa-Fa. He's very nice. But he needs to make up his own mind. If you push him, he might leave us."

"He will. But when he does, he'll take you with him. Sometime, soon or in a couple of winters, he'll leave. He must return to his own people, and be a leader for them. You'll go with him; it is your destiny...and his. He's no ordinary man. He's been made by the gods to be a leader, and a great one he will be. No one anywhere will really honor him until he becomes that man."

"How do you know that, Fa-Fa? Perhaps he'll stay."

"He'll go. He can only be an alien here. The men think he's part god, and that will never change. And he does not wear the breechcloth that identifies him with us. He can never be part of this people, and he knows it. His heart is back in his own country. But he will learn some things from us, and one sun he'll take his knowledge back with him. You will go with him."

There was another long pause, and he was about

to open the curtain and enter when she said, "If he mates me, I'll go with him anywhere. But I fear he'll not see me. When Hawkeye tells everyone he's a god, it makes him uncomfortable. I think he'll leave before he knows me well enough to be willing to mate with me."

"Have no fear, pretty one. He sees you. Perhaps you should offer The Hospitality. If he put his seed in your body, and you made it enjoyable, maybe he'd find good reason to mate you. The gods know every other young puppy in this village drools at the chance to ride you."

He Who Conquers could stand it no longer, and pushed the curtain aside and entered, stamping his feet from the stooped position required by the low ceiling.

"Ah, you returned."

He nodded and smiled. "It snows deep and drifts in the wind. The women feed the fires often. It'll be a while before anyone will be out and about. The wolves are content to sit watch. It's getting cold, too."

Rain Water nodded. "You'll sleep well this darkness. You've had a long sun."

He nodded. "But I needed to be alone for a while. Your men think much too highly of me."

"It makes you a little edgy, does it?"

He nodded. "More than a little. I'm no god, and I'm not Death Wind. I'm only a man with much to learn. The Great One has been too generous to me."

Rain Water nodded soberly. "Yet you are different. You are so much taller and more graceful, and you bring good fortune to this people. It lends to the myth they would believe."

"It's good to hear you call it a myth, Old One. I hoped you knew better than the rest. It gives me encouragement that not all the people are so gullible."

He snorted with a laugh. "Gullible? Perhaps most are, but you give them too much evidence. I've always been a cynic, but I'll keep your secret, even though no one will ever hear me say you're just a man. You see, even I think you're different, quite different...even a bit special. It's why I wish to see you mate Scent of Violets."

"Fa-Fa! I've asked you...."

"Hush, Pretty One! As you wish, I'll say no

more." He moved over found his mat, and in a few moments there was the steady breathing of the sleeper.

Scent of Violets sat quietly, staring at the fire that was sinking into coals, listening to the old man get settled and fall asleep. When he slept, she said, "Fa-Fa is too bold. He has gotten very pushy." She was upset and distressed.

He Who Conquers studied her face while she spoke and then stared at the fire. "It's the way of the old. They learn when they are young, meditate on it when they get older, and become set and very outspoken when they're old. It's the same with the old everywhere."

She nodded. "I'm sorry for what he says."

"Are you?" He saw her head come up with a look between surprise and something else...anger? Before she could retort, he added, "Don't be angry. He thinks a great deal of you to be so forward to a stranger...a little like an overly-protective mu." He smiled slightly. "My mu is like that."

"Your mu, she still lives?"

"She lives, but I'll not see her alive again. Next time I speak with her, we'll be beyond Sipapu."

Her eyes lifted again, studying him in the dim light. "How do you know that?"

He shrugged innocently, not wanting her to know of his visions...not yet. "I just know."

"Do you see things, like...events of the future? You know what I mean...visions. Do you have them, too?"

"Too? What do you mean, too? Do you see visions?"

"I have never seen one, but I think Fa-Fa does."

He nodded. "I think he must, too."

"Do you?"

He shrugged again. "Dreams, that's all I have."

She stared at him for a short time. "Visions."

A third time he shrugged. "I have no idea what a vision is, so it's hard to know."

She got up, her head only a whisker under the roof beams, and went to her room. He stretched out on his mat and covered himself with the feather blanket. He was so very tired...so...sleepy...with the heat beginning to massage his aching muscles...the coldness moving out....

And then he was wide awake. Someone stood outside the door. Who was it, and why? He lay still, trying to breathe as a sleeper, listening, waiting for the curtain to move, tense, hand on his knife. After a long time, whoever it was went away, and he heard the swishing of the snow as the person left. He relaxed again, and in a moment slept.

He awakened to sounds of a fire being reset by Scent of Violets, and wondering if what he had heard in the darkness was real or imaginary. He had only to open the curtain, push aside the covering-stone and see the footprints to confirm it, but was reluctant to do so.

Somehow, it seemed like a bad omen if he should see prints in the snow, as though another witch had come into his life to drive him from this people. To see the tracks would prove that someone came, and it would not be just a figment of his imagination. That seemed important...to know it was not a man...to alleviate the fear that someone had come for him and then had second thoughts.

He watched Scent of Violets with pleasure, but wondered about the reality of the visitor with trepidation. He would have to leave it to the Great One, but he would soon know if it might not be dangerous here, too...like back home.

14

He Who Conquers stood atop the great rock that bent downward and then plunged into the canyon before folding back into a large cave to become the protection for Open Stone. From where he stood, the world looked white, and the people below swarmed throughout the village while children played up and down the canyon. He watched them with curious fascination, because the new perspective made them seem more like ant-people than fellow humans. The browns, blacks and whites of clothing added to the engrossing illusion.

Sun had melted the snow where he stood, and parts of the rock still steamed under the suddenly warm sun. Snow had fallen for two suns, until it was above the knees of
the people. Now, seven suns later, the people were basking and enjoying while they had the chance, having gotten tired of the sudden imprisonment.

Standing where he was, he felt elated. The bison had moved away, though he had picked up their scat and tailed them far enough to know they had left the area.

Whether they returned or not made little difference, because the meat storage pots were full to overflowing, and there was more than necessary for snowtime. He still could not believe his good fortune in seeing them in the storm, especially after the strange whims that led him to go where they were.

It had to be the Great One. He had no other explanation for why he had left the canyon, not to mention how he had twice changed his mind before running toward the place where he only imagined he had seen movement. That inner voice spoke well to him. He was a hero, something more than a man, and perhaps even a god. Sometimes, he even wondered himself....

While it was heady, it was also troublesome. He would never have close friends here, and perhaps anywhere else. Even Hawkeye, whom he had begun to consider a friend, remained aloof. He wondered about the wisdom of considering a mate here, despite what Rain Water said and thought. Yet he had seen some things already to bring back to his people to make things better for them. And then there was Scent of Violets. The stay was definitely worthwhile...until he had gotten what he had come here to find. But what should he do about her?

He saw movement far away along the ridge, a man coming his way, trotting. He watched, walking a short way back toward him in order to be farther from the edge should the confrontation be unfriendly.

It was one he had seen at Council, a young man he had heard called The Deer. It seemed to fit, because he was running gracefully, nearing the place of rendezvous.

When he was close, he slowed to a walk and smiled, greeting He Who Conquers with "Hola!"

"Hola!" he replied with equal gusto, wondering at the obviously purposeful meeting.

"I saw you up here and thought it might give me a chance to meet you."

"You're The Deer. I take it you got the name from your skill."

The man smiled. He appeared friendly, and He Who Conquers relaxed a bit. "I win all the races at the competitions; you run, too, don't you?"

He Who Conquers nodded. "Some."

"You're being modest. You walk like a runner, and you're built like one who could leave me in the dust."

He gave a half-shrug. "I enjoy running."

"So do I. Would you race me? Not right now," he added hastily. "After the snow melts, on a good sun."

"Why? If you're the champion, why race one you don't know? Would you take the chance of being beaten?"

A grin came. "You must be good to be so sure of winning."

"I can run. What would be the purpose of such a race?"

"I call no man my friend unless I can run faster than he. I was told you're something more than a man by some of those I've beaten, but I'd never believe that...unless you beat me."

He nodded amiably, but his thoughts were that this one was much like Boy with the Eye of an Eagle, both self-centered and selfish. "And if I beat you, it would prove that I'm a god, is that it?"

"Maybe. At least I'd have a reason for not questioning the conclusions."

He Who Conquers enjoyed his candidness. "You don't need to question such a thing. I'm merely a man, even if I beat you at a race...if we run."

The Deer was breathing easily despite the run through snow near his knees. There was no doubt he could run, and he had some stamina, at least. He might be a very worthy opponent, and it had been over a winter since He Who Conquers had last run against someone.

"We'll run," The Deer grinned. "You're a runner, and you like competition. I'll have Village Crier announce such a race, and make it a big event." He turned away and started to walk, then stopped and looked back. "I was only kidding about not calling you a friend only if I win. A good run might make me your friend."

He began to trot away, and He Who Conquers watched him run until he was far away and near the place where he would disappear. He went the opposite way of the only way he knew to get on the top apart from the toe-and-hand holds. The man could run, but he felt confident. His legs were longer, he was quicker, and he had more stamina than The Deer realized. It was impossible to know what the man had considered before issuing the challenge. Some sun he might learn what the real motivation was, but at the moment it seemed unimportant.

A race. Probably one that would take much of a sun. There was a ring of excitement to the thought. Then he shuddered. Would everyone consider him a god if he won? If they already did it would make little difference, but it might be the thing...especially if he won by a large margin...the final factor that might convince them. To himself, it would mean little, since he had already beaten every challenger by goodly margins, even the man from the village of He Hears Voices. Then again....

He shrugged. No matter. He would run, and he would run to win. It was a matter of honor. And it was the fierce sense of competition he felt. It might be a difficult task, but he felt confident in his ability and condition.

He began to move in the direction The Deer ran, heading back to the village, and he felt the desire to run. He was instantly in motion, only he ran with more than a trot, pushing himself into a sprint through the deep snow. By time he slowed for the drop into the canyon where the tracks led, which began as a wash, he was breathing hard.

He grinned as he dropped down quickly toward the floor of the canyon. He was feeling good, and a race would be something to help make snowtime shorter.

As he climbed down a drop-off, made treacherous by the deep snow that filled the canyon, his mind suddenly remembered the man who had stood outside his doorway on that night after the bison kill. Had he been friend or foe? Why would he have come to the doorway and stood a long time before deciding he would not enter? Had he been listening for conversation? There was no way he could hear breathing with the wind swirling the snow around so fiercely? Why was he there?

Had he merely wanted to visit, and changed his mind when there were no signs of life from inside? One thing was sure, he had been there. The depressions in the snow after the long darkness of snowfall had been quite clear. His gut feeling was that it had not been intended for a friendly visit, but unless something came about later, there would be no way to ever know. Of course, if it were friendly, he might never know, anyway.

A race! Had The Deer challenged him in good faith, or was it a setup? Being far from the village, he would certainly be open to attack, and no one would ever know--or care! The inspiration that came opened a new light on what the race might portend, even though The Deer seemed very friendly. Maybe the race would be a far greater challenge than he had thought.

Yet, why would anyone here want him injured or dead? Had he not brought to the village good fortune with his coming? Perhaps that was the problem. Jealousy had many sources. It might even be that someone had an eye for Scent of Violets and thought him a threat to his dream.

Certainly she was worthy of dreams. He had already been dreaming! What was more, he liked to look at her while they were together in the dwelling. His thoughts were most exciting when she was around, and it gave him a good deal of pleasure to be in her company.

She was witty, she was candid, and she was intelligent. What was as exciting, she was beautiful. And what added to the dream was that she seemed to want him for a mate, willing even to travel with him should he leave.

But was that fair to her? Did he want that responsibility? After telling Little Dove what he had about a traveling companion? Moreover, he wanted the Great One to confirm his mating of whomever it was to be. So far there had been no sign. He could love her, of that he was sure. And more than that, he knew he would be a good provider and help bring her clan the status it had lost over the past generation.

Suddenly, he stopped. An idea edged into his mind, one that he had just for an instant seen in an ugly image and thrust aside because of something else, a thought first broached by Hawkeye. Scent of Violets was still a virgin, she was not popular in the village, and she was nearly alone. Only an old man stood between her and possible trouble. And when snowtime ended, and the vernal equinox came--the time when the Goddess of Fertility was honored--she would be a candidate for the sacrificial rites!

Was that possible? There was no talk of a young lady being captured from another people, the usual method to supply an eligible young woman for the great ritual, and if none were to be had, a young lady from within the village would be selected. Could she be the prime candidate, not just a possible one? Her acquiescence was only a formality, as she would probably accept the role as village intercessor. It was a rare honor. And in her state of mind, unmated and fourteen winters, she would likely choose to be honored....

That was a whole new aspect for him to consider, although as yet it was not up to him to either save her or let her go. Still, it was something for him to consider. Would he dishonor the Goddess if he should desire her to the point where he would consider mating her to keep her from being the honored gift?

He reached the bottom and moved into the main canyon with his mind still working on the host of new ideas. Mostly, it pondered the race and why the challenge had come, but thoughts, or were they dreams, of Scent of Violets was never far from his mind, either.

When he entered the village, children were still playing snow games and women were still fretting over the meat that was taking a long time to dry because of the snow. Few men were out, most of them warmly ensconced in a kiva sharing stories of their traditions or working on tools, weapons, religious things, or personal effects.

He felt the outsider, and remembered the words of Rain Water. He was unlikely to be invited into one of the kivas, which tended to be very clannish, and he had no clan here to claim a place. Not even Hawkeye had asked him to his! And Rain Water had as yet not been to a kiva.

He was not the son of anyone--or nephew, either; the lack was becoming evident. What was more, he was an enigma to them. Everyone considered him something other than a man, even wondering where he came from. He had not "come from" anywhere; he was dropped like every other child! But that belief alone would keep him from ever becoming one with this people.

He stood with unseeing eyes that were pointed toward the round game of tag going on among the children, his thoughts taking him far away. The Top. The threat to his life no longer seemed so serious, not from this distance. He had begun to doubt the reality of the threat, his thoughts becoming lonesome for familiar people and places.

By force of will, he denied himself further self-pity, and turned to study the partially built stone structure that stood far back and up high, in the corner of the great cave. He climbed the footholds up the steep rock onto the cave floor, and noted the single wall of stone mixed in size and held together with mortar not so different from--in fact the same as--the daub in the daub-and-wattle structures. At least, it looked the same.

This was a new idea, but one with much merit. There was no lack of rock, large and small, for this type of structure on The Top. All they needed was the expertise. He would see to it he would get it, perhaps going to Wide Canyon before he returned home, since there were stories of their use of stone. He would know how to keep the heavy walls from sinking into the soil, how to lay corners and joints, how to place the beams and support posts, how to mix mortar, how to finish doorways, and how to keep the walls from crumbling. Whatever there was to know.

Rain Water could show him some of that, the rest he could see for himself while the workers were at it after the snows melted. When he returned to The Top, it would become one of the things he could teach them. The other would be making pottery that would withstand intense heat for a long time so they could cook beans. Corn became a tiresome food, and squash needed a neighbor.

It was late in the sun, cooking fires sending smoke from the smokeholes of most of the dwellings including that of Scent of Violets. He found a place for relief, then headed for the dwelling and something to eat.

Alone when he entered, she smiled and said, "Fa-Fa has gone to a kiva to share lies."

He returned her smile. "Of Rain Water, I'd never suspect lies. Perhaps there are times he'll stretch truth, or forget the true details, but not to lie." In his mind, he could almost see her being held by two masked clansmen, naked, head up proudly, facing the post to which she would be securely tied before the knife....

He swallowed and wondered again if the Great One would be angered if he interfered with such an image, would in fact mate her and take out of their hands the one whom they might desire to see used to honor the Goddess.

She giggled. "Then you don't know Fa-Fa. I've heard some of his stories; they do more than stretch truth."

He sat against the wall and smiled, his blanket around his back to shield the skin from the cool wall. The room was very warm, the fire heating their food nearly smokeless. "The Deer challenged me to a race." He said it quietly, and was surprised to see her response.

"What kind of race?" Her head had come up and her eyes looked instantly troubled.

"Foot race. Starting far from the village."

"When?" There was an edge in her voice he could not read.

"We set no time, why?"

She continued to look at him, animation suspended. "He's a treacherous man. He's suspected of killing two men while on hunting trips, but never was it proven."

Then his thoughts in questioning the motive for the race were probably not out of line. What of his thoughts regarding her possible danger...if one considered being sacrificed to the Goddess a "danger"...were such thoughts also very real? "You think he'd have such a thought for me? Why?" He had almost lost his trend of thought.

She stared at him a moment, temporarily distracted by his lack of concentration. "He's our most successful hunter. Up until their deaths, so were the two men who disappeared while hunting with him. And now you are. You see the pattern."

He nodded. "Clearly enough."

"Don't race him."

"I must. I accepted his challenge, and you know what would happen if I were to renege. I have to run."

"Then you must honor remember my warning. He'll kill you if he ever gets the chance, and to be far from the village would give him that chance. There are few here who would ever question your disappearance."

He nodded again. "I can believe that." But in his mind's eye he could almost see the knife plunging into her throat, then the head fall to one side with the severing of the muscles on the left side of the neck, blood shooting over her shoulder....

He could almost taste his own bile thinking on that for an instant. And he had the power to keep her from....

She dropped her eyes to the meat she had spitted, again noting his distraction and wondering about it. "I would, but my voice isn't heard. Fa-Fa could do nothing. I would be alone to mourn the loss."

"Would you?" His voice was both questioning and light, the latter to hide his interest in her feelings.

"I would."

He grinned to lighten the subject. "At least that would be one, if you tell the truth."

"I do. I like you. You're a gentle man, and easy to have around. I...would mate you...if you wanted."

He felt his heart flip, words forming in his mind but unspoken. Finally he said, "The Great One hasn't said." His voice sounded raspy and choked. Part of his emotion came from the image of the knife scene.

She saw the advantage. "But you would like to? Fa-Fa said I was pretty, and you would see that. But I told him you wanted more than a pretty woman, and that made it difficult."

He smiled slightly, but decided to say nothing. She continued to spin the tongue of buffalo slowly, then looked up with concern in her eyes.

"Fa-Fa said you would not stay among my people, that you'll leave here abruptly and perhaps before snowtime is over. Will you?"

He shrugged. "I'm a stranger here; there's no way I can ever be accepted as one of your people. They have strange ideas of me, which makes it unlikely I can stay. I'm not yet sure when I'll leave, but it's probable. However, there are things for me to learn, and I seek knowledge. If things change, I might stay...I'd like to. Only what happens in the future will make the decision." How true that was, he thought to himself. Things might change more than either of them would prefer.

She looked almost melancholy. "Then you'll go." How like the response of Little Dove! "If what you say is true, what Fa-Fa says then is also true."

He again did not respond to her insight. By his silence he confirmed her fears.

"I wish to go with you."

"And leave your people?" He was not convinced she could do that, knowing the home-orientation of a woman. And why not? The dwelling belonged to the her. Yet he had the nagging thought that he really did want her to go with him. How could he think such thoughts after what he had told Little Dove, about his honor and all that?

"I can leave them. If I were to mate a man from Open Stone, I'd in time be accepted again; however, there's none I desire, and as it now stands, I'm not well-liked. When Fa-Fa had me reject the available men, the women began to hate me. They think I'm uppity, and maybe I am."

He Who Conquers chuckled. "Maybe, but any woman likes to think her son to be superior to the daughters in whom he might show some interest, and vice versa. I think time will never change that."

She smiled at his insight. "Perhaps, but mating will usually break down that barrier with time. Rejection never will."

They fell silent as she stuck a sharp stick into the meat to test it, then let the meat sit while she prepared the rest of the meal. He sat quietly and watched her, enjoying her presence as well as the sight of her near nude body. And the aroma of the meat was next to the gods! While the fire burned and the meal was warming, the room was so warm she was down to the attire of the warm season.

A noise came from just outside, then the flap was thrown back and Rain Water struggled through the doorway, sitting immediately and leaning against the wall. He looked tired, almost to the point of being wan.

"You need to rest, Fa-Fa," she said softly.

"As soon as I eat," he responded with nothing of his usual aplomb. "I understand," he turned toward He Who Conquers, "that you will race The Deer."

"It is so."

His voice was very tired, but he spoke with feeling. "Then you be most careful once you leave the sight of the village. He's a man of devious behavior, what one might call deceptive. The face he gives you rarely lets you know what he's thinking, if you get my meaning. He'll stoop to anything to be a winner, or the best at what he does by removing the competition. Never give him your back."

He Who Conquers nodded. "We were discussing that not long ago. It seems you and your granddaughter are in agreement."

"Then listen well. We speak the truth."

"I hear."

The old man leaned back and closed his eyes, and silence fell. In a few moments, he slept sitting up, his head falling forward onto his chest.

"Fa-Fa is failing fast," she said softly. "I don't believe he'll last through the cold season."

He Who Conquers swallowed, then said, "If he returns to Earth Mu, there's no one here for me...except you. I live in your dwelling, and I'll have to leave." Would the Great One intercede and let him know what he was to do about this pretty woman?

She looked up with alarm, but kept her voice low. "No! No, you need not leave. It's the usual custom among our people that if a man comes to visit, a woman is given to him to serve his needs until he leaves. The people think Fa-Fa has given me to you already, so if you stay they'll think nothing more of it. I don't wish to be alone, even if you'll not mate me...or couple with me, either."

He nodded. "If you wish, but I want only to save your reputation."

She giggled, a sound he recognized as being her response to something that tickled her. "My reputation? I still wear a chastity belt, but my people think I'm no longer a virgin. What reputation?" A note of cynicism crept into her voice. Then she smiled weakly. "Besides, among our people, it's an honor to couple with a visitor, and moreso since he's considered a god. It's as though the woman is still a virgin. If she conceives, it's the greatest honor of all."

He said nothing, not sure how he should respond. And had she given any thought to the possibility of becoming the village intercessor through her own sacrifice? How did that color her thinking?

"You will stay under any circumstance. And since no one has told you our custom, it seems they don't really consider you a man, but something of a god. If it were otherwise, you would now be enjoying a woman companion. It's not my place to speak to you to correct that, but if you think you have been slighted, I'm here. I've not been entered by a man, but for you I wouldn't even hesitate."

He shook his head. "I won't Open you. It's contrary to the custom of my people to be given to any man while you're still a virgin, unless the man is a spiritual leader. Besides, you've been too good to me already. To use you, even though it's a custom, would be despicable."

She smiled. "I appreciate your saying that. It makes me think the more of you, though if Fa-Fa goes to Earth Mu, you might find me crawling onto your mat with you one darkness." She giggled again.

He smiled. "And I might kick you out!"

She handed him a cup of hot tea and a bowl with soup, then sat back and said, "I'd take that chance," watching as he ate. Rain Water awakened, ate sparingly, uncharacteristically saying nothing of the good bison meat, and went to his mat. Then He Who Conquers was given meat. When he was full, he belched loudly twice and sat back as she smiled widely.

"You're full?"

"I'm satisfied," he responded.

It was her signal, and she ate her meal as he watched. It was impolite to speak to one eating, and the quiet was broken only by a crying infant in the next dwelling, and later by a mu shouting at her daughter.

When she was done, she stacked the bowls, then

said, "When do you plan to run?"

He shrugged. "As soon as possible."

"Plan your strategy well. And don't forget The Deer does have some he calls friends."

"I won't forget." He got to his knees next to the door. "I'll be back shortly."

With that, he went out, standing in the shadow of the building and looking around before moving away and into the darkness beyond the village. At the short box canyon where Council met, he stopped and looked around again, then entered the canyon and waited behind a rock to be sure no one followed.

It was some time before he felt secure, and he advanced to the rocks beyond the fire ring, where he sat and wrapped his coat about himself. He wanted time to think without anyone around, and he wanted to put together a strategy for the race.

The single agreement was that The Deer was far from interested in just a race. He was a man of duplicity and treachery, suspected of killing two fellow villagers. He had the need to be superior to everyone in his chosen areas, namely competition and hunting.

His own strategy must arise from his awareness of the man and his possible assistants. He had to think through how he would run, how he would respond to conflicts, and how to read the proper time for action. The question was how much he dared use his own physical endowments in the case of life-threatening challenges.

Of course, the biggest problem was to anticipate what type of trouble they might give him. Surely they would not use a spear or bow-and-arrow, for either was bloody and messy, and it would require they dispose of the body, a difficult thing to do. So it had to come in the form of rocks or a beating, both of which could be blamed on falling rocks. In a canyon with steep walls, such things might be rare, but far from impossible. So his task was to presage all the possible scenes.

He started to get up and head back when he saw the shadow of someone cross the opening of the canyon, which was bad enough except the person was taking pains to be sneaking. That made it worse. Had he been seen coming into the canyon, perhaps by someone who waited for him to innocently walk out? Or was it merely a young lover on a clandestine rendezvous?

Or were they--if there were more than one-- thinking he might have gone on to the top of canyon that led up to where the great buffalo kill had come? That seemed likely, so he stayed put.

He was warm, he was comfortable, and he was soon sleepy, though he fought to stay awake and be alert. Suddenly his head snapped up, and he realized he had been asleep. Though it was dangerous to let himself sleep, he had little energy left, and enjoyed sitting where he was.

Again he fell asleep. Somewhere in the darkness, he suddenly awakened in a sweat, the result of another vision, the repeat of the first one he had seen. Again there was the two people stopping to couple near the place he had killed Yellow Sapsucker, and the inability to see the face of his mate. It was Little Dove, and then it was not; it was her mu, and then it was not; and there came the fragrance, but again he could not identify it. What was it? But again, before he could dwell on it, there were his decomposing parents. Shortly, there was the run, and then he was again with his mate. Again her hair hung forward as the face looked downward, and from the side he could not see her; but there was the fragrance, not an odor, but a fragrance. What was it?

He sat shivering, but not from the cold. It was the hideous picture of his parents, and then the smiling, waving Boy with the Eye of an Eagle, or was he Eagle Eye by now? Why would a hated enemy smile and wave while he was coupling with Little Dove, or was it she?

Confused again, he stood and headed back, careful to check the trail from every direction before he left the canyon, and then he ran at full sprint for the village, stopping behind the buildings to relieve himself before entering the dwelling and finding his mat. There he lay, wondering and pondering, thinking that it was not a great deal different from back on The Top. His life was in danger again! And he was in a quandary about the vision, and at the moment, specifically the fragrance.

Somewhere in his musings, he fell asleep.

15

Sun God returned bright and warm, and water ran and dripped from the high faces of the cliffs, the sandy canyon bottom ran heavy with water, the snow swiftly disappeared, and people were busy outside. Old men again sat in the sun to ease their aching joints while they argued over anything and everything; old women did their chores in the sun; the village women finished the meat curing and storage; children ran hither and yon through the canyons, trying to stay out of sight of mus.

As the snows disappeared, He Who Conquers left the village before Sun God appeared each dawn and ran, up canyons, down canyons, along the top of the mesa that bordered Open Stone, and across the mesa tops. He ran hard, he trotted at a punishing pace for long distances, and he never slowed to a walk. After six consecutive suns of running through the countryside, he felt more confident that he was ready for the test that was to come shortly. As he was returning from a run, Hawkeye signalled him; he was given an invitation to attend Council, and he was pleased. He went.

Hardly had the meeting gotten underway when a very short man stood, looked directly at He Who Conquers, and nearly shouted, "He is a spy!"

He Who Conquers had never seen the accuser up close, but he knew immediately he had not been invited to just sit and watch the proceedings. After making the accusation, the man dramatically pointed a stubby finger at him and smirked.

He was numb, his eyes locked on the man who accused him. The man was perhaps two-thirds the height of the average man, and he had heard the man referred to as The Runt. Whether or not it was his real name, he was unsure. The voice was almost a screech, and it was this as much as the accusation that made him freeze.

What was this? Had Hawkeye known this would happen, in cahoots with some undercurrent of which he had not been aware? He was given no time to recover his wits, and he continued to stare, his thoughts a jumble. Confidence was slow to return, but he never looked away from the man. Somehow, he could not give the man any room to think he had gained the upper hand, but he was to stunned to offer a defense. It was the suddenness.

"You're a reader of minds, perhaps," he said slowly, hoping he seemed strong enough to mean what he said, "you who accuse without sense or logic. Are you like a woman, who sees through eyes of jealousy and seldom uses reason."

The man reminded him of a squirrel, sitting on a limb with chitters and a twitching tail. The thought almost made him smile, except he was still groping for ideas.

"You are a spy! I've seen you after darkness falls, wandering about and looking at everything! You're here as a spy! You're one of the Others!"

That broke the ice for him. To accuse him of being an Other was so absurd it gave him a sense of direction. He let a smile come, but his eyes remained humorless. Men watched carefully and rode every word. "I'm an Other, yet carry nine of their scalps? I think your brain is as runty as you are." He felt a cheap satisfaction in using the simile. There was a tittering of laughter scattered through the men, and he felt his courage returning with a rush, and with it his senses. Interesting how a cheap shot like that could focus the mind.

"If I were a spy, you'd certainly never have seen me, Runt. If by some chance someone else spotted me, no one would have caught me, anyway. I'd have been long gone. Besides, what purpose would I have for spying? I can see everything I want from up there." He pointed to the top of the cliff across the canyon from the dwellings.

"You think you are the wind, that you can disappear? Or a god, that you soar on the winds? Perhaps an eagle, or a hawk?" The Runt was being theatrical as he spoke.

He began to enjoy the banter. He was still on trial among this people, and for the time he would be with them, it would never end. Was Hawkeye privy to this crazy scene. If so, was his invitation the start of a premeditated plan to discredit him?. If so, why? Had he not proven himself among them, and had not Hawkeye been mightily impressed? Had he changed his mind so quickly? He let his eyes flicker over the man again, then turned and waved a hand at the man, a sign of dismissal.

"You are a small man more ways than in your build." If the Runt could be theatrical, so could he! "You seek to be a big man among your people by using your mouth. Do you also reach up to slap women and children on their buttocks to prove how big you are?" He gave a derisive laugh, and turned for the entrance to the Council.

"I'll race The Deer in two suns. You'll learn soon enough why I claim no one would have caught me. And if you have a scalp or two to prove you are also a man, I'd like to see them." Again, like an actor at a ceremonial dance, he turned dramatically on the small man. "In fact, you have no scalps. Perhaps you are the one who's a spy for The Others. You accuse me to draw attention from yourself. Would you send a message in the smoke to let them know the best time to attack? Or perhaps you signal someone who watches from a ridge."

Hawkeye stood and waved for silence, He Who Conquers turning to watch him; the Runt froze, and even

in that he was like an actor. The Deer smiled and
leaned against a rock, but He Who Tracks stood and
went to the side of Hawkeye.

"This is absurd! To accuse this man of being a
spy is about the stupidest thing you've ever done, Runt!
Your head is caught between your legs! The man has
killed five Others to save me and those who hunted with
me! He killed two deer that you will enjoy over the cold
season. He found the bison, and killed six of them for
us. He has become a friend of Rain Water, though I
doubt you have the wisdom to see what he is to this
village already! If you have nothing more important to
do than go around falsely accusing a welcome visitor,
then I feel sorry for you! Go find a rock and sit down.
Leave the meeting to men with intelligence."

He turned and spoke softly to He Who Conquers.
"I find this council meeting completely against everything
I believe. I sorrow that I invited you, not knowing this
would be the main subject. I ask that you leave. I have
somewhat to say to the men, and I prefer to not have
you here."

He Who Conquers nodded, pleasantly surprised
to have Hawkeye so distraught, and He Who Tracks
standing beside him to offer support.   He stood a
moment uncertainly, then realized the import of what
Hawkeye had said. He walked away swiftly, heading
directly for the dwelling where Scent of Violets would be
already asleep. The old man would be snoring, having
felt too tired to attend Council. But there was something
here he had not understood, some undercurrent that
bothered him.

It was Hawkeye. His invitation, and then the
way he stood back until the accusation had been
completely repulsed before taking the lead.   And the
smug look on The Deer. It was a set-up. But why?
What had he done that was so bad, or stupid, or....

Nothing came, but he was deeply troubled. He
went to his mat, but lay long into the darkness without
sleep.

* * *   * * *   * * *

Sun God came, melting away the last of the haze
to provide his heat from an azure sky. When the rays
reached into the canyon, He Who Conquers and The Deer

were already far from the village, walking along like two old friends, chatting and looking around. For He Who Conquers, it was a necessary acting job.

He had spent the previous sun trying to analyze the feeling of the people, so disturbed that he gave little time to the possibilities that might arise in the race. Rain Water had noticed his preoccupation, and given some insights from his own background as a rebel, but seemed as troubled at He Who Conquers at the Council actions. Yet, it was he who proposed that Scent of Violets keep an eye to see if any of the allies of The Deer went down the canyon at any time after the two left. If so, Rain Water would give a lad an arrowhead to climb to the top and send up a smoke.

He Who Conquers watched the trail closely as it followed the creek, making mental notes about the places where they would have to climb a bank to keep moving swiftly. Part of the time they would actually run in the water. He had no desire to turn into a wrong canyon, though that did not seem to likely.

"You traveled far to get here," The Deer said, being the perfect conversationalist that Rain Water had warned him about. "So did you run a lot, or just walk?"

He Who Conquers caught the implications of the question, and shrugged. "Mostly walked." It was a lie, but he had carried a significantly large pack, which The Deer had seen, and it was very plausible. "I only ran a couple times, the one time to escape the Others." He remembered his lie to Council and covered it.

Both runners carried only a knife for defense should they meet something dangerous, and He Who Conquers felt reasonably sure he was superior in its use, especially since he knew how to throw it so well. It was a ploy he had long planned to use should he get into a knife fight.

They trotted for a time to keep the muscles from tightening due to a constant walking motion, and stopped twice to drink water from the creek. He Who Conquers was most careful of how he drank and his proximity to The Deer at all times, usually a step or two behind as if he were not sure of the direction they were going.

A large cave appeared as the canyon terminated

in a dead end. The sun was near its zenith, and they stopped and sat in the sun to eat the small lunch each carried. When they had finished, they lay back on the sand and rested, though both spoke occasionally.

"Well, are you ready for the grind?" He Who Conquers finally asked, feeling rested and ready.

The Deer grinned, and there was something in his eyes that gave He Who Conquers reason to be alert. "Whenever you are."

"Then I say let the wolf howl."

They stood, and he allowed The Deer to walk a few steps to indicate a place to start. When they stood ready, about four paces apart, The Deer grinned. The creek bent to rising-sun and a smaller runlet came in from setting-sun. The snow had increased the size of both.

"You say the word. I challenged you to run."

He Who Conquers acted entirely unsuspecting, and said, "Alright, when I say go, we go." At a nod from his opponent, he said, "Toe the mark, ready, go."

He said it conversationally, and, when The Deer took his first step, he sprinted. It caught The Deer by surprise, and at first he stepped up his pace to try to keep close, but apparently decided that was foolish. He dropped back into his best gait.

He Who Conquers quickly shot ahead by about two stone throws and then settled back into his normal long-legged pace for distance running. He was a bit winded, but when he finally managed the second wind, he felt good. The practice running had given him an unquestionable lift, and he felt strong. His pace, due to his long legs, was wide and consistent. He counted both his pace and breathing for a time, to be sure he was holding to his best rhythm.

When he turned along the main canyon where it intersected with a lesser canyon, he trotted along the edge of the water, and glancing back saw nothing of The Deer.

He began to wonder if he had mistaken the intentions for the race, although he was in no way ready to feel secure yet. He was glad for the compactness of the sand, a result of the recent moisture, which gave excellent footing. Again he was glad for his use of moccasins. The Deer ran in sandals with straps around the ankles to keep them on securely, but they tended to be stiffer, not allowing the feet to roll with the strides.

There were some dwellings scattered along the sides of the canyon floor, and people had watched them go down the canyon. Now these same people stood silently and watched him run past going up.

He stopped and sipped some water, then immediately hit stride again, still seeing nothing of The Deer. If not for the stream of water, he would have wondered if he were lost. He knew he was well ahead, and had no worry of a threat from him. It was only what might lie ahead...and it was then he saw the smoke far ahead, coming from above the great rock under which Open Stone lay, in a long single thread that reached high into the heavens.

He missed a beat, and had to bring his pace back into control again or lose his precious rhythm. So, he now knew The Deer had sent out friends to delay and probably challenge him, which would have to be soon. He was nearing two-thirds the way back.

He could almost see the smirk on his lagging opponent. He would be smugly confident that the race was his because his challenger could not finish. The thought made him angry, and again he had to fight for control or lose his rhythm.

He turned a corner, and there, sitting against a wall of the canyon, was a young man he had seen but never met, a pouty, obese face on a body that had been working hard to lift the rock for the next competition. He was suddenly very happy for the soft sand that had made his approach quiet, and it gave him a couple extra steps before the young man saw him. He came to his feet with a lunge, but having chosen his seat on the inside of the corner, to be unseen until the runner turned the bend, he was too late. He Who Conquers sprinted past, but the effort had a devastating effect on his legs and breathing. He had run long enough that the sprint was almost more than he was capable of doing. The air coming into his lungs burned, until he could almost taste blood.

The young man hurled a rock, but missed badly, and followed, at the same time emitting a shrill whistle that had to be a signal to someone ahead. At the next curve of the canyon, he met them. Two of them, standing not two strides apart. He had seen both, but did not know their names. They looked like brothers, their body features much alike. Both held large rocks.

They were expecting him to pull up, to be startled into a confrontation, but with the third man not far behind and The Deer still coming, that would prove to be fatal. He acted as though he were going to stop, then jerked his knife from its sheath and ran right at them.

It astonished them, and they jerked back. He swiped at one with his knife, then drove his shoulder into the second as he broke between them, the knife narrowly missing the one on the right, and then he was past them at his full sprint, but zig-zagging, now almost gagging for breath but frightened enough to bring more adrenaline.

It took the two a moment to recover. The one on the ground had to scramble to regain his rocks. The other hurled his, and it grazed his left shoulder, almost hitting his ear. The second bounced beside him. The one who had fallen was unable to throw his stones before He Who Conquers was out of range. They broke into a sprint, but were several paces behind as he raced up the canyon, his legs beginning to feel like lead after the long run, including the two sudden sprints. In spite of that, he pushed himself while the hair on the back of his neck prickled and his breath came in jerks and gasps, his thighs growing tight. He was beginning to see ravens in his head, and wondered if his legs were going to continue to function. He was all out of rhythm, almost terrified, and running with nothing but sheer will power.

He could not remember the landmarks well enough along this stretch to know how close to the village he might be, but he kept pushing, forcing each long stride that he knew would have been able to far out-distance such men if he was at full strength. The water led him.

He glanced back once more over his right shoulder, and they were actually farther behind than he thought! In fact, it seemed they only ran half-heartedly! The realization gave him a new shot of energy, though he kept the pace the same.

Then came the thought that perhaps there were yet more men ahead! If so, he was a dead man. He had little energy left, and could not rely on his knife to save him from so many.

But as he turned the next bend in the canyon, there was a spire along the cliff to his left. He knew immediately that he was approaching the end, nearing the village, and it was that which had slowed them down. They had missed their chance. He was safe.

Another slight bend in the high-walled canyon, and yet another, and then he was in sight of the village. Almost everyone was outside, doing something to occupy their time while they waited for the lead runner to come into view.

As he neared the end, there was no sound. Instead, except for a couple of dogs that began to bark, it was almost a stunned silence. Rain Water sat against the first building in full sunlight, and Scent of Violets sat on the edge of the roof of the dwelling, feet dangling just above him.

Rain Water came to his feet when he saw the runner, then turned to Scent of Violets and helped her drop from the roof to stand beside him. She raised a fist in the air, a signal that she was welcoming her favorite coming in as the winner, and Rain Water gave him a nod. He had a look of pride in him again, though he appeared to be washed out.

His legs felt like new willow shoots, unable to carry him any farther, and he was gasping for breath. There was nothing left for that final sprint most runners enjoyed when they saw the finish line with its cheering spectators. Only no one was cheering save Scent of Violets, whose clapping and encouragement sounded muted in the great outdoors.

He ran to the building and leaned against the wall with his two hands, his feet out behind him and spraddled. It was agony. He could not remember when he had last felt like this. The shoulder wound was the closest, though that was a different kind of pain.

Scent of Violets brought him a small olla with water, and he took it while giving her a grateful glance. He took only one swallow and leaned back, aware that the villagers were staring at him, but also wondering what had become of The Deer. It was eight or ten stone throws to the first bend in the canyon, and no one had appeared yet.

"You've been hurt!" Scent of Violets exclaimed, and for the first time he noticed the blood on his shoulder from where the rock grazed him.

He smiled tiredly, but said nothing, while she ran to her dwelling for some cloth to clean the wound. While she was gone, he looked at the grinning Rain Water.

Rain Water, who appeared so feeble the last halfmoon, was animated again. He clapped He Who Conquers on the right shoulder and went to speak to some of the men, where it appeared he collected a bet from one. Betting on a race was a favorite pastime, and the glum faces around indicated whom most considered the favorite.

Even the face of Hawkeye held no glee, one who thought He Who Conquers was possibly a god had still bet against him! Inside He Who Conquers laughed, but outwardly he was too tired to respond. All he felt was pain...all over. It was yet a long while before The Deer showed at the bend in the canyon, still running but much slower. Not only had he lost, he had lost badly.

He Who Conquers took two more swallows of water, still leaning against the wall, watching his opponent stagger into the village, his exhaustion nearly bringing him to the ground. Scent of Violets returned and began to daub at the blood and cut, and he heard her say quietly, "He deserves to die, the coyote!"

He glanced at her, a smile to thank her for the ministrations to him. Her studied disregard for his smile was betrayed with a smile of her own. It was then he saw the blood on the face and arms of The Deer, and a sudden wave of fear and nausea swept through him.

Several people nearby turned to look at He Who Conquers, and he immediately knew what had happened. The Deer had made his friends bloody him so he could blame it on He Who Conquers, and taint the race! He was not going to be a loser without a solid alibi! He had gotten one up on He Who Conquers!

Horrified, and for a moment stunned, he stood

and stared at the gathering crowd, knowing exactly what was being said. Disgusted, he muttered loud enough to be heard by Scent of Violets, "That lying loser had his friends mess him up so it looked like I attacked him! He is both a coyote and a liar!" Then he turned and entered the dwelling of Scent of Violets.

She followed him in, and a moment later Rain Water entered. He lay on his mat, still struggling for air, and stared at the cold firepit.

"So how did it happen?" Rain Water asked, a touch of suspicion mixed with the honest question.

He Who Conquers lay a moment, then said, "I don't know. He must have had his own friends beat him so he could say it wasn't a fair race! He's both a liar and a coyote! He'll not accept that he was beaten fair and square!" He was agitated, his two listeners silent until he calmed. "I was so far ahead of him I could never spot him from one end to another of straight stretches of the canyon. I had sprinted at the beginning to give him no chance for treachery, and he had his friends lying along the canyon. But they were too lazy to go very far, and when I got past them, they were too close to the village to chase far, and, except for this rock bruise, I got away clean. So when The Deer comes along, he has them bring some blood to his head and make it look like I injured him to win. He's a liar...a lousy liar!"

He sipped the water again, his breath less labored. Rain Water stared at him a while, then said, his voice almost to the point of mirth, "He lost the race, and still has to endure pain from having injured himself? This is good! The man knows he's a loser, and has the village thinking he's a victim!" There came a chuckle, which stopped very suddenly. "You know what he's done, my son? He set it up so no one will care if you're found dead somewhere. No one accepts a cheater. It would be fair retribution. He has just become even more dangerous."

They sat in silence, the full implications of that sinking in, when Rain Water suddenly coughed, grabbed his chest with both hands and pitched forward on his face. Scent of Violets emitted a cry of alarm, and He Who Conquers moved swiftly to the old man. Lifting the almost airy-light body, he turned the man and laid him flat on the floor, the head on his mat.

"What is it, Old One? Are you alright?"

The old man had his eyes closed, his hand reaching out, clutching, grasping, and Scent of Violets put her hand in his.

"The gods...they...they take me," he whispered, with both sets of ears close to his face. "The witch of darkness...dark comes...getting into the cold...I go. My son, mate...." He choked, then seemed to rest a moment. "My son, you must...you...mate...." Again he went silent, swallowing hard, then gagging, his left hand digging at his bony chest.

"Fa-Fa...please...."   Scent of Violets had tears running down her cheeks.

"Hush!"   His voice was firm but weak.   "You must mate He...."   Again he coughed.   "Mate He Who...Conquers." He was rigid, the pain racking him. "Promise me, my...my son!" His body went rigid, then totally relaxed. Breathing stopped, and the old man was dead.

Scent of Violets laid her face on his neck and wept. He Who Conquers sat on his knees, staring at the eyes that saw nothing, then with his right index finger closed the eyes, feeling a frog in his throat and unable to swallow it. He had no chance to tell the old one what the man wished to know, and wondered what he would have said had he had been given time to reply.

Could he mate this pretty young woman without direction from the Great One? And what of his staying in the village now, after what had just happened? He was as imperiled as he had been back home! And he lived in the dwelling of a young lady who would now be just as endangered as he!

Scent of Violets wept, heavy sobs shaking her body like the quakies in a windstorm. Unable to take it, he took his spear, axe and knife and went out into the dark.

People were inside, as he wished. Quickly he went up the canyon toward the cliff and the open spaces where the bison had come. There he ran into the darkness, trotting slowly, unsure of where he was going or why. He was exhausted, his legs feeling heavy and unsure, but he went straight away from the village. All he knew was that he needed to talk to the Great One, to see if he heard and was still assisting him.

For a long time he continued to trot, half-stumbling over the rocks and knots of grass, until he came to a rock that rose straight from the flat ground high into the heavens. He stopped at the base, wrapped himself, and sat down. There, for a long time, he just sat and let his mind play with the many things that bothered him. The feelings of the villagers after the race, mating, Scent of Violets and the old man now dead, home, some of his successes and subsequent troubles, his dream and his fear.

Then he was speaking aloud.

"Oh, mighty Great One! I am pierced to the heart!
    I am troubled, and I am confused!
I no longer know which way to turn,
    Nor do I recognize any direction at all!

Why have you brought me these troubles?
    Why have you made things so difficult to know?
It seems that everything I do goes sour,
    Until I wonder if life is worth living!

He paused, fighting back feelings of frustration and anger, suddenly sure that the Great One was like all the other gods, playing with a man like a bird plays with a mouse it has caught. He leaned his head back and closed his eyes, visions of night fears running through his mind as he realized he was far from his dwelling and it was late in the darkness. The witches of the black skies were everywhere; for the first time in over two winters, he felt something akin to the terror he had felt with he was a young lad on duty in the fields after sunset.

Pulling his heavy cloak tighter, his body aching almost unbearably from the long strain of the race and not aided by the long way he had just come to be alone, he fell asleep. And again his mind went into action while he slept.

He was running again, through canyons and

across fields where wild animals watched him run. Then he was in a great canyon, not terribly deep but quite wide, sweat dripping from his face as he realized he was in danger, and he began to run. Then he was on The Top again, and walking hand-in-hand with his mate, the fragrance there and then gone. There was his mu, her screams making him shiver, and his fa dead and decaying, with his still-screaming mate dead beside him. Both were missing their scalps.

And then he was standing beside a burned-out village, which he studied for a time before he realized it was his own. The horror of it was terrifying, but beside him stood a woman, which he recognized as his mate. Had he brought her back with him, or was he already living there? If so, had he fought the Others that had wreaked such destruction?

And his mate was calmly waiting for him to speak, but again he could not see her face, though he smelled the fragrance of her. It was beautiful, intoxicating...and enchanting.

It was full sun when he awakened. In the darkness, he had seen so much, been so far, considered so many things, that he felt more tired than he had been before he slept. He got stiffly to his feet, wondering why he was here and hardly remembering how he got here. He moved around the rock and looked up at the round-domed mountain nearby, and sat down again.

And he slept. Again came the dream, a time of dusky meditation, and more sleep. Then yet again the dream, and another blurry wakefulness.

Then he was fully awake, and without thought, in the early sun, turned around the rock and headed back.

It was late into the sun when he climbed down the steep path and stumbled into the village, and he ignored the many stares as he entered the dwelling where he had last seen Rain Water alive. It was empty. The body of the old man was gone, as was Scent of Violets.

Violets! That was it! The fragrance he had smelled in his visions was the delicate violet! All along, the Great One had been pointing him to his mate, and he had not deciphered the clue! This was the one he was to mate, this woman in whose dwelling he had been living!

He sat numbly against the wall, staring at the cold firepit and wondering if Scent of Violets would return. If she did, would she still want to mate with him? He knew total confusion again, unsure of how he would broach the topic with her, wishing Rain Water still lived in order that he could promise what the old man had so wanted to hear.

Leaning against the wall, his blanket pulled about him, he fell asleep. There, Scent of Violets stood beside him while another young lady was tied to the post.

16

He was warm, very warm. And he could smell meat--the meat of bison--roasting over the fire. That was when he realized he was awake, Scent of Violets leaning over the fire with tears streaming down her face.

"I'm sorry about Rain Water," he said quietly.

She glanced up, then back down. "He is in Earth Mu."

Startled, he nodded but said nothing. Were these people so different from his own? It took up to four suns for the spirit of a person to find Sipapu. After that the smoke of the fire would lift his body to the gods, who would welcome him and give him life again inside Earth Mu.

"You were gone so long I thought you might not return." He realized she was looking at him timidly.

"I just had to speak to the Great One."

"And he spoke to you?"

He was on dangerous ground, for as yet, no one truly believed or understood what he knew to be true. "He did."

She was silent, but he could see she was trying to understand and to formulate her next question. Instead, she seemed to change the subject entirely.

"You must be famished."

"I am."

"You haven't eaten since last you were here?"

He let a smile touch the corners of his mouth at her concern. "No, why?"

"That was five suns ago!"

For a moment he was blank. "Five suns? But I just went...I mean, it was...." He realized he was not at all sure of what he meant. "What do you mean, five suns? I slept last darkness at a prayer rock to no-sun."

"Over one darkness?" Now it was she who was nonplussed. "No, it was five darknesses since you left."

His mind reeled. Five? No way. He slept, and had his vision, and awakened to return here. "You jest. I went to no-sun and slept...." He'd already said that.

Her eyes pierced his as she sought to understand him. "Fa-Fa went to Earth Mu at the rising of Sun God, and he laid four suns on the death bier before he was buried."

For the first time he understood. He'd slept with the visions for five suns, oblivious to time, understanding why he was so hungry. "I was gone...five suns? But I thought...I mean...I slept but one darkness...I mean...." There was nothing left to say. She understood and he did, too. "No wonder I have this great hunger!"

Her tears hung to her cheeks, but her eyes were dry as she laughed softly at his bewilderment. "Your Great One must have had much to say!"

He stared into the fire, too perplexed to feel the humor she tried to share with him. She watched, not sure of what he was thinking, the smile leaving her face.

"You know The Deer claims you injured him before the race started." She had to get his mind elsewhere.

"I knew he would make some such claims. He's trying to save face by being a liar."

"Many believe him."

"Is that a surprise? He's one of you; I'm the interloper."

She looked up at him from the meat she still

turned. "You must go now?"

"It's no longer possible to stay here."

She nodded. "I will go with you."

"You're sure that's what you want?"

She saw immediately that his attitude toward her had changed. He made no excuses, gave no arguments. "There is nothing here for me any more. Did you not hear Fa-Fa's last words?"

"I heard him."

"What would you have replied had he lived long enough to hear?"

"I would have said yes."

Her hands, busy turning the spit, stopped. "I shall be your mate?"

"If it is what you're sure you want."

"But you do not?"

"I wanted to from the time I first laid eyes on you, standing beside the doorway as I came into the village. But the Great One had given me no sign. No, that's not true. He did, but I wasn't able to interpret the sign."

"And now you know?"

"It was a fragrance. I smelled it many times during visions the Great One gave me. But until last darkness," he paused, realizing that darkness had been through five suns, "I never could recognize it. It was the delicate violet. I'm sure."

She looked up and the tears were flowing again. "You wish to mate with me?"

He nodded. "Yes."

"Then you will take me with you when you go?"

"Yes."

"I sing again. I wish I could tell Fa-Fa."

They lapsed into a shy silence, and she handed him a large piece of bison tongue. He picked off a small piece and dropped it into the fire for the gods, then ate, drinking tea as he ate. She sat and watched until he was stuffed and gave her an appreciative burp, then she ate.

He watched her clean the utensils, and put some small pieces of wood into the fire to keep it going. He lay on his mat, propped on one elbow, studying her face in the light of the flickering fire. "You are sure you wish to travel so far? It will be both tiring and dangerous."

"With you, at least I would die happy. Here...?"
She let her voice tail off.

He felt tongue-tied, his mind in a jumble of
thoughts and apprehension as she completed her tasks.

"The people talk about us," she said softly. "The
ladies are clicking their tongues, and the men laugh."

He smiled. "Is it fun to be the center of
attention?"

She stared at him a moment, then grinned.
"Now that you mention it, it is."

He chuckled and she giggled. "Perhaps they are
right."

She laughed. "After this sun, they will be."

He watched her rise and come to him, laying
beside him, and on this sun when death stalked the
family, they removed her chastity belt and burned it.

"You would be The Stick at my Opening?" she
giggled. "I have no relatives for a ceremony. Will the
gods still smile on you if you do it?"

He took from his neck the pouch from Little
Dove that he had worn since leaving The Top, and
handed it to her. She appeared surprised, then squealed
with delight at the small, pregnant figurine.

"The Goddess of Fertility will surely honor this!"
She hugged him and then fell into his arms. They rolled
on the mat, and it was there they awkwardly succeeded
in completing their mating.

* * *   * * *   * * *

"I'm taller than my people, as I'm taller than
yours. I have thinner and longer legs; my eyes are hazel
instead of dark brown or black. My hair is more brown
than black. My cheekbones are less pronounced. I'm
sort of a freak among my people, even as I am here.

"I desired from my earliest realizations of
manhood to mate with one in my village who was like
me. She was taller than the women, more delicate than
the wild rose, more petite than the forest orchid. Her
laugh was like the wind singing in the trees, and her
smile could make a dreary sun turn to brightness. She
was made to mate the son of the chief, and I ran away
to avoid living where she would be the mate of someone
else.

"You've made me realize that the Great One saved me for you, and you'll be the one I love. When I woke up the past sun, I felt like life was worth nothing. Now I live again."

She lay in his arms while he spoke, his eyes closed and his fingers lightly caressing her bare back. She wanted to hear more, to not break the spell, and did not respond with words.

"I have found many times that in the worst of situations, the Great One has given me the ability to escape some calamity. Yet I've not found happiness, because danger always lay just outside my own doorway. The near-mate of my childhood love, Eagle Eye, tried to kill me before I left The Top. He was jealous that Little Dove loved me, and not him. I was shot in this shoulder from behind, and I killed the man who did it, not knowing who it was until he lay dying. It was the older brother of Eagle Eye. When I left, Eagle Eye recruited four other men to come with him, to track me and try to kill me. One was pulled under the moving waters by the gods, I think, and I escaped rest. A few suns later I found the hunters with whom I came to your village.

"The chief of our village gave me my name; before he did, I was called He Who Runs with the Wind. I've never lost a race. It was my name because everywhere I went, I ran, and I ran faster and farther than anyone else."

"If you called The Deer a liar, and challenged him to a shorter race, in full view of the entire village, you would win?"

He nodded as he spoke. "He's no faster than some on The Top. He could never win."

"Then that's what you must do. You have to call him a liar and make him race against you where the village can watch the entire race. And your challenge must be issued where many hear it. Make it impossible for him to refuse to run. Dare him, shame him, whatever it takes. It might change everything for you. The only ones you need fear then would be The Deer and those of his clan. No one else would bother you."

He thought on that awhile, then said, "You, my lady, are like a sly fox...no, more like a lynx."

She smiled. "What is The Top like? Is it a

mountain?"

He chuckled. "It's a mesa, like these around
here, with many canyons cutting out of it, and a big one
separating it from another to mid-sun. There are many
trees, like the ones above Open Stone on the mesa top.
The canyons are not as deep as this one except near the
moving waters, and there are many caves. I think, some
sun far away, The People will live in those caves...to
escape the Others who attack from time to time."

She still enjoyed the hand that almost absently
continued to caress her, not wanting to leave its soft
touch. "You'll go back there?"

"Yes, sometime. My visions point to it
happening, and I see myself as still looking like I am
now."

"I'll enjoy seeing your people, and being your
mate there."

He chuckled again. "You are a dreamer, my
pretty one. Not many women would enjoy any place
that's not where they were dropped."

They lay silently, until darkness fell outside.
After a long time, they coupled again, and fell asleep
with no thought for food. In the darkness, they
awakened, having changed positions very little.

"Why must you stay here any longer?"

"It's Snowtime. I wouldn't wish to be out on the
country I saw and have a deep snow fall or one of those
icy winds when it's so cold." He grew serious. "Besides,
I have a few things to learn here before I return. Your
cornfields are larger, and in the sand, too. I have to
know why."

"Many winters ago, the *Mountain-That-Smokes*
tried to swallow a god, and the god grew angry. He
hurled a huge stone into the top, and the dust and
smoke from it settled over this entire country. The skies
grew dark, and many feared the gods had come to
destroy us all. But when it was clear again, the ground
was more fertile than ever before, and our crops were
always healthy. The Goddess of Fertility gave us good
seed, and we planted wisely. And the God of Rain came,
and his water was heavier and stayed in the ground
instead of leaving so fast.

"That is why our crops are so strong. The gods

gave us new soil. Is not your soil as good? The great cloud of dust went far away into no-sun and rising-sun?"

"I don't remember. Anyway, we need more knowledge on how to grow good crops, and we need to know more about cooking for variety, and we need to know more about pottery that can stand heat for a long time, as yours seem to do, and we need to know about masonry. The list of things I don't know goes on. I hope to learn."

"Much of it I can show you. Some of it is strange to me. Will you have time to learn it all before some would try to harm you?"

"I'm getting very hungry," he said teasingly. "Then you can start teaching me what I need to know."

"I'll teach you while we travel," she said with a giggle. "Otherwise you might decide to leave me behind."

"Never," he responded, giving her posterior a gentle pinch. "There are other things you must teach me, too."

She wriggled away from his hand and slapped playfully at it, then got up and fixed them a pre-sunrise breakfast.

* * *   * * *   * * *

"You're a liar." He said it quietly, but in the tense emotions of the courtyard, where most of the villagers still were congregated because of the warm sun and many activities, it was heard by many.

The confrontation had been evident since early in the sun. When He Who Conquers had entered the courtyard, The Deer had bristled with defensiveness. But nothing had happened until several had made cutting remarks about a sneaky runner, one who would do anything to win a race, even to surprising his opponent with injuries.

"I'm a what?" The response from The Deer was quick and sharp, for he had as yet said nothing to He Who Conquers, preferring asides to his friends.

"You're a liar." The voice was the same, just slightly louder.

"And I say you're the cheater! Not being one of our village, whom do you think the people here will believe, you or me?"

"I care little what they believe, because I know what you know, that I won the race fair and square. The truth is, you're a liar. You spread lies to make people think I injured you before we started the race, when you had your own friends do it to save face because you were beaten so badly. You think lying will make your sick conscience feel the better?" He snorted derisively, deliberately setting up The Deer for his challenge.

"You lie!"

"I can prove to the people who lies. Let the two of us run again, all of it in sight of the people of your village. We'll never leave their sight, and run around markers within view of everyone until a certain number of circles are made. You can choose the number of laps, and you can even design the course, so long as it stays where the people can see the entire race."

The Deer snorted his disgust. "You think that'll prove anything?" He was in the trap and knew it, but he could not think of a way out.

"Only one thing, of course. Who the better runner really is. You've tried to say I'm only a better runner because I injured you. I can prove otherwise. Either you accept my challenge, or I'll not only call you a liar, I'll challenge you to something much more drastic."

The meaning was clear. There was a murmuring among the throng of people listening, and one voice called out, "It's fair!"

The Deer stared at He Who Conquers, hatred and anger in his rigid stance and clenched fists. He was caught in his lie unless he accepted the challenge, and if he lost the race, it would be proven that he had lied, as well. The silence dragged, while more calls came from the crowd to support the run.

"We'll run when Sun God comes again. You can lay out the course, or let me, I could care less. You say I cheat, I say you lie."

His entire conversation with the agitated The Deer was quiet and calm, completely opposite the manner of his opponent. While the crowd buzzed, and The Deer stared, He Who Conquers turned away, turning to the dwelling where Scent of Violets continued to mourn.

She had missed the entire confrontation, but she

pushed her hair back and smiled.

"I'll race The Deer on the new sun. He's afraid."

She nodded. "He'll try to cheat."

He Who Conquers smiled. "In sight of the villagers all the time? I think not."

"Never underestimate desperation."

He grinned. "I have mated a lynx."

She shook her head. "I'm only cautious. I don't want you injured. After all, an injured mate doesn't function well!"

He laughed, then went out to leave her to mourn. He knew it was best to stay close to the village, and be sure people were around at all times, or he might have a run-in with The Deer or his friends. He jogged out and back, out and back, aware of a few people who kept track of his progress. After he had run for some time, he found a sunny place and lay down, and it was there Hawkeye found him.

"Hola, my friend."

"Hola, Hawkeye. You're betting on the race?"

"You wish to wager on your own race?"

"Are you betting I'll lose again?" He smiled to show he was humored by the bet Hawkeye had lost. He was still guarded with the man, the Council still on his mind.

The grin came. "No, not a second time. I know The Deer, and I knew he'd cheat if he could. That's what I based my bets on. That and the fact you didn't know him or his deceit."

"I knew."

"So I learned. No, this time I carry bets for you. If he can't cheat, he can't win. With the people watching, he won't cheat. I've found many who believe The Deer will win, and their wampum is good. You keep it up, you'll make me a wealthy man."

He Who Conquers laughed. Had he been privy to some information that could jeopardize his life. And what of his role at Council? And why had he not invited him to his kiva for talk or games? And why had he not offered to spend some time with him? Something was not right, but he was not sure what.

Then he realized there was nothing new under the sun. He was already living on borrowed time.

Everything he did was just marking time until The Deer and his friends tried something. Every time he went out in the darkness it would become a new wager, with his life the ante.

Still, he had much to learn. He could not leave yet or he would be sacrificing the information he wanted, the knowledge he so desperately needed; so he would have to be careful, be sure to have someone with him whom he could trust, whoever that might be. And he wanted to use more of his time enjoying his new mate... indoors!

* * *   * * *   * * *

Little Dove looked across the room at her mate with venom. Her infant, named Son of Vision because his birth had been seen in one, nestled in her arm and fed at a breast.

"Your friends laugh at you!"

He was more angry than she, and it was debatable which detested the other more. Their raised voices had been heard many times to the amusement of the village.

"You think that's funny!"

"Yes, I do! You're slovenly, you're lazy, you have no decency about you, and you have a vile temper!"

"And you think you don't?" His voice was a shout, though hers was very quiet, even though said through clenched teeth.

"If I have, it's because you made me that way!" Her infant lost the nipple and she had to guide him back. "Why don't you just get out! Go play with your friends! Maybe Man Who Chases Spirits will let you romp with one of his priestesses!"

"I don't romp with them! You speak like one who defies the gods! I meet the needs of the Goddess of Fertility, nothing more! Don't give me reason to leave you permanently!"

"I wish you would! I have no need for such a child in my home!" Her emphasis on the word child made him flinch. "I already have one to take care of. You can't even make your male member work anymore!" She said it loud enough so that anyone outside the door would hear.

His face was rose-red. His jugulars stood out

along his neck, and his eyes bore into hers. "You should talk, woman! You're about as capable of being a woman as a newborn!"

Again her voice was slightly raised as she repeated, "It's because you made me that way! I have yet to find you a male worth loving! You certainly can't please a woman with your flaccid member! I've felt nothing of you for moons!"

He nearly struck her. His hand was raised, but at the last moment he dropped it, jerked around and left the dwelling. His attitude told her he would not return this darkness, and she smiled to herself as she looked down at her suckling child and teased the right cheek with her index finger.

"Well, little one, we're rid of the snake again. It's just you and I again. Don't you wish you had a fa who was worth the dirt he walked on? But of course, you do. He's not here, though he'll come before long. You just grow up to be a real man. One who can please his mate and who can be of value to The People."

She leaned back and took a deep breath, then changed her son from one breast to the other. "I wonder if your real fa has found a mate. I suspect he has, because he's too much a man not to attract the eye of a woman. Perhaps she'll know better how to please him than I. The man in your life makes me wonder if I can ever again mean anything to a real man."

She heard sounds outside the doorway and in a moment her mu entered.

"Your mate left looking a bit tight. You fight again?"

"Do we do anything else? He's become so insecure he can no longer make his male member work. I wonder that he hasn't looked for another mate while he's still young enough to take his pick."

"He hates He Who Conquers too much to allow you the freedom. He's just too conceited to know how to handle himself, and too proud to ask for advice."

"I think it's time to put his things outside and make him go away. I've tried to make him do it on his own, but he lacks manhood so much he has no idea how to be one."

Her mother nodded. "It wouldn't hurt my

feelings. I weary of your word games." She let her bony
frame down, feeling every joint ache. It had gotten to
where she felt chilled even when it was warm, and it
grew colder with each darkness. "You've been most
venomous." She said it without accusation.

Little Dove smiled and her face softened. "I do
make a good rattlesnake, do I not? He has no idea that
I plan each confrontation before he arrives so he has no
chance at all."

"He never had a chance with you."

"If he weren't such a little boy, one who knew
how to deal with people better than himself--and you
know who I refer to--I would have tried. He gave me no
choice. I've hated him since long before he took the
manhood rites."

"I know."

"Will I ever have He Who Conquers again, Mu?
Will I be mate to a real man? Will I know what
coupling can be between mates who love each other? I
yearn for him to enter me again, give me seed that's
worthy of a man. I want his children." A sob was in her
voice, but she held control. "Will he ever lie with me
again, Mu?"

"You've asked me that too many times, my sweet.
I have no idea. The gods have never chosen to let me
know."

Little Dove looked down at her son and was
silent for a while. When she looked up, there were tears
on her lashes. "I love him, Mu. I've never been able to
stop. And if he brings a mate back with him I'll...well,
I...it'll be very difficult to know how to act."

"Perhaps you'll know how to act because he'll
love her. When the time comes, you'll know what to do."

"Will I? I wonder."

17

The sun crawled over the horizon and turned the sides of the canyon aglow with its gold and reddish hues. Up early, He Who Conquers was quick to slowly jog around the track to be sure of its perimeters and where it lay in relation to the village. Then he saw something that brought a knowing smile to his lips...the trail led around a pinnacle-rock, across the opening to a short canyon that was full of stones.

The three markers were stones marked with white paint, easily identifiable to one running and turned to give a long view as a runner approached, and he quickly moved them so the trail cut in front of the rock, chuckling as he did so, then finished the check. As he arrived back at the starting line, three men came from their kiva and stood in the sun, stretching and yawning.

The Village Crier appeared, and climbed to the roof of his dwelling, glanced around, cupped his hands around his mouth and in a stentorian voice, which echoed down the canyon, announced the new sun. "Sun God comes! He gives us another sun of strength. This is the sun when we see the race to prove the fastest man in the village. Arise, you who still sleep, and greet Sun God with vigor." As if on cue, people came from dwellings and kivas. Morning prayers could be heard and activity began everywhere.

The Deer came, shaking his arms and jogging in place, his eyes giving He Who Conquers the once over and then ignoring him. There were scabs on his face and right shoulder, a sense of satisfaction to He Who Conquers, who remembered the thoughts of Rain Water about one who not only lost, but who also had to endure the pain of senseless self-inflicted wounds. It would all be to no avail, for shortly he would prove the man a liar.

The crowd grew, a quiet crowd with sleep still in their eyes. It was cool, but there was no snow and the skies were clear. It was, he thought, the perfect sun for a good run. He still had some of the stiffness he had felt after the long run.

The Runt, the man who had accused him at Council, was one of three judges, Dog Man and a man known as Big Rock the others. A rope lay for a starting line, and the two runners took their places. Big Rock came to them and stood in front, eyed them, then said, "You've both studied the route. You'll circle the route twice. The rules include the right to trip or throw your opponent if it'll help you win. Are you both ready?"

At the signal--a shout--they started to run. As before, he sprinted to keep The Deer from any trickery, only this time he knew it would be grueling. His legs still felt the effects of the long run, and before he was halfway to the big rock, he felt the muscles in his thighs begin to protest. The consolation was that The Deer would feel the same. His early sprint had been insufficient to catch the former He Who Runs with the Wind, and he was laid back and thinking while he ran.

He Who Conquers was well in front when he came to the rock, and took the new route he had created by moving the stones. Behind him he heard a curse, and knew there were men behind the rock waiting for him. The Deer meant to see he never came out from behind it!

The Deer pushed hard trying to catch up after discovering the changed route, and when He Who

Conquers was turning into the second lap--the last--the gap had closed to five strides. People shouted to them, most giving encouragement to The Deer, but he heard his own name among the cries.

He Who Conquers made no attempt to push hard, but kept his pace, now counting as he ran. Behind him, he could hear the forced breathing of The Deer, and knew the man could never finish at the pace he was going. Keeping his pace consistent, his long legs stretching well, he allowed the tiring man to almost catch him, which came as they neared the rock for the second time. Then he kicked out for the final stretch, his longer strides quickly moving him away from The Deer. His muscles tightened, but he had no intentions of slowing. He would have plenty of time to relax when the race was history.

There was some shouting from the people near the finish line, and Scent of Violets was jumping and clapping. Seeing her was like taking a fresh breath of wind, and he pushed himself to all he had left. As he crossed the line and pulled up, he felt the muscle behind his right knee draw tight. But he tried not to show it, though the pain was sharp and almost took his breath away.

The Deer had collapsed almost a stone throw from the finish line, sprawling on the ground and trying to roll over, gasping for breath. His immediate response was disgust, realizing it was a staging, a poor act, an attempt to get pity and attention. Maybe even an attempt to throw a shadow on his loss.

Scent of Violets was beside him, watching the fallen runner. "He makes all losses a travesty. Everyone knows he's not worthy to be called a man." It was said softly for his ears only.

"Yet they prefer him to an outsider."

Scent of Violets took his elbow, feeling him compensate for the pain in his thighs, as well as the limp from the knee. "You're hurting. Come, I have some ointment that will help."

He followed her toward the dwelling, the muscles screaming in protest. It was Hawkeye who overtook them, with Dog Man beside him.

"It was a good run. What do you have left to

prove?"

Scent of Violets bristled. "He's a man! He proved it to everyone!"

He chuckled. "My, but we are defensive! Listen to what I say, pretty lady. He's a man, and I was wondering what he would do next to entertain us. Is he not something special?"

Placated only slightly, she snapped, "You say it nicely, but you meant to be cutting."

"The suspicious mind of the woman! He's my friend! Why would I want to demean him?"

He Who Conquers grinned. "Are you two like the bucks in rut? Why the hostility? I only did what needed to be done."

"And did it well," Hawkeye added. "I came to offer you congratulations, although I doubt you need it. I only wish I could still run, much less win races." He grinned his humor. "Age is a relentless adversary. And the older one gets, the more witches seem to come. Perhaps it's because of my growing weakness."

He turned and looked near the large rock where He Who Conquers had moved the stones to change the course.

"The posts you see out there, stuck in the ground, used to be one of my favorite pastimes. A target on top, a run at top speed on a path three steps off parallel to the post, throwing the spear while running...with the hope of hitting the target. Have you done that?"

He Who Conquers nodded and grinned. "But I miss more often than I hit. The standing throw for distance and accuracy are more in my line."

Hawkeye chuckled. "Honesty protects you from the troubles The Deer suffers now. But I was good at it... very good. You can ask around. Now...I just watch." His voice took on a wistful tone. "Youth has its glory."

He Who Conquers laughed. "And age its privileges. All of life cannot be full of every talent at the same time. There's something to be said for experience."

"Well said. I'll take your leave. I best see what The Deer suffers this time." He winked as he left.

He Who Conquers continued his pained walk for the dwelling, Scent of Violets walking alongside with her

hand still on his elbow.   Just as he arrived at the
doorway, a youth, who looked much like The Deer,
stopped him with a call from only a few steps away.

"Hey, you with the limp!"

He Who Conquers ignored the unpleasant
greeting and allowed Scent of Violets to enter, preparing
to follow.

"Hey, you hard of hearing?"

Again he ignored the youth and entered the
doorway, letting the cover fall back in place. The youth
came to the doorway and stood beside it.

"You must be deaf, too!"

Scent of Violets stuck her head out and said with
acid sarcasm, "What do you mean, too? Are you? You
surely have no manners!   When you speak to a
champion, you speak with respect. Now, go away, little
boy!"

He Who Conquers chuckled as she pulled back
inside and dropped the hide into place.

"You surely have a way with words, my lynx.
His ears will be burning for two suns!"

She laughed. "He's a brat. That's Little Fox,
younger brother of The Deer. He's like his big brother,
only without the ability to even seem intelligent."

They laughed together as she stirred the coals
and added wood to make the fire blaze again. Then she
started the tea reheating while she pulled out some corn
bread she had previously baked, and a sauce made from
cornflour and the juice of the bison meat, to which she
added corn meal.

While they heated, she sat beside the prone He
Who Conquers and began to knead the thighs, using a
special ointment she had made and kept in a small crock.
She alternately worked on the meal and his legs until he
fell asleep. She awakened him for his food, after which
he fell instantly asleep again.

When he awakened, she had the materials ready
for him that he had requested in order to make a tied
blanket--cotton, feathers and strands from the yucca. His
legs too painful to do any walking, he sat and worked at
the blanket the remainder of the sun, and continued the
entire next sun as well.

A new storm moved in, this one not so filled

with snow but leading in the cold that settled over the area for over a moon and a half. In the entire time, he worked on the blanket, then tanned a bison hide while leaving the hair on the one side. Then he made several moccasins from a deer hide, cutting strips of gut to use for tying them into shape. He made leggings for both of them, and a smaller cloak for Scent of Violets. Finally, he made her a smaller pack than his own.

"Sun God has returned," she announced one sunrise as he awakened to the smell of breakfast. "Your legs should be in good shape again. I suggest we go for a walk, and you can get some exercise."

"And you don't need any?" he teased.

"Of course not! I'm in good shape."

"I know," was his response, with raised eyebrows. He chuckled as he said it.

She giggled. "But, you aren't. Now, eat, so we can stretch our legs."

Snow lay ankle-deep as they walked swiftly from the village, heading to no-sun, where the bison were killed. They climbed the steep trail, Scent of Violets first so he could catch her if she slipped. Once on top, he jogged in place to keep pace with her walking, feeling the weakness in his legs from the long inactivity, but the muscles were no longer sore, and he jogged alternately with walking.

"I wish to be able to keep up with you when we leave," she said, leaving little doubt of her purpose in suggesting the walk.

He nodded. "You can be in good shape by then. It's yet two moons before we can begin, maybe three. We have time to get ready."

"But you've traveled before, and know you can do it. I haven't."

"You'll do fine when the time comes."

They returned at mid-sun. It was still cool, but before they could get to their dwelling, Little Fox came running to cut them off.

"Hey! It's the deaf one!"

He Who Conquers was annoyed, and his reply was sharp. "And what's so significant from a brat that makes me want to listen? You've said nothing worthy of my time."

"Oh, but I will! I think you're a fraud!"

"I care less what you think. I have some doubts about your ability to think at all. Why don't you just go play with the little boys? You know, those of like mentality."

Little Fox lost his congenial appearance, which had been in sharp contrast to his tongue. He swore violently, and before he could say anything more, the two ducked inside their dwelling. Little Fox stood outside their door and shouted epithets at them for some time, until He Who Conquers grew weary of it.

Angrily, he pushed the cover aside and stepped outside. "If you keep that up, you little noisy coyote, I will personally take you down and fill your mouth with dirt! I begin to wonder if you have any intelligence at all. So far, all I've heard is a long list of words a man uses only for special occasions. So get away from here! Tell your big brother to fight his own battles, and not send little boys to do it for him."

He took a quick step toward Little Fox, and the boy stepped back quickly. He laughed. "Go!"

He went back inside, ignoring the lad of twelve winters. The boy threw out a couple more words, then fell silent and left.

"I've made quite a hit among the youth," he said dryly. "But I attract sand fleas."

Scent of Violets laughed. "He has about as much social grace as his older brother. They both act like the main bull of the herd. I think The Deer has been rendered helpless for a time, but little brother thinks he has to champion his cause."

"If he comes again, I might get in trouble with his mu, because I might just take him down and fill his mouth with dirt. He needs to know he's not yet a man."

She continued to laugh. "You'll be in trouble with his mu and his aunt and his second aunt, and maybe his big sister. We might have quite a free-for-all right here in the village."

But the sun passed without further contact from Little Fox, and that darkness the snows came again. The cold stayed with them, and the village became inactive. Then, one sun, Hawkeye and Dog Man came and surprised He Who Conquers, gambling with him almost the entire sun, playing a game of chance that entailed six cross-slices of a deer antler that had colors on each of the faces, and combinations meant scores.

For almost a moon, they played the game often, sometimes in the kiva of Hawkeye, usually in the dwelling of He Who Conquers, and once in the kiva of Dog Man. There, they had several more join them, and in the end it was Hawkeye who won the most.

But snowtime dragged slowly, and witches began to move among the people. Coughing was heard around most dwellings, an old man died while walking from his kiva to the dwelling of his mate, and several older people were so ill they were confined to their mats. Children became irritable and there was crying and bickering; young men became argumentive; young women often screamed invectives at their siblings; men left their dwellings where mus screeched at children, to stay in kivas, seeking quiet.

He Who Conquers and his mate went for frequent strolls in the cold, braving icy winds and knee-deep snow, but trying to maintain a certain muscle-tone that would allow them to travel when the snows melted and the Goddess of Fertility regained control of the earth.

Shortly before the first sign of light a moon later, the God of Snowtime lost his grip, and Sun God regained control. A Chinook came roaring from the mountains, and in but two suns there was no snow in sight. Temperatures moderated, cabin fever was alleviated, and activity burst into the village.

The celebration of the defeat of Snowtime was discussed, men began to think of planting, Rain Man began to send messages to Rain God, Sun Watcher began his watch to the time of planting, and the Hunters began to think of the first hunting trip before Planting. Hawkeye and He Who Tracks spent time with He Who Conquers, showing him how they built with stone, then explaining what they had learned of growing beans.

He Who Conquers and Scent of Violets continued to prepare for the trip they would make. They would not yet return to his people, but would go to another people who lived in a large canyon several suns travel into rising-sun. He Who Conquers determined they would find out whatever those people might show him of rockwork and planting. In fact, he was thinking that maybe they were the people from which his own fa had come. That interested him.

It was Hawkeye who first discovered they planned to leave when he came for a game and saw one of the bundles.

"Yes," He Who Conquers acknowledged to his inquiry, "we'll be leaving." He had no inclinations to say when.

"Why? Are we not a good people?"

"I'm not one of you, and never will be. I'm too different to ever be accepted, both in looks and abilities. I have made enemies among you because I've had the blessings of the Great One. I run too fast, have too much good fortune in hunting, and I mated an eligible young woman whom many a mu saw as a chance for her son. I insulted The Deer and his clan, I shamed Runt in Council, and I've drawn bad ravings from a few individuals.

"Perhaps I've not been what everyone expected, but it's too late to make a different first impression, and first impressions are the lasting ones. There's little chance I'll ever be accepted by this village or be a part of this people. It has nothing to do with your goodness."

Hawkeye nodded. "Sad but true. Everything you say is truth. I'll miss you." Yet there seemed a sense of relief about him as he spoke.

"And I, you. Though you venerated me too much, you've been a worthy friend, and I'm grateful."

"When will you leave?"

"I don't know yet. Preferably after the Ceremony of the Goddess."

"Send me a message by the Trader when you get where you're going. I wish to know you are safe somewhere."

"It'll be done."

When Hawkeye was gone, he turned to Scent of Violets. "When the rains come, we leave."

Surprised, she asked, "You'll walk in the rain?"

"Rain never hurt anyone so long as you keep from getting cold. We have means to stay reasonably dry."

"Why the sudden decision?"

He stared into the fire a time, as if troubled, then quietly said, "There will be trouble if I stay until the Feast of the Goddess."

She watched his face, and decided not to question his resolve. When he had that look, it was decided, and she would go. There was really no good reason to stay longer, anyway. Only the familiarity of her dwelling...and the memories. One does not exist well on memories, and a dwelling would be empty without a man. Her man was here, and he would be leaving. She would be beside him.

18

It was a calm but cold darkness. He Who Conquers felt the restlessness of room fever, inactive too long. He sat impatiently against the wall, considering the thought of going out. He was in a melancholy mood, remembering too much with too much time and too little to do. Scent of Violets was asleep on the mat, her face in peaceful repose beside him, and staring at her pretty face had brought back memories.

Little Dove, so beautiful and so different, yet in personality so similar. What he had adapted to when he mated Scent of Violets had demanded little adjustment. Both were very independent, outspoken, thoughtful and strong. Both had similar distastes, were good at cooking and crafts, had little time for young men with false faces, and respected age.

He had twice caught himself almost calling Scent of Violets by the name of his first love, and it was a distraction to have to stay alert to such a small thing. He remembered the visits of Little Dove to The Rock, and then that climactic coupling that was her Opening.

He was glad now that he had done it, though he had questioned himself and his self-image for some time after. But it was so different from Scent of Violets. With Little Dove, it had been so urgent and much too fast, the response to an impulse after so many instances of control. With Scent of Violets, it was almost like being with an animal. She was stronger physically than Little Dove, and her appetite was deep and frequent.

He teased her about it, and she merely laughed and came for more. She was his lynx, and he was happy with his choice. The Great One had done well for him. He was satisfied.

Yet, this darkness, there was something bothering him and he was not sure what. The desire to be outside, even in the mystical and frightening dark, was so strong he had to go, now. He watched the steady, deep breathing of his mate, remembering their violent coupling of a short time ago. She had immediately slept, and here he lay, wide awake and somehow disjointed.

He slowly moved out the doorway after feeding the fire to keep the room warm for her, then pointed to mid-sun and began to run. A dog followed him for a short distance, but stopped to let him run on alone.

He turned to setting-sun, stopping in a deep, steep canyon, agitated inside and wondering why he should feel such turmoil. He would rather be running full out, wearing himself down, trying to physically throw off the weight that pervaded him.

A flat rock beside an overhang of cedar drew him, and he sat in the shadow of the overhang, knowing that in this place he was nearly invisible. Being a short way up a box canyon from the main one would in itself be a deterrent to discovery.

His insides were crawling. Why he should feel so overwrought, he had no idea, nor did he dwell on the reason. He merely sat, looking up at the blackness of the cloudy skies, trying to find the mind of the Great One and wishing to know what He wanted.

Instead, he suddenly had a strong premonition of impending danger, his inner voice so alive he felt a cold chill run through him. Never had he experienced such a powerful, almost breath-stopping emotion overcome his senses. Numbly, he spun his head from side-to-side and pulled his knife, his eyes trying to split the darkness all around, the stillness so complete he could almost hear his own heartbeat.

There was no sound, no sign of movement, nothing to indicate he might be in danger, and his rapidly beating heart slowed again. Alertly he continued to motionlessly study everything he could see. If he were not in danger, then why the feeling? Was he again getting an insight into the future...The Top...the same vision that had plagued him several times? But nothing moved around him, and there were no messages from the gods...nothing to indicate why he should be troubled.

Scent of Violets! She was alone while he was here! She was in danger, and he must hurry! He slid off the rock, picked himself through the boulder-bottomed canyon and managed the wide canyon floor that led to Open Stone. There, he broke into a run, the pace he had used in the race, the wide-strided ground-eating gait that soon had him within sight of the village.

There he slowed, and when a dog came toward him he spoke softly to it and stopped. He realized the dog had come from near his own door, which might mean someone was there...someone the dog knew and felt no alarm. Quickly on moccasined he approached the door, then stopped just outside and listened.

The flap was in place, but he felt certain there was someone inside, where Scent of Violets slept. Listening as he could, there was no sound of movement.

So sure of it he could almost envision someone in there, he said softly, "I'm out here. If you seek me, come out."

There was no movement, no response. For the first time, he began to doubt what he had felt. Was it untrue? Had he just imagined it? Or had he misinterpreted the feelings he had?

He reached for the cover, and in that moment it was pushed aside and an arm came out wielding an axe, swinging it as a head came behind it. He leaped back, the axe narrowly missing his forearm, and, realizing the awkwardness of the person coming out the doorway gave him full advantage, he jerked his knife, feinted to draw another swing and then slashed behind the swing.

Contact was solid and the only response was a

grunt, the axe falling away. With his free hand, He Who Conquers grabbed the hair of the man and pulled hard, leaping aside as the man came out the doorway in a lunge. The shattered arm was what kept the man from knocking him down, and he leaped on the back of the fallen man.

Without pity, he pushed the head into the ground, keeping the adversary helpless while he tried to identify him. It was a few moments before he knew it was The Deer, and he said softly, "You are fortunate, my friend. I could have killed you just now."

"Why not do it now?"

"I feel sorry for you. You have a witch in you."

"I hope you wander in darkness forever!"

"Our future always goes wanting. Right now, I would say you were the one with the problem. Why were you in my dwelling?" He put some pressure just above the ruined part of the arm, and The Deer groaned. "I think you were going to injure my mate."

The Deer was silent. Again he moved his weight on the arm, his left hand gripping the hair of The Deer and pushing the face harder into the ground.

"Speak!" he hissed, trying to keep his voice soft enough to not disturb anyone. The dog had moved up and was sniffing the two of them, and at the smell of blood it growled low and moved back.

"She's unharmed!" The voice was filled with pain. "I only waited for you once I knew you were not there."

"I can believe the word of a liar?"

"I speak truth!" He groaned again. "Earth Mu, let me up!"

He Who Conquers made no move to honor the request, keeping his weight on the arm. The man groaned, making no effort to move. "My arm...it's broken!"

"It is, only it's more than broken. It's shattered. I guarantee you won't use that hand again, if you live."

"Kill me, coyote. You'll die for what you did."

"I don't kill snakes without reason. You're useless from now on, so you need no release in death." He stood and watched the crying man, who lay as dead except for the pained breathing and quiet sobs. Then he ducked into the doorway to check on Scent of Violets, and found her as he had been told. She was unharmed; and though The Deer had thrown off all her covers, she still slept.

He looked out the door, and The Deer still lay on the ground, though he had turned over and was holding his arm. He glanced at the door, tears streaming down his face, and seeing He Who Conquers, spoke through clenched teeth.

"I'll live, and you will die. When Sun God comes, my clan will come to see you in vengeance for this arm."

"If your clan is honorable, it will do nothing to help you. You prowl in the darkness like a coyote, and no one will believe you."

"You will see. They'll come."

"Let them. They'll see where blood feeds Earth Mu, and know that you've lied again. Go tell them. I'll be here, and I'll laugh. I encourage you to enjoy looking at your arm. When you do, recall your moment of stupidity!"

He dropped the cover and fed the fire to rewarm the room, then lay down beside his mate, pulling the blanket over both of them. In a moment, he slept.

They came, seven strong. They were outside his doorway while he was drinking the last of his early tea. At the sound of their approach, Scent of Violets looked up at him in alarm.

"Must we escape from here earlier than we had planned?"

He smiled tightly and shrugged. "We'll know soon."

"He Who Conquers, come out!"

He recognized the voice of Little Fox, who was charged with seeing justice extracted from one who had injured one of his clan, being the brother of the one injured.

He put down his cup deliberately, then pushed the cover aside, remaining inside on his knees, looking out the doorway.

"You've gone too far. Now you attacked him for the second time, this time in the darkness. It is time you paid for your behavior."

He Who Conquers smiled. He saw that several

of the villagers, including many elders, were up early, and had gathered to hear the confrontation. Hawkeye was among them, and he hoped that would furnish a chance for justice to prevail.

"You're the accuser. What have I done?"

"You heard it. You attacked my brother in the darkness and ruined his arm. Medicine Woman says it can't be fixed, and that the death spirit might come to him."

"I attacked him? Where was this to have taken place?"

Momentarily at a loss, Little Fox stepped forward. Bluster would be his way of covering facts.

"Does it matter?"

"It does. When a man finds another man inside his dwelling with a war axe, it matters a great deal. Would you not agree?"

"And you accuse him of being inside your dwelling? Where were you?"

"I was out running. When I returned he was inside, but I heard him. He came out swinging that axe." He pointed to the axe which had fallen next to the wall, and still lay there. "I don't plan to let another threaten my mate while she sleeps, nor kill me within my own dwelling. Yes, it does matter where he was injured."

"You lie."

"Then explain three things, you of little sense. Why is his axe lying on the ground beside my dwelling, why does his blood stain the doorway and wall of my mate's dwelling, and why do you stand on the very place where his blood seeps back into Earth Mu?"

Little Fox, jittery already from fear of being wrong in front of the entire village, jumped back and looked down. There was no mistaking the dark blood spots that were dried or frozen on the ground under his feet.

In the silence of the shock, He Who Conquers continued, "He came here to attack me. There's the proof. If I went to his dwelling, then I would deserve judgment. But he came here. He's the one who was trying to kill, and if I so desired, I could have killed him right where you stand. I let him live, because that arm will forever remind him that he tried treachery and failed. He will remember long and well."

No one moved, and no one spoke for some time, the two verbal combatants staring at each other, the rest shifting from foot to foot and looking away. Little Fox continued to stare, but no words came.

"If you come to me again, be sure you have something to stand on besides hard feelings. Next time, I'll challenge you to a *Death Match*, even if you're too young to be very brave. You bray like a bull buffalo, but you're nothing more than a small rabbit. Go away, Little Fox-let, and leave me alone."

The final shot changed Little Fox. He drew in a deep breath, and his anger came in a loud shriek. "You are a liar, and you are a sneaky rattlesnake! I'll see you dead before the Goddess awakens Earth Mu!"

He Who Conquers laughed, pulling his head back inside and letting the cover drop into place. Scent of Violets handed him a second cup of hot tea, and he leaned back and sipped.

"We'll go before that," she said softly.

He nodded. "But he'll lie in ambush like the coyote he is. It's as it was back on The Top. Surely The Great One has some more significant thing in life for me than to live where others try to take my life, as if there were not already enough uncertainty." He sipped again. "When the next winds blow warm, we leave."

She nodded, then gave her sly smile. "Will not the darknesses be much warmer with a lynx beside you under the blankets?"

He chuckled softly, the tension beginning to drain from him. "It will be, at that. It surely will."

He was interrupted by a voice from outside.

"He Who Conquers, I would like a word with you?"

He again set down the cup very deliberately after taking a last sip, and pushed aside the cover. The gray sky and cool air was behind the speaker, a tall man whom he had not seen before. "I'm He Who Conquers."

"And I am Sun Watcher. I will talk with you."

"Inside, or out in private."

"Inside is fine."

The man squeezed in, his tallness belittling his broad shoulders and huge chest. He sat just inside the door, leaving the cover to one side.

"I'm of the Corn Clan, of which is The Deer."

He Who Conquers immediately knew there was trouble. "You are a cousin?"

"He mated my sister."

"And you've been selected to be his avenger."

"I have."

"Where I come from, when a man has been attacked and wounds or kills his attacker, there is no further revenge planned. Why are you so different?"

"There are those among us that think The Deer tells the truth. I was selected to come to you."

"Do you believe he tells the truth?" His voice proved how incredulous he was.

The man stared at him for a time, uncertain what to say, then responded, "It matters nothing what I think. I was selected to be spokesman."

"And executioner."

"As you say."

"So you come to talk, we'll talk."

"The clan met and agreed to give you an alternative." He was embarrassed, which told He Who Conquers he was not convinced of The Deer being too reliable.

"Which is?"

"Either you fight a Death Match with one selected from our clan, or leave our village immediately."

"Why would I want to kill someone for nothing? And should I be forced to leave when it's too cold for humans away from their dwellings?"

"You have that choice."

"Would you be the one I would fight?"

He nodded.

"Then we have a problem, do we not? I don't wish to kill you, since I think you believe me and not The Deer. Yet if I go, my mate must go with me, and it's not a good time to travel, Sun God not yet able to keep us warm. What would you do if you were in my place?"

He shrugged, but again said nothing.

"I would hate to kill you, but I would if we were to fight."

"You are so sure?"

"I have reason to be certain. However, you seem

like a good man, and I hate to see that happen. You really give me no choice, though I think I'd like to speak with my mate before deciding something that deeply involves her, and might mean life or death to her."

"You have until Sun God comes again to decide."

"And then how long before having to go, if that should be our choice?"

"You must be gone by the fourth sun."

"Then you go, and we will consider it. I'll give you my answer before Sun God rests."

The man left without saying another word, and the two sat in silence, He Who Conquers sipping his tea again.

"What will you choose?" she asked quietly, knowing he would like to speak but was not sure where to start.

"I must let you make the choice, my lynx. It's a very serious thing to be traveling during snowtime. If we were caught in a storm, we could die quite quickly."

"But if we stay, you must kill or be killed. It's really not a nice choice."

He sipped and shook his head, but said nothing.

"We must go, then. We'll have to take our chances. Perhaps the gods will be good to us."

"I'll entreat the Great One for his favor. It's too much to ask that the snows stop, but perhaps he can protect us."

"It's good Fa-Fa isn't alive. He would choose to have you kill Sun Watcher, and that would be bad for the village. No one would be able to give the proper time for planting, or even for the celebration of the awakening of Earth Mu, or the Goddess of Fertility."

"Then we'll go. I'll speak to the Great One when the darkness comes." Again he stood beside his mate and watched the ritual welcoming the Goddess of Fertility back to earth.

* * *   * * *   * * *

She stood outside her door, Son of Vision working at her left breast, her eyes on the group of men gathered at their meeting place down the hill from the village. They had been arguing loudly for a long time, but the strong winds blowing from the village past the men had kept their words from prying ears. Something was happening, and she was not sure what it was.

"What is it, Mu?" Her mu had just come hobbling across the courtyard from a chat with another woman. "What are they discussing?"

She laughed. "Nothing that will affect you. Some men were seen from The Rock, and they want to go see if it is Others. Your ex-mate is anxious to justify his name and be a hero by doing what He Who Conquers did before he left."

"He thinks he can kill Others...by himself?" Her voice was somewhere between disbelief and incredulity. "He has visions of grandeur!"

"Don't most men who cannot achieve what men should? When they cannot grow up and accept themselves as men without having to prove their prowess with women or in battle, you expect them to be irrational. Some sun, Others will come, and those who are most vocal will run the fastest. Eagle Eye will be among them."

Little Dove nodded, her eyes serious. "They will come, Mu?"

"They'll come. I hope we can manage to be hidden when they do. If they're seen, I plan on taking you and Son of Vision to a cave to hide. There are many women ready to do the same."

"If we have warning. What if we don't?"

She shrugged. "We die, or run and hope."

"Our men can't keep Others out of the village?"

"Are you encouraged by what you see of them? They're fat, they're lazy, they're unable to decide on a course of action, they haggle over everything...you think they'll be able to make a rational decision when they're confronted with a real threat? Not long ago I defended them!"

Little Dove involuntarily shuddered. "And once we were a proud people who knew how to defend ourselves."

"Once, we attacked Others!" Her mu sat down with a jerk on a folded blanket, letting the sun help her get warm in the lee of the buildings. The wind was raw.

"Now...." The voice of Little Dove trailed off as she saw two men scuffle in their heated argument. "Some sun my man will come again. He'll make this people... stronger." There was a wistfulness in her voice. "I hope I live to see it."

    "As do I, my sweet. As do I."

19

"You're a coyote!" The charge rang in his ears. His anger, already on a short fuse because of the tension that had been building in him since the ultimatum, flared because Little Fox was screaming the words at him in front of most of the villagers. He had been walking back to his dwelling after letting the Corn Clan know he choose not to kill Sun Watcher, and would leave. It had not been an easy decision because he knew it opened him up to being called weak and afraid. It had also entered into his mind that this might have been the same situation which his fa had faced, and could become a stigma of like consequences. It had taken far more strength to withdraw than it would have taken to fight, but who would consider that?

The men of the Corn Clan had taken it calmly, until he had left the kiva and was halfway across the courtyard.

The words burned, changing the color of his neck and face, enlarging the veins along his neck, the result of a sudden and intense wrath. He stopped in the middle of the courtyard when the invective was hurled at his back, his ability to think replaced with fury. For a time he simply stood, fighting the desire to turn around, knowing he was at the end of his patience and losing his self-control, wondering in a moment what would happen to him if he should physically attack the overgrown infant.

Then came that grating voice a second time, and he slowly turned to face the youth. He lost all awareness of the villagers who stopped to watch.

He stared at Little Fox, wishing to slap the pocked face that held the ugly grin of cockiness, knowing as certain as he stood there that nothing would be gained by doing it, but no longer in complete control of himself.

His voice was deadly quiet, so soft those behind him did not hear well enough to understand, but a few heard it plainly. "You're like one with six winters of mentality. Does your mouth never stop? You're so much like your lying brother, one wonders if there's anything inside your head but air."

"You're only a coyote! You fear your own shadow!"

"Come. Come here and say that to my face instead of from a distance. Or are you the one who fears?"

Little Fox, his grin intact, jauntily approached, thinking he was safe as long as he had people around. He stopped two strides away and repeated his accusation, loudly enough to be heard by everyone.

No one remembered exactly what happened next, for it was so fast it was confusing. He Who Conquers moved into Little Fox with the speed of an angry puma, his right leg snaking behind the knee of Little Fox, and his open palm coming up under the chin, lifting the head and throwing the young man backward and off balance. The leg presented the barrier to his backstep, and he went down hard, flat on his back.

What everyone saw was Little Fox going down, and He Who Conquers on top of him almost before he hit the ground, his knife out and under the chin of the youth, its tip creating a small dimple against the throat.

In the same soft voice that was more a hiss, only

Little Fox heard what he said next. "You've strung out my patience. I can't ignore your taunts any longer, since you don't seem to have the intelligence to know when to stop. For an arrowhead, I'd push this knife deep enough to sever your trench of blood, but you're still so young. Maybe some sun you can grow up and be a man, if you'll learn to think before you speak. But I'll make you one promise if you'll agree."

The young man was sweating, great beads almost instantly on his forehead and upper lip, and he nodded ever so slightly, trying to swallow and feeling the pressure of the knife tip.

"That might be the smartest thing you ever did in your rather short life. So I'll give you my promise. If you say one more word to me...or about me...before I leave, you will die. Is that perfectly clear?"

Again Little Fox tried to nod, limited by the pressure of the knife. His bugging eyes never left the eyes of He Who Conquers.

Slowly he lifted the knife and made a thin cut into the skin of his chin, side-to-side. The blood was instant and ran down the chin onto the neck. He smiled.

"Good. Now I'll let you up...when I'm ready. When I do, you will run, not walk, to your kiva. Is that clear? You run, and I mean run like the Witch of Fire was almost ready to grab the back of your breechclout."

Little Fox closed his eyes, tried to swallow again and failed, but he made the almost imperceptible nod.

Moving off the youth, but keeping the knife under the throat again, He Who Conquers got out of the way, then withdrew the knife and hissed, "Run, coyote, run!"

Little Fox rolled, scrambled to his feet and sprinted for his kiva, and He Who Conquers, still on his knees, watched soberly. Then, when the youth disappeared amid the chuckles of many, he got up and went on to his mate, who smiled and stepped aside for him to enter before her.

When they were inside, he said quietly, "We'll go before the new sun. I won't stay any longer with so many feeling uncomfortable by my presence."

"I'm ready, my conqueror. We'll go when you say."

He smiled wanly. "You seem almost anxious to go from your own people. You're certainly atypical of women."

She shook her head, smiling in return. " I have nothing here. We've discussed this before."

He was silent, looking out through the open flap and seeing several men discussing what they had just seen. He knew he had given them something to talk about, and it amused him, erasing the anger that had gripped him. One old timer was giving his rendition of what happened, and it was obvious that he had not followed the action from the motions he used. A second disagreed and gave his interpretation, and though it was closer, it, too, was wrong. They grew heated in their disagreement.

He had accomplished what he wanted, and he looked back at Scent of Violets as she asked, "Why didn't you kill Little Fox. He's had it coming for a long time."

He laughed softly. "To what purpose? Everyone would have remembered me as a killer of children. But now they will remember me for something very different. Little Fox ran with the speed of a real coyote, and no one'll think ill of me. On the other hand, they'll remember the fear I put into the feet of a fool."

She grinned. "It was rather funny. What did you say to him that put such fear in him?"

He shrugged, chuckling. "Only he and I will ever know. I'd venture to say he'll tell no one. There is no way he can ever convince anyone he wasn't running in sheer terror, and it'll mark him for a long time--perhaps make a man of him, though I doubt it. He's too much like his brother. They can't think farther than the end of their own noses. Both will remember me well."

She poured him a cup of tea from a larger pot that was hot and stood on the edge of the firepit. He took it and sipped, leaning back against the wall as she stared out the doorway.

"How will we get away without being followed? Or do you think they'll let you go without opposition?"

"They may watch for us to go. We'll leave before the darkness is half gone, and we'll go into no-sun where they won't think we went. The main way out is down the canyon, we'll go up, then swing around into rising-sun later. It'll be a long trip."

She sipped her tea, contrary to Tradition which dictated that a woman did not eat or drink until the man was through. He smiled. She had other things about her that defied Tradition, too, and while he wondered about it, he was amused. After all, he often was in defiance of Tradition. It seemed natural to him.

"Will we go straight to your people?"

He shrugged. "No, the Great One hasn't given me a good feeling about that...not yet. I wish to go where my fa was dropped into the world, and see if I can find out why he's considered a coward."

"How...?"

Again he shrugged. "It seems like there might be another side to the story, which I would like to know. If his experience there is anything like mine here, it would change my opinion of him." He almost added **"and myself**," but chose to hold that to himself. "Besides, they might have something I should also know." For a moment he stopped, then added, "Then, too, there is the matter of my...bad dreams."

"The ones that awaken you in the darkness?"

He nodded, staring into the fire, remembering the vision, the hideous sounds and the sickening sight of his parents, the puzzling actions of Little Dove and Eagle Eye--whom he still thought to refer to as Boy with the Eye of an Eagle, and who still owed him that turn at The Rock. The humor of the never-to-be-claimed debt, were it not against the backdrop of those abhorrent visions, might have made him smile.

"A vengeance by Others upon my people for what I did to them when they came the last time." It was a new idea that came to him as he spoke, for he had never thought of it that way before. The thought struck him with a new force of sobriety. "They'll reek a horrible toll among The People. The gods will sleep, and let the Others toy with them. Only, I'll return at the propitious moment and be used of the gods to strike at them again, and to convince them that their pleasure among my people will come at a very high price."

She stared at him, seeing his eyes locked on the fire and his voice almost hypnotic in its quiet intensity. She wished to ask him another question, but nothing

came, the look on his face too far away to allow her to
speak.

The spell left him as abruptly as it had come,
and he glanced up at her with a sheepish and humorless
grin. "I fear what that means. It's a heavy load to
carry."

She nodded. "Your Great One plays with you
like all the others. Can anyone find peace with the
gods?"

He gave only a slight smile. "It is something I've
often wondered. It answers itself, because we're often
attacked by witches and evil gods. There can be no true
peace among us, or within us either."

"That leaves us with a rather morbid outlook, if
you ask me."

"One must merely seek the gods again and again.
We send our smokes of repentance, and our messages of
hope. We can only try to keep a god on our side, the
evil ones away from us, and though the Great One may
toy with me, he still does amazing things to help me.
These things I can't forget."

"Like what happened out there just a little while
ago? Was that some kind of help?"

He grinned. "Another obstacle, another victory,
no matter how small."

"And it was the last incident before we leave."

He grinned, humor returning. "A lynx ought to
know what it is to be challenged by others. No lynx
protects its territory without knowing any and all
intruders. Without intruders, there would be no need to
protect anything."

She smiled.   "What territory were you
protecting?"

"My own name. It's not easy to live up to such
a name."

She nodded, the trace of a smile on her lips but
her eyes alive. "He Who Conquers. Apt, don't you think?
But it's yours. You seem to manage."

"As I said, when one establishes a territory, there
will be challenges. I wish to protect what is mine."

The twinkle in her eyes preceded the slightest of
coy smiles. "My conqueror, and my protector. But a
female lynx protects itself, does it not?"

"You wish to do so?"

She laughed. "Against men, you will be my protector. But against you, I will protect myself as I wish."

He laughed loudly. "I promise to test that."

"And I will attack you as I have in the past. You will not win unless I choose to let you."

He was laughing so hard tears were forming, when she suddenly leaped across the firepit and landed on him, pushing him sideways onto the mat while laughter held him helpless. Nipping his neck, she forced herself between his legs and lay on him, her hands holding his wrists and pushing them to the mat above his head.

"Give up?" she asked playfully, kissing him around the eyes, the cheeks, the mouth.

"No! I never give up!"

She chuckled and said, "You may not wish to, but you already have. You're still flaccid."

He began pushing against her wrists, gaining control of his laughter, watching her eyes change from giggles to concentration. Slowly he forced her arms back until her grip began to slip, then he gave her a bear hug and saw her begin to laugh.

"Oh, my! He's no longer a limp string!" she laughed. "It's too late! I'm conquered again!" She facilitated his entry, then lay heavily on him and grinned down into his face. "To travel with you will be most exciting. I only wonder how far we'll manage to travel each sun."

He laughed again. "When I get on the trail, fooling around ceases. We'll travel far before each darkness; count on it."

"Perhaps. But that will be a while yet. The new sun is still a long time away. Can I win again?" She began to move. "I think I will."

* * *   * * *   * * *

It was crisp. There had been a hard freeze, leaving the ground solid and quiet. Three dogs watched He Who Conquers step into the blackness and look around for whoever might have been assigned to keep tabs on them. He saw no one. He hoisted his pack onto his back and helped Scent of Violets situate hers, then pointed the direction to her and followed her toward no sun. While she led and kept alert for their trail obstacles, he watched the backtrail for any sign of pursuit.

When they were well away from the village, he spoke. "The hard ground will be a big help. They'll find it very difficult to follow us, especially with these hide boots we wear. They'll waste time going the wrong way, and maybe never find us."

She was breathing hard from climbing, but said brokenly, "My conqueror is wise to make us this footwear. As cold as it is, I'm already warm."

He chuckled. "We still have far to go, my lynx, and the ground is much too cold for your interesting challenges."

She giggled, but said nothing, and they lapsed into silence as they finished the climb to the top and began to walk. He felt none too secure, and continually turned to study the backtrail, having no trouble catching up with her after his brief pauses.

They had walked for some time before he said, "We will rest a moment. You're not used to the trail or the pack. I'll backtrail to see if anyone follows."

She slumped to a rock and he helped her escape her pack, dropped his beside her and headed back down the trail while she wrapped a blanket around her shoulders. For some time he walked, then stopped where the trail turned and dropped, studying the dark recesses of the canyon. After several moments, seeing no one and knowing he had given anyone who might wish to follow plenty of time to get this far, he was satisfied that no one followed...yet. He turned back and trotted to where Scent of Violets huddled beside the packs.

"No one follows."

"Did I not say my conqueror is wise? We go again?"

He helped her to her feet and fixed the pack again, then shouldered his own and led up the trail, being sure he kept a pace consistent with what she could handle. When Sun God made his first appearance, they were still trekking toward no-sun, stopping regularly to allow Scent of Violets time to rest and drink some of the water they had brought. The gray skies vanished, Sun

God conquered the God of Snow, and the travelers began to shed clothing in the labor of walking with a pack. As they turned to rising-sun, the spaces ahead seemed without end, and Scent of Violets, who had never before been where she could see so far, marveled and wondered, a bit fearful and greatly expectant. "My conquerer, when you said you came a great distance, I had no idea what you meant. Where do your people live?"

He pointed at a low horizon of mountains toward rising-sun. "Beyond those mountains."

"It's far! Will we ever get there?"

He laughed. "Before you are too wrinkled to give birth, my lynx."

They topped a rise and stood looking down at the sudden drop from the mesa top onto the desert he had crossed once before. It would be a tough climb down, but from there it was a trail he knew. But to get down was the problem. Now he knew why the trail from the village went up the side-canyon.

He shed his pack and traveled to no-sun, found nothing, and came back to mid-sun. Yet it was nearly dark when he found the way down.

"We'll stay here on the rim. It will be colder down there than up here. There'll be few comforts for us either place, but here we can see farther."

She nodded but said nothing while they dug into their packs for food and water, two cups and a small pot in which to heat water for tea. While the water heated, they wrapped themselves in their blankets and sat watching the flame of cedar and sage.

"You're very tired," he said almost in a trance from the flames. "You should sleep well."

"I'll die. I had no idea what tired legs were."

He chuckled and they ate sparingly, enjoying the hot tea. When they were done, they relieved themselves and wrapped in their blankets between the folds of the hairy buffalo hide.

"This is one tired lynx, my conqueror," she whispered, snuggling against him and pulling the blanket over her ears.

He laughed softly, enjoying her closeness. "What, no protecting of territory? What happened to all those threats?"

She giggled sleepily. "They got lost in the distance back along the trail. You've taken me too far."

He awakened in the darkness, feeling the cold air being sucked into his lungs but enjoying the warmth of the covers. He was slightly tired in his legs and hips from the long walk, but knew his mate would be much worse. She still slept, and he eased himself away from her to don his leggings and his cloak, then started the fire from the few coals that yet lay beneath the dead top ashes.

Starting water to heat, he considered what lay ahead. The trail was still long, and he was not at all sure where it would lead. He wondered about Wide Canyon, lying out in the middle of flat and unassuming country, with growing trepidation about the advisability of going there. Would they welcome strangers, and what would be his reception when they found out who he was?

He had studied the work of stone and mortar, and listened and studied how to prepare a foundation. He had brought with him an expert in the making of pottery, and counted on her to teach his people how to improve what they made. She knew something about cross-pollination to achieve better corn, and how to heat beans until they were edible. What else was there for him to learn from the people of the Wide Canyon?

Scent of Violets continued to sleep, and he sipped tea and stared at the skies toward rising-sun, which were showing the first indications of Sun God. What would he find when he finally returned to his people? Would it be what he had seen in his visions? Would the Others have come and gone just before his arrival? If it was immediately before, why did he see his parents as advanced in decay? Yet, why had no one sent their spirits to the gods so they would find Sipapu if it had been a while? Or had everyone been killed?

No, that was not possible, because their voices had been strong in asking him to come to them, and the hands stretched toward him were many. Were they too few, too weak, or too frightened to send the spirits of the dead up in the smoke of the gods? Where was the chief, or Little Dove, or...? Little Dove! Would she die with the many? Was that why she smiled and kept her distance while Boy with the Eye of an Eagle waved and nodded?

But had not her mu said she would be there when he returned? Perhaps she had seen something he had not, or he might have interpreted the scenes wrong. If so, what would it be like living in a village as small as theirs with a mate while Little Dove lived so near?

And what of her having a child by him? Could he stay away from her if the child was his? Yes, he knew he not only could, but would, because he had no other choice but to act as though it were not his at all. Only she and her mu knew the secret he held, or perhaps that should be the other way around.

The scene came again. While he watched the skies growing lighter, his eyes remembered. He saw the dead, the fields, and Little Dove and Boy with the Eye of an Eagle, and Singing Waters and Son of Happiness. Then he saw something else, a scene he had not seen before. There were many warriors--they had to be Others--sitting around a fire, laughing and holding up the scalps of his people. They were boasting of their victory, of their coups, and of their many scalps. His eyes burned, and his stomach churned, and his hands gripped his bow so hard his fingers hurt. He sat above them on a hillside, watching, wondering....

He was brought from the severe reverie by movement behind him, and Scent of Violets sat up, holding the wrappings tightly to herself.

"Why are you up already?" The voice was full of sleep.

"Already? It's time to be back on the trail."

She groaned, laying back again. "I'm not sure I can move. I had no idea I had so many muscles that would hurt...or could hurt so much."

He chuckled and poured her a cup of hot tea. "Here, this will help you get started. Drink it before it gets cold."

She sat up again and took it, and they sat close, sipping the hot liquid and glancing often at the skies that promised a bright sun again.

"Will we walk far this sun?"

He laughed. "You'll have to be the judge of that. Just remember, though, that every step we make gets us nearer where we go. Every lost moment makes it that much longer to get there. And this is still the time of cold and snow."

She groaned for his benefit. "I'll follow, my conqueror, but I'll not be very speedy."

He laughed again. "You were not exactly speedy last sun."

She swallowed a sip of tea, then said, "But you never complained."

"Of course not. I thought you did very well. After all, we travel together, and we only travel as fast as you are able to go."

"Then I will push myself a bit harder."

"Only if you plan to run over me. I'm making sure you don't over-exert; if you do, we might end up losing time waiting for you to recover."

"But the way is so far. I had no idea...."

"I tried to tell you. Do you want to go back?"

"I appreciate your jest, but no, I'll die before I go back. I am committed."

He grinned. "You'll do fine. The trail leads that way, but we don't have to be there before Sun God sleeps!"

20

To Scent of Violets, it seemed they had been traveling forever. Each new sun was like the last, their routine well-established from their first rising until they again climbed wearily into their buffalo robe and blankets again. Yet it had been only eight suns since they left her village. They had traveled into rising-sun continually, keeping Mesa of Death on their right, staying near the bottom of its skirt. Their step had strengthened as she became trail-broke, her pace more consistent and wider. They passed the end of the long mesa and then some strange red rock formations as they neared a long valley whose rising-sun side was rimmed with rising hills and eventual mountains.

"This is the way?"

He turned his head to speak over his shoulder. "It's the directions given by the Trader, I hope. He spoke of the huge Mesa of Death, and of red rocks carved by the gods at play. I've seen nothing else that might indicate anything different. I know our direction is right, and I'm pretty sure we have to cross those mountains.

I sort of remember seeing them when I came, but the direction was so different."

Confident he was right, they left the mesa behind and crossed, though the openness of the area, surrounded by hills and mountains from which they could be seen, made He Who Conquers more wary and concerned. For two suns they crossed the great expanse before starting to climb the barren hill that reached for the mountain.

The next two suns were spent climbing, finally into trees and steeper mountains, past strange rock formations and through snowbanks that sometimes blocked their trail and sent them on long detours. Whenever one of these massive drifts occurred, they always went to mid-sun for a means to cross.

At the crest, near sunset, they stopped to view the huge country still fronting them. They could see the smokes of several fires far out, some being clusters of smaller fires, indicating a village.

"We'll avoid any contacts with people until we near Wide Canyon. Hard to say what type of reception we might receive from isolated peoples." They camped just off the rim, and then headed down the next sun.

Their sun was nearly spent when they cleared the mountain, enjoying the warmer climate that came from the lower country. A single tree, gnarled and misshaped, was their companion for that camp.

The next two suns were uneventful hikes, staying to no-sun from some village smoke and crossing several heavily-used trails. On the third sun, they paralleled a wash for a time, then stopped near it as the sun dipped behind the mesa.

"Can we stay in the arroyo?"

"It'll be safer. We'll find a place to drop into it, and see if there's a small place where we can make it better for sleeping."

To get down was no problem, a rut opening steeply into the bottom, and they took it. Once down, he noted the softness of the sandy bottom, where they spread the robe and began their routine of making something to eat. They were still eating from an antelope he had killed two suns before.

"It's a good place to camp, my conqueror. The sand will make a nice bed."

"Better than the rocks we slept on last darkness,"
he responded. "We have some protection from the wind
that will blow soon."

"Will this be a good place if it blows?"

He laughed. "So some sand falls on us. It'll be
better than having the blanket torn from us like last
time."

She shrugged. "I suppose. But my hair already
feels like a dirty broom."

He grinned. "A hazard of the trail, my lynx.
When we next come to moving water, we'll bathe."

"That's a promise?"

"It's a threat. I'll push you in if you don't go in
on your own accord."

She laughed softly. They never spoke or laughed
loudly, not knowing if anyone might be around. "I'll wait
for your push!"

They ate and bantered, and finding their spirits
good and their bodies strong, they coupled before falling
asleep. It had been a good hike that sun, and they were
encouraged by the nearness of Wide Canyon.

When they awakened, she was quickly up to
make hot tea, while he climbed the side and studied the
land from a rise near their campsite. He saw nothing,
though he studied the sagebrush country around them as
far as he could manage.

He returned to the fire and was sipping tea when
she asked, "Did you see where we must go?"

He shrugged. "We probably have at least two
more suns to go. It's hard to remember the exact
instructions of the Trader, but maybe I'll see something
he spoke about before long. Somewhere there is a road
we will hit." The general flatness of the country erased
landmarks, and made a traveler skeptical.

She nodded. "At least we'll not have to go as far
as we already have."

He grinned. "Not even when we travel to my
people."

They finished eating and packed for the trail,
habit making it unnecessary for verbal exchanges. He
hoisted his pack, and turned to help her when he froze.
Scent of Violets, puzzled by his lack of helpfulness,
turned to see what was wrong, and noted the cocked ear

and intent look.

"What is it, my conqueror?" she whispered.

"A voice. I thought I heard a voice."

They both listened for a time, then decided he had heard nothing, perhaps the wind or an animal far off. He took her pack and held it for her when again he stopped.

"I heard it, too," she whispered. "It sounded like a man...maybe someone in pain."

He nodded, setting her pack on the ground and shucking his own. Taking his weapons, he motioned her to keep silent and stay with the packs, and climbed the side to the top, stopping when his head was high enough to see. There was nothing.

He remained stationary for some time, then climbed out and stayed low in the scraggly sage, moving away from the gully. Among the sagebrush, he stopped and squatted, his head just high enough to see over the top, but like before saw nothing. Then came the voice.

It was a plea for help. The voice was weak...very weak. It came from out in the sage, far enough to tell him that the person was unaware there was anyone near. It was a mournful plea for anyone who might hear.

He moved in the direction of the sound, not making any noise, staying low. There was a sound of someone rubbing against brush, and some gravel rattled. Then he saw movement and stopped again. Low to the ground, he studied the areas between the sage until he saw more movement. Someone was on his belly, his direction quartered away from He Who Conquers toward early mid-sun. He stood and moved warily, his spear at ready, his knife in the left hand. Was it a trick? It was an old one if it were, a man playing a decoy to get someone close enough to kill.

But this man was no decoy. He was bloody about the head, and it was obvious he was a Broadhead, making it no trouble for him to approach and check more carefully. The man was lying on his stomach, his bloody hands stretched out above his head, resting, his head turned away and lying as in sheer exhaustion, sleep or death.

After a few moments, the head came up, and the weak voice cried out again. "Help me! Anybody, help me!"

When the man's face swung around, he saw that the eyes were glazed over by scabs, the face covered with dried blood. The back of the head was bloody, and the hands and arms were leaving a blood trail on the ground where he had traveled.

The man was in bad shape. He was a big man, and was near-naked. His breechcloth had slipped down to mid-thigh, he had no footwear, and he had no headband and no covering for his torso.

"I'm here, friend. Rest a moment." His voice made the man stop in his quest for new handholds, his only means to make any progress. He'd been snaking along the ground for a long way.

"Who speaks?" The question was as weak as were the cries. His head slowly turned back and forth, tilted to one side to catch any further sound. It was obvious he could see nothing, nor did he know from where the voice had come. And the dialect was strange to him, no doubt.

"He Who Conquers. I'll help you."

"I'll plead with the gods to grant you long life." He tried to wipe some of the scabs from his face, but his hand refused to do his bidding. "I'm Bear Wrestler."

It was pitiful in its weakness, or He Who Conquers might have chuckled, the irony touching him. He was soon to be in his third village in but a single winter...all because he wanted a longer life! And here was someone near death praying he would find it! There was humor in everything!

"Just rest there a bit. I'll find my mate and we'll give you water and food."

The man laid his head down, and He Who Conquers sprinted back to the campsite, then led his mate to the man who had not moved.

"Earth Mu!" She was shocked to see the condition of the man. "How does he yet live?"

"He's strong, and the gods must still be playing. We can put a blanket on the ground and let him roll onto it, then you clean him and I'll see if there's water around here."

They dropped their packs and she spread a blanket beside the man, then He Who Conquers dropped beside the man and asked, "Do you understand me?"

The man spoke softly, "I hear."

"We have a blanket on the ground beside you. I'm going to help you roll onto it."

"It will feel good."

He knelt beside the man and began to roll him onto his back so he would be on the edge of the blanket. The man groaned at the movement, and was half over when He Who Conquers felt the desire to vomit. The man had been crawling for a long time, and his chest, stomach and legs were scratched, bloody, and covered with cactus spines. The breechcloth had been dragged so low, the man's maleness was uncovered, and was as bad as the rest of his front.

"Clean him, my lynx. I'll find more water and return."

"Can you fix a fire so I can make tea for him. He needs to have something to drink to ease the pain."

He nodded and set about making the fire near the blanket, and when it was going, he took the two empty deer-stomach waterbags and headed to rising-sun. For a time he went straight, then turned slightly toward no-sun, and it was yet a while before he suddenly came on what he wanted, a small trickle of water in a shallow creekbed.

He knelt beside it and dug out a hole where he could lay the bags and let water fill them. Then he raced back to where Scent of Violets worked on the man.

"He let his spirit visit the gods," she said as he knelt beside her. "He drank only two swallows of kinnikinnik tea."

"You have done well on his face. That must be a knife slash."

"It is. He's lost sight of that eye. The knife cut right through it. It laid open his cheek and nicked the ear."

"He's lost his scalp!" He had suddenly noticed the bloody top of his head, and it appeared there was no hair.

"Yes. And the back of his head was smashed, like someone hit him with the edge of an axe. Someone wanted him dead pretty badly."

"Any sign of arrow or spear marks?"

"Not that I could find, but he won't be able to use his male member for a while. His entire front has cactus spines in it, and I think we might have trouble getting them out."

"I'll work at it. You keep washing what you can of the blood. His hands look like raw meat."

"Worse. It's a miracle of the gods that he even lives."

"He's a man of men. Perhaps the gods will take him before he awakens again."

"No, he'll live. He has hate to keep him alive; it'll make him live."

"He's so big. There's no way I can carry him anywhere."

"Even his male member is huge! Look at that! It's like the wrist of a girl!"

He Who Conquers chuckled. "It holds many spines. You wish to take them out?"

She smiled. "If you wish. But yours is all I wish to handle. I'd rather you did it."

It was nearly mid-sun before they had cleaned the man, and He Who Conquers had again gone for water. When he returned, he said, "Have you noticed the skies? Clouds come, and they bring snow. We need shelter."

Alarmed, she asked, "Here? How?"

"Where else? I see nothing close where we can drag the man."

"I need to make poultices for his head and hands."

He grinned. "For his male member, too. He needs help everywhere."

"Then you figure out how to make us a shelter, and I'll make poultices." She had the readily available plantain leaves in her basket, which she shredded with her fingers and applied directly to the abrasions, and more-so to the back of the head and the slash across the cheek. He watched for a moment until she looked up and said, "Do you plan to have the three of us huddle under a blanket during a snowstorm?"

He grinned and stood up, looking around. There were no trees except beside the small trickle of water, and that was much too far. The sage was too scattered to build a shelter like he had the first sun after leaving The Top.

He moved away and circled, then circled wider. It was useless to search such barren land, for there was no shelter to be found that would be any help...nothing at all.   He returned to his mate and the unconscious man.

"There's nothing."

"Is there any way to get him back to the arroyo? We can rig a shelter there."

"It's a long way to drag him."

"But better than out here, which is nothing."

He glanced at the big man.   "How do you suggest we move him?"

"First, we let him sleep, while we get back to the arroyo and see if we can find a way to build some shelter.   Then we can come back for him.   With the blanket here, he'll not go anywhere if he awakens before we return."

He grinned.   "You certainly have a way with words and ideas, my lynx." He picked up his pack while she put her's back together and followed him to the ravine.   Dropping into it, they went down it for some time, finding nothing, and retraced their steps and went up it.   There they came to a sharp bend, and caught in it was a pile of debris, mostly limbs, soil and rotting sagebrush.

They wrestled the limbs free and carried them to a place where a side stream had entered, causing a steep but smaller creek bottom.   Here they stopped and worked some of the branches into the wall, and others were leaned against them.   Three trips back to the snag gave them the framework for a hut.

Next came the sagebrush, and he took his axe and began to chop at the base of one after another, pulling them apart so only one branch came with each piece.   Scent of Violets took them and carried them to the framework, where she wove them together and into the branches, leaning more branches against it to hold them in place.   When a side was done, she buried the bottom of the frame and braces in sand.

It took them a while, but by the time the clouds were overhead, they were done and had their own belongings inside. Having saved two strong branches, they tied a blanket between them and carried this to where the man still lay, though it appeared he had awakened and changed position. A poultice had rubbed off, but she ignored it as they carefully struggled the man onto their makeshift *travois*. He Who Conquers lifted the end near the man's head, struggling to get a solid hold and position himself to pull, and then he began to drag it. He managed a short distance, then stopped, then went again, and in but a little while was sweating profusely.

"He's big. This drags heavily."

"He is big, my conqueror. It'll take a while to get to the arroyo."

"You have any ideas on how we can get him to the bottom of that arroyo?" He grinned. "You seem to have all the ideas here of late."

She laughed. "We can drop him over the edge, but that might not do him so much good. No, I was thinking we could slide him down the sand in one of the side-washes."

"Why not go ahead and find one so I can drag him directly there?"

"Good idea! Why didn't I think of that?"

"Too busy with better ideas, I guess."

She laughed again and left him, and when she was gone he began again. Finding a better technique, his progress improved, but in a few strides he could feel the weariness in his legs. Looking over the sagebrush, he could see Scent of Violets walking swiftly along the edge of the gully, searching for a way down.

He rested, then pulled, and rested again, and while he sat in the cooling wind with his eyes on the clouds, she arrived.

"Right over there. There was a small wash, and I caved in some of the sides to make a kind of slide. The trouble is, it'll be a bit of a drag up the sandy bottom to the shelter."

He grinned. "I'm a slave. But I'll make it."

"Let me work the one side. Perhaps it'll go better."

He shrugged, and they tried the system of two pulling. It was much more effective, and they soon had him down the side, dragging him through the sand to their shelter.

They finally had him inside, and in all the tugging and labors of the trip, he still slept the sleep of the gods. They started a small fire and situated their mat and blankets, then made more tea and ate more antelope, this time in a broth with a cornflour thickening.

"It'll be necessary for one of us to stay awake with him at all times. We have no idea what kind of person he is, and he has the witch that burns within him. Perhaps when he awakens he'll need water and attention."

She nodded. "And you've worked hard, my conqueror. You sleep first and I'll awaken you after I become too sleepy."

He was almost instantly asleep, the wind whistling through the sagebrush sides to cover any sounds from either inside or out. When he awoke, his first conscious thought was of the strange light in the hovel. It had to be light outside, there was an eerie quiet, and there was a thin layer of fine snow on his blanket. His mate lay beside him sleeping, and the fire burned low but was still flaming, indicating a recent refueling.

He rolled his head, and Bear Wrestler was laying on his side, his ugly face toward the fire, watching He Who Conquers with the one eye that still functioned.

He Who Conquers glanced again at his sleeping mate, then said, "I slept past the arrival of the new sun."

"From what I hear, you worked hard on the last one."

"You're not light," he said with a grin. "It took some time and effort to get you in here."

"Where are we?"

"In a wash-out. I have no idea how far it is to anyone or any village."

"Who are you? I spoke with your mate a while ago, but never thought to ask."

"He Who Conquers. I guess you were in no shape to remember our first meeting."

"No. I remember nothing." He paused, then said, "Except I woke up with blood all over me and my head did not let me walk. I tried to crawl...but nothing more."

"You crawled. I have no idea how far. My mate and I heard you as we were preparing to travel into rising-sun again. You were calling for help, but it was so weak we could hardly hear."

"But you found me, treated me, and brought me here. Your mate told me. I'm grateful."

"You were attacked by someone."

He nodded, wincing from the action. "One I thought was my friend."

"He slashed your face, and bashed in the back of your head. The gods must want you to live."

"I want to live!" he replied bitterly. "The man will die."

"He took one eye from you."

"And my scalp. For that alone, he must die."

"But you'll have to fight him as soon as you get back to your village. It's the law of honor. You'll still be as weak as a featherless bird. He'll crush the rest of your head before you can do anything."

"It's a point of honor. I'll not live, or he'll not live."

"A Death Match. I have to say none was more called for. But I fear for you, Bear Wrestler. You need time to recuperate before you fight him."

The man was silent, staring into the fire with his one eye. The scabbed slash that angled up his broad cheek and through the left eye turned his already homely face into a mask of ugliness.

"I must fight him for you."

"It's for me to do."

"To die? No, my friend, I found you and saved your life. You couldn't have lived much longer, with the cold coming and having no clothing, not to mention your weakness. Earth Mu has much of your blood, you know."

Bear Wrestler was agitated, but pain kept him immobile.

"I'll fight the man. It's my right, by virtue of finding you alive. I claim the right."

The man lay still for a long time, though it was plain he was busy thinking thoughts that stirred him. Neither spoke until he finally said, his eye again studying the fire, "You'd take the privilege of doing what has kept me alive? I must kill him. It's all I thought about while I could still think."

"But if I claim the right of honor because of saving your life, is it not you who kills him? Or is it not so among your people."

Very softly, the voice came from a resigned attitude. "It is so. I acquiesce."

"Then I claim you as my brother. We'll be as one when we return to your people. Where do you live?"

"Wide Canyon."

A tingle went through He Who Conquers. He now had the means to find the place he sought. "Then you must tell me of our mutual enemy. Who is he, what's his name, and why did he attack you?"

Again there was a long silence, during which Scent of Violets turned over, putting her posterior against He Who Conquers, but still slept.

"He's called Long Knife. He's nineteen winters, and a renowned hunter who handles the knife with skill. He's been seeking to take the chief's role from his fa for a long time, being the eldest son of our chief and my aunt. I've been clan chief for four winters. I don't believe Long Knife should be chief ever. He hasn't the intelligence nor maturity to use sense instead of muscle." He lay quietly a while, then went on. "He wanted to go hunting for a long time, with the snows keeping us close to home. So I consented. And this happened. He had planned this...so long."

His voice was almost monotone by this time, exhaustion overcoming him. He stopped talking, his eyelids drooped, and he slept again.

He Who Conquers lay quietly for a time, then got up carefully and went outside through the antelopeskin doorway, and was shocked to see the amount of snow. And it was still coming. It was almost to his knees already, but he realized it would be deeper in the arroyo than up on top because of the winds.

He stepped around the hut and looked both up and down the wash, relieving himself as he did. He had stood for only a moment when he became alert. There was no mistaking the smell of bison on the wind.

Quietly he went into the hut and got his spear,

bow and arrows, and knife, and went out again after taking another look at each of the sleeping companions. He climbed out of the gully and stood still, trying to again catch the scent. It was there, weak but certain. The wind was from no-sun, the direction he headed, weaving through the sagebrush in snow to mid-calf.

The smell went away, then came again, stronger. He began to trot, and soon the rank smell was potent and constant. Then he saw them, a small herd of about ten hands. They faced into the storm, the only animal known to do that. It put their tails at He Who Conquers, who walked boldly toward them, until he got within ten paces. There he stopped, then readied his bow and arrow and stepped forward carefully, the spear in the right hand, the left holding the bow with strung arrow.

Two steps, then three, then four. The driving snow held them immobile and without their usual alertness. Another step, and yet another. One swung its head and looked back over its shoulder, but he was stationary. The animal looked at him a while, then turned back, and he took another step.

He was so close now he could almost swing the spear like a club and hit one of them. Instead, he stood the spear in the snow, point up, and brought up the bow. His arrow entered a calf near the back of the herd, going in just behind the front leg and piercing the heart. The calf stood silently and unmoving, let out a small bawl and collapsed onto its knees, then slowly rolled onto its side. It was going to be a long time before Bear Wrestler could travel to his people, and it would take more meat than the calf, so he strung another arrow and killed the cow that stood next to the calf. Then he shouted, grabbed his spear and jumped up and down to scare the rest of the herd. His efforts looked useless for a while, until finally the lead cow moved away and the rest followed. They only went a short way and stopped, again standing with heads into the driving snow.

He dropped beside the calf and went to work. He would on most occasions have saved the entire animal for different tools or utensils. But he cut off the head, made a long incision and dragged out the viscera, took his bite of liver and sip of blood, then left the entire viscera in the snow. Tying the front legs together, he began to pull the entire animal back to the hut, and while he tugged and pulled against the deepening snow, a new thought came to him.

It was a warm country...ordinarily. That meant that if warmth came quickly, this amount of snow would melt quickly and rush out in streams. Their hut stood in the bottom of a gully where water had run deep and fast, for that was how the arroyo came into being. A trickle started in higher country, and by time it coursed down a ravine, there was no way of diverting the waters.

He was nearly exhausted when he came to the gully just before the hut, and he sat on the beast while the sweat ran. Finally he stood, looking toward but unable to see the mountains in the falling snow, wondering about how long the hut could stay where it was before they would have to move out.

He tumbled the animal over the edge and let it fall into the bottom of the gully, then followed it down. He stood for a minute to contemplate the situation when Scent of Violets appeared.

Her smile was wide. "The Great One has rewarded you again, I see!"

"There's yet another. I'll have to take off the hide and cut the meat from the bone to bring it back."

"You will save the hide?"

"We'll need it. We have to leave the arroyo when the snow begins to melt or we'll be seeking Sipapu before we choose."

She nodded. "I thought of that when I came out to see where you were. You were gone a long time."

He grinned. "And I must be long gone again. I'll let you cut the meat from this one and fix us a good meal. I must go claim the cow."

She nodded and turned to the hut for her tools, while he headed back for the second animal. He had the feeling he would need that meat...and the hide.

21

Snow continued for another sun, and then wind came to blow snow into the gully until it was difficult for them to get out of the hut. They tramped snow often to keep it from piling so high their hut would be like an underground tomb. Then it quit.

For ten suns cold squatted on the land, her frigid skirt bringing an icy stillness almost deafening for the three snowbound people. Each sun, Bear Wrestler showed improvement, Scent of Violets cleaning the wounds, sparingly making her leaf poultices because the leaves were nearly gone. They talked of life at Wide Canyon from the perspective of the man whom they had begun to know, and He Who Conquers became interested in seeing their methods of construction, which apparently were very different from those at Open Stone, and constantly improving.

Bear Wrestler was a congenial person, somewhat naive and very gentle, almost meek, a man not given to fighting for that which might be his, whether by right or by might. He would rather people liked him than that he have his way, and it was a new concept to him that people would respect him more if he stood up for his rights. They worked hard to convince him that no one respected a man whose attitude showed weakness, or who wavered like the young willow.

Plying him with questions, they found that Long Knife was pushy, demanding and conceited, not from what he told them, because he never spoke ill of the man, but from his descriptions of how the man treated him and others of his canyon. The perspective of Bear Wrestler was that the man was a natural leader who needed to grow up, but probably would not, and therefore should never become chief. Scent of Violets and He Who Conquers drew their own conclusions of a man nineteen winters who acted the way he did.

Then the snow of the land began to melt, slowly at first, under the warm sun which proved again that the God of Cold and Snows could never win the eternal war against Sun God. Water began to run under the snow in the bottom of the small gully in which their hut sat, though the snow nearly filled the long rut. It became necessary for them to save whatever they could and get up on level ground. They took the main braces and supports with them, and cut new sagebrush, Bear Wrestler too weak to do more than help Scent of Violets weave the sage into each new branch so she could place it into the structure.

The world became a quagmire of mushy snow, then of mud, but each new sun was warm. In four suns, bare spots began to appear. For two more suns they stayed in their hut or wandered near it, and on the next one began their trek toward rising-sun, angling slightly to no-sun, letting Bear Wrestler lead since he knew the way and was the slowest. They let him exert himself as he saw fit.

He had to stop often to rest, and his paces were short and deliberate. Nonetheless, they made progress, not concerned about speed. Gradually they angled toward rising-sun, watching the slowly rising landscape change little, a rolling flatness with occasional gullies or rock formations, until they suddenly came over a rise and saw a few dwellings nearby, and behind them a wide valley, rimmed with a drop of rock that was just deep

enough to be a barrier. Below, the valley was dotted
with structures, a couple of which were quite large. To
their right stood a small butte, like a sentinel (Bear
Wrestler explained it was a holy place, and several holy
men spent much time on top), beyond which was flat
country that extended out of sight into mid-sun.

A stairway was built into the rock to their right,
and they followed Bear Wrestler down the stairs, no one
paying them any attention as they walked from the wall
of rock and crossed the valley, aiming at a large structure
that was up against the opposite wall and not far from
the sentinel butte.

Heads turning this way and that, they missed
little as they followed the bear of a man toward his own
dwelling somewhere in the structure to which they
headed. It was yet before meridian-sun, yet they saw few
people, though there were many dwellings.

They dropped into a narrow but deep wash that
ran down the center of the valley, climbing out not far
from the structure to which they were pointing, a
complex of stone and mortar which opened toward mid-
sun, looking directly at the small butte.

For the first time, they saw people, a crowd of
them, the majority on their knees facing the small butte
but quartered away and on the far side. Most knelt,
some nearly prostrate before a nude girl tied to a post.
She was standing defiantly, hair hanging forward over
her face as she looked down at the two men who were
on their knees before her, faces looking up at the girl,
hands raised over their heads. The one on the left held
a knife.

The two men were masked--Spirit Men--and they
were colorfully garbed, the one with the knife wearing an
entire puma-hide which hung over his back, the head--
missing the lower jaw--on top his head. The one on the
left wore a garment that had feathers all over it, making
him the color of a golden eagle, a head of the great bird
on the top of his head. Neither had a piece of skin
visible except the hands.

They were chanting, their eyes never leaving the
girl, while the people stared and made small murmuring
sounds. There were upwards of a hundred fifty people,
obviously not all from the small village nearby, and not

one paid attention to the three new arrivals. Bear
Wrestler stared at the girl for a few moments, tears
began to roll from his eyes, and suddenly a great cry
wrenched from his throat as he moved in a staggering
run toward the front of the crowd.

The effect on the villagers was as electric as if
the God of Lightning had just hurled his fire among
them. The spell was broken as people leaned back on
their knees and turned to stare at the man they thought
was dead.

It was a staggering moment, a man whose stature
alone brought fear to many, believed dead, his face a
pictograph of scabs, racing in great strides toward the
Gift to the Goddess, voicing his displeasure. A woman
shrieked, then jumped to her feet and ran past the two
startled visitors, heading for a dwelling, followed by two
young children who began to wail at the sudden change
of attitude of their mu and the people.

But the greatest change came to the girl on the
post, whose head came up with a jerk. She took one
look at the three arrivals, locked on the approaching
giant, and screamed, so terrifyingly He Who Conquers
shivered. The Spirit Men leaped to their feet and began
to dance around the post in an attempt to refocus the
people on the rite taking place, shaking their rattles and
intoning louder, motioning for the drummer to play
louder and faster, but to no avail. The crowd had lost
their focus, staring at Bear Wrestler as though he were
a ghost, a spirit from the netherworld.

He Who Conquers and Scent of Violets followed
the big man uncertainly, wondering at the sudden
mayhem. Bear Wrestler, uttering his unintelligible roar,
arrived at the post, all evidence of his weakness vanished
in the great urgency of the moment. The transfixed
crowd stared, mesmerized by the man who had come
back from the dead, fearful that he might punish them if
they interfered. He dropped to his knees before the girl,
his hands gripping her bare shoulders and the top of his
head leaning against her stomach. It was a bizarre and
moving scene.

Even the Spirit Men stopped to watch the
spectacle, realizing they had lost control. The man was
mumbling and blubbering, and the girl continued to

scream incoherently. No one moved to confront Bear Wrestler.

Something inside He Who Conquers turned over, fear walking into him as he took Scent of Violets by the hand and pulled her with him, pushing his way to the post where Bear Wrestler hugged the girl. He had no idea who the girl was, but he could not doubt the man was deeply involved with her somehow. His fear for Bear Wrestler was both immediate and deep, not knowing what the two Spirit Men, the people of the village or the deities might do because of his defiance of the rite that had been in progress. The Goddess of Fertility would surely be angry if her rite were desecrated.

When he arrived at the post, the girl had quit screaming, now racked with great sobs. He caught the great similarities between her features and those of the man at her feet. It had to be his daughter.

He knew. The village had failed to find a virgin from another village to serve as their offering to the Goddess, and his daughter had been taken; since Bear Wrestler was absent and she had come from his clan, it seemed obvious that Long Knife had been active since his return with the claim that Bear Wrestler was dead. It was possible that the girl had even cooperated with them in her grief, thinking that her sacrifice might somehow help him in the lower world.

With a great roar that was neither speech nor coherent thought, Bear Wrestler lurched to his feet, a wild look in his face, as though to attack whoever was nearest. Seeing He Who Conquers beside him, his expression lost its ferocity, and tears came from eyes that were never to show tears...the domain of the woman. Then his hand suddenly jerked the knife from the sheath of He Who Conquers and he sliced the ropes that bound the girl to the post, turning as he did to face the crowd.

"Long Knife! Where are you?" His voice was a loud and demanding cry.

There was no response, He Who Conquers sweeping the audience to see who Long Knife might be. The demand came a second time, but again there came only silence. Bear Wrestler, agitated almost to the point of a rampage, turned to his daughter and spoke something so low no one could hear. The naked girl stared at her fa a moment, then sprinted through the crowd and disappeared in the building up the rise toward the wall.

Still there was no movement among the villagers, even the Spirit Men frozen in suspense. Bear Wrestler heaved a great sigh, then turned to his two new friends. "Come. We go to my dwelling."

The people stepped aside docilely as the three walked directly to the same doorway to which the girl had gone. Inside, they found the girl lying on her mat, her thumb in her mouth, weeping softly.

"My daughter, Blue Grouse." His voice was gentle, almost like he had not just been through a shock. The girl sat up, holding a blanket about her throat. "Did you wish to be on the post?"

She shook her head, unable to speak.

Turning to He Who Conquers, he said, "It was all wrong. She didn't wish to be on the post, though it is an honor to die for the Goddess. Long Knife has done this. He tried to wipe out my family in one sweep while I was supposedly dead."

He stood uncertainly for a moment, then said, "Was I wrong to do what I just did? I'm not dead, and she didn't choose to die. Is it not in our traditions that the girl who gives herself to the Goddess must wish to do so?"

"It is among my people."

"And here." Turning to his daughter, he asked, "Who made you do this thing?"

Her voice was hoarse from the screaming, and she spoke brokenly through sobs. "They told me you had died...that a puma had killed you...that I was now alone...I had nothing to live for...I might as well die for a good cause...the Goddess would let me go to you again, Fa...I was scared...." She began to weep again, unable to continue.

"I would have been proud for you to have died for the Goddess if that were what you wanted...but I knew...I knew someone had lied to you...that you wanted to die because of me...my daughter! By the gods, I swear Long Knife will die!"

To now He Who Conquers watched in silence,

not wishing to interfere. Now he broke in.

"It is I, Bear Wrestler, who claims the right to confront Long Knife. I am your friend and your brother. You cannot fight yet...not until you are stronger."

Slowly, the man, on his knees as was He Who Conquers, turned his head and stared for a moment, his eyes showing strong denial and disdain, his body rigid with anger. The stare stretched out, seemingly into an eternity because of eyes that bore such hate; then it was as if a warm wind began to blow across thin ice. The change was dramatic.

He nodded. "It is so. I have forgotten."

He Who Conquers dropped his pack and went out the door, his glance quickly noting the people were restless but waiting for a sure sign the rite was not to be held. The Spirit Men stood near the post, watching the doorway and seeing him before he saw them.

He headed directly for the two men, neither of which moved while he approached. The eyes of the entire village followed him.

"I am the brother of Bear Wrestler," he announced loudly for the benefit of the crowd. "I found him crawling along the ground, nearer dead than alive. The back of his head had felt the broad axe, a knife had sliced across his face and taken one eye, and above all, his scalp had been removed...with a knife."

The dramatic effect of his last statement brought a murmur among the crowd.

"While he is injured and near Sipapu, Long Knife returns to claim that the man is dead...yet he carries the scalp of the one who thought him to be a friend! A man of such treachery does not deserve to live!"

He turned to the Spirit Men. "It will be necessary to find another sacrifice. The girl did not wish to die except to find her fa in the next world. Is that reason to give a life to the Goddess."

Turning again to the people, he said loudly, "Long Knife must die for his treachery! I challenge him to a Death Match! I am the brother of Bear Wrestler, and he is too weak to fight. Earth Mu has much of his blood, and his strength is yet like the new-born fawn. As his brother, and I must fight for him. Long Knife will face me on the third sun! If he fails to show, let it be done to him as to all coyotes!"

His challenge was received in silence, at once filled with an element of fear. He was unknown...and he looked different. It was enough to lend an element of intrigue to the fear, because one so different had to be favored by the gods.

If Long Knife failed to accept the challenge, justice would demand that he be marked--the tail of a coyote cut into his forehead--and ostracized from the people of Wide Canyon.

Without further words, he headed for the dwelling of Bear Wrestler. His entry found a very somber man, one who was near the point of terror, sitting in the corner with his knees drawn up and his hands covering his face.

He looked questioningly at Scent of Violets, then at the daughter of Bear Wrestler. The latter was staring at her fa, as unaware of He Who Conquer's entry as was Bear Wrestler. Scent of Violets motioned him to follow her outside, where she whispered, "He fears the Goddess for having stolen the sacrifice."

He nodded. "And well he might. Yet the Spirit Men were wrong to continue the Ceremony under the circumstances." They returned inside.

It was so still, both inside and out, that He Who Conquers began to wonder if anyone would ever speak again. It was a long time before there were sounds heard outside, muffled talking and a few persons passing the dwelling.

The sun was nearly set and no one had yet moved inside the dwelling, Scent of Violets dozing on his shoulder, when a voice came from just outside.

"Bear Wrestler! Come out!"

The man's head snapped up as though he had awakened from a shallow slumber at a sudden sound. The expression that crossed his face was of terror, and was still evident when he stepped outside the doorway to face the speaker. He Who Conquers sat on his knees looking past the hide, his hand on his knife. He was mildly surprised to find the speaker was Spirit Man, the one who wore the eagle feathers. "You have desecrated the Ceremony of Fertility, Bear Wrestler. However, we have consulted the gods, and the Goddess has told us you have four suns in which to find a suitable sacrifice, or your daughter must die and you with her." He stared at Bear Wrestler awaiting a response, then reiterated, "You have four suns."

He turned and headed toward a kiva, when He Who Conquers went through the doorway and stood up. "Spirit Man, you are wrong!"

The man stopped and then slowly turned to face He Who Conquers. "Who are you, that you correct Spirit Man?"

"You are wrong." His voice was now quiet, but there was a deadliness in it that brought wariness to the one accused. "How is it that you break tradition? Who gave you the right to use the daughter of Bear Wrestler for this ceremony?"

"She volunteered."

He Who Conquers smiled humorlessly. "She did. Under rather unusual circumstances, don't you think?"

Spirit Man began to approach deliberately. "Who makes you the judge of that?"

"Another man, who has rights like anyone else. As the brother to Bear Wrestler, I demand to know."

"You have no right to know."

"I have. And you have no right to demand that Bear Wrestler bring a suitable sacrifice. For one of a village to be eligible to die for the Goddess, she must be willing and under no duress. Can you honestly say that was true of this girl?"

"Duress? What is duress?"

He Who Conquers chuckled coldly. "You are Spirit Man, a man sensitive to man and god. You read the spirits, you sing the songs, you understand the oneness of all things. You tend to man when he is in pain. And you tell me you cannot truly define duress?"

Spirit Man squinted in anger. "You have nothing to say in the matter."

"Your people will be glad to hear that. I'll make it a point for the next four suns to go around to as many as possible and explain what you think of them individually. They'll be glad to know that their daughters might be the next gift to the Goddess, even if they don't want it and the girl isn't willing."

"Just who are you?"

"Does it really matter? If I were the son of the chief or of the poorest man, the matter should be judged in itself and its merits, and have nothing to do with who anyone is. The fact is, unless you, the leader of the spiritual community, can't do what is necessary to please the Goddess, you have no right to send this man out to do it for you. What you do is give him a task that is not possible for him to do at the present time, and for which he should not be held responsible. If you are to be just, and I would like to think that would be your aim, it is Long Knife that should be sent. After all, he's the one who committed the wrong, a treacherous act of attempted murder, and he's the one who should atone for the act before he faces me in a Death Match."

"Perhaps the Death Match should come first."

"Suit yourself. Only you will then have to send yet another, and there are only so many suns in which you can appease the Goddess without incurring her anger. And I gave Long Knife three suns to face me."

Spirit Man stared at him a moment, unsure of how to continue against this cocky visitor, and decided against it. Looking past He Who Conquers, he spoke to Bear Wrestler. "Ignore what I just said; we will be back to talk of this further."

Bear Wrestler stood with his shoulders slumped as though he carried the weight of the mighty rock on his back. He stared after Spirit Man until long after he had entered his kiva, finally turning like a blindman and groping for the wall to support himself as he entered the door and slid to the floor, prone.

"I've done nothing right before the gods! I shamed my clan, condemned my daughter, and brought my friends into a village that will kill them because of me!" His voice was low and filled with regret, a cry of agony. Silence fell with the darkness. He Who Conquers and Scent of Violets sat in the dark and listened to his labored breathing, while his daughter sat in the far corner and wept softly.

Finally, He Who Conquers touched Scent of Violets and went outside, and she followed. They stood a few steps from the doorway and she said, "What can be done to help this wronged man and his daughter?"

"I don't know." He Who Conquers was silent a

moment. "I must find this Long Knife."

"But," she protested, "you have no idea how good he is, what will happen if you win, or what might come of all this. He is the son of the chief! Perhaps we will all die?"

"Then it will be because the Great One has ordained it. Otherwise, nothing can harm us." After a pause, he added, "I have no choice. We found him, and he lives because of us. He was dealt with in a way that even an enemy does not deserve, much less one of his own people. And, like you said, the son of the chief, no less! We came with him. I must now stand beside him. If he dies, I die. If I die, you will die with me."

Scent of Violets said nothing, both of them aware of the silence that hung over the village. Only the voice of a barking dog broke the stillness.

"I wonder where Long Knife is?" The abrupt change of topic brought an end to their tense silence. She said nothing. "I wish Bear Wrestler could answer the challenge on his own behalf, but he cannot. And wishing is for the weak and the coward.

"If there is to be a Death Match, the Goddess must wait. We must first protect Bear Wrestler until we know he is wrong, or vengeance is done. We have saved his life, and he is now my brother. I must keep him alive, and us with him."

"What happens if you fail?"

"As I said before, I die. And if I die, we all die unless we can somehow sneak out of here...which I doubt.   And to sneak out would make me a coward...like...like what they always said of my fa. If he was a coward, then I must know what happened and why he chose the path he walked. If he was given no honorable choice, then I must make amends."

"Then you must act quickly."

"Bear Wrestler must be allowed to sleep. I doubt he could do anything required of him. With the new sun, I must find Long Knife, and we must get this over."

"Whatever is to be, I will stand with you!" She gave his arm a gentle squeeze. "I will do what I can for his daughter. She feels the guilt of one who may be attacked by the Goddess for some wrong she has done. It won't be an easy task to convince her otherwise."

He wrapped his arms around her, and they stood in the darkness without any feelings cf security. Both were aware they had gotten themselves into something more than met the eye when they first found the wounded man. Here was a challenge that outweighed any they had ever faced. While it was frightening, they had to, each in their own way, deal with their thoughts. They relieved themselves before they returned to their mat and slept.

22

He Who Conquers was up with the rising sun, outside where he could study the quiet village and listen to the gods who might speak to him. He heard nothing, and the Great One was silent as well. He stared up at the butte which seemed to be the spiritual center of the people who lived here, and wondered if Sun God dealt with these people in the same way as he did with **The People of The Top**. Birds had begun to sing, a meadowlark repeating its melody over and over, while some smaller birds worked on the ground not far from where he stood. A hawk floated high overhead, the first time he had seen one in a long time. What did the Great One have for him this sun?

A man came from a kiva and saw him standing alone, but made no attempt to be friendly. He relieved himself and stood facing the butte for a time. When he turned, He Who Conquers stood two steps behind him. He nearly jumped from the surprise.

"Would you tell me where Long Knife lives?"

The man shook his head. "In another center."

He nodded, aware the man would say no more. So. The many structures were called centers. Now all he had to do was find out how they differentiated each center, how they named them, and find where his enemy called home. The man went back into the kiva.

His mate came out, relieved herself and came to stand beside him. "You will hunt Long Knife?"

"He lives in another center. The man I spoke to wouldn't say which one. Bear Wrestler will when I talk with him later."

They ate, the four of them, in silence, but it was interrupted by a shout outside.

"Bear Wrestler!" The man blanched, then flushed with anger.

"Long Knife!" He breathed the name, and before he could physically react, He Who Conquers went out the door.

His first look at the attempted killer showed a man with no particular identifying characteristic...except a pouty look that was evident even in the surprise that covered his face. The surprise was replaced by a moment of indecision, covered quickly by a determined look that he could not interpret.

"Who are you?" Long Knife stared at the lanky, sinewy man four winters his junior, sizing him as though he were an broken axe that needed study.

"I'm the brother of Bear Wrestler, the man you tried to kill. You are Long Knife, a man of obviously few redeeming qualities, most assuredly none of which includes honor. You tried to kill the man from behind, an act worse than a coward. I will feel nothing when you die for what you did. You will face me in a Death Match when the next sun rises."

Long Knife curled his upper lip. "So, you're the one who thinks he can kill the champion of The People. I find that most amusing."

"The gods ordain your death. Murder is not something they condone. Cowardice is punished, as well. A battle of honor, yes, but not murder."

"You consider yourself my conqueror, then. Well, we shall see."

"No one who lives in your treachery is worthy of being called a man." He let his hand brush the scalps that hung at his left hip, and saw the other's eyes fall to them. Nine scalps made a sizeable bunch. The man stared at them, then wrenched his eyes away.

"Who gave you those, your fa?" Long Knife lifted his upper lip again, a cold cynical smile."

"If he had, it would have made him more of a man than your fa, wouldn't it? But each must prove himself a man, no? But, though you wish otherwise, these I earned."

"Children and women, no doubt."

He Who Conquers smiled as coldly as Long Knife. "No doubt. But that's for you to learn too late."

Long Knife again silently evaluated his foe, a tinge of uncertainty in his eyes, though he fought to subdue it. No humor showed as he replied, "Anyone as cocky as you has never truly fought a warrior. I'll take my chances."

"That's exactly what you'll take. No, treacherous one, you lose. No coyote fights his battle against an opponent who has strength. You may be able to lift the rock, and perhaps you're very good with your knife. But for this one, you fight a losing battle against one who is both lighter and quicker."

"Interesting." He wheeled on his heel and strode off. As he did, he spoke over his shoulder, "See you at first light."

He Who Conquers watched him go, blank for the first time. The man was unafraid, was self-assured, and walked like an athlete. He was a champion with the knife. It was a sobering thing. Yet he felt confident, for he was in the right. The Great One had taken care of him before, and he would once again.

When Long Knife was long out of sight, heading to no-sun, He Who Conquers turned. Bear Wrestler, his daughter and Scent of Violets all stood watching, having heard the entire exchange.

"He's certainly sure of himself," Scent of Violets offered, a note of uncertainty in her voice.

"He's very good," Bear Wrestler replied. "I hope you are as good as you indicate, my brother."

"With the new sun, we'll know for sure, won't we?" He moved toward the doorway, and they all went inside to finish their breakfast.

The sun seemed to last forever. He Who Conquers was restless, and after midsun left the dwelling, found a quiet spot where he assumed he was alone, and practiced. A small doubt had come into his mind, mostly because the man was so self assured. He had never met a man who seemed so unafraid, and the only two times were The Deer, who was the liar and coward, and White Hawk, who was exactly what he seemed. Which one was Long Knife? Had he been hasty to assume he could win over a foe simply because he felt the gods ordained it? Now that he faced reality, where he was facing a man who could and would fight to kill, was he truly good enough? Just because he could out-fight those on The Top, in a duel where no real harm was imminent, was he better than this man?

He practiced against an imaginary foe for a short time, then sat and let his mind wander. Was this Long Knife the son of the man his fa was to have fought? How could he find out? With whom could he discuss this? Bear Wrestler was too young to have been around, and it could be that the incident here was never as big as what his own people had made it. Perhaps no one remembered!

He began a slow return to the center, not sure of where he should start. Before he had gone a stone throw, an elderly man could be seen leaning against a rock in the sun, watching him. He walked over and sat beside the old one, only once having looked at the man.

Neither spoke, the old one fingering an empty pipe but watching He Who Conquers peripherally. A long silence ensued, He Who Conquers knowing that tradition told him to wait for the elder to speak first. The old man spoke.

"What's your name?"

"He Who Conquers."

The man nodded once slowly. For a long time he seemed to be weighing that. "You are from The Top."

"I am." He had often wondered if other people referred to his home as The Top also. The thought was fleeting.

"The Trader came through just before snowtime. He said a young man named He Who Conquers killed four Others and then left The Top." He flicked his eyes over the young man beside him and again put his eyes into the ethereal sky overhead. Did he expect him to boast of the conquests, or merely acknowledge he was the one? He said nothing for a time, being patient as he could manage.

"It was I. The Great One has been good to me." He let that sink in for a while, not planning to say more.

"I thought it might be. You have many scalps. I have to assume you won them all." There was an edge in his voice He Who Conquers could not understand. Was he being friendly, or had he some cynical retort coming? And how could he turn the subject to what he needed to find while he was here. But you did not hurry elders. You respected them, waited for them, listened to them.

"I did, but not all in battle or a Death Match."

"Well said. You have earned a fight."

"Earned?"

Sharply, the voice was cooler. "Earned. You have become a brother to a man who has few friends."

"As do I." He need not elaborate. This old man was far above the level of word games. He knew. How or when he had learned these things did not matter. It was enough that he knew.

"It is so." Now the old man turned and looked at him with a sharp, penetrating scrutiny. "You have a look about you that reminds me of someone I once knew. It is why I came here." He took the pipe from the edge of his mouth and held it, gazing at it a moment, then turning once more to face He Who Conquers.

"Who is your fa?" He knew already. He Who Conquers felt momentarily tongue-tied. Did he dare admit it? What was the agenda of this old man? Where was he coming from, and leading to? If he told him, what would the old man do with the information, or rather, the admission?

Too late, he heard himself say, "Blue Teal."

The eyes penetrated deeply; they burned, ate and swallowed. Never had he felt so naked, as though every thought he had were on the *Story Rock*, for everyone to see and evaluate. He felt a need to run, to streak down the wide side canyon in which they sat, to get away from this one who knew him without ever having met him.

"Are you proud of your fa?"

He shrugged. "I don't know. He is considered a coward by my people. I don't know the truth. That's most of why I came here. To right a wrong, or find the truth with which I will have to live. Right now, no, I'm not proud of him. Neither am I ashamed. Until I know...."

"You speak truth. I will tell you truth." He put the pipe back in the side of his mouth, but kept his hand on it. "Your fa was a man of talent and honor. He could hunt with the best, he fought with the best, he knew more than most, he traveled to get salt, cotton, obsidian, seashells, turquoise. Whatever was necessary. His mate was a homely woman, but very skilled and very charming.

"Then one sun he claimed a deer kill that our present chief, White Feather, also claimed. One thing about your fa, he was not a man to take second place if he felt he was first, as he did in this case. He would not back down. No one knows who was right or wrong.

"Meanwhile, your fa's mate had eyes for the man who is now our chief. She liked him and had tried to woo him without success. However, White Feather had lost his mate when she dropped a child, which, incidentally, was stillborn. Now Short Grass decided to make her move. She said your fa told everyone that he had shot the animal, but told her he had not, that he merely wanted to beat White Feather once.

"I don't know the truth, but I suspect it. I think she lied. It's now irrelevant. White Feather, then the son of the chief, challenged your fa to a Death Match, the first ever remembered here."

He again took the pipe from his lips and rubbed it, already having polished it to a sheen with his habit. "Your fa was aghast. How could he fight the man who was to be chief, especially since there was no other heir? It would wound his people, and leave a scar deeper than any he could ever wish upon those for whom he cared."

"This place, Wide Canyon, is a vast business world. It is the hub of a trade traffic that grows from both necessity and desire. To be chief is to carry unlimited responsibility and a huge burden. White Feather has such talents, and your fa did not wish to end such talent and throw the entire canyon and its future into turmoil."

He changed position, and again leaned back. "He left. No one knew where he went. Short Grass mated White Feather, and Long Knife is their only son. They had six daughters. White Feather is very old, and Short Grass is one winter older than he. You'll fight their son, a generation after your fa refused to do the same. Ironic."

He Who Conquers had thoughts running rampant. So his fa had done what he himself had done, left his people to keep from a Death Match with the son of the chief. Yet here he was, about to fight the battle his fa refused. The difference, obviously, being that this was not his people. His people were on The Top.

He could not run, nor did he choose to. He had been taken into a circumstance completely different from what his fa had faced, and he had no feeling for White Feather or his lying mate, Short Grass. The only point that mattered here was Bear Wrestler. Whether he and his daughter were really worthy of being called friends had no bearing, because no matter what brought about the failed attempt to murder him did not justify such treachery. No honorable man ambushed a member of his own community. Challenge him to a Death Match, perhaps, but not ambush. Anyone who would do what Long Knife had done was not a brave and honorable man, and no doubt had far more doubts than he let on when they were discussing the situation.

"Are you saying I should not fight Long Knife? That maybe I'm less than my honorable fa if I do?"

For the first time, the old man showed the faintest smile. "You call your fa honorable. That pleases me. I was his friend. We often hunted together. But I was laid up with a broken ankle when this hunt took place, and it was not for me to determine who was the most honorable in their disagreement."

"I understand."

"Perhaps. That, too, is irrelevant. But you came here hoping to prove your fa an honorable man, not to see what the truth really might be. Only in that did you err. But it is an understandable mistake, for a man always sets out to prove himself worthy, and that is as it should be. A man who wishes only to 'find himself' is a liar, for he seeks nothing that would prove himself a man. He's like the willow that staggers in every adversity." Again he changed his position, this time sitting forward, but the pipe remained in his caressing hands.

"So. Now that you know what I know, you may choose to believe whatever you like. I believe what I wish, and it makes me wish to see your fa again. Alas, it can never be. He's old, and I'm old, and there's much distance between us." His eyes seemed to mist a bit, and he paused. "What is between you and Long Knife is of no consequence to me. I'm too old to care."

He Who Conquers had found it all. Everything he had truly come for. Yet something bothered him, and he was unsure of what it was. He stared at the far wall of the narrower canyon, one where there were no trees and little but sparse grasses. None of it entered his mind. He was too busy wondering about all he had heard.

"I will fight Long Arrow. His perfidy shows him to be a man incapable of good leadership. Someone else should be chief of this people, someone who has honor and integrity, who wants to serve his people."

The old one leaned back against the rock wall of the valley, closing his eyes, the pipe again between his teeth. He was done talking, and He Who Conquers got to his feet and began the long walk back to the center. After a short walk, he began to trot, then to sprint, and finally to trot again. Winded, he reached the center just as cooking fires were being lit, when people were standing around with the adventures of the sun behind them. Yet, his appearance stopped all talk, and drew stares he had no means to interpret.

When he stopped at his doorway, Scent of Violets came from the dwelling and took his arm, steering him toward the rock wall behind the village. When they were alone, she stopped and faced him.

"He is gone."

"Who, Bear Wrestler?"

"No, Long Knife."

"Long Knife? I don't understand. Where did he go?"

She smiled, almost apologetically. "Away. No one knows when he left, or where he went. He took his mate and two children with him."

He was stunned. "You mean...he just ran away?"

"That's exactly what I mean. He ran."

He turned and looked at the butte. "But...he's supposed to be the next chief!"

"But now he won't."

"Are you sure it's permanent? Maybe he just left for the sun, to prepare himself for the fight."

"And take his family, and all his personal things, and food and clothing? Not too likely, I would say."

He was blank. He stared at his mate, then turned to stare at the butte, then the valley wall behind it. Was the man that much a coward? How could he know he was not the better fighter? How could he leave his people, his future position, his power? How could...?

There would be no fight. Disappointment and relief were confused in his mind, and he wondered whether this was good or bad. Or was it either?

He took her hand and they went back to the dwelling. Of one thing he was sure, they would now stay here for some time. He wanted a chance to learn a few things, and to talk to a few people--old people.

* * *   * * *   * * *

He was far back from the stake, kneeling like those around him, eyes riveted on the girl tied to the post. This was the new Gift to the Goddess, a young woman who had in the past winter been visited by the Goddess who started her flow of blood. She was a heavy girl, whose body reminded him of a mixture of gourds, varying sizes in a semblance of order. Irreverent as that seemed, he had a second one that he thought even moreso. How did the Goddess view the maidens who were given to her? Did it matter that they were fat or thin, tall or short, pretty or ugly? If it did not matter at all, did it matter if the people made no sacrifice at all?

He stopped and nearly choked. That was as close to blasphemy as he had ever been. How could he think such thoughts? Yet, had this people, like his people, offered sacrifices like this before they began to live by planting? What did they do when they put out their seeds and then left, coming back at harvest after spending the growing time chasing animals and fighting other tribes?

His eyes caught movement, and he realized there was a man on top the butte, an old man who stood with arms raised as if in supplication. He faced away, and the position of his head showed he was watching something or someone. It had to be Sun Watcher, either that he saw or whom the old one watched. From them would come the signal of the exact time for the ceremony to begin. Funny, but he had not noticed anyone on the butte when they had arrived at the aborted ceremony.

Behind the crowd sat two men with large drums, hollow logs overstretched with deerskin, and large sticks, eyes glued on the man atop the butte, poised to take the signal and begin the cadence. Two other men stood near a large pile of debris, ready to touch the burning coal to start the bonfire that would end the rite and begin the celebration of the people.

He Who Conquers, from where he knelt, could see it all in one sweeping glance. He watched Sun Watcher carefully, and the man's arms were raised while he waited for the precise moment. Then his arms came down as he prostrated himself, and the drum began to beat, a slow rhythm at first that soon became a hard throb.

From behind the rock came two men wearing bird masks and painted bodies, walking slowly but in rhythm to the drum, and untied the girl. While they did their task, the two Spirit Men danced slowly around the post four times. She was placed on the ground, where Spirit Man danced around her four times, still slowly, then stopped at her feet, shaking his gourds and chanting, his feet still moving. Then he dropped down between her legs, held apart by the two men, and drove his maleness into her. She made no sound, though she arched her back at the suddenness, no doubt painful without the necessary lubrication.

Spirit Man thrust roughly, still in rhythm to the beat which had been increased. Then he stood and danced around her, again four times, before stepping back to the post while the second Spirit Man then emulated what he had done. It was assumed that at least one of the two men would leave his seed in her, for no one could be given to the Goddess without knowing the seed of a man.

When the second was through, the two men again tied the girl to the post and went into the crowd to become part of it. Both Spirit Men began to dance, away from the post, and then back, and away again. Four times they left the post, and then returned.

Now they again moved around the post, once, twice, thrice, and four times. On the fourth, the first came close to the girl and lifted her face with a hand under her chin, his voice ringing out in syllables to the rhythm of the drum. He left her, and the second went across in front of her, and no one saw the suddenness of his knife. When he rounded the post in his dance and the people could again see her, her head hung sharply to the left and blood ran over her shoulder and breast. When the first Spirit Man came around again, he carried a small open bowl, which he held to the death wound, catching the blood as it pumped from the gaping slice. When he had taken enough, he began to move swiftly through the audience, smearing a bit of blood on every forehead or cheek, hesitating only a moment before finishing his task at He Who Conquers, Scent of Violets, Bear Wrestler and Falling Skies.

When he was done, he moved to the pile of debris and tossed the bowl into the heap, and the two men lit the fire. At the same time, the body of the girl was cut from the post by the second Spirit Man and all the men, including Bear Wrestler and He Who Conquers, followed the male procession to the huge open kiva before the village.

While the women and children began to dance at the bonfire, the Spirit Men cut off the small breasts of the girl and dropped them into the fire going in the fire pit. Then they knelt before the body and cut out the womb and sex organs, which were taken back and hung from a limb on the post where she had given her life. The body of the girl was then cut into small slabs, and a piece given to each man, who skewered the piece given them and went to the bonfire where they roasted the meat and ate it.

The ceremony was over. What remained of the body was put into the huge bonfire so the smoke would please the Goddess. The men joined the women in dancing, while the exhausted children lay on blankets and fell asleep. The dance continued long into the darkness, women dropping out as they tired, a man quitting with each one. Together they would go to the edge of the firelight and couple, paying no mind to who was mated to whom, with the expectation that the Goddess would bring fertility to the coupling. Scent of Violets continued until many of the men had quit, and when she stopped, He Who Conquers did the same. Holding hands, they walked into the darkness, found a place on the soft sand, and made love.

"I am now with child, my conqueror," she whispered when they lay quietly on the blanket she had carried. "Your seed has given you a son. The Goddess is in me."

He smiled. "It will be a son to lead men. Next, you will give me a daughter, who will keep the Totem of the Hawk alive."

She giggled softly. "You plant your seed often, my conqueror. I'll fill our dwelling with children as you fill your quiver with arrows."

He was light-hearted, and chuckled quietly. Then, as they lay side-by-side enjoying the touch of the fingertips, he suddenly was filled with nausea...an overwhelming feeling as strong as the time he found The Deer in his dwelling. The flash of insight was of Scent of Violets, heavy with child, ravens flying around her head, her eyes closed and her face as pale as cotton. As quickly as it had come, it left, but in that brief moment his entire future was tainted. Fear for Scent of Violets would be his every moment he saw or thought of her, even though he had no idea what the exact meaning was. It was more than enough to know it was evil.

His thoughts were ended abruptly by a shout from back near the village. They put their breechcloths on and hurried back to discover the cause of the excitement.

They found Bear Wrestler very exercised about some thing, but he was nearly incoherent. It was the voice of another that told them of what had happened.

"He just discovered that Long Knife has become the coyote, and run away!"

He Who Conquers had already had his shock. He was only surprised that Bear Wrestler had not been told. The man was deeply disturbed that his satisfaction was to be unfulfilled. His bitterness would continue, unless another of the clan could be made to pay for the crime. Yet, who might that be, since there were only two other eligible men in the entire clan, and neither was a good friend of the coyote?

For He Who Conquers, it was the work of the Great One. No longer would he be forced to leave immediately. In fact, with his mate having the seed in her to bring him a son, they could wait until she had dropped her child. The hawk had been true twice in two suns. The Great One still worked with him!

23

The people were planting. Sun Watcher had given them the exact time, Spirit Man had consecrated the first seed and planted them, Rain Man had begun his pleading each sun, and holes were prepared. Scent of Violets found her early suns filled with nausea which passed before midsun, and He Who Conquers was shoulder-to-shoulder with Bear Wrestler, putting seeds into the ground.

It would be several suns before the planting was over, as digging sticks were forced deeply into Earth Mu before a hill was ready to receive several seeds. Corn, squash and beans were planted side-by-side, in hills that followed no pattern. The seeds were watered as they were planted, but would then be left for the work of Rain Man unless drought-like conditions lasted too long. Then they would use water dammed in the gully that ran down the center of Wide Canyon, hoping more run-off would find its way into the supply before the present supply could be used. There had been a bumper crop the previous two suns, and the storage rooms were already full. Still, it was a large and growing society, and there could never be too much. It was part of why the trade business had been put into such a wide and intense outreach.

Discussion was already being made about a journey for trade, using some of the stored grain and seed to barter for the symbol of wealth, things. Colorful birds, shells from the great waters, salt, colorful rocks and useful stones, cotton and other commodities. Among the leaders, there was discussion of laying out more roads and building outlier trading centers. In the future, the "things" of trading would be used to bring in more corn as necessary.

He Who Conquers finished seeding, doing part of the task of Bear Watcher, and returned toward the dwelling. Almost a moon and a half had gone past since the ceremony, and the strength of the big man was slowly returning, though he often complained of the witch that caused pain in his head--the reason He Who Conquers returned alone. He was nearly to the doorway when Scent of Violets came out and met him.

"They couple," she said simply. "We can walk."

He shrugged. "Again? I thought he had a witch that caused pain. Why doesn't he sleep? Besides, it would be better for him to take a mate. Perhaps his pain isn't in his head."

"She doesn't want him to mate. Falling Skies has decided her fa is better than the young men in the village. The pain he says he suffers may or may not be real, but she talked him into coupling as a way of treating his aching head. She says he sleeps better."

He shrugged. "If she were not so homely, someone might mate her in spite of the aborted ceremony."

"That's doubtful, but it's his problem, too. No woman wishes such a man unless she has no other prospects. Besides, the size of his maleness scares most away. His daughter cried even after they had coupled many times, and bled a lot. He's not just big, he's huge. Now that she's used to his size, she won't settle for one smaller."

They walked a while, then he said, "Bear Wrestler wanted me to couple with her. I refused. My lynx is all

I need."

She giggled. "I'll keep you tired. Perhaps you can fill your needs with her when I grow too big for you to get close to me."

He made a face. "I'll use what time you give me to recuperate. You're all I can handle."

Again she giggled. "I want children...lots of children. Who knows when the Goddess will visit me? I don't want to take chances and miss the visit."

"Besides, by the time I'd need her, she'll be with child or have become a priestess."

She nudged him with her elbow. "A priestess is but another name for a woman who's horny and has no mate. She becomes a priestess so she can take men often. You will some sun have to visit a priestess, too, don't forget. Every male must give a son or daughter to the gods."

He grimaced. "It may be a tradition, but I hope the woman is better looking than that one."

This time she laughed. "You may want her to be pretty, my conqueror, but I prefer she be as ugly as a bear sow. There will come a time when I dry up, and you'll wish for release, and the priestess will receive your company as often as I."

He wrinkled his nose, the humor a bit forced as he remembered the ravens and her paleness. Still, who could remain long in such morbid thoughts when his pretty and light-hearted mate was walking beside him and making the world pleasant.

"Do you think Bear Wrestler has become a poor companion?" she asked in an abrupt change of subject.

"What do you mean?"

"He has gotten so morose. He sits and scowls much of the time, and no longer rises to humor. I wonder if he doesn't couple with his daughter often to remove some of his frustrations."

He nodded. "He does not make friends. I'm not sure he's ever tried. He never seems to find any joy in life."

"Neither does his daughter. She speaks in short sentences and mostly says nothing. I wonder if we'd not be better leaving their dwelling. Besides, if the people find that a man couples with his daughter, they will be severely punished. It could happen we would be forced to take the punishment with them."

He shrugged. "It hasn't been pleasant to stay with them like I hoped. Perhaps it's time to consider a place of our own, or return to my people."

She looked at him and stopped. "I'd thought of that, but didn't want to say so. That must be your decision."

"Since you're with child, a trip would not be easy."

"With a baby, it'll not be much better."

"But it's easier to carry a child than to carry a woman who carries her child inside."

She giggled. "True, my conqueror. But when you're ready, I'll go."

He held her close, then released her. "It'd be best to wait until after you drop the child, get through your purifications and regain your strength."

"But what will that mean? We have no dwelling, and Bear Wrestler is getting harder to live with by the sun."

"I can still stand him, and I've sworn to be his brother. It is best to weather the storm as long as we can. Meanwhile, we'll ask around for a dwelling of our own. We can make plans to leave during snowtime when there are fewer things to do, when we're confined. Time goes faster when we have something to do."

"Except he's becoming more critical. He even speaks ill of you sometimes, and that makes my fur rise! What if he senses we're leaving?"

He turned and started back, still holding her hand. "We can only assure him we aren't, and sneak away as we did from your people."

"But he'll know where we're going! Won't he follow?" There was more exasperation than fear in her voice.

"I'm not that naive. He'll try."

"Then what?"

He shrugged and stared at the high rim of the canyon. "Let the gods ordain it."

She was silent, then stopped and looked behind them. "I've seen three caves that would keep us. Could we stay in one of them?"

"What would you say to our hosts?"

She looked blank, then grinned. "That I want more privacy with you?"

He returned her humor. "In this place you think that would carry water? Like a leaky olla!"

"Well, might it be worth a try?"

They started walking again, when he noticed a man on the rim to mid-sun, standing and watching. He kept an eye on the man for a time, wondering at him, thinking through the possible reasons for a stranger--and he knew it was a stranger--to be simply standing and looking. No one did that, unless he had reason.

"Who is it?" she asked, following his gaze.

"A man with a burr under his breechcloth."

"A what? What do you mean?"

"He's a man looking for a missing daughter." He was sure he was right, though it was only an opinion.

She stared up at the man while they walked. "He seeks retribution?"

He nodded. "He comes to find the ones who took her, and to take what is his."

"And will he be appeased when he finds she has become one with the Goddess?"

"No."

Alarmed, she looked up again at the man on the rim. "So what will he do?"

He shrugged. "Who knows? If he's stubborn, it could demand action from Council. A man is to accept the will of the Goddess."

"What would the man demand?"

"A daughter of the village."

"Whose?"

Again he shrugged. "Would you give your daughter?"

She stared at the man. "Would it come to that?"

"You have no daughter, but someone else has. It could."

She again stared up at the solitary figure, trying to grasp the import of his presence. "Yes, if someone demanded my daughter, the Goddess would have her." The words came slowly. "I owe her. Without the Goddess, everything I have would not be."

He nodded. "But when a girl is stolen away, is

it not difficult to see her used to appease the Goddess.? That man wonders why one from within the village wasn't used."

She nodded. "But that's tradition! Even though Bear Wrestler was wrong to interfere."

"Right or wrong, that's not ours to decide. But that man is supposed to accept tradition. Obviously, he has some other thoughts on the matter."

"But he can demand repayment?"

He stopped and watched the man for a time. "Council will have to answer that one, not me. I can only speak for what happens in our area. Traditions differ, but it seems like the man might be from another place, where they think differently."

"So what will Council do?"

"Probably send the man home. To give him something would be to desecrate the Ceremony which was already held.

"Then why is he even trying?"

"He is angry. When a man lets anger rule him, there are many things that can go wrong. An angry man can't use his head or be logical. Maybe he has no mate. Perhaps he's like Bear Wrestler and his daughter. And maybe he's just the kind of man who never learned to think."

She nodded. "Well, I sure hope Bear Wrestler appreciates what you have done for him."

He smiled and turned again toward the village. "He knows. It's enough. And it wounded his pride that he was too weak to challenge Long Knife. He's not a highly intelligent man. Pride is most of what he is."

"Sometimes I wonder if he remembers, the way he talks." She stopped to mess an anthill and watch the ants scurry around. "What will become of Falling Skies if the villagers find she couples with her fa?"

"They'll both be marked and sent away. No one will allow a marked man or woman to live with them. The gods would not smile on them if they did."

"But we know, and we live with them."

"We are not one of them. They would probably just ask us to go."

"And the Trader would spread the story of He Who Conquers everywhere. Your name would become a source of amusement."

"The Great One won't allow that. I do it because the man is my brother."

She shook her head. "I don't understand how Bear Wrestler and Falling Skies intend to get away with what they're doing. They know it's wrong, but they both seem to be driven to continue. It even disgusts me, and I feel I'm more accepting than these people will be if they find out what's happening."

He chuckled softly, watching people scurrying about in the last rays of Sun God, as they neared the village again. "The Spirit Men opened her. If she has a child, who's to know it didn't come about because of their seed. Still, it's dangerous. If time elapses before she's with child, everyone will know."

"Unless they think you might have been coupling with her."

He glanced up at the rim and the man was gone. "It wouldn't help him, then, to move to our own dwelling, will it? Still, I'd feel better if we did. What he does is wrong, and I don't feel it necessary for us to cover him."

"I agree."

He chuckled. "The Goddess was appeased, was she not? And we are helping with the planting, as we'll help with construction and other things. No one can say we aren't carrying our fair share, and just a bit more."

"I'll begin asking around for a place of our own. You're already doing your fair share."

He continued to chuckle. "I searched for a mate, and found the best of the lot. Now it is time to show this people that their loss of Long Knife and his family has been compensated well."

They approached the dwelling when He Who Conquers spoke again. "Remember, people are fallible, and the gods surely know that...since even we know."

It ended their discussion, and they stopped beside the doorway. Scent of Violets pushed aside the hide to find fa and daughter sleeping, curled into each other's arms and still enjoined in coupling. Without a moment of hesitation, she grabbed their blankets and mat and backed out of the dwelling.

"We can't stay there," she said disgustedly, as

they walked along the edge of the cliff, found a soft spot and sat against the wall of the canyon a short distance away.

The sun had set, and the skies were darkening, but neither moved while the coolness came. They were hungry, and He Who Conquers was tired from the long sun in the field; it did his disposition no good to find themselves in this situation.

They huddled together inside their blankets without speaking for a long time. She dozed, leaning on his shoulder, then jerked and woke herself.

"Will Bear Wrestler awaken to know what he's been causing us?"

"What?"

"Here we sit, his guests, in the cool outdoors, while he, because of his poor manners, sleeps inside with one whom he should leave alone."

"I doubt he will realize anything."

"Then I think it time to say something. Sober him to the truth. Shake him up a bit. I know you won't say anything, but I can. This just is not acceptable. Not for me, and certainly not for you."

He chuckled softly, watching cooking fires burn down as people retired to their mats. "Perhaps you're right, but can I leave a brother when he'll need me?"

She failed to respond to his humor. "Yes. For one, you still have no certainty that Long Knife will ever return. It is all speculation, and in my mind, doubtful. Second, you owe him nothing; he owes you. It was you who found him, and together we saved his life. Then you were the one to gain more time for him by challenging Spirit Man, otherwise he would have had to find the girl. And he's the one who has become despondent, and taken his own daughter for a mate. No one will take his side in a dispute. You have done for him what he makes no attempt to do for himself, and he certainly doesn't appreciate what you did for him. Instead, he loses himself in self-pity. I think we have good cause to take a long walk and enjoy ourselves, and let him fend for himself this time."

He mulled that for a time, then said, "Perhaps you're right, but I offered myself, he didn't coerce me."

"So? I think your sense of duty is over-strong.

For me, do this. Come."

She stood and folded her blanket while he still sat, watching her and thinking. She tucked the blanket under her arm and extended her hand to him, and he took it. Soon they were walking up the canyon in the direction they had never been, unsure of what was there.

It grew dark, but the flat canyon floor made the going easy. They passed dwellings tucked up against the canyon wall, and others that stood out on the floor. No one was out, the turkeys had all gone to roost, though twice dogs barked and approached, then stood and watched as the two passed. Finally they came to the end of the valley, alone and far from the last habitations, where they spread their blankets.

Under the blankets, they laid wordlessly, lost in private thoughts, until almost unconsciously they began to caress. Her lightheartedness brought a giggle when he brought his lips to her breasts.

"What do you suppose fa-fa would have said if he saw us now?"

"Nothing," he responded teasingly, "because I think he would only have sat and wished it were he and your mu-mu. He was a lonely man."

She pulled his face into her breast and hugged him firmly but gently. "I could only wish he knew we mated. He wanted it so much. But then, maybe he knows."

"Spirit Man could contact him and let him know."

"I suppose." She paused to relax her hold, and he moved up over her and kissed her. "Maybe it's best to keep it a secret and tell him myself."

He grinned. "The lynx speaks again."

She laughed quietly, taking his maleness in her hands and caressing it. "Does a lynx also tease its mate like this?"

He chuckled. "No doubt. Women are much like cats, and cats are great teasers. But I've never met a man who preferred it any other way."

She laughed again. "You make it sound like a woman can make a man do anything."

"You doubt it? Spend some time and study the male, and you'll discover that if a woman makes demands, a man will kill himself to please her. Women control all."

She spread herself and guided his entry, then they lay calmly. He moved only a minimum to feel the union.

"A lynx never lets the tom stay in her long," she teased. "It's over very quickly."

He grinned down on her. "The tom is a dumb animal, right? I have more intelligence than that!" She lifted to meet his gentle movements, and he spoke softly in her ear, "The human species is the only one that mates front to front. It surely is more enjoyable. An animal only masturbates in his coupling, only when the female is in heat, and loses all the enjoyment because she cannot respond...or doesn't know how."

She laughed again. "So, does that make the human female better? Or smarter?"

"Yes, on both accounts." He began to increase the rhythm, and she moved with him.

Suddenly she stopped, sober. "If I'm with child, I can't be in heat. If I'm not in heat, why do I let you do this?"

He burst out laughing, and each time he tried to speak, he would start again. Finally he was calm enough to respond. "Because you, my lynx, are always in heat, and you don't do this only to make babies!"

"Oh! So I'm always in heat!"

He was laughing again, and she joined him for a long time. When they were through, he was flaccid, tears in his eyes. She had no trouble getting him started again, and after a time they lay spent, and slept without separating.

He awakened to the first touches of light and sat up, to discover her lying awake watching him.

"You've been awake long?"

She nodded. "It was pleasant to lie beside you and realize what I have. You're a mate in a million."

He grinned, leaned down and nuzzled her. She held him there for a while, then pulled him against her.

"You will stay with me until midsun, and you'll make love to me again before it gets full light. I won't let you go back to the dwelling until I'm sure Bear Wrestler knows that he's been wrong."

He grinned and lay beside her. "You have a most

persuasive way about you. Did I ever tell you that a woman never loses?"

She smiled, but she was as serious as she was tickled. "You will make love to me...now. I'm bribing you to stay here with me."

He laughed and began to caress her, and it started all over again.

They tucked their blankets under their arms and began to walk back, unhurriedly, their eyes taking in the marvel of Wide Canyon. It was almost midsun; they were both thirsty and hungry. They slaked their thirst in the first gully, which held only a trickle of water. The long hike to the dwelling of Bear Wrestler lasted until the sun was well past to midsun.

Bear Wrestler and Falling Skies were gone. There was no sign of a meal, and Scent of Violets went about making one for them. He sat with his back to the wall and watched her.

"Was your mu like you?"

She looked up and smiled. "Not that I remember. Not many secrets live in a small dwelling. She and fa argued often, and she would make him sleep elsewhere. Usually he slept in his kiva. I never understood why they were not more intimate, and determined I would do it differently, not scream at my mate like she did at fa. One sun he took his spear and went hunting after she had laughed at him and called him names. He never came back. Mu cried many times, but no one knows what became of him. The trackers lost his trail not far from the village. Mu was sorry for what she said, and prayed often for his return. I think she was a very unhappy woman. She was with child when he left, and when she went to drop the child, the witch took her to the underworld, and her baby with her. I don't think fa knew the Goddess had taken his seed.

"I never wanted to be unhappy like that. I decided I'd love my mate so much he would never want to go. I used to sneak to the doorway and watch fa-fa and mu-mu make their bodies one, and longed for the time when I could show my mate the joys of such love and tenderness. But I never knew any boys in our village who had the slightest idea of what tenderness is. All of them were coarse and vain.

"Then you came. Fa-Fa was impressed with you immediately, and let me know his feelings...and you, too! But when you first arrived, and you looked at me while I stood beside my door, I melted. I went inside to avoid showing you my response. If you had come to me then and asked to couple with me, I would have done so...so fast you would have been unable to walk away for a moon!"

He laughed. "You are a true lynx. Let me tell you of the lynx. The female stakes out her area, and then keeps all the males out, until she's ready to bear young. Then she drives away those males she thinks unworthy of her, and mates with only one. When her kits are born, her mate helps to feed them, and when they're old enough to care for themselves, the female drives them away, and their fa as well, so there will be enough food to keep her alive. She hunts with cunning, knowing how to use the wind, and even more importantly, the eyes. She's seldom in trouble. When she eats, she's careful to have enough for another meal before she eats it all. Before she is out of food, she hunts. The cougar, unlike her, gorges itself and has nothing, then must hunt to survive; she's smarter. She's intelligent to the weather, seldom caught out in a storm. She knows how to sleep more and require less food in time of bad weather, and seldom must hunt when her prey is holed up and hard to find. She's not as strong as the bear, not as great as the puma, not as fast as the wolf, not as keen as the deer, not as fierce as the badger, not as numberless as the shaggy bison. She's seldom seen, often overlooked, infrequently hungry, and more successful on her hunt than animals that are superior to her. She's intelligent, cunning, strong, quick, and most often, the victor. She's like my mate!" He finished with a laugh.

She laughed with him. "You are good with words, my conqueror. You're more intelligent than any of my people, more compassionate than any man, more mysterious than any I've seen or heard, and more considerate by far than any man I ever saw in our village or this. You've become my mate, and I melt when you're with me. I always dreamed of one who would be this way, but thought it a vain dream after seeing all the young men in our village. I was almost to resign myself to mating for children, and ready to despise the mate. I'm glad you came to me, and that I had not yet committed myself to a man."

He grinned as she handed him a bowl with corn porridge, a corn biscuit, then a cup of tea. He leaned back and ate, his eyes following her as she continued to prepare more food for him and herself. He was satisfied. His mate was better than anything he had dreamed...if only it were not for the ravens.

24

They slept in the empty dwelling, unaware of what had happened to Bear Wrestler or his daughter. With the new sun, He Who Conquers went to find him or discover his whereabouts. The first three people he asked turned away without answering, disgust in their faces. Something drastic had happened in his absence. Standing near a kiva, he saw the approach of a man he believed to be Spirit Man, though he wore no ceremonial garb--the only way in which he had ever seen him. He waited until the man was near. "I seek Bear Wrestler. My mate and I were gone for a sun, and he's nowhere to be found."

Spirit Man eyed him carefully. "You're He Who Conquers, owner of the scalp of nine Others. Why are you still here?"

The man was ignoring his question in an attempt to intimidate him, but he desired an answer and knew he would get none if he became defensive.

"I came to learn what I could to take back to my people, and met Bear Wrestler on the way...or rather, found him seriously injured. Surely you know the whole story. Am I such a person that I should not be welcome here? I like it here, and until Bear Wrestler is back to full health, I protect him against Long Knife."

"I heard. You've been with us over two moons, and even helped plant. What knowledge do you yet seek?"

"Is knowledge limited? Whatever I can learn, of building, of crops, of things that make life better, of how your Council operates, plans and hopes, everything."

Spirit Man watched closely as He Who Conquers spoke. "Why is it necessary for you to have all this information, this knowledge? And what do you want of Bear Wrestler?"

"I wish to know all I can, for whatever purpose and without a purpose. It's good to know, to have knowledge, to understand and be as wise as possible. And I swore to be the brother of Bear Wrestler. I seek him."

"He's among all of us."

He Who Conquers nearly staggered. "He took the...the Rite of Perfection?" He knew his voice, much less his body language, betrayed his surprise.

"He did."

"Why? Without even speaking to me?" He expected no answer from the man who was clearly hostile.

"He looked for you when the man came to claim his daughter."

"Who came?" He knew, but he did not want Spirit Man to know he had seen the man on the rim.

"The brother of the girl who became our Gift to the Goddess."

He stared at Spirit Man, feeling the lump in his throat. He wanted to ask a question, but his voice deserted him.

"His daughter was claimed by the brother, to be mated to him. I, of course, had to explain that she had been opened in the ceremony. He took her as his second mate."

"And this was enough...to make...Bear Wrestler...?"

"He said he had no one. He wanted me to tell

you that the dwelling of his daughter is yours until you choose to leave." Spirit Man had eyes that said he wished that time was up already.

He Who Conquers stood uncertainly, his gaze on Spirit Man, surprised the man was being so open and candid with him, and at the same time feeling he had somehow let down the man whom he had befriended.

"You're sad; it's natural. But you should know he was certain of his mind in the matter, and that he owed you much. Yet he chose the rite." Was that meant to be a dig at his absence? It was.

He Who Conquers nodded and began to turn away. He was stopped by Spirit Man.

"He asked that you not be allowed to take a part of him."

"Why?"

"He said you were his brother. That you were already one with him. I wished to speak with you before telling you this. He said that whatever was in the dwelling was now yours."

He Who Conquers nodded. "He became a good friend. I only wish he'd said something to me of this." Yet he knew that Bear Wrestler could never have spoken to him about this. He was not a man to whom words came easy, and his mind would not have thought through all the innuendoes.

Spirit Man studied his face, then nodded. "You came here under odd circumstances that only the gods know. You backed Bear Wrestler in his error of claiming his daughter from the Ceremony. You stayed in his dwelling, but said nothing about his incest. Yet you protected him as a man should his brother, you shared in the Ceremony, and you have helped plant. I do not like you, but you already know that. You don't like me either. Still, we can work together as we must. You're brash and somewhat cocky, which is abrasive, especially to people who don't know you well. To allow you to stay, however, may not be so easy. Long Knife was well-liked, and you drove him away without a chance at vindication."

He refused to be intimidated by the man; it was a battle of wills, and he was determined to win. "Thank you for your openness. However, I came because Long

Knife is a treacherous man. I doubt your word that he was well-liked, for no one yet has confirmed that. In fact, what few men speak of it, all have nothing but disdain and dislike for the man. Perhaps I'm brash, but I'm tired of people trying to tell me everything I must be. And I was not wrong, you were wrong in using the daughter of Bear Wrestler as the Gift. She was in mourning, she was being robbed of her will to live by the Witch of Pain, and she was afraid to die. She should never have been considered. It's an honor to die for the Goddess, but the maiden must wish to die because of that honor, not to escape the Witch of Pain."

Spirit Man stared at him, his eyes cold. "Come to my kiva when Sun God sleeps. We must discuss this further."

"I'll come."

His legs heavy with his uncertain feelings of grief, he turned back to the dwelling. He felt that somehow he had let Bear Wrestler down, not being there when he was needed. The man had taken the Rite of Perfection, no doubt because of total despondency. The witches were chastizing him for coupling with his own daughter, and his self-pity would not allow that she was being mated, and taken out of his life. It was too much for the man, who no doubt had felt extreme guilt and knew what the gods would or were doing. To escape, and to yet remain among his people, he had taken the great step.

Perhaps it was more than that. A leap. He had made a fast decision so no one would change his mind. And this people would be altogether too willing to accept it, putting him away so no one would ever be intimidated. Was it an act of a coyote or an eagle? Was he a coward, or soaring with the gods, when he made his decision? Who could know? As for the people, he would have to reserve judgment on that as well.

Falling Skies was mated and taken from her people, which meant she would not own the dwelling in which she had lived. Should she drop two daughters, the first would be given to the Goddess as soon as she was of age. As a stranger among them, Falling Skies had no rights and no claims, but her children would be fully accepted.

No doubt it had hurt Bear Wrestler, too, knowing that. Yet, would not his guilt be the worst? Perhaps that was why he was getting so morose, so much like the animal after which he was named.

Guilt. He Who Conquers knew how that could affect a man, for it was in great measure what he was feeling now. If he could know what the motive had been, maybe he could shake it. But....

"Did you find him?"

He nodded, and his expression told Scent of Violets to ask no more questions. He slumped down inside the dwelling, leaning back against the wall and staring at the leather pouch in the corner. He had seen it when they returned, but had no desire to touch it. Not yet. Now it was like a serpent, ready to strike. Scent of Violets gave him some tea, a mint tea which had a soporific effect, and in a short time he was sleeping where he sat. Scent of Violets huddled next to him to keep his head from flopping and waking him.

As she sat, she thought of what he might have heard, but came up with nothing. Whatever it was, it was dire for him to have come back so obviously distressed. Sleep would be his best medicine, and she would see to it he slept well.

When he awoke, the sun was slanting strongly, showing just above the rim of the canyon, throwing the color of the rock walls into golds and deep yellows. He sat up with a start and looked outside, then leaned back and rubbed his eyes sleepily.

"I slept long." She moved away to start a meal when he started out the doorway. "I'll be gone for a while. It'll be long dark before I return. Sleep if you must."

Unsure of his sudden preoccupation, she sat for a long time to contemplate what she ought to do. Why was he so curt? Why leave without saying where he was going? What had happened to make him feel as he did? Again she knew it was something grave and out of her league, though she wished to discover what it was. Would he be ready to talk when he returned?

An alarm sounded in her mind. What if he failed to return? What was it that had him so disturbed? Did it pertain to life and death? What would become of her if he should not come back at all?

She leaned back and wondered if she, too, ought to drink some of the mint tea!

He Who Conquers walked a short distance up the canyon, then back, and it was dark by time he returned. He went straight to the kiva, where Spirit Man sat alone. Where were all the men? Was he to be the only one here? He sat quietly, and Spirit Man, sitting cross-legged before the firepit, could have not heard him enter for all the sign he gave.

His eyes were closed, and he sat as though mesmerized by the heat, though the coals were darkening and there was only a small indication of any fire at all.

Knowing to remain silent, he watched the unmoving man for a long time, hearing sounds of women putting children to their mats or speaking sharply to a member of the household. A dog barked twice and was silent. There was no wind at all.

"He Who Conquers, prostrate yourself before the gods."

He looked at Spirit Man and then at the three images that sat on the banquette to his right. He rose, then laid on his stomach before the gods, his hands over his head with palms on the floor, Sipapu near his right side. After a long time his mind began to move over the three gods represented on the banquette. The God of Male Fertility, the God of the Four Winds, and the God of the Four Seasons.

He had not been terribly faithful to them, for he had been captivated by the Great One--Sun God? He wished he knew--who was over them all. Yet, perhaps he had failed to appease these lesser gods because of his attitude. Did that mean he might be wrong? Would the Great One protect him if any of these gods might toy with him?

And what if he had made one of them angry? The thought was almost terrifying, and he had to fight his thoughts to put that idea to sleep. While he wrestled with that, Spirit Man spoke.

"The gods speak, and they wonder if you know them, my son. Do you know the gods before you?"

"I do." He named them.

"Have you offered them anything lately?"

"I have been traveling, and have not had opportunity. I have spoken often to the Great One. He has smelled my smokes of thanksgiving many times."

"This 'Great One' of which you speak, I'm unfamiliar with him. Who is he?"

"Your God of the Sun." He knew this would satisfy Spirit Man, and it would require fewer explanations. "He's over all, and therefore most important. I speak to him; he's my protector."

"You talk to Sun God? It's not possible."

"I've done it, so it can't be impossible. He's shown me many things yet to come, and given me life many times when I would otherwise have already been beyond Sipapu."

There was silence for a time, then Spirit Man spoke again, his voice touching on impatience. "You think it was Sun God, but it might have been another. Or perhaps many others."

"It was the Great One. I live before him, and all the other gods pale in comparison."

Spirit Man almost gasped at his audacity. "It's they who are angry at being ignored."

"They can't touch me, not while the Great One looks down on me with favor."

"But he sleeps now."

"For you perhaps, but he's listening to me at this very moment. He hears you as well. Would you try to appease lesser gods when the Great One is over them and wishes you to address him?"

"No one has addressed him for many generations. He has gone from us for the present, and will return one sun to again make us a part of himself. You can't speak to one who's not there."

"You only think he's not there. Where do you think he went? He shows us his face each sun to remind us he is present, and he can't therefore be ignoring us. Why must we ignore him just because someone in our past told us he left us?"

"It's known to Spirit Men everywhere."

He Who Conquers rolled and sat up. "It's taught them from one generation to another, but none question or test the teaching, as though what one man thought generations ago must always be true. But is it? Sun

God is the Great One. He rules Earth Mu, he oversees the lesser gods, all gods quake when he makes his demands. It's foolish of us to ignore him when he sees us each time he enters the sky. How can he be far away and still warm us regularly? I think it's important for us to honor him, and him alone. When he is satisfied with us, what can the other gods do to us?"

Spirit Man mulled this in silence. "The God of Male Fertility could render you infertile. The God of the Four Winds could keep the winds from blowing. The God of the Four Seasons could turn the entire time of man into one long time of snows, as it was in antiquity."

He Who Conquers shook his head. "No, they won't take away my fertility, or fail to bring us the rains, or turn my world into snow. Not while Sun God receives my praise. He'd destroy one of them if they did. Have I not been speaking to him for almost ten winters? Yet my mate is with child, the winds blow both cold and hot, and the seasons follow each other. If these gods could overcome him, would they not have been toying with me already? They don't touch me, because the Great One sees me."

Spirit Man stared at him. Was this blasphemy, or was this an infusion of new truth? Should he accept it and test it, or would he be wiser to ignore it and continue as he was taught? What would happen to him if he tried to change the teachings of his people now, after all they had heard from him? Would they believe him? More likely, he would be made to run the gauntlet. Of course, it was always possible this man had been given a different song for his own life that affected no one else. Sometimes men heard different voices and felt different drums, and the gods honored them, but that didn't mean all men were to think or act the same way. Perhaps Kokopelli was the greatest example of that.

"You give me food for thought, but I can't accept it. However, I won't dismiss it without discussing it with other men who study the gods." His abrupt ending of the conversation was evidence he had closed his mind and was no longer interested in hearing more.

"He spoke highly of you. He says you are a special envoy of the gods, and a great hunter."

"He flatters me."

The man shrugged. "Who can say? You are different, and it's usually because the gods wish to deal with a person that they make him different." He paused. "Our people need meat. You will find meat for us."

"If the Great One chooses, there could be a herd of bison near the entrance to the canyon. Who can say?"

"I have spoken to the men who belong to the Hunters. They've tried to find animals for two winters with limited success. This new planting season, when the snows ended and before the Goddess was honored, they found nothing. You will find meat for us. It'll show that Bear Wrestler still lives."

"I'll lead them, but they must accept me as their leader." He was remembering the bison he had seen while they stayed in the hut during the snowstorm and cold. If there were some there because of the Great One, there would be more around.

"They will. But if you fail, you'll not leave the canyon."

It was a volatile threat. Perform--which shows the Great One is indeed what you claim--or die.

He stood, then looked down on Spirit Man. "Your threat is no speck of fear. The Great One will protect me, even if there's no meat. I'll lead the hunt, but if anyone touches me or my mate, I'll kill him. I don't trifle with what the Great One has given me. That includes my mate and my life."

He left the kiva without looking back.

His mood was changed when he entered the dwelling, and he chuckled to himself when he found Scent of Violets asleep, with evidence that she had drunk some of the mint tea she had served him before he slept. He drank the half-cup of tepid remains, laid beside her and went to sleep.

With the dawn, he was outside with his axe and spear, sharpening them on the sandstone rock that stood up behind the center, fronting the canyon wall. Somehow, the thought of a hunt, a real hunt, excited him, and with the planting done, he had time to put things in motion. He would have the Village Crier announce the plans with the new sun, and leave in two.

In the back of his mind he wondered if the bison he had seen were still in the area. Perhaps some other group had found them and driven them away.   No matter, he would lead the hunt, and they would travel far if necessary.

He smiled as he thought of the threat that Spirit Man had not even taken the time to couch in subtle language. He had an idea of how he could handle the situation, and felt little fear, though he wondered at the hostility of the man.

Returning to the dwelling, he ate with Scent of Violets, then opened the leather pouch left to him by Bear Wrestler. He simply upended the sack and let the items fall on his blanket.   Then he stared at it in amazement.

Fifteen arrowheads for big game, and several for birds or smaller animals. A single spearhead of excellent finish. A necklace of amber and seashells. A highly polished charm on a leather cord, the stand-up image of a man praying. Three large seashells, such as he had never seen before. Deer antler chips with small figurines etched on them for use in games. Two hollow turkey leg bones to use as straws. And finally, a carefully woven poncho that was fading with age but still in good shape.

Scent of Violets watched him sort the items, her eyes big with disbelief. "He was a rich man, yet would not give a gift for a mate!"

"Would you have mated him?"

She shook her head. "He was not my choice of man, but I was a bit more choosy than some."

He grinned. "I feel flattered." He took the amber and seashell necklace and put it over her head, then sat back and admired its effect as it hung below the image of the pregnant woman and lay between her enlarging breasts.

"Nice!   It expresses that you are a wealthy woman."

"I can wear it now?"

"All the time.   Does it not give you the status that you want?"

"My man is generous. I like it! But what is this about status? Have I ever asked for it?"

"Just between you and me, it looks better than I have seen on any woman around here.   You'll be a woman of importance and substance, even when you return with me to my village. And whether you asked or not, I have never known a woman who despises status."

She laughed softly. "You prepare me to be the mate of a chief?"

He smiled as she stood and moved toward the door. "The mate of a rich man. A man wants to see his mate honored by other women, and envied by them as well."

She wrinkled her nose at him and went outside. He put the things back in the pouch, then followed her out. She was squatted in the sun, checking her medicine basket.

"You have used up much of it," he observed.

She nodded, then looked up at him. "You are to lead a hunt?"

Surprised, he said, "Have you been communicating with the spirits again?"

She giggled. "No, I was told. When do you plan to go?"

"In two suns."

"There'll be some women along?"

"There always are a few, to help handle the meat."

"I plan to be one of them. I need to find more medicines."

He nodded. "I thought you might want to go. I have to speak to Village Crier before midsun."

She stood up, closing the basket. "It is why I checked my supplies. I have few left after nursing Bear Wrestler." She left the opportunity for him to explain what had happened, but he said nothing. She was curious as to where Bear Wrestler was, though she had a good idea. Falling Skies still had her puzzled.

He turned back to the dwelling and checked his pack, going through it thoughtfully and thoroughly. Satisfied, he went out and found Village Crier, whom he told of the hunt. Then he sent the young man to announce the hunt to all centers that had an interest in meat.

At midsun, twenty-seven men met. Spirit Man was present, but took no part. A man named Running Hare was headman of the Hunters, and he sullenly sat back and said nothing. Gray Fox and Birdsong showed the most animation, and he appointed them sub-leaders under himself, impressed with their attitude and apparent intelligence.

He explained what he intended to do, then announced that they would depart on the second sunrise. Everyone who intended to go was to come see him in person during this sun, and they would make medicine on the next. Some women would be welcome to come along, though he planned on no more than five or six. These would service the needs of the men and help in the skinning and care of the meat.

He retired to the dwelling, but sat in front to mend his buffalo blanket. One by one, men came by, a few bringing a mate, and he memorized the names and kept count on the ground beside him. When Sun God dropped behind the canyon rim, he had the commitment of twenty-nine men and seven women, not counting himself and his mate.

He was satisfied. They were sufficiently large to handle any Others they might meet, and large enough to get animals if they found any. It was getting exciting already!

25

Spirits were mixed among the group that left the village. He Who Conquers was not with them, but the twenty-nine men and eight women who carried their packs included Scent of Violets. He Who Conquers, having given careful instructions to Birdsong and Gray Fox to head into no-sun until he found them, had left immediately after they had made their medicine. When he left, the men had put together their supplies and weaponry, the two men directing and checking to be sure all was in order. The trip could be a long one.

The Hunters followed the two leaders out of the canyon, assured that He Who Conquers would rejoin them within two suns, but were to continue until he found them. They had the eight women among them, and there were thirty-three dogs to help carry the meat.

He headed for the highest promontory, a small mesa above rising-sun, traveling light and fast. Running most of the time, he cut back and forth into valleys where he could see if animals had passed in the recent suns, and over hills where he stopped to study every place he could see.

Finding nothing of interest, he climbed the desert-mesa toward which he'd been aiming, and skirted the edge all around to find any sign of animals. Nothing. That darkness found him sleeping on the mesa without water. It was a cold darkness, chilling from a cool wind that whistled through the sparse grasses about him, with nothing for protection.

He ate meagerly, then dropped off the mesa and headed back at an angle between no-sun side and setting-sun, where he had seen a haze on the horizon that could have been dust. He slept that darkness among the sage.

Near midsun of the fourth sun, he topped a rise overlooking a wide valley that was broken with an arroyo down its center. There they were. A sea of moving animals, foraging their way in the direction from which he had come, hundreds of bison, filling his vision and giving rise to an exciting anticipation. He had found them; the Great One was still walking ahead of him. He wondered if his old friend, Son of Happiness, was remembering to burn fagots for him.

Next was the planning of the hunt, to make sure of success, that meat got back to the village. Carrying the burden of meat, using travois, they could have a great kill without concern for having to abandon meat. It could easily take them ten or more suns to travel back to the village, and as warm as the weather had become, the meat would most likely spoil. That meant they would have to smoke and sun dry the meat before transporting it. Trees were not close, which would cost time fetching huge quantities of wood for racks and the fires they needed.

He could see where a good kill might keep them away from the village nearly a moon. Still, it would be well worth the trip if they could kill four hands or more animals. And it would be a good laugh to see the face of Spirit Man when they returned.

He dropped down the side of the hill, studying the land as he went, staying far from the animals while learning how the valleys lay, and where the tops of hills would conceal men trying to sneak close. When he was satisfied, he headed back up and over the hill, pointed to mid-sun, and began to run.

Through the entire sun, he failed to meet the hunters, wondering where they might have chosen to travel and what their speed might have been. He slept near a streambed, digging into the sand almost waist deep before he found water, watching it fill the bottom. He drank until he was bloated, filled his gut bag, and again headed into mid-sun.

It was only a short run before he met the group. They were past their initial enthusiasm, walking much slower with the stiffness of unused muscles suddenly exercised, and the fatigue led to a decline in anticipation. They had stopped to drink and eat when they espied him coming, and while they waited for him, many stretched out on the ground.

"Hola! We'll have meat!" he called as he got close.   "You found them?"

"As many as the grains of sand under your feet."

"How far?"

"Nearly a sun's travel from here. We should hurry. They feed their way to rising-sun."

Enthusiasm   rejuvenated   even   among   the complainers, they ate quickly and traveled again, following the steady and quick pace of He Who Conquers. It was dark when they stopped. The women nearly dropped from exhaustion, but managed to throw together a cold meal, and all were grateful to stretch out and sleep.

He Who Conquers stood watch, dozing until near dawn. He was wide awake and alert when the first stirrings came from the camp, and Scent of Violets joined him with a cup of hot tea and a bowl of corn soup.

"We walked far, my conqueror. How much farther are the animals?"

He took the cup and sipped. "We did very well. We'll be on the hill looking down at the herd before midsun."

"You have a plan?"

He grinned. "We can walk right into the herd...if it hasn't moved on."

"It will be where you saw them. Your Great One is watching over you most diligently."

He shrugged.   "I honor him; he makes people

honor me."

She snuggled against him in the cool of pre-sunrise. "There'll be work for everyone shortly."

He nodded, enjoying her softness against him. "I suggest you take your little asides for medicines while we rest or while the men prepare to move into the herd. There'll be a huge amount of work once we make the kill. The Great One will give us all the animals we can handle."

She sipped again and looked at the hill toward which they had been walking. "Climbing that hill will itself be a workout."

He chuckled softly through a mouth full of soup. "That's the easy part. Wait until the travois-dragging begins--coming up the other side of that hill for a starter."

She gave a mock groan. "I will not be able to couple for a moon after this!"

He laughed quietly, finishing his soup and setting the bowl aside. "Perhaps I will need to take a second woman."

She shrugged. "If you have the urges of a bull elk when all the cows come into heat, go ahead."

He continued to laugh, even while she finished her tea, took his empty cup and bowl, and headed back to the womenfolk. Shortly, they were all hiking again, the men carrying huge packs and the women smaller ones, and each dog carried supplies. Scent of Violets trailed behind, stopping here and there to gather her herbs.

It was halfway from midsun to setting sun when the men lay behind the break of the hill and surveyed the huge herd that strung across in front of them browsing, many lying down. They were speechless, staring at the mass of animals.

"So how do we get to them?" Gray Fox continued to eye the brown sea enclosed in dust in complete amazement.

He Who Conquers had the attention of every man when he spoke. "See that gully down there, the one that looks short and turns back against this hill? It is not. It mostly runs toward snowtime sun-set. It actually runs directly into the herd. Right out there, where you see the six animals lying near each other, the farthest two are actually on the far side of the gully." There were almost as many animals on the far side of the arroyo as on the near side.

"But if it runs into the herd, won't they see us while we're in it?"

"No, it's quite deep. But our biggest problem is wind. It mostly comes from the same way as the gully, which takes the smell directly into the herd. We'll need to use the sun and attack in two places. We can keep one of the women on this spot where she can be seen from down there, and have her keep the two groups coordinated."

He paused. "Which woman will take the task of keeping us working in tandem?"

A man named Bright Bird spoke while his eyes still perused the herd below. "My mate will do it. She's always telling me where to go."

The men chuckled. He Who Conquers grinned. "She'll be most important to our success."

"Don't tell her that! By the gods, I'd never hear the last of it!"

They laughed again.

"We'll eat, then lay out our strategy. On the new sun, we attack." He continued to stare at the herd.

"We still have a lot of sun. Why not attack now?" It was Running Hare, leader of the Hunters, a man who had given no indication he would join the hunt, yet had tagged along, his voice showing his disdain for the young man who was taking his place.

He Who Conquers smiled coldly. "The animals have been here for many suns, gradually moving along. They'll still be here on the new sun unless someone scares them away. If we hunt now, we'll have many animals down, and darkness will come before we can properly protect them from wolves. Not to mention that we haven't yet made medicine. You of all men should know of such things." His dig was caustic, and brought the sought response; he had no liking for the man. The fact he had even come, he fully suspected, was merely to watch him fail at the task given him.

The man snorted, but had no reply. His attitude was not lost on the men, who avoided his eye by continuing to watch the flowing herd. He Who Conquers knew he had to be sure the man stayed in camp after darkness. Even at the cost of his own people, he was jealous enough to try something. The consequences of his actions were unimportant to the man when it came to protecting his own power, and He Who Conquers read his attitude clearly.

The remainder of the sun was spent instructing each man of his role in the hunt, and explaining to the mate of Bright Bird how she was to signal them and what each signal would mean. Scent of Violets spent the entire time filling her basket, and came back just before sunset. Her nod told He Who Conquers that she had been most successful.

Most of the men went to no-sun where there were trees, cutting and hauling wood for a fire, drying racks and poles for travois. With darkness, a small fire was lit and the men danced, calling upon the gods for success. He Who Conquers found a place and slept, while Scent of Violets watched to see if Running Hare had ulterior motives. When she awakened He Who Conquers about middarkness, the man still slept.

Refreshed from the good sleep, he lay and watched, while four men sat in the darkness and kept their eyes open for Others. It was nearly dawn when he saw Running Hare rise. He rolled, coughing lightly, then appeared to sleep again, and in so doing alerted Gray Fox.

When Running Hare slipped into the darkness, Gray Fox was close behind, followed by Birdsong and He Who Conquers, who were careful to not be seen or heard.

Once away from the camp, Running Hare moved faster, until his followers were almost running to keep pace. When he reached the bottom on the far side of the hill, he gave a puma scream, then walked forward five paces and did it again. Some snorts came from animals in the herd nearby, but there were no sounds of the herd moving.

Behind Running Hare, Gray Fox grunted like the javelin, just as He Who Conquers and Birdsong joined him.

"He tries to frighten the herd to moving."

"The cries probably won't do it unless they also smell the puma," He Who Conquers replied. "Usually," he added as an after-thought, emphasizing how notional the bison could be. Sometimes a snapping twig could set off a stampede, and other times they might stand as they had at Open Stone.

Running Hare had heard the javelin, and turned his head to listen. Gray Fox, enjoying himself, scratched the earth like he was rooting for food and grunted again. Running Hare stood silently and watched the blackness of the animals before him, then screamed one more time.

"They will stay," He Who Conquers said, loud enough for the man to hear.

Running Hare spun like the puma he imitated. "You!" His one word was like a speech under the cloak of darkness.

"And I," added Gray Fox.

"And I," added Birdsong.

Running Hare tried to peer through the darkness at the disattached voices. The three men sat on the ground in one clump, making it difficult to distinguish them, and Gray Fox had an arrow strung.

Slowly Running Hare walked back, his steps slow and measured, gradually distinguishing the dark figures.

"Why are you here?"

"To see why you left camp like a coyote. The important thing is why you are here. Why do you try to frighten the herd?" Birdsong, older than Running Hare by one winter, spoke with harsh accusation in his voice.

"You think I want to scare the herd? You lie!"

"Then why did you come here, and why the puma screams? You think we have no intelligence?"

Running Hare stopped two paces away. "I came to see if the herd was jumpy. Knowing they are not will make the hunt much easier."

Gray Fox chuckled softly. "See, Birdsong, I told you while we danced that we lacked the intelligence to lead such a hunt. Who else could have thought of such an important thing? And who else would have thought to sneak away, just before Sun God comes, to speak with the herd? And even more, who else would have made sure he left when there would be no others to see that he was leaving? I mean, you and I know nothing when it comes to hunting."

Birdsong chuckled at the cynicism. "You have a most unusual insight into our shortcomings, my friend. I suppose we can return to our mates and get warm. Very likely, the hunt will be a great success without us. With such a thoughtful leader, we would need only four or five hunters to kill the entire herd!"

The two laughed at their own humor. Running Hare stared at each of the men, and He Who Conquers watched the leader of the Hunters carefully. The man was rigid with anger, embarrassed to have been caught. No one would ever believe him. Running Hare stepped past the them and stomped into the darkness, heading for camp. The three followed.

With the dawn, the hunters were at the bottom of the hill, in two groups widely separated, one hiding in the arroyo pointed out by He Who Conquers. Birdsong led one group, Gray Fox the other, and He Who Conquers sat on a flat surface between the two. Birdsong and Gray Fox watched the mate of Straight Arrow, who sat on the crest of the hill where she alone could see He Who Conquers.

When it was light enough to see well, he signalled her, and she gave the sign for the group with Gray Fox to begin their stalk. After a time, she gave the same sign to Birdsong, and He Who Conquers lay on his stomach under a piece of bison hide and began to crawl toward the herd.

The gully was perfect, and the lack of wind in the early sun was ideal. The men were among the animals before the herd sentinels became aware of them.

He again signalled Hummingbird, and she gave the sign. The men were on their feet, scrambling out of the gully without a sound, and among the animals with spears flashing. Reaction of the animals was swift. A bellow, then another. A cow turned and rammed into the two animals ahead of her. In a sudden cacophony of bellows, the herd began to move.

Arrows flew, spears jabbed, and then were flung. Animals bawled, one went down, then another. The air filled with dust, screaming men, noise, and then the alarm of men. Some bulls and cows had turned to defend the herd, and attacked. A man flew through the air, hooked by a bull and tossed like a Kachina doll.

He Who Conquers seemed to be everywhere, his spear finding the bull just after the man was flung away. The bull turned on him, and he darted aside and grabbed an arrow from his quiver, jamming it into the cavity of the great bull as it went past and turned.

The bull came again, enraged now, feeling the wounds inflicted by the spear that protruded from his chest and the arrow that stuck in the ribs. He Who Conquers waited until the last moment, then flung himself aside, and again put an arrow into the beast.

The bison stopped, turned more lethargically, pawed the dry earth, then sank to its front knees. Just in time, He Who Conquers saw the second bull, and dodged the swinging head as the animal went past. It was Gray Fox that flung his atlatl home and sent the huge animal skidding onto its nose. His cry of success split the dust-filled air.

As sudden as their attack, the animals were gone; hundreds of bison had split in their panic. Many rumbled away toward rising-sun, others toward no-sun. For a long time the earth shook, and the great cloud of dust drifted slowly away. Then it was quiet, and the men stood as though mesmerized, saying little in the aftermath of their savage attack. The sun was not yet over the horizon.

Animals lay dead or dying in every direction, and many that escaped carried arrows and spears. One was seen far out on the flat land, standing alone; not far from it, another lay on its side and struggled to get up.

Suddenly the cry of victory began, Birdsong's ululating voice breaking into the quiet like a voice from the gods. Another joined him, and then another, until all the members of the successful hunt spun and danced among the dead animals in jubilation. Only Running Hare failed to join the festivities, standing aside and watching. Women came down the hill, and the men dropped to their knees to begin the ritual. Out came the stomachs, and the men shared contents of their kill with those who had made none. Hearts were cut out and put in the fire that was lit by the first women to arrive, and then cow genitals were added to the growing flame. He Who Conquers cut the liver from the first beast he had killed and took the bite to show his dedication and appreciation to the Great One.

Near the arroyo came a shout, and the men ran to see what it was about. The arroyo was nearly blocked with the bodies of bison, dead ones, some with broken legs, some healthy but caught in the melee of carcasses. The twelve to fifteen visible on the valley floor would be almost tripled because of those in the arroyo.

Then came the lighthearted but heavy work of skinning the animals and deboning the meat. Men made their second trip for travois poles and firewood, and women built many frameworks for hanging strips of meat over smoking fires. Dried meat, in addition to keeping the meat from spoiling, would be much lighter for the trip home.

The entire sun, men and women worked side-by-side on the meat, and men cut into the skulls for the brains that would be used to cure the hides later. These were put inside a few cleaned stomachs to allow them to age for tanning. Horns were cut off and stacked for ceremonial use, and male parts were removed to be part of a ceremony come the next darkness. One of the cows had an udder of milk, which was put into another gut-bag for all to enjoy later.

Efficiently, the animals were deboned and the meat cut into strips for drying. The huge mounds of meat, stacked on the hides of nine animals, brought spontaneous outbursts of singing and dancing from both men and women.

Long into the darkness, they celebrated and ate freshly-spitted tongue. Their dancing was jubilant, their songs long and bawdy. Even the man who had been thrown by the bull sang, though his broken ribs and dislocated shoulder kept him from dancing.

Then from sheer exhaustion, they slept. Weary, the next sun was spent cutting strips of hide to make the travois, and resting, while the smoking fires were kept at their maximum.

The next sun, six men stayed in camp with He Who Conquers, while the rest headed into no-sun for more wood. The men who stayed kept three alert at all times, the rest tending the fires and guarding the meat from the wolves that were now beginning to become bolder.

Unnoticed, He Who Conquers slipped away into that darkness, went far up the hill and over, where he found a place to speak alone to the Great One.

His voice was quiet, but firm.

> "O Great One, again you have given me victory.
>   I claim no great deeds, save following you.
>   You gave success to the hunters,
>   Happiness to their village,
>   Food for their snowtime.
>   Indeed, you are worthy to be called
>   The Great One!"

He lay quietly for a time, then added,

> "My heart is troubled, O Great One.
>   I am troubled over the visions I have seen,
>   Of what is to happen among my people.
>   I am also troubled over what I feel
>   Is about to happen among the men who are here.
>
>   Will it be from within, or from Others?
>   Will they fight among themselves?
>   Or might this sense I feel be of the
>   Presence of Others?
>   Are they here?"

Again he was quiet, wondering at the suddenness of his own words, and for having spoken without thinking. But the words had sent him on full alert, his eyes alive as he looked up and around at the hillside that divided him from his followers.

After a time, he came from his spot like a shadow, and moved along the hillside, around the peculiar rocks that projected from the earth. He had no idea why he felt the alarm, but he followed the instincts that had twice given him life when he was endangered. Nearing the crest above the camp, he stopped.

There was movement ahead of him, above him, silhouetted against the dark sky filled with the distant fires of the gods. Unable to identify what he had seen, he squatted among the rocks and waited.

Patience ruled. It was of little importance that one accomplished too much in one sun, only to be idle on the next. Such folly made little or no sense at all. One learned to live with unpredictable weather, lack of water, skimpy food supplies, unwelcome illness, the movement of the seasons. There was no way to overcome the cycle of nature, and learning this taught them to accept life with tolerance and patience.

He sat. He could not see the camp, and noises from it had stopped. If the six men were still celebrating, they were doing so with much less gusto. It was more likely they had called a halt. He hoped their sentinels were alert.

On his hands and knees, he worked uphill toward where he had seen the movement, and stopped again to watch. He knew he would be hard to see by one on the crest, and hoped there were none below him--if there were enemies around. His gut feeling said there were. He was sure that was no animal he had seen.

Staring hard and using the peripheral vision he found so much better for sight in the darkness, he finally made out the prone figure of a man who was watching the camp below. Was he alone, spying for a larger group?

Knowing he had the advantage of the situation, he moved slowly along the hill. There were none down the ridge from the man. Back he went, staying low and moving with careful deliberation. No one was visible, but he could not tell if there might be some over the crest, unlikely because that would skyline them to the camp.

He dropped down and sat among some rocks, keeping his eye on the single one he had seen, and contemplating what steps he should take next. It was going to be a long darkness, with much to do.

26

Just how long, he was soon to discover. He had been watching for only a short time when the man stood, looking down towards the campsite. Alert, he watched, his nerves tingling. Something was happening. No one, short of a maniac, would stand on a ridge in enemy territory.

The man said a few words--he could barely hear the voice from his vantage--to someone, and then a head appeared, then two more, and then five more. For a moment he watched the eight come to the crest and pass the single man, and as they did, he could see that two of the men were captives. He tried to determine who they were, but with no moonlight it was impossible.

The man continued to stand, watching the eight go up the ridge for a time, then turning. In but a moment, more heads, then bodies, appeared. Four, with one prisoner. Two, with another. And finally, five more, with two prisoners. When these passed the man on watch, he turned and followed.

Twenty-four in all, six of them captives. Eighteen

Others. He registered this, wondering if there were more and where they might be, but afraid if he waited too long they would disappear into the darkness and he would lose them. His decision was made out of necessity, and he followed them, staying along the side of the ridge where he would be least expected.

Forays in the darkness were rare. The fact they had done it showed how sure of themselves they were. To die in the darkness was the worst of terrors, for the spirit would wander forever looking for Sipapu. It was said that few ever found the trail.

They headed into no-sun, no longer concerned with sound, talking and laughing, jabbing at the men they drove with them. But where were the men and women who had collected firewood and saplings for the drying racks? He shuddered. Were they back yet, and thus dead? His own Scent of Violets was among them. No, they had to be at least a sun, maybe two, getting wood. They would return to an empty camp where wolves would be feasting, and the guards gone. Which meant the Others planned on making yet another trip to the piles of meat. For now, they had to be entertaining the idea of having fun with their captives at their campsite.

Along the bare ridges, they finally dropped down among some trees, went through them and up another hill, across the top and down into yet another thickly forested hillside. Here they began to sing aloud while they approached a single man who sat beside a fire.

He Who Conquers stopped and hunkered down beside a stump, three stone throws from them, and watched. He identified the humorous Bright Bird first, then Birdsong. After a time, he guessed one was Running Hare, and then saw the face of Sun Watcher. The other two remained unidentified.

Two of the men, Sun Watcher and Birdsong, were tied to a tree near the fire, their hands stretched high until their feet were almost off the ground. One of the unidentified men was tied to Running Hare, the head of each tied to the feet of the other, hands tied behind their backs. The final two were staked to the ground, spread-eagled.

He watched the activity, keeping an eye on the

Others to see if there were more than the nineteen he had already seen, but he could see no more. Two of them went out as sentinels, one standing beside a tree one stone throw to his right, the second up into the trees across the meadow. After a while, another went out to his left, far enough into the trees to be lost from sight.

The rest bedded down, one sitting beside the fire to keep it going and watch the captives. It was quiet, dark, and cool. Nothing moved except the man and his fire.

For a time he stayed immobile, then moved away from the fire and circled toward the one he had seen to his right. The man was careless--which he presumed came from the cocky attitude of the entire group-- spending most of his time watching the fire and the area around it.

As he aligned behind the tree next to the man and began to sneak forward, he wondered about what the Others planned. They had captured six men, and how they had done it he had no idea. These were the men who were to keep the wolves off the meat and the fires going, three asleep and at least three alert at all times.

It was thinking of this which gave him the incentive to do what he felt had to be done. Darkness was far advanced, he did not have a lot of time to do what he must, and he would have to work fast...but carefully. One slip and he would lose everything.

It was no problem getting near the first man. He was lethargic, unsuspecting and half-asleep on his feet. Walking to the tree with knife in hand, making little sound in the short grass, his knife sliced the throat of the guard with the swiftness of the lynx. He caught the body to keep it from creating noise, and scalped the man and stuffed his severed maleness into his mouth.

Then he circled to his right, above the camp across from the other two sentinels, until he was behind the tree which held the two men. His approach was bold and swift, the two hanging full-weight on their wrists by now. When he was behind the tree, he caught the attention of the two with a touch.

When they looked at him, he put a finger over his pursed lips and whispered, "Slowly get your weight

on your feet.   If I cut you loose, can you hold your
position?"

Birdsong nodded, and Sun Watcher whispered, "I
think so."

"You ready?"   He watched them to be sure they
were poised so they would not lose their balance.   Then
he sliced the ropes on their feet, then the hands.

"Hold the position until I give you the signal."

He glanced past them at the man beside the fire.
The man had glanced his way just before he got to the
tree, but the men tied together were on the far side of
the fire not far from where the two were staked, and he
faced that direction.

He Who Conquers stepped around the tree,
hoping the two guards on the hillside could not see him.
He moved softly for the few paces to the guard and again
sliced the throat, just as the man began to turn his head
at the whisper of sound behind him.

He stepped over and cut the ropes on the
remaining men, identifying the unknown captives as Red
Hawk and Thunderstorm, and gave them the signal to
stay in place a moment longer.   Then he looked for the
chief or subchief.   In a moment, he located the man, and
was surprised to see him so near and without men on
either side.   In but a moment he had cut the man's
throat, and added the third scalp to his belt.

Standing among them he glanced around one
more time, ready to give the signal to the six to follow
him out, when he saw one he recognized.   The man
wore a puma cape, with the neck of the pelt on top his
head.   He had seen the man among the Others who had
been on The Top when he took his first scalps.

Wondering how much time he might have before
discovery, he gave the signal to the men to get up and
go out of the camp in the direction from which he had
approached it, the only way in which he felt sure they
could go unseen.   Then he knelt beside the man and cut
his throat, took the puma hide and the man's scalp.
Then he left a large "X" across the man's stomach, and
followed the men out.

As he moved away from the fire, he heard a
shout from the trees across the meadow.   One of the
guards had glanced back at the camp and seen him.

"Up!" he hissed to the men in front of him. "Move it!" He ran past them and led the way up the hill at a near-sprint, knowing the men might have trouble with legs that had been tied tightly for some time, but also certain that speed meant life.

They followed, their labored breathing soon warning him that the pace was too fast. They topped the ridge, where he turned and slowed to a trot. They were away safely for the present, and there would be no pursuit until the new sun, but that was only a short time away. Already the heavens were showing signs of Sun God.

They walked for a time, then trotted again, then walked. As Sun God appeared from behind a band of clouds along the horizon, they were dropping down the hill above the camp. The fires were out, and there were several wolves working at the meat.

The men raced down at them, shouting as they ran, hoping their noise would drive the wolves away. Most turned and ran off a short distance, but two stood their ground with fangs bared. He Who Conquers shot one with an arrow, then charged the other with his spear. Before he could reach it, it broke and ran to join the others. They sat just out of reach, tongues slobbering.

Two of the men got the fires going again, the four others getting their weapons. They killed two more of the wolves before the rest ran far enough away their arrows would no longer reach them.

Tending the fires and resting the remainder of the sun, the men were at first subdued, then animated over what had happened to them. At sundown, the wood-gatherers came, dragging a huge supply while they carried even more. The dogs were loaded as well.

"The fires are a welcome sight!" Gray Fox called while they were still a ways out, the group showing signs of the ordeal they had just completed. "We found tracks we were unable to identify, and thought Others had you for sure."

Bright Bird shouted their reply, "Others came, and Others went! The gods came, and swept them away!"

Birdsong chuckled despite his exhaustion. "Only

one god came. He carries scalps!"

"Not funny!" Hand of Stone soberly rebuked the levity of the men. His eyes accused those about him. "Don't defame the gods with mortals."

"Who makes jokes?" Bright Bird snapped back, his humor gone as suddenly as it had come. "You want to see the rope marks we all have? We were dead men! Two of us were tied to trees, two staked to the ground, and two bound together head-to-foot. They planned to play with us this sun. Then came a god. His feet never touched the ground, and he carries four scalps, including the one belonging to their chief. He cut us loose and led us away. You joke if you want, Hand of Stone, but I think the winds of the gods came."

He Who Conquers glanced at Scent of Violets, and again she was staring at him like he had seen her do when Hawkeye told of his arrival at her village. He stared back, humor in his eyes but seeing none in hers. His faint smile came only because his eyes could not contain all his feelings of humor.

Several turned to stare at him and the scalps at his right hip, but he ignored them as he laid down his spear, dropped the puma hide beside it, and sat on his mat at the feet of Scent of Violets. He felt tired and wanted to sleep, his hunger not strong enough to out-do his fatigue. He laid on his side and was almost instantly asleep.

"No man can claim to be a god," Hand of Stone argued.

"Has he claimed to be?" Bright Bird responded. "Has anyone heard him make the claim?"

"He claims to listen to the Great One," Birdsong added. "I think his god is very strong, and he's like him. I've known no man like him, and you have to admit, he's physically very different from us all."

"I agree," Red Hawk said. "I would never have believed what I saw. He came like a night witch. He cut our ropes and killed the guard, the headman and the man with the puma hide...without making a sound. And he can run like the wind." He stopped and looked at the faces staring at him. "I was ready to drop and he was running like he could have done it for a whole sun!"

"He's still a man!" Hand of Stone insisted.

Gray Fox chuckled. "Most likely, but a favorite of the gods, no doubt about it. What do you say, Running Hare?" The question was meant to drag something from the most sullen member of the party, on the heels of his rescue. He knew it would be interesting to hear the words of one who had no liking for their leader.

Running Hare was caught by surprise, preferring not to be put on the spot in the matter. He shrugged. "He saved us, what more can I say? I planned to die well, to be a credit to my people. I live."

The grudging admission was more than anticipated, and Birdsong was humored by it. Then his eyes grew serious. "We won't again be caught off guard. It was laziness that got us into this trouble. Nine will stay to guard the meat, and the rest will go for more firewood and rack saplings. We have all the travois poles we need. We have to get this meat dried soon. Does anyone yet believe we're safe out here away from our people?"

"Will they attack again?" Thunderstorm asked, fear evident in his voice.

"Not for a while. They need to make new medicine. Perhaps they'll not even come again. But we'll need a lot of time to take care of all this meat. It gives them the time they need." He paused, then added, "The gods smiled on us this time. If He Who Conquers had not gone off to seek to his Great One, we would all be dead right now...or soon. And we need at least three more suns."

"But their leader was sent to an eternity of wandering in darkness! They will come again?"

"Maybe." Gray Fox' eyes showed his ambivalence. "But right now, we have work to do. We best not let this immobilize us. We have to eat and rest, then choose which will go for more wood. We must stay busy."

In a short time, they had eaten and were lying on their blankets. He Who Conquers slept, oblivious to the rest.

When He Who Conquers awakened, the sun was at its hottest, Blue Grouse, mate of Bright Bird, tended fires under the racks, two men slept, and three sat watching from vantage places on surrounding hills. Four more men sat on blankets and watched. The wood carriers were nowhere in sight.

He sat up and glanced at the big pile of wood, wondering how much more they would need. A young man just past his Ceremony of Manhood, called Strong Like the Cedar, stared at him for a time, then asked, "Are you from the gods?"

He Who Conquers gave him the slight smile. "No. I'm just like you, a man."

"There are some who doubt that."

He noted that Scent of Violets had left him some jerky and a biscuit, and he picked them up. "Their mistake," he said simply.

Strong Like a Cedar nodded, still sober. "How did you manage to do what you did, if you aren't a god?"

"Do what?" Of such things, he began to realize, came the stories heard around the fire of kivas during the long cold season.

"Walk on air. Cut them loose without sound. You know, help them escape."

Again he gave the slight smile. "Walk on air? If you go back there, you'll find my tracks. Cut them loose without sound? My knife is sharp. And we walked and ran to get away."

"But they said you could run fast all sun! No man can do that!"

"Neither can I. Longer than those men, most likely, but not all sun. I stop and rest, too."

The man sounded relieved. "It sounded so mysterious. You make it sound normal."

"It is normal. Men, when they're rescued from sure death, are never sure exactly what they saw. Their eyes are covered by a layer of fear."

The man nodded. "I can believe that." He paused, then added, "You came from far away, they said."

He shrugged. "The legs are capable of taking a man far."

"You didn't soar with the eagles?"

"I cannot fly, any more than you." He smiled, glancing up the hill to see the first of the wood carriers coming into sight. "I walked...and ran. It took me a half moon to get to Open Stone, and we walked many suns to get to your people."

Again the look of relief, or was it
disappointment?

"Ask my mate. She can tell you I'm just a man."

A laugh. Then they stood and watched the
people coming, carrying huge loads. The fires could be
built to a maximum for a long time with what they now
had. Perhaps they could have the meat cured in but a
few suns. It was a good thought, with the Others aware
of their stationary nature. No one would take it for
granted.

The entire sun was spent working on the meat
and hides, and four sentinels were sent out, taking
positions of concealment where Others would not see
them--unless they were already watching. Then they
bedded for the darkness. The dogs would be their
sentinels, allowing all but two to sleep.

He Who Conquers and Scent of Violets coupled,
and when she slept he slipped away into the darkness.
One woman watched the fires and did not see his
departure.

He stopped to let Gray Fox know he was
returning to see what the Others were doing, and headed
to no-sun. Unfettered, carrying only his knife, axe and
blanket, he ran. It was a considerably shorter time for
him to arrive at their meadow this time.

The Others were still there. All fifteen sat near
the fire, and one man stood facing them. Though it was
dark and had been for some time, they had no one on
guard. The signs of ashes showed they had sent the
spirits of the dead to their gods, and there were signs
they had spent some time making new medicine.

He circled to get where he had been when he cut
the first men free, then approached until he could hear
the man clearly. The words were unintelligible to him,
though the man spoke at length. He faced the speaker
and was behind most of the listeners.

When the man finished speaking, he sat facing
them, and one with his back to He Who Conquers stood.
His voice was low, almost nothing but a murmur. While
he spoke, several of the men spun their heads and stared
into the dark. A man added fuel to the fire, which
leaped to life again. The orange faces he could see held
sobriety and fear, and he chuckled to himself. The

medicine they had made must have been without good signs.

When the man stopped and sat, another stood. He Who Conquers backed up into the trees until he could barely see the fire through the trees, and the face of just the one man who looked his direction. Then he began to chant softly, a sing-songy chant in the language of his own people.

> Life is short, like a vapor,
>   It lasts like smoke from the fire;
> When death comes near, we quake with fear,
>   The Death Witch takes whom she wants.

He watched the men tense, and the speaker stopped to turn and stare into the trees. Heads turned with torsos, as they all heard the voice that seemed disembodied in the darkness. He wanted to laugh, but held himself in check, and softly repeated what he had already sung. Then he laughed, loud and long.

Not a single warrior moved. Frozen in fright, they stared into the darkness. When he went silent, they remained still, listening for a repeat. He said nothing more, watching.

Several voices spoke, and near bedlam occurred as they tried to over-shout each other. Then they went quiet, and the one who faced him spoke softly to them. They listened to him, though some continued to turn to listen to the darkness.

He moved, staying out of the shafts of light that managed to find their way through the broken trees, until he was far from the spot where he had first sung, yet no farther away from the fire. Then he sang again.

The reaction was immediate, but still nothing more than trying to listen to the direction. Six of the men stood, looking in his direction, and two more joined them. They began to walk his way carrying their spears. He laughed loudly again.

Moving quickly, he went directly away, then angled enough to keep out of their sight. Finding a clump of brush, he strung an arrow. He waited until they were about ten paces away, knowing that, as dark as it was with no moon, they would never see him, and aimed the arrow at the man who was in the lead. It was only an image of black, but his arrow was true.

The man went down with a cough, though it was impossible to see where the arrow struck. The other five stopped, three dropping to inspect the fallen man. He let a second arrow go at the closest man, who was staring in his direction. Again the man simply coughed, then staggered a step before collapsing. The one who still stood turned and sprinted away, and on his heels came the three who had knelt beside the first dead man.

He ran forward and scalped the two bodies, then put a large "X" on the stomach of each, and cut off their genitals which he stuffed into their mouths. Then he wiped his knife clean on the breechcloth of one of them, retrieved his arrows and moved back and circled.

He returned to his original spot and sang his song once more, while the thirteen men continued to stare fearfully into the dark, unable to see their antagonist and wondering if he were other than human. He laughed, and continued to laugh as he headed back up the hill. He felt good. The Others were frightened now. It was clear their medicine was bad, and they would be no more trouble to the hunters.

But as he walked back to his group, his elation faded with a memory. The run through valleys. The hideous laughter of his mu. The dead and decaying bodies of his parents. The burning village. He no longer felt good. Death stalked from many angles, and he could feel only a coolness about him. And there was Scent of Violets, with ravens fluttering above her distended belly. She was about to give birth, but the ravens....

27

"Everywhere I go, they think I came from the gods just because something out of the ordinary happens. Why? Why must I always be so different? It may be good for some to be held in high esteem, but it's then always expected. I weary of trying to be perfect."

Scent of Violets smiled at his discomfort. "But you are different. It isn't just appearance. Why don't you just accept the fact and live with it?"

"I do live with it...continually. It's not pleasant to be thought of as a...a misfit or something!"

"You still have many things to learn about life, my conqueror. Any man who excels will receive recognition, but when his achievements are so outstanding, everyone knows he's different. Your achievements are...surprising. Often." She paused and looked at him. "Sometimes even I wonder when I hear the things being said about you. You did some things while you were coming to my people that no ordinary man could do. While you are there, you just 'happen' to discover a herd of bison, when my people had sent out hunters for two winters with only a few seen here and there. You outrun the fastest man in our village by so far he appears to be walking. You come here, find a man who should have been dead and keep him alive, then by your mere challenge frighten away the people's champion knife fighter. Then you find the Wide Canyon people more meat than they have seen in several hunting trips, and rescue six men uninjured from Others, and take six scalps doing it. If it were not for your male member and your male needs, I'd begin to wonder, myself. You don't think you're something a bit above the ordinary, my mate?"

She shook her head as though she could not understand him, either, and shrugged to emphasize it. He stared at her, then grinned.

"When you put it that way, it does seem a bit extraordinary." His grin disappeared. "But the Great One does it. I feel fortunate to be in the right place at the right time, and then to have the skills he gave me."

"That, my conqueror, is just the point. The skills are above our people, and those who live here, too. We don't train in doing the things you do, and the time we have to spend in the fields doesn't allow it. Plus, hunting game is quite different from stalking people!" She smiled. "And are you sure it's all the doing of your Great One? I tend to think you over-play his role and underplay your own. You've honed some skills not seen in our villages."

He shrugged. "But I never spend time working on the things I do. Like sneaking up on Others, I never trained to do that. I've practiced hard with my weapons, but what I do to sneak on Others is nothing any of these people could not do if they had reason. Perhaps it's something innate, brought to me by my ancestors. Our traditions tell us we once were like the Others." He remembered being on the hillside, just returning from time with the Great One, when he happened to see the single man skylined on the ridge. A different angle on the hill, or not being alert, would have sent him right into the midst of the warriors coming up the hill with their captives.

He leaned back against the wall, tired to the bone from the hard sun in the field. They had returned to the village almost two moons ago, and he had found himself the center of attention, gossip, and admiration. He received a multicolored feather from Spirit Man for his achievement in leading the successful hunt. In the fields, he put in extra time, not shirking his duties and in fact exceeding what was expected of him. He was filled with fatigue each sunset, though he felt his strength increasing. He felt the hard work bulking his body and giving him strength.

While he worked he watched Scent of Violets beginning to blossom. Her breasts had increased, and she was showing the swelling of pregnancy.

But with her development came memories of the dream, or vision, though he hoped it was just the former. Seeing her naked under the claws of the reaching ravens was sobering, and each time he thought of it, dread returned. He almost wished she could not have children, his love for her growing so strong he preferred to have none than lose her. If he told her his vision, she would merely laugh at him because she wanted to shower him with children. To warn her would not stop her, of that he was sure, but it would make her unhappy. How often had she spoken of filling his quiver with children...it had become her main goal in life.

He could not bring himself to tell her of the vision, preferring to suffer in silence and let her be happy in childbirth. Would she have more than one child before the vision was fulfilled? He answered his own question, because when his mate stood beside him at the time they returned to his people, she had a child in the cradleboard on her back. This birth would not be the one for bringing trouble...he hoped....

"You just think too much," she said, breaking into his morbid thoughts. "You need to sleep, and not get so tired. When you are tired, you're hard on yourself."

His eyes were closed, and he was leaning hard against the wall. She had just finished eating, and was leaning against the opposite wall watching him. Usually he sat with his eyes on her, admiring her development and studying her bare stomach each time they could sit for a time. She enjoyed having him admire her body, and made sure he had the opportunity. As the Sun God warmed the earth, she was able to shuck all her clothing whenever she was inside, wearing the skirt-like breechcloth like all the other women whenever she was outside.

"You had best sleep, my conqueror. The mat is ready. Just fall on it and let go."

He smiled and his eyes opened. "You tempt me beyond my endurance."

She giggled, and he crawled onto the mat and fell asleep. When he awakened, it was raining, more than raining, it was pouring. People were outside with soapstone and yucca root, taking a bath in the hard drizzle, laughing and playing in the welcome moisture. Scent of Violets was with them, rinsing soap from her skin. He went out to take his bath amidst the entire laughing, playful villagers.

"You look better, my conqueror. You slept long and hard."

"Rain does that to me," he grinned.

She nodded. "When I'm clean again, I'll sleep most of the sun. I suppose you'll go to a kiva and gamble."

He laughed. "Why not? I've been lucky. The things Bear Wrestler left for me are still mine, and a great deal more besides."

"Just you quit while you are still ahead."

"Now, how can I be a good gambler if I quit when I'm ahead? Besides, this would be a most boring time if I just sat around and slept."

She laughed with him, in good humor after the bath. "You lose some of it, you quit. Mind what I say!"

He continued to laugh, then grew quiet as he saw Red Hawk and Bright Bird coming toward him.

"Hola!" Red Hawk said as they neared. "We come to see if you want to lose some of that wampum you won a few suns ago."

"Hola!" he replied. "The thought did cross my mind. Minus the losing part."

The two men laughed. "I feel lucky this time," Bright Bird said. "Your chances are not real good, the way I feel."

He Who Conquers laughed, glancing at his mate as he did. She was already talking to a woman from two doors away. "What you feel and what's real are like enemies. When does this big challenge begin?"

"At mid-sun. We're scouting to find several. We'll see you later, and let the chips fall as they may."

He laughed as they walked away and finished rinsing himself before returning to the dwelling to eat. She followed him inside, and finished heating what she had prepared earlier.

His visit to the kiva, where eleven young men met to wager their possessions for the chance to win more through the tossing of ten antler chips, began as a rowdy, funfilled, festive occasion. It slowly evolved into serious business, losses by the unfortunate, bitterness at losing so much so quickly. By the time the sun had reached its meridian, though the rain continued to fall, only three remained. He Who Conquers had just held his own, Bright Bird had forged new winnings, and Roadrunner had won early but now was losing, becoming more and more belligerent.

Some of the losers had left, but three, including Red Hawk, stayed to watch the ongoing struggle. Bright Bird, feeling confident and being of a carefree nature, had set the pace quickly with heavy betting, and never slowed. He Who Conquers won the next toss and collected. He was more moderate, and Roadrunner made some caustic remarks about it as he tossed in his bet. Bright Bird, laughing at Roadrunner, raised everyone, which caused another round of odds. He Who Conquers was satisfied to match the bet, Roadrunner raised it, forcing Bright Bird to match or raise him; he raised with a flourish. He Who Conquers matched and raised slightly, Roadrunner matched, and Bright Bird laughed and raised again. Roadrunner blustered, his balance fast depleting. He Who Conquers matched again. Roadrunner sat for a time and contemplated, then matched. Bright Bird goaded them for their fear, but only matched. He threw the chips.

He Who Conquers won again. It made his winnings almost equal to Bright Bird. Roadrunner growled, leaning back and taking a long drag on his pipe of kinnikinnik-leaf tobacco. He was beginning to show the effects of the narcotic lift.

"By the gods!" he exclaimed as he laid the pipe aside and checked his ante, "I was doing great until this foreigner started cheating!"

He Who Conquers reacted with a jerk and an expression of annoyance, but said nothing. The others watched the two with bated breath.

"What foreigner?" Bright Bird asked, trying to soften the blow. "I took everything you had the last three times we played. You think I'm a foreigner?"

Roadrunner was past placating. "You know what I mean! I have eyes!"

"And just how did I cheat?" He Who Conquers asked softly, hoping to avoid confrontation with the heavier, slightly older Roadrunner.

"You think I'll show these innocent ground squirrels the tricks of the trade, my friend." His voice dripped with sarcasm as he leaned back against the banquette and grinned, but his eyes showed a hateful humor.

"I cheated? The fact is, you've twice flipped chips when you were counting, then recounted to show your advantage. And you think I cheated? I think you're just a poor loser and want to cover your own buttocks."

The grin disappeared. "You accuse me of cheating?"

"If the moccasin fits, wear it."

The cold stare was returned by He Who Conquers, who knew now he was not going to escape confrontation. He should not have spoken. Roadrunner held the stare for some time, trying to overcome his opponent, but the hazel eyes held his without wavering. Seeing his advantage slipping, he jumped to his feet.

"By the gods!" His voice was a shout. "I hate being cheated! Especially by a foreigner!"

He Who Conquers continued to sit, appreciating the fact he had won the tug-of-war with the eyes. He smiled at Bright Bird and sipped his tea casually, but the relaxed manner infuriated the other.

"No one calls me a cheater! Nobody!" His eyes flitted to the others in the room, then back to He Who Conquers. "My honor has always been above reproach! You doubt that?"

He Who Conquers simply stared back, saying nothing and giving no sign he agreed or disagreed. His mind was in turmoil, hidden by his outward calmness.

Why was this happening? What had he done to deserve
the accusation which he had turned around? He was
always open and honest with these people, and he had
seen no signs of malcontent until now except for Spirit
Man and Running Hare. How could he always raise the
hackles of someone? He had no idea what burrs had
stuck to Roadrunner's breechcloth.

"I'll not accept the charge without proof!"

"What proof? No one can prove anything...one
way or another," Bright Bird broke in, still trying to help
avoid trouble. His face was a mask of concern.

"He called me a cheat! There's only one way to
prove who's right and wrong!"

"No, Roadrunner! He's my friend! Please, no
Death Match over something as small as this!"

"Small? You say, small? My character has been
defamed! He accused me of being dishonorable!"

"Whoa! Wait a minute, Roadrunner! You
accused me, remember?" For the first time He Who
Conquers raised his voice, but only slightly.

"And it was true!"

"It was a lie." He dropped his voice to the cold,
quiet level of before. "It was you who cheated, yet you
lost."

"You call me a liar, too? You heard that, Bright
Bird. He called me a cheat and a liar! I won't take it!"

It was too late to reconcile, the ebullient Bright
Bird now miserable. It was plain he feared Roadrunner
would kill his new friend.

He Who Conquers remained quiet, unable to
believe the suddenness and intensity of the hate. It was
obvious Roadrunner had been storing feelings for a long
time, looking for an appropriate time to vent them.

"On the next sun! We'll meet with our knives!"

Red Hawk gasped. "You forget he has killed six
of our enemy! He knows the knife very well!"

Roadrunner laughed, a rasping sound in the close
confines. It was a bit forced. "While they slept! I'll be
wide awake!"

"But you challenged him," Straight Arrow said
calmly. "It's his right to name the weapon."

Roadrunner's head snapped around and down.
"You stick up for the foreigner...against one of your own

kind?"

"I only remind you of etiquette."

His hostile eyes swung back to He Who Conquers. "You choose a different weapon?"

"I'd rather not fight." The statement was calm.

"He's a coward! You hear that? He's a coward!"

"I said I'd rather not. I didn't say I wouldn't. It's just that...well...I don't enjoy looking at the blood of one whom I thought of as a friend."

There was a sudden stillness in the kiva, the weight of the statement locking minds into instant surprise. It took a moment for the full shock of the statement to find a response.

"You think a skinny runt like you can beat me?" It was plain to each of them that the statement had struck him hard. He had convinced himself that he had He Who Conquers slinking like a coyote, totally misreading the outward calmness. His voice held a tone of uncertainty when he added, "On the new sun we meet! Your mate will need to find one who is a man!" He grinned lasciviously. "Perhaps me."

He swept up what was left of his ante and charged up the ladder to disappear in the duskiness that preceded sunset on the suddenly dismal sun. The others remained, the game forgotten and no longer important, stunned, saying nothing.

After a time, He Who Conquers put his ante into his pouch very deliberately and stood. "Thanks for siding as a friend." His glance touched each of them. "As the Great One is my witness, I cheated no one, and I am grateful that you, at the least, stayed neutral. It disgusts me to think of taking a knife to one I thought to be a friend."

He turned to the ladder when the voice of Red Hawk stopped him. "I saw him cheat twice, in case that means anything now. I said nothing, because I fear his temper."

"Rightfully so," He Who Conquers responded. "It seems he has held hard feelings about me for a long time. I never knew it, though he's never been very friendly." He put one foot on the ladder before adding, "His blood will run, and I'll feel no joy for having put his dreams in Sipapu."

Silence returned as he went up the ladder and headed toward the dwelling, his legs heavy as he considered the terrible consequences of having played a game. Perhaps, he soliloquized, it would have come to this now or later. The man almost seemed to relish the idea of the fight, which indicated he had done some meditating on the matter. He had planned this, and only awaited the proper time to spring it.

The question was why? What did he have to prove? How could he have such hatred locked inside? He was not terribly bright, but he certainly seemed like a good enough fellow. Why, why, why? The question railed at him like a nagging pain as he stopped outside the doorway and relieved himself before entering.

The man was a bully, and he had won respect through fear. He had been a brawler all his life, holding the championship in wrestling for five winters. But to bully into an ultimate test of life...why? He had never made a threat to the man, had never tried to challenge him to prove who was best at anything...except the game of chance they had just played. What would it prove if the man killed him? Maybe a boast of killing the "foreigner", but one the people had come to know and idolize. Was that it? Did he dislike the recognition given to one he could not accept as one of them? To this extreme?

Not likely. There was something else behind it. Or someone! Did someone want him gone? Out of the way? Long Knife was gone and no one had heard of him since he ran. Was he somewhere near, wanting to return, but feared to do so while He Who Conquers was still there?

That was possible, but how likely? He was considered a coward, a coyote, by the entire community. If he returned, he would be *branded with the mark* and run from the area. So with that possibility unlikely, who?

Unable to come up with an answer, he pushed the hide and entered the dwelling. Scent of Violets lay asleep, the fire low but the room very warm. Her nakedness immediately raised his uncontrollable masculine feelings. He squatted beside the door and stared at the woman who had become like a part of his body, of whom he thought frequently throughout each sun.

She was innocent in sleep, the mischievousness gone, the face in total repose, the enlarged breasts rising and falling slowly in the calm breathing of sleep. She lay on her side, the enlarged abdomen resting on the mat, the left leg thrust forward onto a knee to help hold her body in balance. He stared at her a long time, not thinking of anything but the beauty of his mate, studying her in a way that would forever hold the image in his mind.

Beside the fire was his meal, and a cup of hot tea stood on a rock that sat in the edge of the pit. It was obvious she had been thinking of him as she went to sleep, and the thought was titillating. He smiled to himself and sat against the wall, eating and perusing her, and his thoughts turned to their relationship.

He realized that he had been studying her for a long time and had not thought of coupling. Why was that? What made a man look at a woman--a naked woman--without thinking of such an enjoyable and demanding thing? How often he had seen other women naked, from bathing to draining water, and not desired them. That was no surprise to him, for he realized how much he wished to be a lover, not a coupling machine. But this...?

It was growing dark fast, Sun God at rest. Her body became less and less visible as he finished his meal and slowly finished his tea. He wanted to keep considering the matter that had held him when he entered, but found the thoughts displaced by the new thoughts she conjured.

He still enjoyed her candid ways, her animal drives that continued even while she was carrying a son. She was insatiable, and he knew she felt it was her sure way of keeping him with her. He chuckled to himself. It surely was, although he had never entertained thoughts of anything else. She seemed to think he would start making regular trips to the women of the gods as soon as he returned to his people, and his feeble denials only made her giggle.

He decided not to reveal that he had to be twenty-five winters before he became eligible for such trips, and then it had to be at the invitation of Spirit Man. He would continue to enjoy her frequent demands and be excited by her wild and vicious wrestling.

If. He did have a new threat, and it came at rising sun. Perhaps she would have need of another mate...but he doubted that. The Great One had given him certain abilities, and with them, a set of goals to accomplish. He still had many to do.

28

He was restless. His sleep was often broken by his vivid, frightful dreams, those visions that told him of an unfinished future, those awful events which would place him in leadership of his people. But this time, the dreams began differently, for he was no longer running through canyons, but instead was walking toward The Top. The Top...as he had seen it once when he looked back while leaving...the steep skirt of green, the sheer rock facing, the trees that broke the skyline...and smoke! Smoke rising from a place back from the edge, a thick, black smoke that rolled into the abode of the gods and hung suspended in the windless, endless blue.

His travels were over. He would go no farther, but the realization brought no joy. He knew what the smoke portended, and he had little wish to see it fulfilled. The razed village when he walked into it, the many dead, and somewhere among them his parents and one other he had seen for the first time. Chief Roaring Lion. His bloody genitals were crudely stuffed into his mouth, his stomach cut open, his scalp missing, his eyes but jelly set in oozing sockets.

The sweat had come again while his mind comprehended the story, and his body was exhausted. He lay still, feeling the weight on him. He not only did not wish to move, he could not. His limbs were rigid as dried sticks. He slept again. He rolled, he tossed, he awakened and dozed. The first light found him squatting against the front of his dwelling, wearing only his breechcloth, his moccasins, and his headband. His knife and axe were in their sheaths, and his hands lay inert in his lap. He stared at the peg that stuck in the center of the courtyard, to mark the center of the limited arena.

He had no idea how it got there, as he had heard nothing, but it was not there when he went to his dwelling to sleep. Yet, there is was, the symbol of conflict, of his inability to avoid trouble one more time, though his stay with this people had not been smooth from the very beginning. But it had seemed mostly controllable, until his innocent visit to the kiva on the previous sun. He had not realized the depth of the underlying animosity toward him.

Then the thought hit him. Perhaps it became clear because he was still unrested, and his mind was therefore more focused, not as lively as it often was when he was feeling good. Roadrunner was being used, he was someone's fool. It was not Roadrunner who hated him, because the man had no reason--at least, none of which he was aware. He had been fed a host of lies and implanted with the hatred of someone else. The problem was that in his desire to be known and believed by his people, he had forgotten to open his eyes to the men with whom he rubbed shoulders.

Running Hare. Spirit Man. Hostile men with a voice of authority much beyond the common man, men with studied reasons for disliking him. Running Hare, who lost face on the successful hunt and would never resume his former place as their leader, even when He Who Conquers left. Never again would he see the elevated stature of honor he had previously held. Then again, he had been unsuccessful several times recently, and might have already lost his lofty perch, though he would have been unaware of the loss. But there was no question about it, he had reason to hate. And he did.

And Spirit Man. He had not wanted the intruder
among his people from the beginning, and found an
argumentation that had turned his own spiritual odyssey
into question. He was unable to refute the dogma
presented to him by a mere young man, and it led to a
doubt about his own spiritual honesty--which he might
overcome if the person who was the focus of his trouble
no longer existed, for it would be proof that the gods
didn't accept him. It was why he had appointed him to
lead the hunt, knowing that, with the recent lack of
hunting successes, it would be a failure--with Running
Hare along to disrupt any possible success. That would
bring to the foreigner nothing but disrespect, and death
as a spy or witch. But it proved to be otherwise. His
accomplishment had rendered the life-or-death threat
harmless, and made Running Hare, close friend of Spirit
Man, the loser. Even worse, He Who Conquers had
taken the threat as lightly as a joke, in so many words
telling the Spirit Man to never threaten him or what was
his. The threat had been reversed, and though Spirit
Man was the only one who had known of the exchange,
in himself he now felt belittled and demeaned, trying to
avoid contacts in a small village where contacts were
inevitable. He was a hard bone to swallow, this brash
youth who turned a traditional spiritual journey into little
more than shallow mind games.

How blind he had been while he worked so hard
in their fields, as he played games with them, while he
watched them storing the meat he had led them to find.
If he were to become a successful leader of his people, he
had to be more aware of the currents running among his
people, to keep on top of their looks and expressions,
interpreting correctly what they were thinking before
they even knew of it themselves. Perception. How much
he had yet to develop, and learn.

Movement in his peripheral vision drew his
attention, and a man came into view, mincing along as
though trying not to disturb someone sleeping beside
him. He was close to the stake before he noticed it, and
he stopped as if it were a snake. His eyes stared at it for
a time, then lifted and ran across the buildings until he
espied He Who Conquers watching him.

He Who Conquers had never seen the man

before, so it was with curiosity that he watched the man approach, only then realizing the reason for the man's style of walking. He used a stick to aid his walk. He was an old man, and the witch of pain had attacked his back and shoulders, causing him to stoop as he walked. The closer he came, the more it was evident the cane was a necessity, not merely a convenience.

"You are a visitor here?" the man asked.

"Perhaps."

His voice was deep and quiet as he spoke. "What is the occasion of the stake? Is there to be a Death Match?"

He Who Conquers nodded. Because of the man's posture, he had at first missed the strange breechcloth, but now he saw it. It was of the type used at Open Stone, and he had not seen it here.

"Then maybe I should stay for a bit of entertainment. I imagine all the centers will watch."

"Likely."

"I came to visit an acquaintance. It seems the visit might prove more interesting than a few casual words." He eyed the squatting youth and then glanced at the doorway. A young woman had pushed the hide aside and was looking at him. "Your mate is strange to this area, too."

"She came with me."

"Where are you from?"

"Lately of Open Stone."

The man's eyebrows raised and he again looked at the woman. "You both are from there?"

"She is. I'm not."

The man nodded. He Who Conquers had not volunteered any information, and the point was not lost on the old man. "Open Stone. I know of the place." He took yet another look at Scent of Violets. "Did you by chance know an old man by the name of Rain Water?" Before either could answer he answered for himself. "No, not likely. He'd be long dead, now."

"He died just after the first snows."

The man straightened up in his surprise, the cane jerked from the ground and then was thrust back down. He fixed his eyes on He Who Conquers again. His bushy eyebrows hid the eyes in the early light.

"You knew him?"

"That's his granddaughter." His thumb jerked over his shoulder to indicate Scent of Violets.

The man almost staggered. His voice was shaky as he responded, "Can it be?" He stared at Scent of Violets again, the shadow of the doorway hiding her features. "Come out, my child, I would see you up close. My eyes are not as they were once."

She hesitated, then came out. She stood beside He Who Conquers, and a hand went to his shoulder for comfort.

"You look like your mu," he said softly, whispery. "I would have known you...." His voice cracked. "But prettier...softer...." Scent of Violets stared at the man without blinking, her eyes cool.

"You are my fa." The tone was as cool as her eyes.

He continued to stare at her, He Who Conquers rendered silent by the drama. "I am."

He Who Conquers was not sure why the man should feel such deep-seated emotions about her. He had left when she was but an infant, and it was unlikely he felt much of a paternal tie. Maybe it was guilt, or the memory of her mu, or some other equally painful thing. The latter two could be one and the same, underlying his escape.

"I have no memory of you." The coolness of the statement was meant to be cutting.

"It's just as well." The man had winced. "Your mu and I never had much happiness. It is good if you have found some. Your mate has raised quite a new attitude in the centers of Wide Canyon." He was unsure of himself, glancing almost apologetically at He Who Conquers. But he gave his daughter no chance for a response. "I found what I wanted here. It would never have happened there."

She nodded once but said nothing. She was determined not to help him if he chose to justify himself.

He turned and looked at the stake, his eyes staying there though it was obvious his thoughts were elsewhere. Agitated, he tapped the ground several times with the cane. Before anything more was said, two men came from a kiva, glanced at the stake and He Who

Conquers, then turned and walked away. Running Hare and Thunderstorm.

He stared after them, then heard more stirring and found Bright Bird approaching, with Red Hawk beside him. Both studied the old man before turning their attention to He Who Conquers and Scent of Violets.

"Three of us plan to go on a hunt in two suns. Are you interested in joining us?" It seemed a bit fabricated to He Who Conquers, but he assumed they had come to speak with him on other matters before discovering the two others with him. He let them know he was grateful they stayed away from the subject. Not even Scent of Violets knew of the match, yet.

"You have some particular place in mind?" he asked.

"The mountains to sun-set."

"I'm interested. My mate would love fresh meat."

"Mine, too," Bright Bird grinned. His manner was relaxed, though his eyes said otherwise.

"Who else will go?"

"The two of us and Gray Fox." He paused. "Birdsong might; he spoke of it some time ago, but not since."

"It's a good group. Perhaps we can even find a grouse or two for variety."

Red Hawk watched the interchange, not sure why Bright Bird was beating around the bush. He held his tongue, glancing at the old man several times. "Who is the old one?" His question brought up the head of the elder.

"I am White Cloud." His voice was again deep and assured.

"I've seen the old one," Red Arrow said, using the phrase of respect. "He's from Great Center." The Great Center was the largest of the centers in the valley, and would probably grow as fast or faster than the others in the future.

White Cloud nodded, studying the two newcomers. "You are the son of Flaming Spear." His eyes fixed on Red Hawk.

"I am."

"He was a great man of the hunt." His eyes glanced toward the unseen mountains. "I saw him stalk a buck and put his spear into it without having to throw it."

Red Hawk nodded. "I heard of that. He spoke highly of White Cloud. He said White Cloud once rode the back of a wapiti that walked under the tree in which he waited."

The old man showed the trace of a smile to indicate his appreciation for the compliment. "The son of Flaming Spear is like his fa. He's a hunter."

He Who Conquers watched the exchange with interest. It was very likely that the open attitude of Red Hawk toward him came because his fa had held an open attitude to a stranger, and befriended him. Of such things came learning and wisdom.

Red Hawk touched his forehead with his right hand, a sign which indicated he was grateful for the compliment. Seeing he would not be able to speak to He Who Conquers about the match, Bright Bird turned to him. "We'll speak to you at sunrise."

He and Red Hawk walked away, and soon he could see the latter asking why they had not gotten to the purpose of the visit. It was unlikely any plans had been laid for a hunt, and Red Hawk was exercised about that, too.

"You'll join us for breakfast?" Scent of Violets addressed the question to the old man. He was leaning on the cane he had fashioned and polished.

White Cloud was taken aback, but regained his composure quickly. "I'd be grateful."

"You two enjoy the meal," He Who Conquers said. "I have something I must do. I'll return when it's over." Without giving either of the two a chance to question him, he walked quickly away, aware that Scent of Violets was shaken by his sudden departure. He would explain later. Besides, it would give them a chance to reacquaint without interference.

He relieved himself, then turned to observe activity begin in the courtyard. Word was passing quickly about the match, and many came to look at the stake to verify the rumor. Spirit Man and Running Hare came again, each carrying a rope, a sure sign they were anxious for the match. He knew now he had been correct about them. They were the ones who had conspired to get the mentally sluggish Roadrunner to do what they feared to do for themselves. On the inspiration of the moment, he headed directly toward them as they knelt to tie the two ropes to the post. His rebuke of Spirit Man before the hunt was about to be recast.

Coldly, he said, "Well, if it is not the evil brothers in a strange plot. I hope you will feel irenic this sunset when you know you goaded a man into losing his life."

Running Hare, who made no small thing of his dislike for He Who Conquers, misunderstood the meaning. "No one will miss you around here."

"Miss me? Why should anyone miss me? I'm only a humble foreigner, but one who enjoys living. I assume Roadrunner did, too, before you two spoke to him. How many people already know it was you who planted this whole thing in his head? I assume there are many. Will they think so highly of you when he lies on Earth Mu, his blood giving her nourishment? I rather think they'll blame you for getting one, who is not too bright, to fight your battles for you."

He locked glances with Spirit Man. "I think I once reminded you that the Great One has much for me to do. Obviously I haven't done it yet, for I'm still here. What I don't understand is why you do this. My leaving would have let your lives return to their former useless states. Now I think my leaving will do far more, perhaps end your respect among your people forever. I suggest that when Roadrunner falls, you both put your tails between your legs and run like the coyotes you are. Join Long Arrow somewhere."

Running Hare came to his feet with a growl deep in his throat. His eyes were murderous, his face red and the veins of his neck distended. No words came. He Who Conquers stared back defiantly, then turned and walked away. He pulled up short when he saw Gray Fox coming, and from another direction Roadrunner appeared.

As if on signal, people began coming from every direction, a solemn and quiet people who appeared to be sleep-walking. Did he detect mixed emotions about the fight and a winner? He had made friends among them, and Roadrunner was not admired by all. It was a strong possibility that what he had said about the people knowing who actually perpetrated the match was plausible. Perhaps more than merely plausible.

"You look fit," Gray Fox said as he arrived. "You know what the rules are?"

He shrugged.   "They might differ from my people."

"Each man has a rope tied around one ankle to keep him from escaping.   Each man fights with one weapon, and the axe is used only when the opponent is on the ground and lives.   There can only one left alive."

"It's the same."

"Good.   Then you'll not have to try to think of the rules in the heat of combat."

He shrugged again, but said nothing.

"Spirit Man will signal the beginning.   When your opponent is dead, you can cut the rope that holds you."

He nodded.

"No one is allowed to help either man.   You're on your own, as is Roadrunner.   Be sure to test both ropes to be sure no one has tampered with them."

He again nodded.   Roadrunner was talking with the two men at the stake, and he joined them, saying nothing as he knelt and tugged hard at the ropes to be sure each was secure.   Then he took the two ends and ran the ropes out to full length, finding one to be almost a stride longer than the other.   He cut it to make both even, jerking each rope several times before walking back to the stake while he eyed both ropes as they lay on the ground.

When he returned, he nodded his approval, handing the short piece of rope to Spirit Man.

He tied the rope on the ankle of Roadrunner, and Roadrunner tied the rope on his.   Then each stood facing the other.   He Who Conquers stood calmly eyeing his opponent, and noticed Roadrunner showed the initial signs of tension.   He grinned, but said nothing.

Each then turned and walked back to the full length of their rope in opposite directions, turned and walked to his left, thus setting up the boundary for spectators.   If anyone ventured inside the boundary, he would be forcibly thrown back by those around him.

The crowd was huge, people still arriving, some from far away. They stood on boulders behind the dwellings, stood and sat on the dwellings themselves, and their quiet was almost alarming.

He was amazed at how far the word had gone so quickly. But as yet, neither Scent of Violets nor White Cloud had shown. He was glad. He would rather she knew nothing of it until it was over. What he could not understand was the quietness of the large gathering.

They returned to the farthest points from each other, and stood staring. Spirit Man walked to the stake and stood with eyes lifted toward the butte. When the hand of Sunwatcher, who could be seen standing on the top, came down, he would signal the fight to begin. The latter would wait for the first ray of direct sun to appear on a mark up where he stood. Sun God would not strike the fighters until later, since the wall of the valley shielded the rays until Sun God had risen far. The fight would probably be over before He saw the bottom of the canyon, which was just as well. It would be cooler.

It seemed forever. They stood and waited, the huge crowd still strangely silent, a few voices heard as one or another would comment on the delay, but it was so quiet he could have closed his eyes and wondered if there were anyone around. Roadrunner nervously fidgeted, toying with the haft of his knife and kicking at the ground with his toe or heel. Then the arm came down, and Spirit Man lifted both hands to indicate the two men, then clapped once and backed away.

Roadrunner came with a rush to close the distance. He Who Conquers merely walked forward and then poised to await the bigger man. Then he half-smiled, realizing he had quite an edge in height and reach, hoping he could be the quicker.

He moved to his left to avoid the straight charge, and Roadrunner stopped two paces away and crouched. The two men moved cautiously to their right, then Roadrunner feinted and stabbed, backing off quickly. He Who Conquers had hardly moved, not wanting to show any of his speed or quickness. He let his opponent make his own move and reaction. It seemed ponderous.

Roadrunner repeated the move twice more while He Who Conquers worked back to his left and backpedaled slightly. The impression he gave was of fear, a ploy he knew would shortly become helpful. He moved back again to the right, then let another feint come and go before he again started to the left.

For the fourth time, Roadrunner came with the same move, and this time he stepped to the right, and with a slash that resembled the speed of a rattlesnake, he left a long red mark across the chest of Roadrunner. He was away before the bigger man could bring his backhand.

A new respect came to the man, appearing as sweat on his forehead. The red mark issued with seeping blood, as he had sliced through the outer layer of skin. For the first time, he became aware of voices, people shouting and urging the fighters on.

He moved forward a few steps, and Roadrunner gave ground. He had suddenly realized he was fighting a man inferior in weight but faster. He was red-chested to prove his slowness, and his eyes had narrowed to slits.

For a time they circled right and left, then He Who Conquers twice in swift cadence stepped forward and jabbed, the second time nicking the forearm that held the knife. Roadrunner stared down for an instant and watched the blood ooze from the shallow cut. His eyes flickered between fear and determination.

Suddenly the man charged forward, his left coming for the knife-wrist of He Who Conquers, the right poising to stab. But when he got where his opponent had been, he was no longer there. He had moved down and to the left, and raised and turned with the same quickness. He was behind Roadrunner, who had not been prepared for the move. He merely laughed, then grabbed the rope and jerked.

Roadrunner went down, and the crowd gasped. In the sudden quiet, the voice of Scent of Violets--a gasp of fear and surprise--was alone in the breezeless air. The deep voice of her father came behind the sound.

"Here, my child! Stay with me!"

He did not dare look to see what she was doing, his eyes intent on the man who was fast getting to his feet, surprised that he had not been set upon while he was down. It was the same thought that went through the spectators.

As he circled, he saw Spirit Man behind
Roadrunner, his face grim. Inside, he felt a moment of
satisfaction, but it was short-lived as Roadrunner moved
again. This time, his blade nicked the elbow on the left
arm, which He Who Conquers failed to protect soon
enough. The backhand that came after the slash nearly
caught him in the armpit, but a backward leap carried
him away by the barest of margins.

In that moment he gained a new respect for his
opponent. The man was a fighter, already overcoming
his fear twice to show intensity and bravery. The
cockiness of the kiva was gone, raw determination
replacing it.

He circled again, keeping his rope slack and not
too close to the feet of Roadrunner. Slowly he
maneuvered the man backward until they were on
Roadrunner's side of the stake for the first time. With a
few feints and jabs, he kept the man back, his superior
reach a definite asset.

At a feint, Roadrunner lunged, and He Who
Conquers moved like the rattler again. Down, to his left,
and a forehand jab. It entered the left thigh, deeply.
Blood cascaded when the knife was jerked free. He
leaped back to avoid the defensive swing from
Roadrunner, then back- slashed and caught the knife arm
just below the elbow. The cut laid the arm open to the
bone, and the knife fell helplessly from the released
fingers. He was without defense, at the mercy of He
Who Conquers, and dying of the blood spurting from his
thigh. The cut had severed the main artery.

He stared at He Who Conquers dumbly for a
moment, unable to comprehend what had happened with
such lightning quickness. His knife lay at his feet, his
arm was useless, and blood was pumping from his leg in
spurts that coincided with his strong heartbeats. His left
hand tried to throttle the flow, without success.

"You won." He said it numbly, calmly.

"I sorrow. You shouldn't have had to fight the
battle of someone else."

"I fought you." The meaning was unmistakable.
He considered the decision his.

"You're a strong man. You could out-wrestle
anyone I've ever known. But you should not have

listened to those who set you up, who said you could win a knife fight. You are not quick enough, and strength alone does not win a Death Match."

He was growing pale, his strength failing him with every drop of blood that escaped. "You are a great fighter; I should have listened to your friends." His voice was weak, almost a whisper, his knees wobbling while he tried to remain on his feet. "Beware the...beware...." His knees began to fold. "Beware...Spirit...beware... the...." He pitched forward onto his face, then slowly pulled his arms under him and tried to rise. His arms shook with the effort. His head tilted so he could look up at He Who Conquers. "Spirit Man...hates...." He shook his head, his eyes rolling back before he again willed himself under control. "Run...Running Hare...wants to...to kill you...." He dropped onto his face in the dirt and this time there was no further attempt to rise. Blood seeped slowly from the wound in the leg, soaking quickly into the sandy soil. There was a great sigh, and breathing stopped.

It was his right to take the head and impale it on the post where the maiden had been sacrificed, but he felt nothing but disgust at the whole affair. It was his duty to take a fistful of blood and soil and smear his chest to mark his victory, and instead he turned and stared at Spirit Man.

"You sent him to this death. You and Running Hare plotted to have him challenge me. You have your hollow victory. He is dead; the Great One has given me victory. Everyone knows you two sent him to do what you feared to do. He fought hard, and he fought with determination and bravery, but he failed; so have you. You caused his death, you smear his blood on your chests. Let the people know where lies the coyote."

He bent down, pulled his axe and chopped the rope. When he stood, his knife and axe were in their sheaths. "When you taste the flesh of this man in your kiva, his spirit will live in you to constantly remind you that you are coyotes, and he the only brave one among you."

29

"You are very tired. We had better rest here for a sun or two, I think."

She stopped immediately, standing with shoulders sagging, her body covered with perspiration and her face a mask, trying to cover her complete exhaustion. "Yes." It was all she could manage.

He helped her escape her pack, then shucked his own and supported her as she knelt, then lay on her blanket.

"I thought you premature in wanting to leave now," he scolded mildly. "It is not an easy trip."

"I knew that when I insisted we leave. I'll be fine. Just let me rest a bit and I'll make something for us to eat while you make sure we are secure here."

He nodded, took his weapons and began to climb the hill to get a view of the country. She lay back on her blanket and closed her eyes as he began to leave. She slept before he was twenty paces away.

As he neared the top of the small hill, which was actually the first set of trees the Others had entered when they had taken the six hunters, he paused and looked around, having just lost sight of her. He edged forward until he could see the other side, then stood and studied the country, slowly moving up to see what was closer to the hill. Satisfied there was no one near, he turned and started back down.

She was sleeping when he returned, and he stood for a moment and watched her regular breathing, concerned for her. She had insisted they head for his people. It was not what he wanted, solely because of her condition. She was heavy with child, and he was afraid she was going to overtax her system. But she had been adamant.

Things had started to go downhill not long after the Death Match. Spirit Man had become openly hostile after He Who Conquers had made his accusations, and many had found willing ears with many people. There were those who began to shun Spirit Man, which was more than the man could stand. He had openly cursed He Who Conquers, even to the use of a witch, unaware of the white feather which was in the possession of the latter. A white feather was protection from witches and curses, which, apart from the pelt of an albino, was the only known deterrent.

Running Hare had started an undercurrent of slurs on his own, charges which also found a few soft ears. It was not hard to convince people that He Who Conquers was a man, and because he was only a man, the amazing things he did had to be caused by a witch. It was very likely he was owned by one. Black feathers were found tucked into the crevasses of his dwelling, and once a live rattlesnake was dropped inside his door.

Only a single moon had passed before Scent of Violets determined it was best they leave, and go secretly. Not a single person was to know.

Just after dark, while the moon had not yet appeared, they left. Dogs still barked at anything that moved, and did not cause enough alarm to investigate. They were out of the canyon without being seen. However, the worst was yet to come.

She was sure they would be followed and he

shared her fear. They went straight into no-sun for two
suns, but she failed to get stronger with time, as on the
trip from Open Stone.   She knew she was fighting to
keep any pace at all, which made her desperate.   She
would refuse to stop to rest when he did, continuing to
walk until he gave up and followed.

From a hill he had seen five men following, far
back but coming at a trot.   The trail had been easy to
follow. Knowing he had to delay them, he tied blankets
to their feet and turned sharply into rising-sun, toward a
line of mesas.   Then he went back and lay along the trail
to see if they found the new direction.

Scent of Violets, without the blankets to hinder
her, continued to walk while he went back, and when he
saw that they began to cast back and forth trying to see
where the trail went, he knew they would be delayed for
a while.

He caught up to her soon, and they walked
almost a sun.   Then he again tied the blankets to their
feet and they turned again to no-sun.

This was the sixth sun of their journey, and
Scent of Violets was covering less ground with each step.
He often insisted they stop, and though she refused
several times in this sun alone, she finally consented. He
found no sign of Others, or of any man, except the
knowledge that five men trailed them.

It was a dilemma. What could he do to shake
them, when there were surely some expert trackers
among them? Even then, they knew where the two were
headed, and could feasibly get ahead and ambush them.
To his chagrin, he was not in a good position to try to
ambush or attack them, having to protect his mate. He
sat on a mound where he could see her and yet keep an
eye back along their trail, his thoughts troubled.

Sun God was about to sleep on the mountains
again when he finally decided they were somewhat safe
for the darkness, and he returned to camp and made
them something to eat. He determined not to awaken
her just to eat.

They were along the setting-sun side of the hill.
From where he had viewed the area ahead for Others, he

could see the hills that preceded the Waters-That-Hurry-
to-Sunset. The thought brought little solace. If they
went directly toward the waters, they would be visible for
the two suns it would probably take them to reach them.
With men behind him, that was inviting disaster. And,
to keep traveling anywhere was a waste of his mate's
reserves, if she had any left.

And to top off the trouble, if they stayed put,
those on his trail would likely find them within a single
sun!

He ate slowly, unenthusiastically, mechanically.
His eyes often went to his mate, a shade of anger in
them because he let her talk him into starting now. He
was a bit angry at her for pushing him so hard, but more
so at himself for going along with her idea.

She awakened with a cry. Her arms locked
around her large belly, and she doubled around her
arms. A shock of fear went through him, wondering if
she might deliver the baby here, without having spoken
with the Goddess of Fertility, or Earth Mu, or the other
gods the womenfolk acknowledged. He knew nothing
about childbirth, as did all men. It was cause for witches
if a man learned what was involved.

She gasped for breath and said, "What do I do
for a hammock?"

He was on his feet beside her, then kneeling.
"We have no hammock, my mate! What can I do?"

"Find two young trees near each other and tie a
blanket between them. Cut a hole in the blanket--about
this big." She demonstrated a hole whose diameter
would be about twice the length of his foot.

On his feet, he ran for the nearest trees, and
soon located that appeared to be what she asked, and
with two pieces of rope, tied the blanket between them.
Then he cut the hole with his knife and ran back to her.

"Now you must put the paint on me. I can't do
it myself."

"What paint? We have no paint."

"In my pack. A rolled skin. It has dried paints
on it. Apply a few drops of water to each."

He felt like five thumbs, but he found the pack

and rolled it open. There was the skin. He untied the string that held it closed and let it flip open. There were five daubs of different colors, red, white, black, blue and yellow.

Following her instructions, he put three drips of water on each color, then smeared each into a thick paint. Next he did as she asked, and took the white, which he smeared into a circle around her distended belly. He outlined it in black, then put a large red dot over the navel. Then he put a white circle around each breast, and colored the nipples bright red. A yellow line was then drawn from each nipple to the navel, and from the navel to the top of the pubic mound. Blue arrows were then added from the knee upward, then turned at the hip with the arrow-tip pointed at the pubic area.

While he did the last painting, he noticed how the vaginal opening had enlarged, making his haste even greater. But he had concluded the painting.

She fought to her feet, and he had to first help her, then carry her up the hill. As they neared the hammock, the water burst and gushed down over his legs. Fear lanced him that witches might attack him for being this involved in her birth. Or attack her or the son about to be born. He nearly ran the last few steps to the blanket. At the blanket, she cut a short piece of live branch from a pine, then straddled the hammock, her clothing already off because of the painting. The pains were coming again and again, and each time she would nearly double over.

"Go!" Her order was direct and accompanied with a pointing finger. As he turned away, she put the short piece of branch in her mouth to bite down on when the pains came, then clasped the figurine he had given her in her fist. In her other hand she held the knife she would use to cut the cord.

He was unsure of what to do with himself as he returned to and past the campsite, darkness now complete. He wanted no fire with men behind, and he felt compelled to stay near where she was dropping her child. He could see their camp from where he sat, and back along the trail as well. Deciding their camp should remain where he was now, he quickly dropped down and gathered everything, though it took two loads to get to the place. Only once did he hear anything from the area where she was laboring, but his training told him not to go check, for to see the birth would condemn the child to death. There was nothing for him to do. He sat and stared into the darkness, trying to think about the men behind him, wanting to see where they might be or what they might be thinking. It was impossible. His nerves were too tight about Scent of Violets. It was a struggle for him to even stay alert for sounds which did not belong in the darkness.

Then there was the cry of an infant breaking into the softness of the dark. He stood, looking uncertainly in the direction where she was struggling alone, wondering what to do. There were no calls for him, no words, no instructions...just silence since that first cry. He sat on the rock that had numbed his buttocks already, then stood again. He was amazed. He could begin to see down the hill! Struck by this, he turned and looked back, to see the sky turning light toward sunrise. The entire darkness had passed, and he had been unaware of it.

Realizing how this might mean spending some time here, he dropped quickly to the old campsite, and spent time erasing signs of their stopping. He sifted some sand into the brushed-out tracks, turned two rocks back to their original position, gently brushed some grass to make it stand again. When he was satisfied, he walked from the site toward the top of the hill, backwards in his steps, at the same time erasing all signs of Scent of Violets. At the crest of the hill, he turned and walked to no-sun, sure tracks that would be easy to follow. He stopped at a drop-off, where the wind had carved the hillside into a cliff about at high as he was tall. Then again he walked backward in his own tracks, until he came to a weedy area. Here he took a leap to the left with all his strength, wiped the track clean, and worked slowly back to where he had chosen to make their camp, wiping out his tracks as he went.

From there, he watched the backtrail. Sun God

made his appearance, and birds flitted through the air and around the trees. A small gopher came near and stared at him, then darted away. The sun grew warm, the blue skies showing no sign of clouds, and he was grateful Sun God was still winning the war of the seasons. A sound came from behind him, and he half-turned to look back, a huge smile crossing his face. His mate was slowly working toward him, carrying her infant in the blanket he had prepared for her birthing.

She was pale, but she was smiling "Your son is very small, but strong."

He stood and went to her, helping her into the small circle of fallen trees, letting her down on a blanket. "It's two moons sooner than you expected."

She nodded. "The Goddess decides." Then she closed her eyes. "I'm very tired, my conqueror."

"Sleep. We'll stay here as long as we have to. The Great One will keep us." He hoped his confidence was not misplaced. He watched her fall asleep; the infant, unseen inside his blanket, made no sign of life. He wondered if he even lived.

He continued to watch their trail, until dread touched him as he saw a head appear over a hilltop back along their trail, then another and another, until five men appeared. Running Hare came first followed by Thunderstorm, Hand of Stone, Spirit Man, and then, Long Knife!

He was amazed. Long Knife, who had run! Long Knife, who tried to kill a friend treacherously and failed! Long Knife, a man of cowardice! He had returned to his center, if he had left at all! And now he was one of the party that hunted him and his mate!

He watched them approach along the hill, already holding his bow which was strung with an arrow, his spear beside him should he need it. His eyes missed nothing as they followed the sun-old tracks.

Where he had changed the trail, they stopped. Long Knife and Thunderstorm studied the tracks while the others stared about them, looking at every stone and in every direction. They were puzzled. He had not totally obliterated the signs of the previous campsite, but he had made it very unreadable, and the lack of tracks leading to it or away from it had them wondering.

Long Knife and Thunderstorm went back to his tracks along the top of the ridge, then stood and stared around them. His tracks led to mid-sun, but those of his mate had just vanished. They followed the single set until they stopped at the brink of the sandy blowout, where it was obvious both were puzzled. His tracks had disappeared like those of his mate.

The two returned to where the others stood talking, too low for him to understand. He watched nervously, fearful his new son would cry and alert them. But both his mate and his son slept.

Long Knife was their best tracker, and he circled out to find sign, but He Who Conquers had done a thorough job. Thunderstorm went the other direction, and they each made a complete circle, finding nothing.

Long Knife returned to the blowout, studying the country in every direction, then dropped down into it and cast about for sign. There was none, but while he looked, the others joined him, and all five searched the panoramic view in front and below them, spreading out to find a better place to find something...anything. He could see at least one of them at all times, but none came his way.

Scent of Violets slumbered on, the infant lying on her stomach in its blanket. Neither moved. He sighed with relief, though it was not over yet. He could still see Spirit Man near the blowout. All he could hope for was that none of them would stop to think, to try to put themselves in his place and read his intentions. The fact Long Knife led them was good, for the man did not know him at all, and if he were the one doing the leading, it would be hard for them to out-think him.

Spirit Man glanced in his direction, but looked away again. In a while, he heard one of the men call out, but could not understand what he said. Spirit Man went out of sight along the hillside.

Time passed slowly, Sun God rose in the heavens and warmed the nest where He Who Conquers sat immobile, eyes alert for any further sign of the five, while his family slept. He grew sleepy as the sun warmed him, fighting heavy eyes that threatened to betray his watchfulness. He was tired, and he was hungry. It was the latter which helped to keep him awake.

Finally, after what he surmised was nearly a fourth of a sun gone without further sign of the men, he crept from the camp and worked along the hill to where they had disappeared. Near the end of it he hunkered down and crawled. They were nowhere in sight.

Puzzled and a bit fearful to know he had lost track of them, he lay on the top and worked slowly along until he could see out over the desert. They were far out, looking like ant-people, walking in single file into the great expanse he had dreaded to enter. Knowing they were gone made him breathe easier, but he wondered if they would continue or if they would backtrack again.

They were between him and his people. They could lay an ambush for him if they knew he was behind them, and he was sure they would shortly know that for a fact. Still, it gave him time to make a proper camp and let his mate recuperate for a while before they would again take up their journey.

He returned to his camp to find Scent of Violets eating, and she had prepared him a meal. His son was sleeping again, or yet, although she uncovered the boy so he could see his new son. He stared at the tiny, dark-skinned, ruddy figure with the wrinkled skin and wondered how this could ever become a man. But he grinned to see the fists balled and the feet curled in sleep. His was a son who would be strong, but who would make decisions only after using his head carefully. The curled feet said he would sit and contemplate, and the balled fists that he would not be weak.

"He'll be a strong son," he said wonderingly.

"And his name is Night Hawk, for I saw the great hawk when I was cleaning him. The hawk looked on him, and spoke."

"A good name. The gods will honor him for it."

She smiled. "He'll be another conqueror. But

he'll do it after many things happen that will make him
strong to lead. It's not going to be easy for him to learn
to lead; his mind is strong, but he will think too much
while he's young, and be indecisive until things occur
that hurt him deeply. One he loves and respects will cut
him deeply, and one he wishes to help will turn on him.
Yet he will become a great leader."

He Who Conquers looked from her to the boy
while she spoke, wondering at her words, but knowing
better than to ask how she knew. He was not the only
one whom the gods visited!

"Those following us, they're not here?"

"They went past and are now ahead of us. We'll
let them go for a few suns, until you get your strength
back. When we travel again, we have to somehow get
past them."

She nodded. "I was not smart to push you into
this."   "Too late to worry about that, now. We plan for
what lies ahead. Blaming you, or me for letting you
make the decision, won't help us now."

She nodded. "Still, I was wrong. It puts much
more pressure on you."

He grinned. "Weight is something every man
must learn to handle. I'll do what has to be done when
the time comes."

* * *   * * *   * * *

"He'll come before the snows."

"He'll bring a mate with him?"

"Yes. But all won't be well here when he comes."
"Such as?"

She shrugged. "I will not live to see my son."

Little Dove looked at the old woman. Her face
had become so wrinkled it was hard to see how she
could once have been pretty, but she was known to have
been a very attractive young lady. She was withered and
stooped, her teeth gone and her lips drawn, her nose thin
and hooked. Some of her hair had dropped out, until
she looked like a witch.

"Are you sure? If he comes so soon, why won't
you see him? Where are you going?"

"I go back to Earth Mu."

Little Dove was puzzled. "But you are still healthy! You can live yet another four or five winters!"

The homely, toothless smile was soft. "That is nice of you to say, little pretty one, but I am old and verey wrinkled. There is little left for me except Sipapu."

"But...if you won't see him again...I mean, does this mean that...well...something will happen...here? Mu says something will happen, but she can't see what."

The piercing eyes of the old woman lost their softness. "Do not ask for what we should not know. It is best to remain ignorant of the future than that we see calamity. I have no idea why I cannot see him again, but it is enough to know I shall not."

She turned and waddled away, leaving Little Dove to stare after her with continued puzzlement. She turned to go to her dwelling when Eagle Eye and Gray Dog came from his kiva, directly in line with her trip. She had avoided Eagle Eye of late, trying not to see him at any time, but here she could not avoid it.

"Well, if it weren't for my poor eyesight, I would say there's a woman coming without a woman's private place to see us, Gray Dog." The two laughed, though Gray Dog's laughter was a bit forced. He had wanted to mate her, but was afraid of what Eagle Eye would say to him--especially if the mating worked.

Her response was icy. "If you were the only man alive, I would go the other way. Your testicles are dry, and your manhood like that of a boy before he walks!"

"O-o-o-h! Caustic!"

"And grateful to be rid of you."

She moved past them quickly, feeling her skin crawl for fear he would try to touch her or even make a grab for her. He did neither, but his anger was so great he lost his train of thought. She went directly to her dwelling, and was grateful to close the skin and shut out the sight of him.

Her mu chuckled. "Poison never loses its power, I see." Her voice was dry.

Little Dove picked up her screaming son and pushed a nipple into his mouth almost savagely. "He still upsets me so easily."

"And he loves it."

"I just talked with the mu of He Who Conquers. She says he'll return before the snows...and bring a mate with him. And she will not be alive to see him."

Singing Waters raised an eyebrow, but said nothing.

"Do you know of some reason she'll not see him?"

She shrugged. "I have seen nothing."

Little Dove stared at her as though not sure she should believe her. "It's a puzzle to me."

"Perhaps she'll just seek Sipapu."

"No, there's more to it than that. I'm thinking of what you said a winter ago...about hiding in a cave if Others come."

Her mu jerked visibly. "Others?"

This time it was Little Dove's turn to shrug. "Is it, Mu? Do you really know something more than you say?"

"No, my child, I don't. Perhaps she does."

"She did say it's best not to know the future when it holds calamity." Little Dove looked down at the toddler drawing on a breast, but she said nothing, and after while her mu left the dwelling, leaving her to feed her young and think her own thoughts.

30

Standing on the side of the hill, sitting in a small depression that broke his image against the dark sky, he stared out across the black plain below, watching the small winking eye of light he could see so clearly in the windless, cool darkness. He knew the fire, and who was there. And he knew they had him cut off from The Top unless he made a wide detour around them, a much longer trip. Perhaps more than Scent of Violets could handle, not to mention the possibility of snow.

For six suns they had stayed put. He had killed a deer early the second sun, and they had no problem with food, but it was getting cooler. Snowtime approached. There had again been frost again at rising sun...but that winking light was more foreboding than the weather.

He had watched the fire for two darknesses. It had not moved. Evidently they sat on a knob, or near one, where they felt they had a good view. They knew he was behind them, and they held the position of command, a thought frightening to him, and he fretted about how to handle the next leg of their travels.

Scent of Violets was walking again, gingerly at
first but better now, and their son slept most of the time;
but the remainder of their journey was not shaping up to
be a casual hike. He had to do something about those
men, though he had no desire to confront or be
confronted by them. Yet, if it came to the safety of his
family, he would do what he must. There would be no
need to so much as pause for a decision.

Gloomily he stared at the small orangish eye,
then up at the myriad of fires in the heavens. Twice he
had talked with the Great One, but there had been no
answer. He blinked, looked away, and the fire was gone!
Either they had put it out, or one of them stood in front
of it. His eyes were tired, but he continued to...what was
that? Another fire, nearer and toward rising-sun...no,
two fires. Now what was that about?

Puzzled, his attention changed, and in the deep
and moonless dark he had to study the new threat
several moments before he realized it was really quite
near. There were two fires, very small, with shadows
moving around them. Though he could see the dark
figures, he could neither count nor identify them. Yet it
had to be Others. They were probably moving back
toward their village, where their families awaited,
somewhere toward no-sun. If so, what did this portend
for him?

Of course, it might be a contingent of men who
had been to mid-sun for trading. Salt, cotton, turquoise,
all came from mid-sun trading. But normally these
people stopped at Wide Canyon on their way, and there
had been no one. Yet, if that were the case, he might
find someone with whom he could travel back to his
people. The large packs could be trade goods. But
something was nagging the back of his mind, something
that he could not quite get a grasp on, a premonition....

In two more suns, he had determined that he
and his mate would begin walking again, but traveling
on the heels of Others was dangerous at best, risky at the
least. Yet out there, somewhere near the moving waters,
was the other threat. Either was the potential for
disaster.

He returned to his camp with his thoughts

running in circles, knowing he had to be back on this very spot early to see what that pair of fires meant. Scent of Violets slept, her son curled in against her, and the fire but coals. On the edge of the coals was the flat rock that held his mug of tea, and he pulled his blanket over his shoulders, hunkered down to the coals, and sipped his tea. He nursed the cup for some time, not desiring sleep though feeling sleepy, nearly exhausted from staying alert all the time to protect his family.

Most of the darkness he sat, sipping tea, considering his options. Toward sunrise, he slept briefly, awakening to head back to the vantage point where he had seen the two campfires, firming a course of action—which depended upon the disposition of the men below.

They were up and moving about when he settled into his nest of rock. It was cold, enough so he felt it biting into him, and they again had their two fires lit, though in the sub-light they looked much smaller than they had in the dark. He counted thirty-three men. They were all men, no boys and no women. Each carried a large pack.

They ate while the skies lightened, and from as far away as he was, he could hear them occasionally laugh. Being a large party, they were unafraid. He studied them carefully, poised to race down the hill to meet them should it prove they were people of his own kind.

As they finished, they began to move around, and now he could see them clearly. War paint! One doubled his fist, thrust it into the air, and let out a blood-chilling war scream. They were Others. Almost subconsciously, He Who Conquers slid deeper into the depression.

Without delaying further, the Others lifted their packs and followed their leader toward no-sun—straight at the five men who had no fire but were probably still in the same place!

He moved back, eased around the side of the hill until he was out of sight, and raced back to the campsite, where Scent of Violets was up and feeding her son. He watched the boy draw on the enlarged nipple, humored by the insistent suckling. She looked up and smiled at him.

"He's strong, and very sure of what he wants."

He chuckled. "Good. He will be a man."

"Like you. He already looks like you. He's going to be tall, and he'll have hair and eyes that match yours."

He Who Conquers smiled proudly. He had sired one who would be a leader. He wondered what his other child was like, the one with his mu, Little Dove. Then he sobered. "We must begin walking."

She glanced up in surprise, then nodded.

"It will be hard for you, but we won't travel fast. The five men are far, and will soon have to run for their lives. A large bunch of Others stayed below us last darkness, and they move to no-sun. They'll clear the path for us if we're quick enough to use it."

"There's a lot more to carry."

"I'll do it. You have the boy and a small pack. We won't be hurrying, so we'll be fine."

It was not long before they were moving. Careful to not be seen by the men who were already far ahead of them, they reached the bottom and followed directly in the trail of the Others. He noted they had plenty of food, for they had strewn bones with meat still on them, and birds were already fighting over the carrion.

Their pace was leisurely, and he was careful not to skyline as they followed, though his fears subsided as the Others gained on them. All sun they walked, stopping for Scent of Violets to feed her son or to rest, pacing themselves to keep her from getting too tired. It was dark when they stopped, and he built a small fire in a dip in the landscape, what might at one time have been a dusting place for some large animals, a place unseen from anywhere except the hills from which they had just come.

Again they walked, long into the next sun, before they approached the area where the five men had been keeping their vigil. He found a hollow carved into soft earth by a creek and left his mate and son while he scouted ahead. Shortly he found the ashes of their fire, and signs they had departed running. They ran into rising-sun. The Others had stopped to read the sign, then continued to no-sun. The site was almost on the shoulder of Waters-That-Hurry-to-Sunset.

He scowled as he returned to his family, unhappy

that they had not tried to follow the five. Evidently they sought larger quarry, and wanted it easy to get. Somewhere, not far away, were his five enemies. Unlike the many times when he sat and watched their campfire, now he had no idea where they might be. Chased from their vantage point, where would they go? Across the moving waters? To another high hill? He studied the knolls of rising hills around him, and saw nothing.

He had to continue to follow the Others. It was the wisest thing to do, because the five would no doubt stay away for half a sun or so to let the Others clear out of the area. Perhaps they would return to the same place, but he doubted it. More than likely they were already situated in another place where they were sure he would have to pass. To try to outguess them would be useless at the moment.

They slept on flat ground, but only after he had taken a scouting turn around the area; they were away before first light. The pace stayed leisurely, but they still arrived at the moving waters long before midsun. The Others were already across and far ahead, unseen except for their trail. Above the trail a hawk floated, and for the first time in many suns he felt encouragement from the Great One. He would conquer.

And then he saw the five men. They were on the far side of the moving waters, gathered at the base of the mudwall that climbed to the prairie above and behind them, facing mid-sun, watching He Who Conquers and Scent of Violets as they stood on the edge of the bank above the wide, deceptively placid waters. They might have been there watching him when he had scouted here the previous sun. The thought was disquieting.

They stared at each other for a long time, no one moving, before one of the men stood and walked toward them, toward the river that flowed between them.

"They show us their intentions. They'll watch us and not let us cross."

"What can we do?"

"Stay put until darkness, then I'll do what I have to. The odds are five to one; I think it's time to cut them down."

"You'll cross the moving water alone?"

"It's the only way. They expect me to quake in fear, and I'll let them think it's true. When it's dark, I'll go up the shoreline, find a large branch, and cross. They look to prevent us returning to my people; I've run out of patience."

She stared at him. "You'll speak to your Great One, and then walk the skies like Hawkeye said?"

He grinned. "They'll think that."

She sat on a blanket, slipped out of the cradleboard, unstrapped her son and put him to a breast. "I'll rest until you are through. We've come a long way."

"You've done well, my lynx. Soon you'll have a new territory to stake out." He chuckled.

"Your people, they'll let me take a dwelling?"

His face showed the strain of what he knew was about to occur. "We'll make our own for you." She saw the pain that crossed his face and said nothing more.

He turned, looked to no-sun, and visibly shuddered. A new thought had shaken him deeply. The Others they followed were the ones who would fulfil the vision! They were the wreckers, the destroyers, the forerunners to his own return! That was the evil omen that had been working at the edge of his consciousness!

With a face set in stone and eyes like glass, he stared after them, the hatred evident in his features so strong Scent of Violets had to look away. Whatever the secret he carried, the visions he had seen, they had to be shocking and horrible. Nothing else she had ever seen could have made him look like that.

He finally broke his spell and lay beside her on the blanket. In moments he slept. She watched him while her son fed, and wondered at the twitches and other signs of restlessness. Whatever the spirits were doing inside his head, it was fierce, the scowls and irregular breathing showing her that he did battle with many witches, evil spirits and gods.

When he awakened, she still watched, her son asleep beside her. The warm sun was making the whole world lethargic.

"You slept long, my conqueror."

He nodded, but said nothing. He had experienced another vision, and she could tell it affected him deeply. "You have seen more of the events soon to come?"

He stared into no-sun, the nod so small she almost missed it. His silence was evidence enough that he had no desire to talk of it. After a while, he stood and walked along the elevated shoreline, watching the men across the way, as they lay or sat and in turn watched him.

When he returned, the sun was setting and she was preparing their meal over a small fire. "How did the Others cross?"

He was somber. "They swam."

"So how do we get across?"

"I'll find a way." He ate in a morose silence. She honored his silence, and merely watched him. He lay on the blanket and again slept. She lay beside him as Sun God disappeared and sounds of darkness began to grow.

She was feeding Night Hawk again when he awakened. He rolled off the blanket, fastened his knife and axe to his side while still prone, took his spear and crawled away toward rising-sun. To the men across the moving waters, he was unseen. She stared after him long after he was no longer visible.

He Who Conquers watched the blinking fire across the river, keeping tabs on the five men while he moved along the bank. When he could, he dropped over the edge and walked in plain sight, aware that they could not see him yet in the heavy darkness. Moon God would appear in a while, but would be so small as to be little help.

He smiled savagely to himself. The coyote was about to strike again. "It was your fa who was to have fought Chief White Feather? But you're not like him! He ran!" Red Hawk had known the story well, as had everyone else.

"He didn't run to escape. He ran because he didn't want to fight the man who was to become chief. The man was going to be important to this people, and my fa thought of himself as a nobody. Who was he to try to kill the next chief?"

"But you forced our next chief to run like a coward! Don't you feel the same way as your fa?"

He crossed a washout, then another, and stood

up and ran for a time, hoping he had gotten out of their line of vision. They had last seen him on the blanket, and would not look for him to be anywhere else. He crossed yet another gully, rounding a slow bend in the moving waters, until he was well out of sight. He trotted on until he came to another gully and there he stopped.

"Long Knife is a coward of the worst kind. He tried to kill one who thought of him as a friend; what is more, he did it by ambush! No man who does such a thing can be a chief. Especially of a people so large and so important as those of Open Canyon."

Red Hawk had stared at him for a long time. "You truly are a man of honor. I can almost believe you when you say your fa didn't run from cowardice. Especially after knowing you so well in such a short time. You are certainly no coyote." Gray Fox and Birdsong had nodded their agreement, and Bright Bird had grinned.

"Coyote? By the gods, this man's the most fearless of men I've ever known. Come, Red Hawk. We have to tell the Chief about this and see what he says."

A small log, old but dry, lay high on the bank in the gully. He pushed it into the water and went in after it. Pointing its end toward the far bank, he began to kick his legs to propel the log--and thus himself--across the moving waters. When he felt earth again, he stood and waded to shore, taking the log with him and leaving it where he could easily find it again.

The set of his face would have frightened Scent of Violets. It was the image of a man who felt the threat of death on his small son and mate, who had reached a decision and was no longer working with logic. He had become a hunting animal, his weapons serving as his fangs.

"You are the son of Blue Teal?"

"I am."

The old man's eyes studied him. "Yes, I can see him in you." He studied his eyes and face. "You have the same guileless look. But no one can believe that he ran just to keep me safe."

"I can't make you believe, Chief White Feather. I can only tell you what I've heard, seen and believe."

"He didn't tell you what you told me?"

"No."

"His almighty 'honor'", he muttered. Again he stared at He Who Conquers for what seemed an interminable time. "Yes, I think I can believe that. Still, I wish he'd have come to me secretly and discussed it, rather than running like he did."

"Mighty Chief, he was never one to talk. It got him in difficulties among my people, as well. But his honor was always above reproach, even when others called him a coward or a coyote."

The chief coughed lightly and nodded. "True enough." He leaned back against the banquette of his kiva. "You did what no one here dared to do, my son, chasing away my wayward son. And you fought Roadrunner, whom everyone feared. You brought us meat greater than any we've ever had in one hunt. You worked in our fields, doing more than your share according to some grudging admissions from some of my people. You've proven yourself a capable man, one to be envied. If you see your fa again, tell him I said you were a man among men, and no coyote could ever have raised such a man."

It took little time to round the bend on the wide, flat mud-plain that followed no-sun side of the moving waters, where the sweep of the bend of the moving water had carried it to the far side of the river course. The weeds and grasses that grew in the rich soil gave him cover as he moved back toward the five men. When he saw them and their fire, he became like the puma, silent, alert, filled with concentration--the hunter. Three lay back, at least two of them asleep. Two sat, one staring into the fire and the other with his back to it, watching the far bank of the moving water. The quarter moon threw enough light to keep an eye on the plain across the way, but the deep shadows of the gullies hid them from sight. The one watcher was fully awake and alert.

He approached from behind a small stand of willows until he was within ten strides, then the willows ran out and he was forced to drop to hands and knees in the weeds. Knife in his teeth, he inched forward, wishing for his bow and arrows but aware the string would have gotten wet and become useless in the crossing. What lay ahead was work for his knife and axe. He had only one thought, and that was to kill them all. They had shown him they were his enemies, that his life was threatened, and even more, those of his family. For that, he held no thoughts of mercy. They must all die.

He located Running Hare. He slept, as did Spirit Man. Long Knife stared into the fire, his eyes useless if he should look into the darkness. Thunderstorm sat alertly as guard, and Hand of Stone lay with his eyes open, staring at the moon that was now overhead.

"How're you doing?" Long Knife spoke softly as he pulled his eyes from the coals and glanced at the youngest of them. He was sleepy.

"Fine." Thunderstorm never changed his position, signs of a good man on the trail. It was too bad that one so young and of such ability had to die.

"Nobody moving over there?"

"He drained water a bit ago. He's still there."

He Who Conquers smiled to himself. Scent of Violets had stood to simulate a man, keeping them unaware! She was a mate worthy of a chief, and one sun she would be just that.

"You need someone else to watch for a while?"

"No, I do fine."

"Let me know."

Silence. Then Hand of Stone spoke. "I think we ought to go get him while they sleep."

"Why? Isn't it easier to kill them when they're in the water?" It fit Long Knife that he would not put himself out much. He was as lazy as he was cowardly.

"Perhaps they won't cross."

"Sooner or later they have to."

"They'll not sneak across in the darkness?"

No answer came, and silence settled again. Finally, Hand of Stone slept. He Who Conquers moved to his left to gain better coverage, careful to make no sound and to keep out of the line of vision. Thunderstorm turned his head and looked in his direction, perhaps sensing something wrong, but saw nothing and looked away again.

The eyes of Long Knife dipped, then closed, and the head hung forward. He Who Conquers watched him snap up, then settle down again. Poised, he gripped his knife in his left hand, his axe in his right, and waited until he was sure the time was right.

He was less than three strides away when he came out of the tall weeds with a lunge. His knife slashed the neck of the surprised Thunderstorm, and his axe bashed in the head of Long Knife. With no pause, he swung the axe again, at Running Hare who had raised his head to see what had disturbed him. The axehead struck so hard it buried in his skull.

He shifted the knife to the right hand, unable to quickly extract the axe, and buried the blade into the small of the back of Spirit Man, then ripped when he pulled it back. Spirit Man screamed and rolled over out of muscular reaction, lunging for his axe. Hand of Stone rolled away and stumbled getting to his feet, then sprinted into the darkness. Spirit Man collapsed, his eyes full of hate and clamped on He Who Conquers.

"You! How...?" He died without finishing.

He Who Conquers stood among the carnage, gripped in the feelings of hate and action. He destroyed all the weapons, pitching them into a pile beside the body of Thunderstorm. Then he checked to be sure all four were dead before he went back toward the river, not afraid of Hand of Stone. The man had left without his weapons except for a knife. The remains of five axes and four knives were pitched into the river, along with arrowheads and spearheads.

Standing silently, he listened to the sounds around him, then got into a dugout that lay on the bank and pushed away from the shore, not far upstream from the place he had first crossed, seemingly a lifetime ago. This time, with no panic from being chased, he was soon across and pulling the dugout into the nearest gully to the camp.

"Hola, my lynx. I return," he called softly so she would not be frightened when he returned.

"You're safe?"

"I'm well. Our enemies agreed to leave us alone." He chuckled at his own humor.

Misunderstanding him, she asked, "You spoke with them?"

He laughed. "Let's just say they won't try to stop us on the new sun and leave it at that." I just wish I could tell my fa what he would love to hear. The gods have dealt him a cruel fate.

She shrugged, looking off toward where the campsite had been, but there was no fire to indicate the men were still there. "It'll be good to not waste more time."

He felt good. "I have a dugout they allowed me to take. It's in the first gully. We'll cross with the new sun."

"You don't wish to cross while they're unable to see us?" She again looked at the dark moving waters.

Another laugh. "No, they have agreed to pay no attention to us when we cross. They gave me their assurance."

Still puzzled, she said nothing more, and soon he snuggled in against her and nuzzled her breast.

"You wish to steal from your son?" she asked with a touch of sarcasm.

Again he laughed. "No, my lynx, I have no wish to steal from our son, but these mammaries are large, they are soft, they speak of womanhood, and they draw attention from one who enjoys the nicer things in life."

She giggled. "You may do what you wish with the outside, but leave what's inside for that son of yours. He'll soon wish for what's his."

He ran his cheek against her breast and then nuzzled her in the neck. For the moment, he forgot what was about to happen on The Top, the dark feelings gone in his enjoyment of his mate. For the first time since the birth of their son, she wished for him to couple, but he was afraid he might hurt her. Besides, she was still a long time from purification, and it would be a desecration such as this that would bring the ravens of his vision. Like an ominous cloud, the thought of the ravens returned to him, though his self-control won out. He concentrated on the enjoyment of touching her, though she felt the tension in him, wondering if it were his need of her or that other thing, unaware he had a premonition about her that was a far greater fear than his need would ever be.

31

He stood on the hill above the moving waters, but Hand of Stone was nowhere to be seen. The dugout still sat in the gully below where he stood, the pole lying in the bottom as he had left it. The sight of the moving water always disconcerted him, mostly because he was unable to swim and partly because he felt vulnerable while in the dugout. Not knowing where the only one of the five left alive might be hiding, it was risky to cross for more than one reason.

But he had no choice, he had to go. He dropped over the edge of the gully and went to the boat, Scent of Violets right behind him. The crossing was uneventful.

They began to walk, the immediate surroundings blocking out all sight of The Top. The soil-sided pseudo-mesas rose all around them, the earth cracked with gullies and ravines. Fierce watershed and sparse vegetation had criss-crossed the dry lands with signs of erosion, and the false flat-topped mounds around them held no sign of life. The parched earth lifted dust with each step, and before long the flatness of it stretched to the first mesa formations that lay toward rising-sun.

To people who knew only of the gods and their playfulness, there was no scientific understanding of the geological formations toward which they trudged. The Top stretched toward no-sun, but lesser mesas were visible to their right as they walked. The smaller, disconnected parts of what at one time had been a larger mesa were seen only as evidences of the gods. The erect rock that rose from a billowing skirt looked to be a worn and eroded penis, to receive their careful and awe-filled reverence for the God of Male Fertility. To mid-sun, and farther away, was one which had worn even more, until the rock projection was very small above the rounded base. It was obviously a breast, perhaps from a goddess that had turned to stone there.

Neither spoke as they walked, once they saw the profound configurations that would accompany their trek until they were near their destination, but both awed by solemn responsibility of procreation signified by this playground of the gods. It would not be long before Scent of Violets would purify herself in a ritual bath and the burning of the placenta which she still carried in a small gut-bag, and then four suns would pass before Medicine Woman performed the Purification Ceremony and she could allow herself to be entered again. Her worship of the Goddess would assure them of another child. The homage would be accompanied by the excitement of coupling, which she was beginning to anticipate. But she knew that her desire was still small compared to his needs, and it was this that made her grow impatient.

They slept beside a stream that he called Water-from-Sunrise. He explained that the water came through the mesa to which they headed, splitting it into two parts. Those who lived to no-sun were The People, and those who lived to mid-sun were more recent occupants. However, there was inter-mating now, and some sun they would all be one again, as they had been in the beginning.

The next sun, as they walked, he became more tense as Sun God progressed across the sky. He watched the mesa he called home, still a long way off, his eyes seldom leaving it, all desire for communication deserting him entirely. She followed silently, wishing she knew his struggle. He wanted to go faster, but carefully limited himself to keep her close, and she knew it. Still, she did not want to push too hard, what with their son so vital to their future. Again they slept along the creek, and his dreams came again.

He was walking into a village devoid of life. Bodies lay grotesquely, scalpless and mutilated, carrion birds feasting everywhere. A coyote was slinking away, and from somewhere over the edge of the valley, near where they threw their garbage, he heard the grunting of a bear. The chief lay nearby, his body covered with birds, his weapons near at hand indicating he had gone down trying to defend his people.

Smoke still curled from the burned dwellings that lay in rubble, white popped corn strewn around the ground. There was no life anywhere, and he could not force himself to look away from the carnage.

Somewhere to no-sun from the dwellings lay his own parents, something he knew without having to search for them. Two turkeys strolled from behind sagebrush, stopping when they saw the two people watching them.

He awoke in a heavy sweat, writhing on his blanket. Scent of Violets, feeding her son, watched him in pity. His eyes never opened before he rolled over and fell again into sleep.

This time he stood below the skirt of the mesa and watched heavy smoke rising back from the edge, where he knew his village lay. It was the place where they would awaken on the new sun.

"Please, my conqueror, wake up!" She was pleading with him as he became conscious of her gently shaking him. "Wake up! You groan aloud."

He sat up, his hands rubbing at his hair and neck, sweat again his only blanket despite the frost-laden coolness. He immediately turned toward The Top, reacting to his dream-vision. All was dark. He sat a moment to get hold of himself, then threw off the blanket that covered only his feet and stood up.

Without a word, he walked into the darkness and stood until the sweat had dried and his mind was again his own. Still, he could not shake the dread he felt. To be so close was almost beyond self-control, knowing they were up there, nearly done making medicine and preparing to launch their attack, and here he was, too far away to be of any help. Even a message in smoke would go unnoticed. There was no way he could warn them...as he might expect. The gods were toying with his people, and he was helpless....

"We better walk, my conqueror." She spoke as he was about to squat beside the coals and check on the tea. "You'll feel better if we're walking, and I am ready."

He glanced at her, but he had little control of his feelings. "You need the rest." For the first time he felt the heavy stone hanging around his neck because he had a mate and son. He hated her for keeping him from hurrying, and hated himself because he knew nothing could change the events that were dependent only on the fates directed by the gods, that even if he left her and ran all the way, it would be over before he got there. If he had left seven suns earlier, he would still be too late! It was not his mate, nor his son, nor his trek, but fate. It was out of his control.

His voice was more gruff than she had ever heard, and she was afraid of him. She did not know this side of her mate. He was losing control of himself, witches and evil spirits rolling over him. Yet she was helpless, except to feed her infant and follow. That she would do, for soon he would be himself again, his trek nearly over. Still, she wondered what he hid inside, what he was not telling her, the reasons for the many dreams that made him cry out, that made him grovel on his blankets in anguish, that made him sweat. She felt the dread but had no idea why. Something was about to happen; she had no idea what.

She picked up her son who was awakening, and changed his wet coverings and washed his bottom in the creek. He fought against the cold water, but she clucked to silence him. Then she put him to her breast and let him feed. While he suckled, she dipped up water and drank it, then organized her pack and ate. Soon they were walking, just as the skies lightened behind The Top.

His pace was impatient, yet he controlled it, again silent as he walked, knowing that soon there would come the great smoke. He could almost hear the wild shrieks of the terrible Others, the screams of fear from women and children, of men shouting instructions in terror. He could almost see the one-sided battle, and he was still almost a sun away! Sun God would be nearing The Sleeping Giant when he and his mate entered the village.

Sun God rose, to slowly move across the sky, just beginning his trek to meridian when smoke appeared. He came to a stop...staring...helpless, frustration and anger mirrored on his face, emotions coursing through him that he had no idea how to handle.

Scent of Violets realized for the first time what had been worrying at him. She, too, stared with horror at the thickening smoke, before again studying his face. In but a moment she knew his visions had pre-warned him of this disaster, as he had once hinted to her, and here it was. His troubles were like a map on his face, and all his wrestlings suddenly made sense to her. She could only stare and wonder at his great burden.

They began to climb the skirt, taking an angle that made the climb easier though she wondered how they would get on top when they got to the cliff that surrounded it. But she had faith in his knowledge, since this was his country, and stayed as close to his heels as she could.

It was a laborious climb, partly because of its steepness, partly because she felt tired from a short sleep, and partly because of what they would see once they made it. Just before they topped out, they could see the smoke again.

She noticed the slope of his shoulders, the heavier tread, the slower placement of his feet. He was being torn apart inside, almost like he had never fully believed the vision until he saw it taking place. She had been privy to his sweats, his rolling and tossing, his whimpering and muttering while asleep. She had listened to his cries that last darkness. Yet she knew the actual event was more than anything he could have imagined.

It was after midsun when they finally entered the trees above the rim, and the walk was suddenly so easy she almost felt like running. His steps increased in size, then speed, though the heavy pack he carried kept him

slow enough for her to keep pace. The trail was
downward, and through the trees the smoke had
diminished greatly. They passed a dilapidated dwelling
that stood vacant, and went around a small grouping of
trees. There it was.

His pace slowed as he entered the devastation he
had known was to be his greeting. His feet stopped, and
he stood with eyes that confirmed everything he had
already seen. The tendrils of smoke from what was left
of the dwellings, the chief, the bodies mutilated, two
turkeys, white popped corn on the ground, a dog that lay
dead under a tree, the grunting sounds of the black bear
over the edge of the valley, birds flitting around the
bodies, buzzards circling and alighting beside the carrion.
It was all there, fulfiling everything...almost everything.

His mind refused to accept what he saw, anger
turning to rage, beginning far back in the recesses of his
patient nature, burning into his awareness, and then
overwhelming him. The change in his posture was
striking, and Scent of Violets watched it from slightly
behind him. His legs straightened and tensed, his
shoulders lifted, the hands that were gripping the ropes
over his shoulders clenched, and he changed from a
fearful spectator to an awesome warrior. She could see
the resolve build, the point of no return passed.

A dog came from the valley, tail between its legs,
slinking into the courtyard and stopping to cower before
the man who was dropping his pack, it, too, sensing the
devastating fury.

He Who Conquers helped Scent of Violets shuck
her small pack, then carried them to a tree. He spread
her blanket and laid the buffalo robe beside it.

"You will stay here. It's safe now; the Others are
gone. In a while there will be a few women and old
men returning. You tell them who you are, and that I'll
return before the moon is again a sliver. Get the men to
bury these bodies on the fourth sun. When I return,
we'll rebuild."

She listened with dread, knowing he would be
gone and she was among strangers. But even as she
looked quickly around, something moved behind some
trees.

"There's someone over there," she said softly as

he picked his weapons. He followed her eyes and saw nothing.

"You sure?"

"I saw someone move, unless it was a dog."

He stood and turned toward the trees. "Come. We are friends. I am He Who Conquers."

There was a mild exclamation, then Singing Waters appeared with Little Dove close behind and carrying her son--their son. Both women were crying as they hurried forward and fell in front of him. Others began to come from concealment.

"Earth Mu has answered our prayers! You've come!"

He was perturbed to be delayed, but knew he had to set things in order. "This is my mate, Scent of Violets, and my son, Night Hawk. Singing Waters and her daughter, Little Dove. Where is Eagle Eye?"

"He was with some other young men. They ran that way." Singing Waters pointed down toward mid-sun.

"Coyotes!" The single word burst from Little Dove.

"Stay here beside this tree, or up in those. Gather what you can. I must go after the Others. They have to pay dearly for their folly this sun. When men return, have them bury the bodies, then light a fire so the gods can smell the smoke they love." His voice was filled with bitterness and anger. "I go."

He turned, weapons in hand, an empty waterbag and a pouch with dried venison over his shoulder, a blanket around his waist tied with a rope, and began to trot past the village and up the hill in the direction of The Rock.

Just past the burned buildings, he saw them. Fa lay on his back, his maleness stuffed in his mouth, his scalp gone, his stomach ripped open, birds feeding. An animal had already eaten much of his face. Mu was only a couple strides away, her scalp gone, and her body mutilated almost beyond recognition. He only missed rhythm on one stride and kept going, not wanting to see more. Other bodies lay scattered around, caught where they had fled, scalps gone and covered with birds. A coyote skittered away at his approach, but he paid it no mind.

Up the hill, through the trees, along the ridge, farther up, and then across the semi-bald top until he came to The Rock. There he stopped, and in surprise looked down to see another body. Less mutilated than the ones at the village, it was missing its scalp and had its eyes plucked out and maleness cut off. But he could see clearly that it was Gray Dog, surprised while he watched in the same haphazard way most of the youth watched, his throat slit. Blood on The Rock showed he had been lying back, probably asleep. He had earned his sudden trip to Sipapu.

Ignoring the body, he stood on The Rock and scanned the country, but not for long. The line of Others was to his right, out on the wide valley, heading toward the mountains toward rising-sun. It was no surprise; it was where the Others had gone after he killed four of them. Quickly he dropped down, headed around the cliff, and down along a short section of cliff that broke sharply.

In carefully placed strides, he went down so fast he hardly realized when he was again on firm footing, running in the manner he had used against The Deer. He intended to catch the Others before sunset, and spend the darkness wreaking havoc. They were cocky and careless, and he should have no trouble overtaking them. As yet, he had no idea what he would do once he found them.

A long mesa to his right, his strides constant, his breathing consistent, he found their trail where it turned into rugged hills and gullies, while Sun God circled behind him. He slowed his pace and climbed a hill to the left, then began to walk slowly, knowing he was close to where they would stop to camp.

He heard voices before he saw them. The canyon was shallow, the sun-set side heavy with trees, where he stayed. The bottom of the canyon was rough, but they had found a small meadow and set three fires. There was laughing and clowning around the fires, men waving their scalps and bragging. His eyes slitted as he watched them, wondering which of them would become his first victim.

Darkness settled quickly, and the fires flared as

the men spitted meat. They had apparently killed a deer in the canyon. He watched them eat, then sit on rocks or on the ground with backs against large boulders, talking with a great deal of laughing and demonstrating.

He crept down until he was so close he could smell the odor of their bodies, where he squatted to watch while the fires burned down and men sprawled on blankets. One walked down the canyon to take guard duty, another went up. No one bothered to climb the sides.

It was growing quieter when one of the men got up and walked toward him, getting inside the growth of trees before he squatted. He faced downhill, away from He Who Conquers, and never knew there was anyone around before his throat was slit from ear-to-ear. He toppled back, and He Who Conquers caught him and lowered him to the ground. Then he took the scalp expertly with just two quick slices, cut off the male member and stuffed it in the mouth, stuck the knife into both eyes, made the large "X" on the stomach, and moved back into the trees.

Quickly he circled down until he located a guard, who sat on a rock against a tree, eyes closed. He had no trouble creeping up behind, and slit the throat so quickly the man hardly moved except to relax. He took the scalp again, did the mutilation and made the same large "X" on his stomach. It was to be his trademark, a sign that he had done it. Perhaps the Trader would some sun make mention of the X's.

Climbing the hill again, he circled past them, to locate the second guard. He was whittling on a stick, not bothering to look around. The arrow entered his head slightly above and in front of his ears. He never knew what hit him. After his usual aftermath, He Who Conquers slipped back to where he had been before he killed the first one. There he watched the camp until everyone slept, then moved down to the very edge.

Surprisingly, no one had missed the dead man who had gone to relieve himself, but it made his task simpler. Standing behind a tree where he could see men sprawled wherever there was sufficient room in the rough canyon, he strung his arrow and put it into the throat of a sleeping man. Stealthily he approached, retrieved his

arrow, mutilated the man, took the scalp and left his "X".
Only two strides from another man, he knifed him and
used his learned procedure, then retreated back to his
place.

Five scalps so far, and he still had alerted no
one. And he had not lost an arrow. The Great One was
at work, even with Sun God gone. Did that mean the
two were not the same? Could it be Sun God was
controlled by another? Was that blasphemy?

A man rolled near him, then stood, lifted the flap
of his breechcloth and urinated. When he had settled
down again, He Who Conquers put an arrow into his
throat, a short shot of only four paces from the tree
behind which he stood. He was especially careful as he
mutilated the man, left his mark, and retreated. Six.

Now he had a problem. Every man was only a
step or less from another. He wanted so desperately to
kill the leader, the sub-chief who slept only five or six
paces away, but his head and torso were shielded by a
bush and he had men on both sides of him. He studied
the situation and decided he did not like what was left.

He worked his way back up the hill, then sang
the song he had sung when he had rescued the men of
Open Canyon. It seemed to fit.

> Life is short, like a vapor,
>   It lasts like smoke from a fire;
> When death comes near, we quake with fear,
>   The Great One takes whom he wants.

Before he was half through, he heard voices,
speaking quickly and waking the entire group. He
moved, listening to the turmoil as they lit their fires, then
heard the exclamations when they discovered the dead.

He was above the second dead guard when he
sang the song again and laughed his derisive laugh,
hearing silence fall over the Others in the camp. Then
he again moved, down to the bottom and up the other
side, near the top. Again he laughed, this time not
uttering a word. Then he laughed as he moved along
the ridge.

When he finished, he dropped down and crossed
into the heavier trees, again going well up the hill, where

he stopped and sang his song one more time. Then he lapsed into silence.

He could not see the camp from his vantage and merely sat, listening and watching. His heart was pumping hard somewhere between excitement and the exertion. A cry went up again; they had found the first guard he had killed. In but a moment, the second guard was found. The talking was fearful, continuous, and scattered. They were in twos and threes, trying to find the last man, the one he had killed first.

He left them, climbing the mountain and passing along the ridge, knowing their trail would follow the canyon to the top of the range they climbed. He found rocks and spent time traveling over and through them, the rock slide covering all traces of his trail, then dropped down into a heavy stand of trees and rolled into his blanket.

He awakened at first light, ate dried venison and drank heavily, then climbed the side to the top of the ridge, where he sat on rocks to await the coming of the Others. He would let them see him, then wait to see what them did. When they saw him, if they came soon, he would be standing on the very top of the ridge, blanket over his shoulders and around him, arms folded under it. He would merely watch them.

They came. He had hardly taken his stance and pulled his blanket into place when the first man came into view. They were far below him, and it was the third man who spotted him. The line came to a halt and stared up at him, and he never moved. They were talking, the silence only because of the distance, though their pointing and animation told him of their conversation and interest.

He counted twenty-five. He had killed six, and when he had first seen them many suns before, there had been thirty-three. Two had apparently been killed in the attack, which made him feel better. They had now lost eight men, nearly one in four. It was becoming a costly raid; if he had the opportunity, it would cost them more.

After finishing their discussion, they began to climb again, following the bottom of the ravine as before. The canyon was widening and becoming more open meadow, with grasses and low brush. They were leaving cover for the alpine meadows above timberline.   He watched them as they passed below, then dropped over the side out of their sight and ran toward the distant ridge. Up in the rarified air, he found himself gasping, and had to slow to a walk.   Then he again hurried ahead. He topped the mountain and turned along the ridge, then dropped over the far side and hurried on. When he felt sure he was close to where they would appear, he topped the ridge and again took his stance.

It was some time before they appeared, far down the mountain.   They again walked for a time before one stopped and pointed, and he was again the center of attention. He stood as before, as majestically as he could muster, his heart beating fast with excitement as he realized what his second appearance was doing to them. They were going from curiosity to fear.

It was what he wanted. He wanted them to sweat, to worry and fret about who he was while they began to wonder if he might have had something to do with their dead. He chuckled to himself. They had not taken the time to burn their dead, their fear of the place had been so great. They had appeared much too soon, and he had seen no smoke.

Five of the group broke off and began to climb toward him, the rest moving on in their chosen direction. He stepped back and went over the side, then moved quickly again. It was clear for a long ways, the first rocks far below, but he wanted to be in them and out of sight when the men appeared at the top. He made it, but not with much time to spare. From cover he watched them top the ridge, stop, then move back and forth seeking his trail.

He laughed to himself. He had used the rocky soil well, his moccasins an asset though his tough feet were becoming sore. They could not find his trail! They moved back and forth several times, then met again and stared along the hillside. After a time, they disappeared from view, but he stayed put.

It paid off to be patient. They suddenly appeared again, and stood staring at the side of the mountain, but again disappeared. He sat a long time before deciding they were gone for good this time, and he pulled out some jerky and ate a piece, then drank again.

The sun passed its zenith, and he casually glanced over his shoulder. Fear struck. Great gray clouds were coming from setting-sun, having obliterated every peak in that direction. Snow was coming, rapidly, and he had no leggings. The high peaks were not a good place to be when snows fell, for often snow would get so deep a man could hardly struggle through it, not to mention the cold that, at this altitude, accompanied such snow.

He had to leave, get out of the peaks before the snows hit, or he might never make it. He rose from the rocks and began to climb toward the top, angling away from where the Others had been, having no desire to run into an ambush. He topped the ridge to find no sight of them. They had gone. Now he had but one task, to get out before he got buried in snow.

32

It was down all the way, sometimes fast, sometimes slow. When it was steep, he angled, and when it flattened, he went straight down the canyon. All the time, he ran. His legs took the punishment of his weight plus the downward lunge with every step, but his lungs found it much easier going down.

The clouds had him near panic, for he had seen them like that before, and always it meant snow. Here, near the peaks where the watershed split toward rising- or setting-sun, it could mean a blizzard. All his mind could think about was the thought of snow and the trail ahead. Everything else was forgotten.

When he passed the campsite of the Others, he never slowed, though he saw the bodies as their friends had left them. In their fear and against all their traditions, the Others had simply grabbed weapons and fled. It displayed their complete panic, and the thought made him smile. Already, birds and animals were feasting.

A small wolf looked up and bared its fangs as he

ran by, but he made no moves to threaten the animal. When the first flakes fell, he was nearly to the mouth of the canyon and it was getting late.

He stopped, glancing around for something that would serve as a shelter, but except for a place under some trees, there was nothing. He trotted ahead, dusk making him feel an edge of panic, when he spotted two trees that had fallen part way to the ground and become lodged at an angle against another. Underneath, the needles were deep and overhead the branches were still green and thick.

In a few moments he pulled together a large stack of wood and a few rocks, then knelt and began to build the fire. The snow was coming faster, and he had to shelter the spot with his body as he spun the stick. With the first sign of smoke, he nudged the grass closer and blew softly as he continued to spin the drill stick. The first spark was all he needed, and he nursed it into a small fire, then added fuel. Soon it was a good fire, bigger than he normally wanted, because this time it would be for heat.

When it was burning, he again gathered wood, stacking it carefully against the wind that was beginning to kick up. He added a few larger branches to the sides of the shelter, then broke off several pine boughs and wove them into some holes. The snow continued to increase.

When the shelter was secure and better covered, he went inside and wrapped in his blanket, sitting on the soft needles. He chewed jerky and ate his last wad of gorp, made from corn, dried berries, cornflour and suet. He drank a few sips of water, then whiled away the time feeding his fire in morbid musings. Thinking. Of ravens.

The winds began to howl through the pines, and the snow fell heavily as darkness settled completely. He knew he was in trouble. He had no leggings, no greatcoat, no furs. Only one blanket, a little water, and a few pieces of jerky. Only now did he realize how much his rage had blinded his intelligence--another lesson in self-control so important to being a man and a leader. Even in anger, a man must be able to control himself enough to think clearly. Nothing excused stupidity or naivete.

He kept the fire going until he had a good bed of coals, then lay on his side and slept. It was a short sleep, despite his physical exhaustion. The wind awakened him, and he heard a tree go down. The trees that were part of his shelter squeaked and squealed as they swayed and rubbed above him. He was afraid the tree that propped the other two would fall, and the fear kept him from sleep. He dozed fitfully, awakened, dozed again and yet again. Over and over throughout the darkness he wrestled with sleep.

When dawn came, the wind still groaned and shrieked through the trees, and snow fell and was whipped into drifts. His shelter was buried in snow, the fire keeping him reasonably warm. Smoke still found a way out above. He shaped a place for his hips into the soft needles and snoozed most of the time, awakening to relieve himself or eat snow. The winds died as darkness came, and the snow slowed. Sometime in the darkness it finally stopped.

He awakened to deep stillness, laying for a time trying to think of what had happened, then got up and pushed some branches aside. A chunk of snow fell on him and inside his shelter, but bright snow appeared through the opening. The cold hit him like a shower of ice, reinforcing his certainty that he was in trouble.

He needed food whether he stayed or traveled, and he needed to find coverings for his legs and feet; but the snow was deep, nearly to the belt. He wondered how far down the slope he would have to go to get to shallower snow, and if it were any warmer back near The Top. It would take two suns of travel with this much snow. He could never make it. Bare skin, deep snow, and cold...so cold. What could he do? This country was known for its frequent and deep snow and intense cold, yet he had thought nothing of it when he jumped onto the trail of the Others. He had been stupid, careless, childish...whatever other terms he could think of. But accusing himself solved nothing. He had to think, to plan, to find a way to survive.

He studied the snow, and realized it was deeper around his makeshift shelter than farther out, though out there it was still to the knees or more. He needed to break a trail from his shelter to the shallower snow to see what it would be like, and he began to stomp the snow where he stood, and then away from the shelter. It was cold! In but a short time he had to return to his fire and add fuel. Wrapped in his blanket, he stayed until he was warm, ate a piece of jerky and more snow, then went back out to work on the path.

When midsun came, he had tromped down a well-defined path to the shallower snow, another that led to a deadfall where he could get additional wood, and he had cut an end from his blanket and wrapped his legs. They got wet quickly, but were nonetheless helpful. Now the footwear concerned him most, and his lack of food.

He went back inside to warm and dry himself, then climbed to the ridge where the winds had blown the rocks bare. There was no place between the tall trees from which he could see either distance or game. He studied the trees but saw no squirrels, and not a single rabbit track broke the snow. He was grateful to find the snow shallow, in some places only ankle deep. Following the ridge up to a rock outcrop--from where he could view distant peaks of white--he found no tracks to break the fresh snow.

He remained to study and watch, hoping to see an animal moving, but gave up and went inside to warm up again. He wished to anticipate the movement of animals, but realized how much his people had forgotten about real hunting. He could only hope they had sat tight during the snow, which meant they had to move about soon for food, but foraging would not be good among the trees where his camp was situated.

Where were the meadows that would draw deer or wapiti? Were rabbits likely to be about soon? Even a squirrel would be helpful! But they would mostly be in the timber where the snow was deepest. When he was warm again he left the fire and went down the ridge, studying the area to both sides, until the one on his left opened into a meadow. There he checked the wind and worked around to the other side where the wind blew cold but softly into his face.

It was still. The wind almost ceased to exist, the cold so crisp trees occasionally popped. Nothing moved. After circling the entire meadow, which was long and narrow, he returned to his shelter having seen nothing,

not a single track except mice. Even the birds were
sitting tight. Only a single Rocky Mountain jay flitted
nearby, hoping for something to steal. He ate snow and
laid beside the rebuilt fire, his mind worrying the
location of game. He could think of nothing that gave
any hope. His feet were so cold they had lost feeling.

Sun God neared his resting time when he went
out again, and quickly returned to the meadow, but
nothing had crossed. He swung up the hill and made a
hard, circuitous route back, in places fighting snow to his
belt. He was soaked and cold when he got back to his
shelter, and the fire had to again be built to heat his
enclosure.

He slept, but awakened during the darkness, and
lay awake thinking of his plight, and of his mate. Then,
on a whim, he put on the leggings that had hung over
the fire to dry, took his weapons and went out, his
blanket as a cloak. He was drawn back to the meadow,
where he sat beside a tree about midway down the long
lea.

He was soon cold clear through, shivering yet
reluctant to leave. He had no idea why. When he saw
the first movement across the opening, his teeth
chattered. He stared at the spot, but his eyes watered so
much in the slow-moving, brittle air he could hardly
make out the motion, much less identify what he had
seen. Not daring to move even so much as to wipe his
eyes dry, he blinked savagely until they cleared. On the
far side and up the hill were four does and a fawn.

They browsed the aspen leaves and pawed at the
snow, then moved down the hill and found a place
where the snow was blown shallow. They used their
hooves to clear away snow, fed a while, then moved
down again, until they were almost to his hiding place.
Near where he sat, there was another wind-cleared place
where tall grasses came through the snow. One of the
does moved toward it.

He sat as stone, the arrow now on the string but
his hands so cold he could scarcely feel with them.
Hoping to control his shaking, he slowly raised the bow
and waited for the doe to come near enough. She
stopped, looked back, then approached until she reached
the grass.

She floundered through a deceptively deep spot, and began to feed on the grass where snow was to her knees. She was only four strides from where he sat.

He was afraid. His fingers were so cold he could not feel the string, and he wondered if he had enough control to keep them bent and pulling until the right time, then make them release. His teeth chattered and his body shook with chill.

Deliberately he aimed, trying to control the fingers on the string, pulling to what he hoped, by sight, seemed a proper tension, then slowly trying to straighten the fingers. He had no idea when the string slipped from the fingers, and his control of the arrow was poor. It struck the doe at the snow line of the rear knee. The doe floundered, her rear going down, but she came to her feet quickly, the lower leg hanging oddly to show the joint had been shattered.

She had no idea what hit her, standing a moment to try to see what the problem was. He fumbled another arrow onto the string, missing twice before getting the slot aligned, then quickly pulled and released. Again he felt nothing in his fingertips, but saw the arrow strike the doe in the neck, about a hand span from the head.

The Great One had done it again! He screamed his victory as the doe folded without a step, the sound of his voice hollow in the stillness of the dark, but terrifying to the remaining deer. They bounded out of the meadow with their stiff-legged hop, then stopped in the trees on the other side to see what had scared them. He paid them no mind, but got stiffly to his feet and went to the dead doe, shouldered her, and staggered back toward his hut.

The exertion warmed his trunk, but his hands, legs and feet were still numb when he dropped the doe outside his shelter and went in to start the fire. Then he cut open the belly, dragged out the entrails and found the liver. He took the single bite demanded by the gods, then tossed the rest into the snow away from the carcass. The heart and female organs he laid in snow on a fallen log near the trail but away from the entrance to his shelter. Then he cut out the tongue and a chunk of the rear quarter which he sliced and spitted over the fire.

He warmed his hands and feet while it sizzled, then ate it before it was done. When he was warm, he returned to the animal and began the skinning, but it took several trips to accomplish it in the intense cold. By the time he was through, the hide was already freezing where he had begun. He pulled the hide inside his shelter and placed it above the fire, hanging in the branches.

Then he cut meat from the carcass and brought it inside, storing it in the snow along one side, hacking off more to spit, and he ate again until he was gorged. The sun rose and set behind the heavy clouds while he worked.

He spent the next sun working at the hide, cutting foot and leg wear, sewing it together with lengths of gut. Not having time to tan the hide, it would not last if he had any rocks or dry ground on which to walk, but in the snow it would be more than welcome.

Again he ate until he was gorged, then slept, and was restless the entire darkness from too much rest and too many thoughts. For the second consecutive time, Sun God came out brightly, but there was little melting until the third sun. He immediately put his pack together, along with the meat he had dried over the fire, took his weapons and headed out into the cold. He was anxious to get back to his mate and see what had happened to his people.

He went to the ridge and followed it down, staying as much as he could to where the wind had helped blow the ground clear. He felt good from his few suns of rest and eating, and he had a pack full of food to help him get where he was going. He broke out of the trees well before the sun reached its apex, not sure if he imagined the seeming shallower snow.

Suddenly his left leg gave way and he went down, his spear catching only part of his weight as he fell. Its snap was loud and clear on the crisp air, and through his mind flashed something he had almost forgotten. "The time for the greatest vigilance often comes at the very moment when you feel the best." Why the thought crossed his mind he had only a moment to ponder, because as he rolled to get up, unsure of why he had fallen, he saw blood on the snow. Then he felt the

pain. "Life is as uncertain at the time you feel great as
it is when you feel terrible."

An arrow stuck through the flesh of his leg just
below the knee, side-to-side. He could not identify it,
though it looked like one from The Top! His first glance
was at a bush to his right, and there stood Little Dog,
the younger brother of Sitting Bear, a grin on his face
from ear-to-ear.

His bow and arrow awkwardly twisted in his
pack, his spear broken, he felt naked. He shook snow
from his right hand and grabbed the broken head of his
spear, a piece only as long as his forearm, and fought to
his knees. Little Dog was stringing another arrow, his
malevolent smile more like a knowing grin.

"You! How does it happen you're here?"

But he knew. Family retaliation for the killing of
Yellow Sapsucker. He had assumed it would come from
Eagle Eye. He had forgotten the cousins, Little Dog and
Sitting Bear. Another stupid mistake! It seemed he had
made many recently! Where was Sitting Bear? He was
the oldest, and should be the one here...or was he? How
many were there?

A second arrow was fired by Little Dog, the man
only eight paces away, but it was hasty and high.
Realizing how useless his piece of spear was from this
distance, he struggled with the bow, and had just gotten
it cleared when the next arrow came. He saw the
release, dropped into the snow and turned his back. The
arrow struck the pack and stayed, unable to penetrate
clear through.

Quickly he rolled, ignoring the growing throb in
his calf, an arrow of his own ready to string. On his
knees, he slotted it and let it fly, an instant before Little
Dog was ready for his shot. Even as he saw it in flight,
He Who Conquers became conscious of another presence,
and glanced to his left. Eagle Eye stood beside a scrubby
cedar, hidden to the waist in brush, shooting an arrow
with plenty of time to set himself and aim well.

He Who Conquers dropped again, but not soon
enough. The arrow grazed the top of his head, cutting
a groove and taking a rut of hair from the scalp. The
pain was sharp and instantaneous. Big black ravens
charged him, and he fought to avoid them. Cold snow

helped, his face buried in it. He tried to roll, but found he was unable to move.

His bow was lost in the snow, and he felt the arrows from his quiver slide over his left ear as it ended upside down. His left arm was twisted under him, but his right was at his side, and his fingers closed over the haft of his knife. He was not sure if he could move after having failed in his first attempt, but the ravens had gone and he was mostly alert. Pain was coming from both his head and leg, but he tried to ignore both while he waited for Eagle Eye to come check on him.

It was a long wait. Eagle Eye called to Little Dog, but got no reply. He Who Conquers lay still, scarcely breathing, wondering if his arrow had found its mark, if the silence was only a cover so he would not be able to concentrate on but one enemy, or if Little Dog had only signalled rather than speaking. The pain in his leg was throbbing, and the one on his head was stinging like fire. And where was Sitting Bear?

A swish of the soft snow alerted him to the presence of one of his antagonists, and he stopped breathing while he tried to judge where he was. His right hand gripped the knife so hard his fingers hurt, but he almost lay on the hand and his pack was on top of him as he lay nearly face down.

"He's dead!" the voice above him said. "I got him! You want to do the honors?"

Eagle Eye was speaking, but no one responded. Did he only think Little Dog was alive, or did he know it? His antagonist grabbed a handful of hair and jerked the head up, but He Who Conquers knew he could not take his scalp. It was known among The People; to show it around or brag would be foolish. He let his head flop loosely as though he had no life.

"Little Dog?" The hand released the hair and his face fell back into the snow. Eagle Eye had stood and was looking away, in the direction of Little Dog. His voice showed concern and was pointed in that direction when he added, "Where in Earth Mu are you?"

He stepped away, hesitated, then headed in that direction. He Who Conquers rolled slowly and got to his knees, quickly scanning the snow for his bow. The impression of its location was over a stride away, and he

moved toward it on his knees, feeling like he was in slow
motion. The bow was only a hand's depth, and he found
it, then reached back for the arrows that lay in the snow
where his shoulder had been. He picked up two,
dropped one in front of him and put the other on the
string, then aimed and released.

The back of Eagle Eye was only four strides
away, a wide target; the arrow stuck near the spine just
below the left shoulderblade. Eagle Eye staggered
forward two steps and collapsed, rolled over and tried to
sit up. He failed on the first attempt, then managed with
the second. Facing He Who Conquers, hate written in
every line of his face, he mouthed soundless words before
managing, "You live!"

"Never turn your back on your enemy. You were
to have learned that while you were young." His voice
sounded as though it came from somewhere else.

"Too late...too...too late I remember." His eyes
closed and he forced them open by sheer will. "You
killed Yellow Sapsucker, too."

"He put the arrow in my back." He watched
Eagle Eye fight for life, almost pitying the one who had
been his antagonist for so long, tried to kill him several
times, and almost did on this occasion. His pity faded
when he remembered.

"Lit...Little Dog! Where...are you?"

"He's dead." He hoped it was true, feeling like it
must be since there had been no response from him.

"How can you...can you be so fortunate?"

"The Great One...he watches me."

"You...you...." His eyes closed and he slowly
tilted backwards until he half-sat and half-lay in the
snow. There were no more signs of life.

He Who Conquers stared around him, wondering
about Sitting Bear. Where was he? If Little Dog was
here, Sitting Bear should be, also; but there was no sign
of anyone else. The stillness had returned.

He watched the motionless Eagle Eye for a while,
then turned and sat, and remembered the arrow that
stuck through his leg. The pain was intense, and it
continued to bleed. He dropped his pack and with both
hands broke the arrow. With the snap came ravens,
engulfing him, swirling about him, burying him....

When he revived, the air felt warmer. The snow was wet, he was cold, and the broken arrow still stuck from his leg. He jerked it out with no delay, and for the second time the black birds swirled and carried him into the darkness of Earth Mu.

He again became conscious of pain, his head pounding and his leg throbbing. He took snow and packed it around the leg and put some on his head. It came off red. He had to get to shelter, and the first one he thought about was the one he had left. Could he make it back?

First he had things to do. He crawled to Eagle Eye, the body already stiff and cold, retrieved his arrow and took the foodsack he carried. Then he crawled over to where he had last seen Little Dog. He was slumped down like he was doing obeisance to the gods, the arrow through his throat. He took it out, then took his foodbag as well and returned to where his pack lay. He struggled his arrows into the quiver, then shouldered his pack. Carrying his bow in one hand, the broken end of his spear with the spearhead on it in the other, he tried to stand and walk. He hopped a few steps, unable to put weight on the leg, but the effort made him dizzy.

He looked around and, with a determined hop, headed for a small stand of aspen. He had to stop three times before he got to it, but stayed on his feet. He found one that was gray and dead, still standing, that fit his hand. He bent it only once and it came free.

Putting his bow over his shoulder and sticking the spearhead through his belt, he used the aspen as a walking-stick and began to work back along the trail he had taken, remembering to cut across a couple of places where he had taken a more circuitous route. The skies were turning black under a heavy cloudbank when he entered the opening to his shelter, dropped his pack, started the fire, wrapped himself in his blanket, and slept.

The darkness was long. He ate snow twice, the witch of fire burning inside him. He awakened and dozed many times, only to awaken with chills on each occasion. He kept the fire alive, but felt so weak he could not get out meat to eat.

The light finally came, though the gray skies

held. He spent the entire sun alternately dozing, packing snow around his feverish leg and head, and eating snow. As darkness fell, he continued to shiver and then sweat, until he lost track of time. Sometime in the darkness, his vision returned.

Scent of Violets and the ravens. Evil birds hovered over her swollen belly, and he wondered when he awakened if she would still be alive when he returned. He wept, feeling the depression of loss overwhelm him, and was ashamed of his tears. He felt weak and lonely, and in the feeling he wished he were not a man, but a child, sitting at The Rock in the freedom of youth. How much simpler life was then.

33

When the vision came, the witch that brought heat to his body left. He remained inside the crude shelter five suns, waiting for strength to return, watching it snow twice for brief periods. On the sixth sun, the wind cold and biting under lead-gray skies, he burned the two empty food bags, donned his pack, took his weapons including the broken spear, and left the shelter to begin his trek home.

He forced himself to take it easy, lightheaded and reminded of his injuries by the cold that bit into the scab running through his hair, despising his inability to step on the left leg. He made the crutch from a pine sapling, and, though he tried to pad the "Y" at the top, it was soon chafing the underarm raw. Progress was slow.

It was after midsun when he passed the two bodies, partially buried under the light snows. He gave them only the most cursory of glances, feeling nothing. They had come to take his life; instead, the Great One had given him theirs.

At dark, he camped under a cedar, sitting next to

a fire he kept going as he dozed many times but never really slept. Tired, annoyingly aware of the light snow falling, he resumed his travels with first light. His armpit was painfully sore, and he folded his blanket over the crutch to pad it. It helped soften the rough wood, but the awkwardness of it made progress even more difficult. The Top loomed ahead, shadowy and mystic in the falling snow. He watched it slowly grow more immense and awesome as he neared, but he took little time to think of anything but wishing he were already at his destination. He stopped several times in the cold sweat of weakness, each time to set his mind and continue. By the second darkness, he was exhausted, but buoyed by the fact that he could, in the last light, make out individual trees on the slopes.

He again curled into his blanket, his head on his pack and a fire before him, to spend the restless darkness taking short naps that ended with teeth chattering. He lost track of the times he had to rebuild the fire. With first light, he was chewing venison as he hobbled slowly and clumsily, stopping occasionally to dig out another piece. He ate snow often, but the feeling that it was all a dream never left, even when he arrived at the bottom of the slope that led up into the mesa. He did not stop, or even slow down, as he began to gradual ascent.

At first the hill was gentle enough to give him no trouble, but soon became steeper than he remembered. He doggedly fought his way through the deeper snow, plodding a step at a time, surprised at the depth of the snow along the slant that looked at the early sun, and sleeping under another cedar in the darkness. If not for the cold, he could have slept for two suns, but he roused often to refuel his fire, sitting close to it to rewarm himself before trying again to sleep leaning against the tree. It was impossible.

Before the skies showed signs of light, the crispness of the darkness making the snow squeak under his feet, he climbed again, until about midsun he topped out and began the more horizontal walk around the head of three valleys before starting the slow descent to where the village had stood before the Others had destroyed it.

The sun came out just before it reached its zenith, and the breeze was warmer as he neared the village. Smoke from two fires climbed slowly toward the abode of the gods before the breeze fanned them out. A child screamed at someone. He came into view of the burned-out remains, and there he saw several people working on firewood.

Two women saw him coming and stopped to stare, saying and doing nothing. When he at last crutched his way into the village, several more turned to stare, making him feel most uncomfortable, like he was a spirit from the gods. No one greeted or spoke to him, no one moved.

He stopped in the courtyard and said to a woman named Small Wren, "Am I a spirit of the gods?"

She nearly shrunk from him. "You have been gone so long. You still live?"

He shrugged. "I think I do." He grinned.

She showed no signs of responding to his humor. "You didn't see Eagle Eye or Little Dog?"

"Should I have?"

"They followed a sun after you left. They thought you might need help."

He portrayed innocence as he shrugged again, shaking his head. "They must have changed their minds. I saw no one who came to help."

"They must have missed you, then."

He nodded. "They guess they did." He almost smiled at the grim humor of his own cryptic remarks, maintaining a sober face. He glanced around, then back at Small Wren. "Where does everyone stay?"

She pointed to the trees where Singing Waters and Little Dove had been hiding when he first saw them. "We built a shelter in there for those of us who still live." Her remark left him wondering about how many survived, and the morale of those who did.

He nodded and turned toward the trees. The shelter they had built was large, enveloping several trees and tall enough for the average man to stand, though he could not. There were thirty or more people inside. It had been hastily erected from branches and pine boughs, one large room with the trunks of many trees visible. Animal hides were affixed to the ceiling over several firepits, to keep melting snow from dripping into the meal areas. Families were gathered in groups, though there were some mixing with others.

"Hola, He Who Conquers!" Son of Happiness saw him from back in the big room, his grin wide as he moved quickly between people to greet his friend. "I didn't expect to see you again!" The inference was plain.

He took the innuendo and ran with it. "It was touch and go a while, but I made it." He could not hold back his own grin.

"Little Dog and Eagle Eye came out to help you. It appears they missed their connection."

Again he spoke to a double meaning. "Must have. I saw no one who came to help." His terminology told Son of Happiness he had indeed run into them.

He felt someone beside him and turned to look at Scent of Violets, who stood almost shyly. He shrugged from his pack and smiled to her as she took it, touching his arm as she did so. He felt the meaning in her touch and watched her walk away. When he saw where she stopped, he turned back to Son of Happiness.

From his belt he pulled the six scalps, which he handed to Son of Happiness. "Hang these on the post in the courtyard. The gods will keep us safe for a while, I think."

"Six!" The same worshipful eyes that he had so often seen glanced at him before he hurried away. He turned and worked his way with a stoop-walk to Scent of Violets.

"You're hungry." A look of concern came as she glanced at the injured leg, but she made no remarks.

He nodded, looking at the form of his son sleeping in the warmth of the cradleboard near the fire. "I'm hungry and tired. The Others made my trip back a bit difficult. If I fall asleep, I'll sleep for a moon."

She smiled. "Then you shall sleep. First I'll make you something to eat, and then you can sleep as long as you like." She busied herself around the firepit.

He sat on the edge of the mat and looked around the big room. Singing Waters and Little Dove, with Son of Vision, had their firepit near the middle of the room beside a tree trunk, from which hung a variety of clothing items. Happiness, now mated to Fire in the Sky, had rejoined his mate in the far corner from He Who Conquers, and his mate held an infant daughter to her breast while she worked at a meal.

"You've met Son of Happiness and Fire in the Sky?"

Scent of Violets looked up and nodded. "They're nice. They have a daughter."

He nodded. "What have they named her?"

"Orchid of the Woods. She's cute as a chipmunk."

He continued to identify the people who had survived. Of the young men his age, only Happiness survived. There were many women, now widows, who worked around their fires in threes and fours. Some had changed dramatically in the two winters he had been gone, a couple of them much more attractive in maturity. A few old men lived, including Keeper of the Corn, Sun Watcher and Broken Nose. The last still had a huge poultice around his torso, and one arm was wrapped, as well. He had glanced at He Who Conquers several times, but always averted his eyes whenever the latter turned his way.

He took the stew given him by his mate, who had found and put aside the meat he had in his pack. It was dried, and would help greatly if food began to run short. He would be sure Scent of Violets ate well, since the life of his son depended upon her well-being. He dipped his finger into the stew, flipped a finger toward the gods in all four directions and began to eat. He kept going until he was stuffed, and his two burps of appreciation came just before he laid back and fell soundly asleep.

He awakened once to quiet, and realized everyone slept. It was only moments before he slept again. When he awakened again, it was because of a crying child and a scolding mu. The sun was shining, coming through a myriad of holes in the thick cover overhead, and there were few people inside. He sat up, and with Scent of Violets gone, struggled to his feet, took his crutch and hobbled outside. He relieved himself, then crutched down to the courtyard.

"Hola! You finally wake up!"

He smiled at Happiness, who came to meet him. "How long have I slept?"

"Almost two suns. Remind me to keep you away

from The Rock."

He laughed. "What's been happening around here?"

"We had a rabbit hunt and killed over three hundred. Then we found four bison in a canyon below us. We killed a mountain sheep two suns ago, and we traded for some corn with the people out on the valley."

"So how is the food situation?"

"We have been fortunate, but we can't make it through the winter without a whole lot more."

"That cache of beans, is it still available?"

"Women have been grinding it into flour, but having a hard time."

"My mate can show them how to make pottery that'll finally last longer than it takes to bake them."

"She already has, but they haven't had good fortune getting clay. She showed them how to grind some of the old, discarded pottery into what she called 'tempering' material. Does it really work well?"

He nodded. "It does. I was amazed."

"I will be, too, if it works."

"It will, skeptic. Believe me, it will. So what's planned for more food?"

"Nothing at the moment. We discussed a hunting trip, but it's been deathly cold. The men turned coyote."

"When this leg heals, we'll go. There were bison hanging around to mid-sun, a sun's journey, maybe two."

"You saw them?"

"A few, and many tracks. A wallow was freshly used, too. I think, unless someone hunts them soon, they'll still be there."

"No one will hunt in snowtime. Not in their right minds."

"Why not? It's a matter of survival, isn't it? I'd rather freeze to death trying to get food than sit here and starve to death."

"Good point, but what few men remain have little vitality left."

He remembered the spiritless remark by Small Wren. "Then they better get some! They plan to just sit and starve, and watch their women and children do the same?"

He shrugged. "You'll have to talk to them, then."

"What of Broken Nose? Is he useless since he got back after trying to kill me?"

"Broken Nose came back with a broken leg, and it healed crooked. He walks with a bad limp, his foot pointing out."

"But he still gets around, right?"

"Slowly."

"Faster if his life depended on it. We best get the men together and have a talk." He studied those nearby, and could see there was little elan in any of them. "I suppose we should visit a few others around The Top and see if more men will go with us." He hesitated. "You will go, right?"

Happiness smiled. "I wondered if you assumed I would, or if I had a choice. I'll go, of course. We need meat."

"How many men are left here?"

"Nine. Two are too old to go."

"Do we have a Spirit Man?"

"Yes, over there. Spirit Man Swift Eagle."

He Who Conquers looked surprised. "Didn't he live on the Top of Many?"

"He mated old Wren Feather." He grinned. "You ought to hear them couple. Sounds like two wapiti bulls in rutting season!"

They laughed.

"So Swift Eagle lives here now. He still makes a good hunter?"

"Oh, yes. Deadly. And he fears no animal. He has more guts than anybody I ever met...except you."

"Me? I have few guts! Just quick feet!"

Again they laughed.

"I'll see if I can call a meeting for sunset. Town Crier was killed, and no one took his place. Maybe that role should be mine. Earth Mu knows I have few other skills!"

"You'll have a noted skill before long, my friend. Count on it!" He Who Conquers watched him walk away toward three men who stood talking, then turned away and hobbled toward the fire pit. The hind quarter of a deer was spitted over the fire, and two young girls were slowly turning it while it sizzled and spit.

Broken Nose stood on the other side of the fire, his head turned to watch two lads wrestling. The sun was warm, and the temperature had moderated greatly. He Who Conquers, not sure of how to conduct himself with one who once tried to kill him, stopped near him and greeted him with a soft, "Hola."

Broken Nose turned like he had been stuck with a pin. He was surprised by the proximity of He Who Conquers.

Unsure of himself, he nodded once, his dark eyes almost unseen under his bushy eyebrows.

"I come to offer peace. I was greatly surprised to see you with the four who came after me; rest assured I hold no animosity. No harm was done...to me," he amended.

Broken Nose nodded. "He Who Conquers wishes for peace? I have no reason to want war."

"You once tried to kill me. You still seek to do so?"

"No. There'd be no benefit to this people anymore."

"There was once?" He kept a soft, neutral voice.

"I thought so. You sought to be chief. There were those who had the right before you."

"I wanted to be chief? You jest!"

Broken Nose studied his face. "It was heard by three men."

"And three witnesses make truth." It was considered a binding truth if three men agreed as witnesses. "But they lied."

"You make a serious charge. Eagle Eye will be furious to hear you charge him with lying."

He Who Conquers gave a humorless grin. "I called him to his face a few times. He never knew what truth was."

"Knew? He's dead?"

"Figure of speech."

"Now who lies."

He Who Conquers let a slight smile touch his lips. "Who can tell? Is Eagle Eye here?"

"You know something you aren't telling."

"What I know is of no consequence. Life has many secrets that are best kept that way."

Broken Nose shrugged.   "Like what you said about being chief?"

"If you want to take the word of Eagle Eye and his two best friends, suit yourself. Did you ever consult the chief about me?" He watched Broken Nose think on that, and then shake his head. "Why? Would not that have made more sense than just the word of a known liar and self-centered brat?" Again he watched Broken Nose for any reaction, but the man merely looked away, uncomfortable.

"Gray Dog died as he lived, lazy and with his eyes shut. I assume the third witness would be Twin Who Lived, who feared Eagle Eye. He thought he would be given a place of honor when Eagle Eye became chief." He snorted. "I would no more believe those three than if they claimed to create mankind."

It was an insult to Broken Nose for accepting their word as truth. He bristled. "Now you say I'm stupid!"

This time there was genuine humor in his eyes. "No, Broken Nose, not stupid. Just gullible. You knew that Chief Roaring Lion was an honest man, an honorable man, and assumed his sons were like him. But the fact is, Eagle Eye never knew what truth was."

"So you say."

"Suit yourself. If you champion the cause of such a bitter and hostile man as Eagle Eye, I can only feel sorrow for you. I think you're much more intelligent that Eagle Eye ever could have become, only you have always felt inferior to the chief and his sons.   You delude yourself. Be a man, Broken Nose. You'd make a far better chief than the chief's sons could ever be...by so far an eagle couldn't reach it. Some sun soon, you'll have more use for the intelligence you own than you ever thought possible."

He turned and hobbled away, again hating the crutch that was a symbol of his injury and weakness. There were several things he had to put his mind to, and having to fight a crutch fit nowhere in those plans.

Happiness was still circulating among the men, so he found a place in the sun and sat down, watching the women before he realized they were grinding old pottery, using a pair of small sledges and large grinding stones. Scent of Violets was among them working clay to show them the new method of stronger pottery.

A dog approached, and he held out a hand to it. It came to him and he scratched its matted fur as he watched the activity. A gray jay was pecking at something white on the ground that he could not identify. His interest was casually aroused, and he watched it for a time.

"Corn," a woman said from near him, noting his preoccupation. "The fire did that to much of our corn. We found it good to eat, and saved a lot of it. You want to try some?"

He smiled and nodded, looking up at a pretty young woman. He had to think quickly to remember her name, Blue Skies. "Is it safe to eat, Blue Skies? Perhaps the gods desire it."

She blushed that he should so easily remember her name. "Spirit Man said it was good to eat. His clan ate a lot of it."

"Then I would welcome some."

She left, and came back with a basket filled with the popped corn. He tried a piece, then looked up at her and nodded. "This is good. You say we have a lot of it?"

"Many baskets. Some burned, but a lot of it jumped out of the storage rooms when they burned. Spirit Man said the gods threw it for us to eat. We gathered it."

He ate another, then took a small handful. "You're not mated yet?"

She blushed again. "My mate was killed by Others. I have a son."

He nodded. "We'll try to find some young men from another clan to mate some of our women."

She shook her head. "The Others made many widows on The Top. Everywhere, the men tried to fight them with only a few from here and there. No one organized them so they could have enough to win. You won't find many men anywhere near."

"The Others were around for a time?"

"Two suns, but we didn't know it. They attacked many of the outlying people first, and came here last."

He continued to eat the popped corn, picturing

in his mind the workings of the Others.

"There are some who think the men of our village should take more than one mate."

He glanced at her, amused. "The women would accept that?" His slight smile showed his doubt.

She nodded soberly. "Many of us have spoken of it. Your mate suggested it."

He was nearly speechless as he stared at her, his humor buried in incredulity. "Scent of Violets?"

Again she nodded. "We need offspring, and she thought it would help if a man took three or four mates."

He sat silently, wondering at the idea. Many wives would not have occurred to him in a lifetime! Monogamy had become their tradition many generations ago, though it was a shaky heritage. It was easy to leave a mate and take another, though not practiced often. Even at that, this new concept was a far deviation from the old mores. He was overwhelmed that the women thought it a good idea.

"I'd welcome you as a mate," she said boldly but with yet another blush. "Scent of Violets will speak to you of me when she gets a chance to leave the women."

He continued to be disconcerted; words failed to come. She smiled as he handed her the basket of popped corn, but she stood beside him after she had taken it.

"You would not want me? I can bear children."

He began to feel warm about the neck and face as she stared at him. "It's too new to me. I haven't thought on such a thing." He looked away to find relief from the eyes that showed pain that he would deny her. "You think the idea a good one?" The enlarged member that strained at his breechcloth indicated he was stimulated by such a discussion, but he was too overwhelmed to even think logically. It seemed too farfetched.

She saw at a glance his reason for discomfort, and the pained expression disappeared. It was replaced by a slight and assured smile. "I do. Many of us do. You always had eyes for Little Dove when you were younger, and she also thinks the idea good. She will no doubt speak to you soon, too." Self-consciously, he stared at the ground, and she took the occasion to watch the lump behind his breechcloth.

He turned his head to look at Little Dove, who stood with the women watching the process of tempering. She shifted at that moment and glanced at him, and his mind went into shock. She still wanted him, too!

But the idea was too new; he doubted that such a thing would work. It had too many thorns, the first being rivalry. Jealousy would become a big problem if he gave too much attention to one or the other, and was he capable of being a mate to two or three women?

The idea was titillating, there was no doubt of it. Except that he loved Scent of Violets. How could he be regularly coupling with other women if he loved only one? No, to be honest, he still felt something more than liking for Little Dove, too, but would it not interfere with his feelings for his mate?

Little Dove looked away, and his eyes returned to Blue Skies. She smiled, no animosity in her eyes though she had seen the exchange between him and Little Dove.

"We have talked, and came to some conclusions about how it would work, but you need to speak to Scent of Violets to find out about it." She gave him another smile and turned away, to leave him sitting with his perplexing thoughts.

34

Son of Happiness squatted beside him with a twinkle in his eyes. "You're popular with the women, old son. I have no one except my mate who shows an interest in me. But then, it's most likely you'll become our chief. A chief is always popular with the ladies while he's young and virile." He grinned. "Sure, I knew about this for a while. Women speak freely...sometimes too much. But I'm more than satisfied with Fire in the Sky. She has fire in more places than the sky."

He Who Conquers chuckled. The idea of having several mates was great fuel for the mind, though he was skeptical it would work as smoothly as the women thought. A full moon with each mate. When one was pregnant, he would no longer go to her until after she dropped the child and her purification rites. If all three were expecting at the same time, he could do whatever he chose, depending on the health of the woman and her proximity to giving birth, and each recognized that Scent of Violets came first.

Scent of Violets seemed to have no qualms about

it, and was in fact favoring it because The People needed children. When there were enough women and men around, the system would fade out for lack of need.

He looked around at the other men who had come to discuss a hunting trip. The chatter of the multimates had taken priority at the outset, and he had let it run its course for a while before he could again recapture their attention and get it focused.

"Be that as it may, we came to discuss hunting. We need meat or we'll starve. What is your interest?"

Broken Nose spoke first. 'Interest, or commitment?"

"First things first. It seems to me we have but one choice, hunt or starve."

"We have enough food if we're careful," Keeper of the Corn said. "To hunt now is suicide. We just need to be better at conservation...eat less. I'm not sure I agree with your premise of hunt or starve?"

"Huh!" Sun Watcher showed his disgust. "I already walk around hungry most of the time. I eat any less and my belly-button will connect with my spine, permanently. I don't favor eating less, believe me. I say we hunt."

"Me, too," Son of Happiness responded.

"It appeals to me, but I doubt I could make it," old Red Deer said ruefully. "These saplings I call legs refuse to do what I tell them anymore."

Broken Nose stared at the fire but said nothing. It was evident his mind was running hard.

"I saw bison to mid-sun, and I think they plan to spend snowtime there. They left many tracks, and used a wallow. I even saw a few." No one looked at He Who Conquers as he spoke, except Swift Eagle.

"What makes you think they'll still be there? How long will animals stay in one place?"

"A deer will die within a few stonethrows of where it was dropped. A bear stakes its area, as does the wolf, the lynx and the coyote. A puma stays in one place unless its food runs out or a stronger one drives it away. Wapiti stay within the same territory unless one bull drives another away. Bison move only to find food, unless something drives them away. Yes, I think the bison are still there."

"He's gone two winters, and he's an expert. It's madness to think we can survive out there on a hunt. Cold kills." Keeper of the Corn looked fiercely at the faces lit by the fire, jerking his robe tighter around his neck.

"You're a coyote, Keeper of the Corn. You always were. Everything he says about the habits of the animals is fact; we all know it. I say we need meat, and if we go when Sun God shines, properly clothed we can live. If we fail to act, none of us will survive snowtime."

"Bravo, Red Deer! You speak big, but you can't walk. You'll sit by a fire while we freeze to death out there!"

"What do you mean 'we', my brother? You won't be there even if everyone else goes!"

He Who Conquers chuckled. "I'm going to hunt. I can't live on a corn cake every other sun, and my mate can't cut down on her intake and keep my son alive."

"I agree! My mate gives suck to a baby, too. I'll go with you." Son of Legends lived with his family a short distance away from the village, one of two men who survived a fight that destroyed his lone dwelling. One of the Others that died on The Top had been killed there.

"You're crazy! You have plenty of food! The Others never saw your food stores." Keeper of the Corn stared at Son of Legends fiercely.

"We shared our corn with you, remember? We, too, are going to run short."

"Your problem is stupidity!" Keeper of the Corn was caustic.

"Stupidity? For being big-hearted enough to share corn so you and I can live? Well, on second thought, keeping you alive is a mistake! But your problem is cowardice! I hope the witch that burns visits your maleness!" Red Deer was thoroughly aroused now. "If you go, He Who Conquers, I'll go with you, even if these legs fail! I'll crawl! At least I can show I'm a man!"

A chuckle came from Broken Nose, the first time He Who Conquers could ever remember hearing him laugh. "Good! Feisty! Stupid, but good! I'll go on such a hunt; it'll be better than sitting here listening to two turkey toms determine their pecking order!"

Several men laughed, and many voiced approval of such a hunt. "When will we hunt?"

"When the next moon begins."

"That will be many suns, yet."

"I just burned my crutch. I still hobble." He almost added, *from the wound*, but caught himself in time. As yet, no one had asked about his injury, assuming it was an accident he had on the trail. He knew that one sun, when he bared the leg, they would see that it was an arrow, but planned to say nothing until then. "When I can walk well, I'll leave."

"And no one can go if you don't, is that it?" Keeper of the Corn was determined to play the witch.

He Who Conquers gave him a dazzling but cold smile. "If the men choose to go without me, that's their right. I only say that I doubt I'd make it right now, at least, not well enough to kill an animal. When I'm healthy, I'll
go. Even if the others leave long before and perhaps have already returned. I plan to carry my fair share of the load around here, as should everyone else!"

"See to your weapons, your blankets, your leggings," Broken Nose said, asserting himself as one of the few Hunters yet alive. "It'll not be pleasant, but I have to agree with the idea. We need meat to survive."

Keeper of the Corn muttered under his breath, giving Broken Nose a scathing look. His voice would inspire many, and Keeper of the Corn was sure none would return.

The cold had settled with the sleep of Sun God, and they quickly broke up the meeting to return to the warmth of the community dwelling. He Who Conquers, limping noticeably without the aid of his crutch, went directly to his mat. Scent of Violets sat beside the fire feeding their son and gave him a cup of tea.

"I think I might be pregnant, again."

He felt the dread of alarm, but covered it quickly. Would the ravens come this time? His grin was weak. "A son again?"

She laughed. "I have no idea, but either would be fine, now."

He sipped the tea and glanced at his son. Before

he could say anything more, she said quietly, "Blue Skies would like another child. Her son is past his first winter, and she's strong." She leaned close. "You need the relief this darkness. She said if you go out to drain water, she will slip out and meet you. The women have spoken about this, but no one has acted yet. She's not sure you want to be the first, so she'll be discreet."

He frowned. "You think this good?" Suddenly the idea that had been so titillating was not sounding so good.

"I do. My needs won't be frequent, now. I've faked need many times to keep you busy, but now there's no need. Go. She'll come soon. I put blankets in a tree up the hill. You'll see them."

He did not move, glancing from her to his son. Was it true, that she had faked it many times? No, he could not believe that. She was too playful, too insistent, too responsive. So what was happening here? How could she change so quickly. She certainly had no such mindset when she was expecting the first child. By the gods, she had no less drive until just a few suns before he was dropped!

She smiled. "Go."

He stood, hobbled outside and relieved himself, still not sure of what to do. If he should couple with Blue Skies, would Scent of Violets be angry when he returned? And how would he feel about himself? How tangled the web of the spider! What would a man, a real man, do in this situation? After all, he was a man. Still, the women had set this whole thing in motion, and his own mate had been the instigator!

He felt the chill, and realized he had to make a decision. It was his to do. He knew what the women had decided, and his mate had given him the word. Now it was his move. Funny how the choice was not so easy as had been the lascivious discussions among the men! Well, if it was his to decide, and he made the wrong one, at least he had decided. Standing here could get one's manhood frozen, along with the rest of him.

He moved up the tilt of land to no-sun. He saw the wad of blankets, and suddenly it was clear. He would do it. Why not? The need was for children, and he felt a desire to couple. His mate told him to go, so if he did and she was unhappy, tough! If it was all a game with them, why not accept it and play the game? It might even be interesting. Surely, not all women were alike! He could handle variety! And in the back of his mind, he knew the innocence of his love for Scent of Violets was gone. Never again would they have the playful banter, the savage animalism, the pure satisfaction of what had been theirs until now.

The realization saddened him. He thought to turn back, but understood immediately that, even if he did, his mate had changed as much as he. Her discussions with the other women had brought her naivete, her guilelessness, to an end. It had become honed, polished, trained. Yes, trained. Taught to think differently. Impregnated with impurity, with learned degradations. She had lost her first love in the basin of need.

He could mourn. He felt a sadness as he realized the time of loving naivete was gone. Love would become more mechanical, more socially oriented. He felt like weeping. Alas, that was not possible. He had to accept the strange ways of the Goddess, and do what was necessary.

He realized he had been standing beside the tree, looking at the stash of blankets, for some time. His emotions had fastened him to Earth Mu. He shook himself as though to rid himself of a load, and then reached up for the blankets. **Blue Skies,** he said to himself, a new feeling flowing over him, **remember, you asked for this.**

Blankets in hand, he turned to decide where he should go, when he saw movement among the trees up the hill, and Blue Skies appeared. She stood and watched as he approached.

"I thought you might not come," she said with a shy smile. "You were so long beside the blankets, I was sure you were changing your mind."

"Something new. Gives a man a question or two to answer in himself." She took his arm as they walked up the hill, slowly in deference to his limp. Entering a thick stand with underbrush, they stopped, then stood awkwardly, each touched by embarrassment.

She took the top blanket from him and spread it

in the small area between brush, then sat on the edge on her knees, and he dropped beside her, not sure how to proceed with one whom he hardly knew. **Innocence gone**, he thought, and the idea seemed lightly humorous.

She reached over and took his hand, though it was very cool, and put it inside her cloak against her breast. "I'd like to put another infant on that nipple."

"It's hard for me to accept that coupling should come for nothing more than procreation," he blurted.

She stared at him, though it was hard for either to make out the features of the other in the darkness. "Then do it for other reasons. Need? I suppose you feel that. A desire to exercise your manness? I can believe that. Experimenting on a different woman? Most mates wonder what it would be like to be lie with another. Conquest? Some men think to take as many as they can. There can be lots of reasons, He Who Conquers. But I do have one."

He smiled at her humor; at least, he thought it was humor. "Humor me."

She shook her head. "If you had not left here, realizing Little Dove was taken, you'd have had to fight pretty hard to get me to leave you alone. I've wanted you, wished for you, even loved you, since I have memory. You always thought everyone disliked you, even hated you, or at best, preferred to ignore you. You had so many of us grovelling at your feet, you had to be the blindest of men not to know."

It was news to him. Never had he noticed anyone except Little Dove. He was speechless.

"All you could see was Little Dove." She smiled. "You were so blind, you never noticed how often I'd remove my belt and drain water where you could see me, and you never looked twice." She squeezed his hand playfully. "I could have stood naked in front of you, I think, and never have caught your eye. For a long time, I was convinced I was really ugly to not get you to so much as look at me!" She laughed softly. "I think...no, I know...I could have jerked on your seed-stick, and you would have walked on past!"

He chuckled, aware of her soft, full breast and the warmth of his hand against it.

"You gave Little Dove her son. You even Opened

her. Am I so undesirable to you?"

He was astonished that she knew. Were there any secrets among women? "No...you...how...?"

"She told me after the Others killed my mate. She was trying to comfort me about my loss, and said it without thinking. Don't blame her too much; that's a tough secret to live with. Most women would have told everyone long before. Besides, the women of the Goddess couple merely to give children to the gods. Is it any less important that we have children in abundance in order for The People to survive?"

He shook his head as though to clear it.

"Come," she said, realizing his defenses were down. She lay on her back and pulled him down on her. "I'm as good looking as most. I can't be too repulsive."

He still felt that full breast in his hand. "No, you are not repulsive at all. It's only me...my own inhibitions. This is happening so suddenly."

"I always thought you'd be a super mate. Even before I mated Twin Who Lived, I longed for you."

He twitched at the mention of her mate's name. She felt his response.

"I know, he hated you. But he was weak. You know as well as I that he was only a follower of Eagle Eye because he was scared to death of him. But he gave me a son, and I liked him for what he was. He loved me, I think, and I think I loved him. Sometimes I wonder what love is, anyway." She paused and hugged herself to him. "That's immaterial now. But I'd have mated you in a moment before you went away."

He felt the response of his male member to her hug and continued discourse of interest and felt his inhibitions washing away. She was arousing his interests and reaction. She was pretty, she was healthy, and he knew there was not a man alive that would not couple with her under the circumstances. He took her.

"That was nice." They lay in the aftermath. "Little Dove was right, you are fierce."

He chuckled. "And cold. It's time to go back."

"We can do this again?" She held him against her so tightly he made no move to get up.

"What happens if you come with child, and no one knows we've mated?"

She giggled. "I'll tell no one if you don't. But when we build our new village, my dwelling will be yours."

"Until then...?"

"My blanket will be yours. Two darknesses?"

He paused a moment. "Sure, why not?"

"Was it so bad?"

"No. It was quite good, in fact."

"Then I'll be here next time."

She let him roll off, and he left. She remained to fold the blankets and hide them.

He slipped back in and found Scent of Violets awake when he moved under the blanket. She nuzzled him.

"You did it?"

"Uh-huh."

"Good. Sometimes I will want you. I'll let you know. Until then, you go to her as often as you choose."

He still was unsure about how to handle this, but he said quietly, "You're still my first choice. I'll always prefer to couple with you."

"And as long as I'm your number one, I'll be more than satisfied."

"I feel like a wapiti bull."

She giggled. "Just be a stud to the others; be a mate and lover to me."

"Forever," he promised.

Three suns later he had begun to overcome his limp as the leg gained strength quickly. He met Blue Skies at their appointed time, and the next darkness had a passionate coupling with Scent of Violets. She was not as demanding, more reserved...or did he just imagine it? Was she angry at him for doing what she requested? He had no desire or time to dwell on it.

Happiness spent time with him, there being little to do except wile away the time waiting for his leg to heal and the weather to warm. But he began to show his friend how to construct dwellings from rock and mortar, making them more impregnable and not so likely to burn. Only the ceilings would burn, and only from the inside. Happiness was not only fascinated, but also curious enough to ask questions. Mixing mortar, chipping rock to fit better, chinking with smaller stones, double wall construction, he learned it all, and imagined it.

His leg mended, and by the twentieth sun he was walking without a limp, though he occasionally had to favor the leg when something strenuous was required.

Preparations were made for the hunt, twelve men going and accompanied by four women. Blue Skies was one, and, contrary to her word, had made it no secret she had mated He Who Conquers. But with the first announcement, four other men took a second mate. A hunting ceremony was held on the final sunset before their departure, followed by the men separating to another area out of sight and sound of the dwelling with Spirit Man and making medicine.

It was a short time before dawn when they headed for their mats, one by one, until He Who Conquers and Spirit Man, who had walked back silently but together, were the only two left. They sat on the log next to the glowing coals of the community fire in silence for some time.

"You left here with some intense pressure," Spirit Man said after the prolonged silence.

"Yes."

"Why did you return?"

"To bring back some ideas that can make life better here--things I learned from other people. I intended to come back from the time I left."

"Even though you left under rather, what should I say, harsh circumstances?"

"I had hoped things might be changed by time I returned, but I never doubted I would be back in two or three winters."

"And things have changed...drastically."

"They have."

"As you knew they would."

This stunned He Who Conquers. He shrugged to pass it off. But Spirit Man knew.

"We'll speak of that sometime. Would you want to be chief of this people?"

He lifted his shoulders, then spoke slowly. "I don't concern myself with that. It makes no difference if I am or not, because I'll influence my people with new ideas regardless. All I care is that we build better than we have in the past, that we learn to handle beans well to enlarge our diet, that our pottery be stronger and thus more useful, and that we live the best way possible."

Spirit Man chuckled. "You're serious, I take it. Well, I've spoken to a few of the men about making you chief. I've had only one clear dissent, and you no doubt know who that is. He was pretty adamant about not wanting to see this hunt, too."

"Why?"

"If it's successful, you'll have shown you can lead successfully. I hear you already talk of building with stone and mortar, which I've heard from the Trader, but no one knew how to start. Long ago, someone used it to build our water supply, but no one ever thought to use it for dwellings. Now it's about to become reality. And your mate shows the women about better quality pottery. I'd say you've taken the horns of the wapiti and made him kneel. Broken Nose came to me five or six suns ago and mentioned you as the next possible chief."

Surprised, He Who Conquers visibly moved. "Broken Nose?"

"Don't underestimate the man. He's sharp. He says you possess leadership qualities found in no one else in the village."

"But he was one of those who tried to kill me two winters ago."

Again he chuckled. "So he was. Told me the entire story. However, he sees the death of the two sons of the former chief as indication you were correct when you said they lied. He was also impressed with your self-assurance in taking a second mate and in proposing the hunt, especially that you were going even if alone."

He Who Conquers stared into the coals. "He's come a long ways around, then."

"Broken Nose is a selfless man. More than you might believe, and more than I ever understood. Naive, perhaps, but still selfless. He wanted to kill you only because you had--or at least, he understood you had--declared you would one sun be chief. He thought it was presumptuous and a direct threat to the chief and his family."

He Who Conquers remembered the discussion he had held with the man. He said nothing.

"Well, you best get a little shut-eye. I certainly need a some. A trip with the new sun will make this old man wish for younger legs, I think." He chuckled, then stood, and he Who Conquers stood with him. "We can speak more of this when the hunt is over. In the meantime, I'll continue to seek out what the men feel about this other thing." He walked away, leaving He Who Conquers standing alone beside the log.

He paused only a short time, then turned toward the dwelling, and literally bumped into Little Dove. She stood directly behind him, and he had been unaware of her. She stopped him with a hand to his chest after he caught his balance.

"You're hard to catch alone," she said, and he remembered her voice so well from the many times she came to The Rock. It had matured.

He smiled. "I've become too occupied with too much and too many."

She nodded. "The next chief, the women say. Is it true?"

He shrugged. "Who can say? I don't seek it."

"You should."

"Why? It's an honor to be chief. It should be earned by hard work and honor, not campaigning for votes."

She nodded. "True, but you'll make a good chief."

He was silent.

"You've taken a second mate. Is there a chance you might consider a third?"

He looked at her with an expression she could not read. "I took a second mate because my mate urged me to. Scent of Violets has my heart. It will always be so."

Little Dove sat quietly for a moment, her eyes searching his face and eyes. "So you will refuse me?"

"Scent of Violets said it would be fine by her if I took you for a mate. I told her it was up to her to decide. I feel like a rutting buck deer."

Little Dove smiled. "I told her that was how you would feel, because we've been monogamous for so long. But I desire you to give me whatever you will. I've always loved you, and you know that. I knew you feel something special for Scent of Violets, and I never want that to change. I like her...very much. But I want you, and I want your children. And I want to know you still have some of the fire for me you once did. I'll not mate another."

He again stared into the winking coals wordlessly for a time. She remained silent, knowing he often thought for a while before making a reply. It was something she had learned at The Rock.

"I have always loved you. I cannot forget that special first love we had. I'll not lose that, ever. To say I've not thought of you...often...would be a lie. Sometimes, when we first mated, I almost slipped and called her by your name. I can never change." He was again quiet for a short time. "If you wish, I'll take you for a mate. It might be awkward. Three mates will be very difficult."

"We discussed the way it would work."

"I know."

"You think it will be a problem?"

"I can't say. If Scent of Violets wants to couple, anytime and anywhere, I'll give her that right. If it means you or Blue Skies have to wait another sun, so be it. She's the mate I chose, and we've had a special relationship. I'll do nothing to hurt her or make her feel she has to compromise."

"Fair enough. But the turns of a moon each is workable?"

"Yes. But if during your moon, she wants to couple, you will have to wait another sun."

"I can accept that. You alone can give me what I want, and I have eyes for no other man. What we nurtured at The Rock will always be for me my only love. If you couple with me only once in a winter, I accept that, too. Not that it would please me, but I will live with it. I love you, my love. Just so I have hope and can still dream. That's enough."

He nodded. "Then it's workable. I've desired you from time to time, but I've never chosen to do what will anger or deceive my first mate."

"Will you couple with her before the sun rises, before you go on this hunt?"

"No."

She rose. "Then come to me. I have blankets ready." He took her proffered hand and followed her into the trees, aware that this was the moon reserved for Blue Skies, and there experienced something of what he had tasted so long ago. This time, it was of a less vicious drive, and when they were through, she kept him on her and hugged him close until skies showed signs of light.

"You must go, my love. I'm grateful to you."

"I felt guilty taking Blue Skies turn with you. But it was you I preferred as a second mate."

They nuzzled each other passionately. "I will await your return. We'll talk together while you're gone, and decide how to work things out."

"Blue Skies accompanies us on the hunt."

"I know. It's her moon." She smiled coyly. "Makes me feel something special. I can dream again while you're gone."

He smiled as he sat up. "Just so no one thinks they're getting one up on Scent of Violets."

"We agree on that."

He ran his nose over her cheek and left the trees while she gathered her blankets. Only a short time later the men left the village, accompanied by the four women.

35

The hunters were gone nine suns. They found bison on the second sun, trapped in a deadend canyon, and killed eleven. They skinned them and deboned the meat which froze quickly in the frigid temperatures. They put the brains in gutbags for use in tanning the hides later, wrapped the meat in the hides, and made the trip home using travois and eleven dogs, which took three suns.

Once back, the meat was cut into strips and smoke-dried on racks, then stored. Hides were scraped clean, rubbed with ashes, and softened by rubbing and pulling, and working in the brains. The robes were welcomed by the families inside the crude dwelling, and old hides were fastened to the ceiling to aid in the fight against the drips of melting snow.

Snowtime grew mild for a moon, then gave another round of cold and snow, before giving way to the Goddess of Fertility. The celebration was held on the sun of the equinox, declared by Sun Watcher, and the girl offered came from within the village, a girl orphaned because of the raid. She was eleven winters and had just been visited by the Goddess.

With the thawing of the soil, construction began for the new village. Rock was hauled from the canyons; the chosen site, atop the burned ruins, was leveled with a straight, long beam with a wide-mouthed open bowl of water sitting on top to show level. Stakes were driven into the ground to demark the center of the walls at every point where they intersected with themselves or the outer wall.

Happiness listened to He Who Conquers carefully, then sat beside him in the early darkness to ask questions and think on what was happening. The discussions regarding the layout of the first level brought about the first disagreement among the men. Only one man other than He Who Conquers had ever seen rock and mortar construction used for dwellings. On a trip to Open Canyon six suns journey to mid-sun, Spirit Man Swift Eagle had been fascinated by it. He wished for a kiva for each clan, built like those he had visited while he was seeking the wisdom of the gods at his inception as a spirit man. Sun Watcher wanted their own design, with opportunity given to the gods to change their minds, detesting the idea of copying others.

The argument raged for two suns, while the men and women carried stones, and some men followed the example of He Who Conquers and chipped them to rectangular shapes. On the third sun, the men sat in council on the new courtyard that fronted the village, legs hanging over the short retaining wall that was built to hold back the soil taken from the place they leveled for construction.

"We will build the kivas according to the way I desire, because the men of Open Canyon have found that the gods listen to them. The gods are pleased when men build what pleases them; their design obviously does. If you choose not to build that way, then I'll go somewhere else, where men choose to delight the gods."

"Don't make threats to me!" Sun Watcher snarled. He Who Conquers had noticed a jealousy about the power Spirit Man had so quickly gained among The People.

His voice soft, his response almost contrite, Spirit

Man defended his position. "I do not make threats, my friend. I speak what my senses tell me, and I try to make sure no one misunderstands me. What I said was not meant to be hostile or threatening, merely my mind. Besides, we can't help but be somewhat unique, because I don't remember all the exact measurements, and even theirs differed somewhat. I'm sure ours won't be exact replicas."

"And it's good enough for me," He Who Conquers agreed. "It can't be any big deal for most of us, anyway, because we haven't studied things like that. If what he says is true, then why not do it that way? I, sure as Earth Mu, wouldn't want the gods angry with our kivas. Why make an issue of something like that?"

Sun Watcher stared at him, unsure of how to respond to his conciliatory statement, then muttered something unintelligible. For anyone to speak against Sun Watcher could be disastrous, though no one wanted to cross Spirit Man either. For a time, no one said anything.

"Then it's settled." He Who Conquers looked around at the men he faced, tired of their two suns of pointless argument, then looked at Happiness. "You will work with Sun Watcher and Spirit Man to design the size and shape of the kivas, and stake them out. The rest of us will carry more stone."

The stack was huge, and still they traveled into the canyons to bring more, until men griped about it being excessive and women complained that they were too tired. It was time to begin work on laying what they already had, he knew, before they grew into such discontent they would quit. They were far short of the stones needed, but they would find that out soon enough when the huge pile ran out. In the meantime, seeing some of the work done, they should be less likely to continue their discontent, understanding the great amount of stone required for such a project.

He Who Conquers began by showing them the texture needed in the mortar to best hold the rocks in place, so it would adhere properly and yet not be runny. Then he studied the staked layout that now included the three kivas which would be included in the main level. A front entrance into the main level would facilitate the storage of their grains and meat supplies. The three kivas would be entered from their roofs, as usual, which would become part of the courtyard of the second level where dwellings would be built.

The double wall construction began, with men carrying mud and mixing it, others bringing rock and learning how to lay it properly. Some men spent their time trimming the rock to fit, others in choosing which rock should go next. Women helped carry water for the mixing, and some waded into the mixture that was created in a depression of the soil. Even children threw themselves into the mixing of the mortar, stomping back and forth through the mud. One of the men spent his entire time repairing mauls and chippers and replacing broken handles.

The walls began to climb, the rear exterior wall going up first and the inner walls that intersected tied into it so that they grew along with the back one. One sun after another passed, until the lower walls were done. Then came the beams that would support the branches and small tree limbs that undergirded the courtyard. The men spent four suns finding the beams and trimming them, and women and children dragged the branches and limbs from where the men felled the trees.

Then came the mud, again. Heavy, thicker mud, that adhered into the top branches and remained in place, covered with more mud until the thick roofs were done and the men quit to allow it to cure.

Then came planting time. Corn, beans and squash went into the ground, blessed by Spirit Man, timed by Sun Watcher, first given in dedication to the gods for their approval and assistance through the Celebration of Sowing. Sun after sun, they planted, across the cleared valley and down the slope into mid-sun, then up the hill toward the place where their water-gathering trenches were located.

And then it was back to the rock and mortar, the walls going up for the second story where the people would live. Seeing how fast the rock ran out put a stop to the complaints and sent them back to gathering more. Again they roofed, and women plastered the front of the rock to cover the stone facing and give smoothness and uniformity to it. In the meantime, crops were watered and watched, the boys kept guard that rodents did not dig up the seeds, and Rain Man danced to beg Rain God for moisture.

With the start of each dwelling, a prayer stick was placed in the mortar of a corner to assure the gods approval on the family that would live there. With the completion, Spirit Man gave his blessing in a great ceremony, flavored by the roasting of an entire elk.

The large kiva on the courtyard was for the general Council, and the others, whose roofs helped make the elevated courtyard, were for the clans of the people of the village, each totem having a private kiva. One went to the Clan of the Hawk, for He Who Conquers. Then, with the construction needs done for a time, their numbers such that no more construction was necessary, the crops again became their priority, watering, weeding, thinning, protecting, and more watering. While the crops grew and were given care, the men hunted, gradually filling some storage rooms with meat from bison, bear, deer, wapiti, puma, bighorn sheep, and smaller animals.

Women made pottery, excited about the new method and superb quality.   Scent of Violets improvements lent them a new significance, and, as when they first began making pottery generations ago, the women started an unspoken competition for the best workmanship and painting.

As the harvest approached, Scent of Violets dropped a girl; two moons later, Blue Skies dropped a son. In mid-snowtime, Little Dove had a daughter. He Who Conquers was made chief.

For two winters, The People enjoyed prosperity. Scent of Violets dropped her second son, and Blue Skies birthed a stillborn daughter. As the celebration of the Goddess approached, Little Dove had twins, her second and third sons. The first twin died before the third sun, but the second was healthy.

On a lazy sun with balmy temperatures, just before harvest, He Who Conquers felt a need to be alone. It had been a long time since he had been given the urge to go out on his own, on a whim, some inner restlessness goading him. The Feast of Harvest had passed, the rains had ceased to fall, the corn, beans and squash were healthy, and some of the beans had already been picked.

For several suns, he had been discussing with Broken Nose and Happiness the need to store a larger quantity of water through enlargement of the reservoir. The latter He Who Conquers, as chief, had renamed Stone Setter. It was a name to honor his ability to build with rock and mortar, and he had been called to various places around the mesa to show people how to do it. He had even found a few superior ways to make foundations hold better, having already run into a problem on the outside wall toward the hottest sun. A corner wanted to sink, and had already been repaired once.

Having spent many suns working in the fields and discussing water, the restlessness had begun to burn within. He needed to go alone; in fact, he had not run in a long time, and after he was free of the village, he broke into a trot, feeling how much he had lost of his once great ability to run.

His wind was less because he had not extended his lungs for some time; but he ran in spite of it, and when the breath came in gasps, he still ran. He wandered along the same level, circling toward rising-sun, until he became aware he was nearing the place where long ago he had killed four Others. What a long chain of events that had triggered, until he had arrived here, following the Great One so far.

He stopped near the stone, and stood nostalgically. He remembered the warrior who stood so near, who had realized to late that the one he saw in the twilight was not one of his own; the delay cost him his life. He remembered the first guard, and how his hands shook when he handled his bow. The Great One had guided the arrow, for his own skill was useless in the fear and excitement he had felt. And he remembered Yellow Sapsucker, who died just about right where he stood, whose blood was in Earth Mu because of him. He felt no remorse.

He moved forward and sat beside the rock for a time, watching a hawk circle out over a deepening canyon, then got up and moved down the hill to where the four pyres had burned. The ground still showed the black of the ashes, and a few sticks still lay with charred ends or scorched bellies. He looked down at them and remembered.

He stooped and took a small handful of pebbles and ash, and stared at it, the ash a symbol of death--and he had been the instrument. He still had those four scalps, now shriveled but hanging in his kiva--his very own kiva. Now he was a chief; he always knew it would happen, but it had led to a feeling different from he had anticipated.

He was now a man. He had sired several children, traveled far to learn things that were an asset to his people, killed many Others, become Chief of Honor, owned his own kiva, and was accepted as a man of principle, honor and intelligence. No longer did he need to prove he was not a coyote, or that he was a man, though he might again...sometime...to himself.

Still, despite the ache that had begun in many of his teeth, he was strong, active, virile, a leader. No one doubted it--not any more. He had indeed conquered.

Surprised, he looked down at the ash he still held in his hand. It felt strangely warm, almost as if it still held the fire that he remembered--when suddenly there were images moving across the skyline before him. The Death Dance was in progress, the fiercely painted men chanting around the pyre as smoke raised to the gods. Then there were the five Others, lying in the darkness while he escaped with their scalps near Open Stone, and there were four more near Wide Canyon.

And then it was Scent of Violets--lying cold and pale, her womb viciously ripped open and ravens carrying off an unborn son. A scream echoed up the valley to him, and carried across the canyons, and was joined by his own, heard by several as far as the Top of Many, across the canyon from his own village. His hand turned over with a spasm, the ash and stones falling to the ground, a look of horror on his mature face.

His love, the one who truly held his life in her hands, was back in the village, six moons pregnant!

Suddenly he was moving again, down and up, taking the direct route toward the village, something inside driving him to run, sending him sprinting, down and up, and down and up. His breath came in gulps and gasps, his lungs feeling as though they were being torn from him. And then he stopped. Suddenly.

He was near the village, it was near time for the sun to set, and he heard the wails. His legs turned to grass; he staggered and his legs gave way, but he forced himself to get up. He fell again, and this time his spirit was gone, along with his desire to return to the village. He heard the cries, the screams, the wailing sounds of death that lifted against the silence of the setting sun.

He wept, unashamed, never considering the weakness it portrayed in his character. His Scent of Violets, his lynx, was no more. Without her, life was over. The one who had loved him with no reservations, who stood beside him when her people thought him something other than what he was, who walked with him while she was heavy with child, who wanted his happiness so much she would give birth to their son in a tree-hammock while isolated in the wilderness...this one who left her people to be his mate, who tended to his needs both diligently and faithfully, and whose love so vastly transcended what he had ever thought possible--even to encourage him to mate other women because of the acute need for offspring among his people--how could he live without her? No, why should he?

Darkness fell while he lay on the cooling Earth Mu and alternately wept and begged the Great One to bring her back. The skies turned cloudy, and were silent. The Great One had nothing to say to him. His devastation was so complete he began to contemplate going into the wilderness to starve himself to death, waiting for death as the old often did.

He went silently into the village while all slept, even the dogs. The wailing had ceased until the new sun, and he could not bear to be there when it returned. His kiva was as cold and silent as he felt, and he took his possibles bag and hung it around his neck, to be sure he had his spiritual aids. He took his weapons, though he had no idea why, a robe of feathers given to him when he became chief, and a few of the riches accumulated over the winters.

Then he pointed to where he had chased the Others, and began to walk. His paces were steady but slow, and he walked the entire darkness, staggering before daylight and falling under a tree where he slept and dreamed of Scent of Violets, as she had looked when

he first saw her and when she wept for her fa-fa, as she
came to him in their first coupling and when she lay
naked with him so many times, as she teased him about
keeping him exhausted and when she told him of the
idea that he couple with other women for the sake of the
village, though it probably hurt her inside to see him do
it.

   With first light, his wrestling set aside, he walked
on, eating nothing and stopping only a few times to
drink. He slept as restlessly the second darkness, only a
short distance from where he had been wounded but still
killed Little Dog and Eagle Eye. He did not think of
them, and gave no attention to the bleached and
scattered bones when he walked past where they died.
Their weapons lay as they had been left, the wood
shafts and hafts weak and the gut and resin stringing
gone. The clothing was only small rotted pieces. He
saw, but his thoughts did not have time for that fateful
sun when he had put to death the one who would have
become chief.

   The trees he had used as a shelter still stood, but
their branches were nearly gone and they no longer
formed a shelter. He eyed it carefully, then turned and
climbed the ridge. Halfway up he found a deadfall
where another tree had fallen across it. It formed a cave
if he removed the bottom branches, tall enough for him
to sit.

   He did, then crawled under and sat with legs
folded in front of him. There he stayed, weapons beside
him, robe over his back, riches and amulets on the
ground in front of him. Darkness came, then sun, then
darkness and another sun. He never moved, though his
legs ached from the inactivity and he had twice urinated
without moving.

   Birds flitted through the trees, ground squirrels
ran on the tree above his head, a deer wandered past
and bounded away when it caught man-odor, but the
man was unaware. He was locked inside himself,
remembering, weeping, and forgetting--forgetting the new
method of construction he had introduced, the new
pottery they made because of him and his mate, the
ideas planted that they needed more water storage.
Mostly, he wept.

In the eerie first light of the third sun, he saw someone in the trees below him, and the sight of movement drew his thoughts into cohesion for the first time. He watched, fascinated and fearful, until the figure moved again. A woman, in a blanket she held around her neck, moved toward him, her eyes locked on his. She seemed to float, her walk so graceful, and he stared at his mate in disbelief. She lived!

But he could not move. His legs were folded under him; he wanted to get up and go to her, but a power held him in place. Someone held him! He struggled against hands that lay heavy on his shoulders, but he was greatly weakened by his vigil of death. He struggled, then cried out, unaware that no sound came.

And she came, closer and closer, until she stopped scarcely a stride away, staring.

The eyes...they were fierce...they were strong...they were accusing! It was his Scent of Violets, but he had not seen her like this! Again he tried to speak, but could not. She merely stared.

Then she turned. She was leaving! No! Come back! But as before, no sound escaped. He was helpless! She took two--or was it three--steps, then turned.

"I do not know you!" It was her voice, but it was like nothing he knew. It was scathing! Bitter! Angry! "I knew a man, not a weeping, pitiful corpse! I thought it was He Who Conquers here, a man I loved, a man who was all man, but I was wrong! I see no one here but an old body who weeps as a child!"

She began to walk away again, and after passing the first few trees, looked back again. "You do not see me, because I am not. I dwell with my son in Earth Mu. I awaited my mate, but this disgusting thing is no one I know! I would not know this weeping cadaver if he spoke to me in Earth Mu! My mate would have continued to live as before, to love his mates, to lead his people, to give what he is and knows. He never dwelt in self-pity!" Her eyes were red, like fire through an agate, burning his soul even as she spoke. "No lynx would desire to stake out an area near here, because a weak human has no strength except to foul the air!"

He saw her take a step, then another, and then

she was gone. His arms were released, his eyes opened, and his voice returned, but there was no one to see or listen.

He shook involuntarily as a chill ran through him. What had he seen? Scent of Violets? She came to him from Earth Mu! She knew where he was...and why. She knew his sadness...his guilt...his feeling of lostness.

And in his weakness, she rejected him! He shivered. "No!" His voice rang through the trees, and died in the hush that followed. Birds stopped their early chirping and flew away from the weirdly quiet place. He tried to unfold his legs, but found they were almost locked. He had to take his hands and pry them free, then roll onto his stomach in order to try to stand. He fell.

His legs refused to hold him. Circulation long pinched had numbed them into inaction. He reached out to a limb and pulled himself up again, but the legs were like broken blades of grass, and except for his grip on the branch, he would have fallen again. He held himself there until his arms began to shake, and he had to let go. He tumbled awkwardly into a heap.

He lay for a time, until his feet began to tingle with a million pins; pain came to his feet and calves, and muscle spasms jerked them around like an aroused rattlesnake. He had not felt such pain since his wounds at the hands of Eagle Eye and Little Bear. He wanted to scream, and in the very moment when Sun God broke through the trees, he did.

His voice sounded small and dead in the enclosure of the forest. He groaned at the pain, and reached down with his hands to rub the legs as though stripping the contents from an animal gut. Over and over he rubbed, and his groans sounded as hollow and subdued as had his cry.

A twig snapped, and he was instantly quiet and alert. It had been close, so close he should have been able to see whoever it was, but he had not deciphered the direction from which it came. He reached his knife and axe, lying silently, his head turning as on a spit. Who was there?

And then he saw her. Coming up through the trees where Scent of Violets had disappeared, her head turned as she studied the hillside. He watched her speechlessly, realizing suddenly what he had done to himself and those who believed in him. He had let them down. He had begun to destroy himself through self-pity. He was weak, not because he wept, but because he thought only of himself and what he had lost, not of what he was and what he yet had. His weeping had not made him weak, but only proved that he was. He was not yet a real man! He had proven again he was still a boy, a weak, self-centered coyote!

By the gods, would he never grow up? How long must he continue to fool himself, to think he was something he was not?

He struggled to his feet, feeling the weakness in his entire body from the fast and lack of activity, his legs no more than keeping him shakily upright, and as he stood, she saw him and stopped. He stared at her as she at him.

"How did you find me?"

"I followed your tracks. You walked like someone in sleep."

"I was asleep."

Her voice was soft and firm. "I came to find the one I love. Why did you leave?"

"You were dead. I saw the ravens take the child from you and your life went with him."

She was somber, the blanket held around her exactly as he had seen earlier. Tears began to flow, but she came no closer than the five paces that separated them.

"I gave birth six moons ago. My child lives. It was your first mate, Scent of Violets, who died."

This time, the instant she spoke, he saw it was not his first mate, but Little Dove who stood before him. A look akin to terror crossed his face. She saw the look, but could not understand it.

"I am dead."

"No, my love, you live. Weak and hungry, but you live."

He scrubbed his face with his left hand, then looked at her again. "I cannot understand." His hand went to his headband.

"Understand what? That I've come to you?"

He shook again, staggered from his poor balance, caught himself and stood erect. "That I'm not the man I thought myself to be--that you think I am. I was given a name, and it means nothing."

"That is not true. You are a man. Does not everyone fail sometimes? You were given a heavy grief, and you staggered. Are you not now standing again?"

He stared at her, trying to understand. His grief was being swept away; in its wake came remorse and self-hatred. He had been the infant again. He was not a man.

She stepped toward him, until she was only a single stride away. "You have many children, and two mates. You have a people who wonder where you are. You are loved by many, and no one could gain such love except he be a man of honor. Don't tell me you are not such a man, for I know better. I've known you longer than anyone...better than anyone...except perhaps Scent of Violets. I helped make you a man, even as you made me a woman. There is nothing you can tell me that will ever convince me you are other than what I know you to be."

He continued to stare at her, feeling the heat sweeping up his body, such warmth that sweat began to appear on his forehead. He wanted to believe her, but....

"I killed her."

The voice was stunned. "You what?"

"I killed her. It was my fault she died."

"She told me of your feelings." Her voice grew as she spoke. "She once told me you feared for her life with each pregnancy."

He was speechlessness.

"She said you feared for her life, perhaps because she gave birth in the wilds and had no way of remaining in seclusion for twenty suns. That you feared you brought the Goddess' wrath on her and you."

Still shocked, he was mind-numbed.

"She knew that she would die with the birth of one of her children...long before you did."

"No!" His voice was small and weak.

"She told it to both Blue Skies and myself. Question her. She can confirm all I have told you. It was one of the reasons she wanted you to mate with us."

He stared at her, but he knew that every word was true. She had known! All the time, she had known! Yet she said nothing, never showed fear, never...by the gods, she was truly a lynx!

"Will you come back with me? I return to my children and my people. You are my leader, as well as my mate. They need you. I need you."

He reached out a hand and let the back of his fingers rub softly against her cheek. The touch brought reality, a reality which began interpreting what he had seen earlier. She looked back at him without moving, allowing the touch wordlessly. After a moment, the hand dropped.

"Am I no longer a woman? Am I not worthy as a mate?" She let the blanket drop from her shoulders, standing naked. "I have changed little since we first coupled. I have larger mammaries from feeding your children, and my tummy hasn't lost all the fat, but I am much the same. The only difference is that I have you as a mate, not as one who only made me a woman. Am I such a weak person you no longer desire to live?"

He shook his head and closed his eyes. "No." The voice was weak, so quiet she saw it rather than heard it. He opened his eyes again. "No, you are strong. It is I who am weak."

A tear began to roll down her cheek, having hung on her eyelash since she had been back in the trees. "You are as strong as you choose to be. You only chose to be weak out of grief." She took a deep breath, controlling a quivering lower lip. "If you were not a man, I would not want you. It was why I couldn't stand Eagle Eye. He was truly weak, like an infant. He had never grown up; he was yet an infant in character, in maturity, in faith in others. He chose to remain the self-indulgent brat-son of the chief. You were strong, though you think otherwise, but it is that which makes me still love you."

He smelled his own physical weakness and the effects of his suns without moving, but he took a deep breath, almost in response to hers. He reached out and pulled her to himself, feeling her breasts cool against his heated chest. Her arms went around him, and she laid her cheek against his shoulder.

"You're right, pretty one. You haven't changed except to become a mature woman. I have. I let grief close my eyes. I have much, though I lost much--a love that's irreplaceable. But when a man has the love of his people, he has much. When he has the love of a faithful woman, he has everything. The Great One has tested me again, and I failed the test. Still, I'm rich."

He pushed her away and lifted her chin and rubbed her face with his nose, his lips, gently. "I wish to stay here with you for three suns. I will kill a deer and we can rekindle what I mistakenly thought I had lost."

She smiled through the tears. "I was right. I have a man. No woman in the history of our people, now or ever, will know a man as noble as mine." She stepped into him and pressed herself against him, her arms around him, her cheek to his chest. "I can laugh again, because I helped make him a man."

GLOSSARY
AND
AUTHOR'S NOTES

atlatl: A rock-tipped, wood-handled spear used with a sling attached to the hand/wrist. When mastered, it gave the thrower greater distance, more power, and finer accuracy than the simple spear.

branded with the mark: In many societies, a brand was a means of chastising miscreants who broke the social codes or mores. A mark on the face, an ear removed, the nose cut off, fingers or a hand cut off, these marked a person for life for his crime. Sterlization, often accompanied by a mark on the forehead or cheeks, was another. For liars or cowards, breakers of the law, witches, sex deviates, or unwanted persons, to be marked was cruel but effective.

Broadheads: Somewhere between 700 and 900 A.D., the Anasazi adopted a hard cradleboard to hold their infants on the back while mother/caretaker went about her tasks. It was a drastic change from the soft animalskins with fur to the inside. Why they made the change is uncertain. It seems plausible that word reached them from the advanced civilizations of Central and South America, and thinking that perhaps the shape of the head led to such intelligence and success, mothers everywhere decided to increase the brain-trust of their people with similar broad heads. For whatever reason, the method became general throughout the Anasazi world. Strapping the infant's head against the board for the years as an infant/toddler reshaped the head, flattening the back and forcing the skull to grow laterally.

Ceremony of the Stick: There is evidence this type of ritual was found among some of the Amerinds by early explorers and trappers. Assuredly, it differed in pomp and ceremony, but not in the final result--that of making the first sexual experience of a man much easier. That it existed should not be any great surprise, since there are many sexually-oriented ceremonies among the Ancients. Sex rights belonged to the man in most societies. He was the one who had "the need," and he was the one who planted "the seed." Procreation was of infinite importance to the tribes who struggled with nature and whose lifespans probably did not exceed thirty or thirty-five years. That its means should be given major import is not surprising. A woman was to be the submissive recipient of "the seed" and the one who relieved a man of his "need." It would be a natural for something so basic to eventually become a religious or civic ceremony.

chastity belt: Among many peoples, a belt, worn like a sanitary pad or diaper, became a girl's symbol of virginity. It may have began as an absorbent material during the menstrual flow, and over time took on a larger significance.

Chinook: A warm wind, usually quite strong and often with 40-50 degree temperatures, that come off the mountains in dead of winter, when temperatures are often zero or below. Within a day or two, a foot or more of snow can melt.

coupling: Sexual intercourse, a modern term, was simplified to describe it as simple as possible. To join a man and woman together is to couple.

daub-and-wattle: An early method of construction among the Anasazi. Poles were stuck firmly into the ground, crossed or laced with other smaller poles and branches, then covered inside and out with a thick coating of mud, creating a strong, wind-resistent building.

Death Match: Dueling in some form was found in most societies of the past, as recently as the nineteenth century right here in the United States. Among the Amerinds who lived here before the white man came, fighting to the death was common in disputes of "honor." Honor, a word used and abused, brought many men into conflict. The death match of this novel is described in the narration.

dropped: Among many primitive civilizations (as recently as the 1950's, it was found among the Auca Indians of South America), birth was accomplished by a mother alone, seated in a hammock-like blanket with a hole in the bottom. Through that hole, a newborn dropped to the ground and thus into the world. The mother removed her own placenta, cut the umbilical cord, and did whatever religious ritual was required at the time of and after the birth.

fa or *fa-fa*: Father or grandfather. With a life expectancy of just over thirty years, there could not be many times when four generations were living at one time.

gully-makers: The arid lands of the West are criss-crossed with streams and streamlets, many of which are dry in the summer. Many of these beds are rutted deeply. The reason is two-fold. First, the country is dry, which creates a shortage of erosion barriers, namely grasses. So, second, when the summer rains, often sudden and violent, pour down, they simply wash away the soil in water's tumultuous drive to the lowest possible recipient. What remains are the gullies, or ravines, or washes, or arroyos, various names that are among others given to this phenomena.

lifter of the rock: Lifting the rock was a physical feat for the strong. It was often a symbol of manhood. In a society where survival of the fittest was understood, it was made into a contest. The rock was usually quite heavy, and the object was to lift it--and sometimes to carry it for a specified distance.

mat: The Anasazi lived on floors of rock or soil, both of which were likely to be cool. A mat was often used under blankets to keep the body off the floor. This mat was made of reeds or from yucca fibers.

midsun: noon

mid-sun: (see sun)

moon: The second most powerful light in the world of the Ancients, the moon represented many things. From a being active in creation to fan overseer of the night, one thing is for sure, it was used as a time table. That is the use throughout this narrative. A moon means one month.

Mountain-That-Smokes: Sunset Crater of today.   It erupted about 1050 A.D., and its ash greatly affected the soil for some time, much similar to that of Mount St. Helens of recent time.

mu or *mu-mu*: Mother or grandmother.

no-sun: See sun.

Oath of Retribution: When a person was wronged, injured or killed, it was up to that person to demand satisfaction. Of course, a dead person is somewhat limited in his ability to make retribution. In that case, if it was a wrong or supposed wrong that caused the death, someone from the family or clan was blood-bound to make the demand. The eye-for-an-eye system was very common.

Open or *Opening*: See Ceremony of the Stick

Others: I have, after reading the pros and cons of the

many arguments of the "experts," come to the conclusion
that there were nomadic and marauding bands of peoples
during the time of the settled Anasazi. The Anasazi were
themselves the ancestors of wandering tribes, who
followed the seasons and food supply. That there should
be no other people around except those who settled
down to farming seems to be a belief too simplistic and
naive. The Puyutes, precursor to the Utahs (Utes), the
Apaches or possibly even the Navajos, were known to
inhabit the area by the fourteenth century. Nomadic
tribes left few pieces of evidence of their passing, though
recently there have been some discoveries of just such
things. I present the Puyutes (Paiutes, Peyutes, et al) as
the dreaded Others, who had the attitude of conquest
and earned honor, along with total disdain for sodbusters
(not too different from recent U.S. history!).

rising sun: first sun in the new day

rising-sun: See sun.

Rite of Perfection: A man hates to die without a legacy.
This rite was a legacy. He dies at his own hand, and his
flesh is then ingested by those whom he chooses, a
means of continuing his life on earth vicariously.

Rock of Prayer: Petroglyph Point, Mesa Verde.

setting-sun: See sun.

Sipapu: The Anasazi probably held beliefs similar to but
more primitive than the modern-day Hopi, who is very
likely a direct ancestor (not the only tribe with such a
claim or distinction). Their construction methods and
religious rites suggest this. Sipapu is among the Hopi.
A ceremonial and symbolic hole in the floor of the kiva,
it represents the means by which man arrived on the
surface of the earth from the third level of existence.
The hole, usually four to six inches in diameter and of
inconsistent depth, is universal among them, though the
"real" place was thought to be somewhere around the
Grand Canyon.

Sleeping Giant: The Sleeping Ute Mountain as we know it today, had many tales told of its inception by various tribes of the Southwest. Appearing from the Mancos Valley and Mesa Verde as a man reposing on his back, it has often had "god-stories" and other legends attached to it.

snowtime: Winter. The time between harvest and the vernal equinox.

stone-throw: Meant to be about one hundred feet.

Story-Rock: Most areas of Anasazi ruins have petroglyphs and pictographs. Where they are located next to dwellings, such as at Wijiji ruins in Chaco Canyon, I mean them to be more of a newspaper, or wishbook. When one has to travel some distance, then I refer to it as a Rock of Prayer. It is simply a nuance of mine.

sun: In the narration, sun stands for day. However, when it is hyphenated, it means a direction. Rising-sun is east, setting-sun is west, mid-sun is south, and no-sun is north. Thus, "above rising-sun" would mean north-east.

Sun God: Most early peoples worshipped the sun in some way, often as the greatest of their deities. Because it was seen as the greatest celestial body by the Ancients, this would be quite natural. Its heat kept them well, and with Rain God brought their life to them. He fought battles with the cold season and with clouds and rain, and always won. Sun God is therefore vital, and he was often credited for a role in creation of all, and often enjoyed some form of mother/father worship. Sun dials and elaborate time and season machinations point to the Ancients acknowledgement of Sun God's role in life.

The Hospitality: Observed by old Chinese tradition as well as among many other peoples and tribes, including Amerinds in the day of trappers and adventurers, a man would loan his spouse (or one of them if he had more than one) to a visiting stranger to meet his physical "needs" while he stayed with them. This idea is not original to the author.

The People: Most civilizations and Ancients of the world have regarded themselves as The People, the called ones, the first or the foremost. Some tribal names mean just that, The People.   It was, and still is, a pride in nationality or one's "roots". It is what gives a people cohesion, a reason for existence, importance. National pride is not a new concept, but for many centuries was what held a people together and gave them a reason to live and a means to survive.

The Rock: The idea of The Rock is the author's creation. It is a personal whim, pictured as a shelf of rock on the high point of Mesa Verde, atop the prominent cliff as seen when first approaching this stupendous landmark from the east. From this point, the view of the entire Mancos Valley and San Juan Basin must be breathtaking.

the splits: A knife game we played as kids was certainly not invented in the modern era, though perhaps was not yet played in Anasazi times, either. Two people, facing each other, held a knife. The object was to stick the knife into the ground to the left or right of the opponent, who must then place his foot where the knife stuck. If the knife did not stick, no move was necessary. The knife could not be stuck more than eighteen inches from the foot, thus giving each player a couple chances before the game ended.   Each player received one throw, alternating turns, until one or the other had "the splits" so wide they could no longer stand.

The Top: The author chose a simple term for The People to use to refer to their homeland. The top of the mesa offers a sense of safety and security through its isolation, and from its lofty perch above the Mancos Valley and San Juan Basin could well have provided the people with a sense of superiority. However, its isolation also kept them from picking up on several discoveries until they had already been well-developed and in common use elsewhere.

the Trader: A man or men who traveled widely, trading

rocks, seashells, feathers, foodstuffs, pottery, ropes, belts and any other carryable item, then taking these things to the next place and trading again. At this time, his entire stock was probably carried on his back and the back of dogs. In Book II, the author takes the liberty of having the Trader using llamas.

travois: Two poles, with a hide or blanket stretched between and kept separated by a short pole at the front and back, facilitated the hauling of heavy or long-distance loads. Small travois could be used behind dogs. One or two persons could be used to drag such loads. In later times, the Amerind used horses to drag travois while moving any significant distance.

valley: Mancos Valley and San Juan Basin, that which could be seen from the top of Mesa Verde.

Water-from-the-Sunrise: Mancos River, which splits Mesa Verde into north and south sections.

Waters-That-Hurry-to-Sunset: San Juan River. Leaving Colorado, it begins to cut a deep gorge before entering the Colorado River just above the Grand Canyon. Most of its course is not really hurrying at all, but deceptively placid and wide.

winter: Each winter demarked the end of a year to those who lived by the crop. When spring arrived, Sun God conquered snowtime, and the renewal, with the Ceremony of the Goddess as its beginning, began a new year. No dates were kept regarding birthdays, so each winter demarked the conclusion of another year. Ten winters equalled ten years.

ORDER FORM

For additional copies of this book

ANASAZI SERIES: BOOK I   *He Who Conquers*
(ISBN 0-9639014-0-0)

_____Copies @ $12.95	$_____.__	
For mail order, add $2.50 shipping and handling for each book	_____.__	
Colorado residents add 3.5% tax	_____.__	
Canada and foreign countries, add $5.00 per book	_____.__	
TOTAL	$ _____.__	

Send order and remittance to:

WEB Publishing Company
P.O. Box 528
Westminster, CO 80030-0528

NAME:_____

ADDRESS:_____UNIT:_____

CITY:_____STATE:_____

ZIP:_____

COMING SOON

ANASAZI SERIES, VOLUME II:

NIGHT HAWK

Night Hawk wishes to become Spirit Man of his village. His half-brother, Son of Vision, considers himself the next chief, and murders his father to make it possible. Then he wounds Night Hawk severely as the latter attempts to seek his vision and education, and in the doing inflames the controversy and conflict growing on the Mesa.

These two sons of He Who Conquers (*Anasazi Series: Vol. I, He Who Conquers*) find their future a thing difficult to understand, and even more difficult to control. Their confrontation is a climax that even The People could not have imagined.

If you wish to be notified when *NIGHT HAWK* is available, send in the form below. As soon as the book goes into pre-publication, you will be notified. If you are also interested in other future volumes of this series, check here. ☐

NAME_____

ADDRESS_____UNIT_____

CITY_____STATE_____

ZIP_____

ABOUT THE AUTHOR

Wallace Burke has developed a life-long interest in early America. He came by the interest naturally, being a romantic who had a descendant that traveled west with Daniel Boone, and then went on to settle in what later became Kansas, and other early descendents who went on to Wyoming and Idaho.

Married to Barbara Jean for more than 34 years and with three grown daughters, he has had a great deal of encouragement in his love affair with writing. Six years in the pastorate and six years in child protection with the Jefferson County (CO) Department of Social Services, along with his two degrees, have given him opportunity to develop his imagination while recognizing the facts and suppositions of history.

An avid reader and backpacker, with interests in photography and local travel, his writing has become much more than casual. He has studied and traveled throughout the Anasazi world for over nine years, and brings this background and expertise to his writing, as well as his lectures and slide presentations about the Anasazi world.